He strode throu night, as driven as the hard rain that had begun to fall. She had skirted his protection by wandering beyond his established boundaries. Clare had told him she was bathing.

Rain pelted them, the seeker and the sought, a torrent that would have driven lesser mortals to shelter. Fiona arched back and lifted her arms toward the sky, welcoming the rush, letting it wash over her face and body. Kier fingered the brim of his hat and kept walking, undeterred. Lightning turned the sky blue-white.

Fiona stepped into the tall grasses, dressed, and set out for her wagon cleansed of all but her thoughts of Kier.

Introspection turned to frustration at her inability to free herself from him. He had put her and her son in danger. He had teased her with his affections. Her pride was bruised by the emotional extremes, the way he lured her with his smiles and stares, but never delivered on what his empty flirtations had seemed to promise.

With her every step, her anger grew; with his every step, his desire to ensure her well-being increased. It was at that moment they met, a collision of tension and relief illuminated by the storm that raged overhead.

Custodian of the Spirits

by

Bronwyn Long Borne

The Valley of Heart's Delight Series

Custodian of the Spirits

Cover Art by *Kim Mendoza*

The Wild Rose Press, Inc.
PO Box 708
Adams Basin, NY 14410-0708
Visit us at www.thewildrosepress.com

Publishing History
First Mainstream Historical Edition, 2020
Print ISBN 978-1-5092-2873-7
Digital ISBN 978-1-5092-2874-4

The Valley of Heart's Delight Series
Published in the United States of America

Dedication

For Stuart

Acknowledgements

Fiona Lenihan's journey would not have been possible without the support of family and friends, especially Cathy Kruzic and Christine Loomis.

Special thanks to my editor, Nicole D'Arienzo, for her ongoing guidance and for welcoming me to the garden.

Chapter 1

It was a raw day, the kind when exhaled breath became tufts of vapor, adding to heavy fog that burned tongues, choked words, and chilled to the bone all who suffered through it. Dew collected on brows and lashes. It dampened clavicles and constricted throats suffocated by starched collars and high-necked dresses. Palms perspired beneath tightly buttoned gloves. Corseted bodies stood erect in the oppressive air, their nerves laced as firmly as the ties that bound them.

Two women faced off across an open grave. Dressed in richly ornamented dresses and stiff black bonnets, they were the extremes of the family, the eldest and youngest Mrs. Cushings. The death they mourned marked the start of the closing battle of their undeclared war. Fiona Cushing met the frosty stare of her mother-in-law before scanning the crowd for a sympathetic face. Finding none, she lowered her eyes to the coffin awaiting burial.

The behavior of the Cushing matriarch at her son's funeral struck the new widow as particularly cruel, even for Edna Cushing. To those who knew how these women had become relatives by marriage, it seemed the elder Mrs. Cushing struggled to contain her glee until after the cherrywood encasement that held the remains of her youngest son had been buried in the earth. As the pastor recited Psalm 23, a malignant smile pinched the old woman's lips.

"Mother," Maggie Cushing said, tugging at Fiona's skirt to get her attention. "Father isn't coming home with us, is he?"

Fiona studied the concern in her three-year-old daughter's upturned face. "No, darling," she confirmed in gentle tones. "Father isn't coming home with us." She said the words deliberately, as if hearing them for the first time. Her husband was dead; she had been released from Simon Cushing. Exactly what her newfound freedom meant she did not know.

Fiona clasped Maggie's hand and tightened her hold around the shoulders of her eight-year-old son, Caleb, who stood at her other side. He was strong and proud like the men in her family. Caleb had the look of a Cushing but the soul of a Lenihan.

The widow appeared pale and determined against the black sea of mourners, like a piece of driftwood fighting the incoming tide. Through it all she remained upright, as if refusing to yield to forces that pummeled her with the relentlessness of a gale.

At the reception it was plain to Fiona she had been excommunicated from the Cushings' social circle. People who once called themselves friends of hers and Simon's paid their respects to Edna as the bereaved mother, but sidestepped Fiona where she sat alone across the room. Only a handful of mourners who had nothing to fear from Edna Cushing offered Fiona their condolences.

Even though the windows were open on the April morning, it smelled musty when the sun began to creep through the clouds, steam gasping from the saturated earth as the temperature rose. The stench of sweaty bodies lingered.

Fiona was alone in a room filled with people. She sat erect, unmoving, her hands clasped in her lap. Her black hair was pulled severely away from her face. Her expression was refined, almost impassive.

In her immigrant crossing from Ireland, in her tenure as a servant in the elder Cushings' home, or in the darkest hours of her marriage, she had never experienced the isolation she did in that moment. Before, there had always been someone to reassure her. When she had come to America, her brother had been at her side. When she had married into the Cushing family, there had been a kindly sister-in-law who had taught her the ways of a lady. But now Edna had made certain there was no one.

Fiona longed to feel her children in her arms and their warm breath on her cheek. But they had been delivered to their home after the funeral. She wished to be with them now, far away from this place of dread.

The room was close. She felt hot. Her stomach began to churn. Her mouth was dry. The weight of her corset bore down on her chest. Her pulse raced in her temples, thumping, pounding. She wanted to vomit. She wanted to scream. She wanted to run from the room.

Instead, she followed the visitors with her eyes. Look at me, she tried to will someone to pay her heed. But Edna's caustic scrutiny was enough to make people think twice about acknowledging her daughter-in-law.

After a time, when Edna's well-choreographed parade of humiliations had become too much, Fiona shifted her focus to the detail on an inlaid vase. Its intricate pattern gave her something other than the funeral reception to occupy her mind.

The steady tick of a grandfather clock marked the passing of time. Her gaze fell to the floor. She followed the parquetry to where it reached the wall. A cockroach scuttled across the baseboard to the fringed border of a Turkish rug. Fiona could not turn away from this imperfection in the Cushings' world. It was an unusual sight in this social stratum, where appearances meant everything. Edna would not have tolerated this creature and its implications.

As a servant, Fiona would have handled it immediately, disposing of the insect before anyone could see it. But as the unwanted daughter-in-law, Fiona took perverse satisfaction in knowing if there was one cockroach, there were others nesting in the walls. Hundreds more, scratching the mortar with their tiny feet.

Fiona wondered what the next few days would bring. No mention had been made of how life would continue without Simon. Her children were Cushing blood. Simon's heirs. Surely the family would provide for them.

Perhaps they would move to a smaller house. Perhaps they would move into the elder Cushings' palatial home. Those details mattered little to Fiona. She would be content to live anywhere and watch her children grow with the opportunities afforded all Cushing grandchildren. She had dreams of Caleb attending university, perhaps becoming an attorney or banker, perhaps someday working with his uncles and cousins.

Simon's will was read that afternoon. After the reception Fiona was ushered into the library, trying to ascertain the worst that could come from meeting with

Simon's father, Stanley Cushing, and the Cushing attorneys who would sit in judgment of her.

She had no idea.

The barrage of numbers was dizzying. She moved quickly from uncertain to nauseated, hope fading as her understanding grew. Her husband's recklessness had left him more than $75,000 in debt. The sale of her home and its furnishings would still leave her more than $20,000 in debt. Fiona was at the mercy of the Cushings.

With no income and no hope of earning anywhere near enough money to settle the debt and care for her children, she turned to her father-in-law, Stanley. She knew before she spoke that she was responding exactly as he had expected she would.

"Is there something I could do, some work in your offices that would allow the children and me to keep our home?"

"I don't see how it is possible," Stanley told her, his look of resignation complete. "You came to the marriage with nothing, and you leave with nothing."

"But the children," she pleaded with him, "Caleb and Maggie. Cushing," she said to emphasize their relation.

Stanley was not an evil man, but he was easily led. He had built his marriage on doing as Edna had instructed. Unlike his wife, he had treated Fiona with kindness, which made her heart sink even more when he handed down his pronouncements.

"I spared you from death in Ireland," he said. "Were it not for my generosity, you would have been dead ten years. I brought you to America in exchange for three years' service. After working in our fields,

Mrs. Cushing and I advanced your standing to
housemaid. Your service lasted just over one year, at
which time you eloped with our youngest son, leaving
nearly two years of service remaining.

"I would have been willing to reach a financial
settlement with you, but as you can see, my son left you
penniless. It is you who are indebted to me, for I have
paid what Simon owed to save you from debtors'
prison."

Stanley made a solid argument, so convincing that
Fiona might have agreed with him were not her life and
the lives of her children at stake. "What of the
children's schooling?"

"There is no schooling for field hands' children."

"Field hands?" Fiona said with dismay. "May I not
have my old position in your home?"

"Mrs. Cushing and I do not want to put our guests
in the uncomfortable position of being served by a
woman who once dined among them. Our fields are the
only place for you. If your children join you there, I
will erase the debt in one year."

"Fields," Fiona repeated, the reality of her situation
becoming clear.

Her brother had died working in the Cushing fields.
She had no love for the land, regarding it as selfish and
unpitying, and relentless in its demands on man and
beast. It had taken much from her. She had vowed
never again to stake her survival on the land. The
thought of returning to the fields, to those endless rows
of corn and wheat, potatoes and turnips, made her heart
heavy.

"Your children will work at your side, so you can
keep watch over them and avoid the trouble field

hands' children have a way of finding," Stanley instructed.

"They are your grandchildren, your blood. Will you not take them in to live with you?" Fiona implored.

"They are not our responsibility. They were born of a marriage I and Mrs. Cushing found objectionable. In one year, all of you will be free to seek employment elsewhere. Perhaps in the Irish part of town where a woman alone with two children would hardly be noticed."

Fiona watched him without emotion, wondering how heartlessness came so easily.

"So, what is it to be?"

"May I have this evening to consider your offer?" she asked, gripping her handkerchief.

Stanley nodded. "We expect your answer tomorrow," he said to close their meeting. His expression was smug. "Your house will be dismantled, and its contents sold at auction Monday morning."

Her hopes for her children evaporated. She had nothing to give them and no belief in her ability to provide for them. In one day's time she had fallen from the upper echelon of society to its depths. She had been raised in the fields of Ireland and knew she was more than capable of returning to that life. But she would die before forcing it on her children.

Quieted by all she had heard, Fiona rose from the table and made eye contact with each man who had handed her this sentence: Stanley, who appeared uncomfortable, and the three attorneys, who peered down their noses at her.

"Good day, gentlemen," she said, her voice steady.

To their surprise, she thanked them before turning

to leave. Although she felt like a defeated old woman, she forced herself to face her sentence with dignity.

She passed her mother-in-law in the foyer. Edna gloated, acting with restraint to prevent an outburst of laughter. One who had devoted the recent years of her life to becoming the perfect Cushing was no match for a woman who owned the hollow victory of being one.

In the awkward silence of the library, the senior counsel cleared his throat and began to speak. Edna entered the room and closed the door behind her.

"Many people know Fiona. Her reputation as the bellwether of the Cushing family's charity work precedes her. How will you reconcile her new role with those who are certain to ask?"

"She has gone to Boston to live with relatives," Edna replied.

"What if people see her in Philadelphia?" he pressed.

"Field hands cannot come near the house. None of our society would encounter her."

"What about her children? They bear the Cushing name," the second attorney asked.

"So do many Negro slaves bear the names of their masters."

"They could one day make claims," the first attorney warned.

"She's too stupid to think of that," Edna chortled.

"She was shrewd enough to become one of your most highly complimented daughters-in-law. In fact, didn't your other daughters-in-law follow her example, expanding the family's charitable works?"

"She has no education, no understanding of the larger world. She is ignorant. It is damp and drafty in the field hands' quarters. Accidents happen with draft animals and farming implements. Those half-breed children would be lucky to last a year."

"As your counsel, I must warn you that keeping her near you could leave you exposed," the attorney cautioned.

"Humph," Edna sneered, eyeing the team of attorneys as if they were overly cautious alarmists. "Look at her," she said, gesturing out the window, watching Fiona disappear down the street. "She believes she is beaten. That is our greatest advantage, for she will not be inclined to fight her new situation."

"She has no resources, no family, no friends outside our own," Stanley said in support of his wife. "We have left her with nothing. What choice does she have but to accept?"

"It was a waste to allow her to consider the offer," Edna sniffed, giving her husband a castigating glance. "We cannot remove that woman and those awful children from our lives quickly enough."

"Tomorrow, Mrs. Cushing," Stanley said to ease Edna's distress. "Tomorrow."

****

Carriages flashed by, their finely dressed passengers awash in conversation that came and went in inchoate snippets. The sounds of hooves on pavement, nurses guiding their charges, and the din of the city rang in Fiona's ears.

She walked the streets in a daze, imploring herself to find some way out of this fate. She thought to contact Alfred Cushing, Simon's oldest brother and an ally, but he and his wife had sailed to Paris a fortnight earlier for their wedding anniversary. Alfred had no idea his youngest brother was now dead and buried. Or how circumstances had changed for Fiona and her children.

Suddenly she stopped walking, realizing there were opportunities all around her. She was standing in the heart of one of the wealthiest parts of Philadelphia, among the grand homes of the Cushings' social peers. She knew all of them by name.

Fiona checked her bonnet and ran her hands over the bodice of her dress. One by one she knocked on doors along Powelton Avenue to ask the Cushings' friends for work as a servant in their homes. Fiona knew if she were to secure a position as a lady's maid or housekeeper, her children would be spared field work. She would somehow find a way for them to become educated, either by a benevolent governess or from scraps of knowledge Fiona could gather.

She asked politely at the first few homes and was reduced to begging at the last few. Most people refused to admit her. Those who did addressed her through the same staff of house servants she was desperate to join. All of them said no.

Her knuckles raw from knocking on doors, Fiona thought to try their pastor, the very man who had officiated at Simon's funeral that morning. He was the only person she called on who would speak with her directly.

"Reverend True," she said. "I fear I am in a difficult position." She told him all that had happened. It took the whole of her training as a Cushing to maintain her composure, especially when he responded.

"Mrs. Cushing," he began, his tone so insincere Fiona cringed. "You are a woman of virtue. You have been a tireless minister to the needy and sick. You have many gifts, and now you must use them to your advantage. I cannot help you."

"Cannot or will not?" she blurted in a tone as foreign to her as it was to him. She was startled by her forcefulness.

"My apologies, Mrs. Cushing, but—"

"What price your loyalty?"

"Pardon me?"

"What size gift to your parish did it take for you to turn me away?" Growing desperate with the lateness of the hour, she shed decorum. Her body shook with anger.

"Stanley and Edna are senior benefactors of our parish. Surely you know that," said Reverend True.

"And what they're doing is wrong. How can you, a man of the cloth, so easily turn your back on my children and me in our hour of need? We are hardly strangers to you."

"Your marriage was not blessed by the church. Had you and your husband recited your vows before God—"

"What sum was paid for my children and me?" she demanded, cutting him off.

"You should leave, Mrs. Cushing. I am sorry I have nothing to offer."

"Could I not work for the parish, as a cook or a cleaning woman—anything—so my children could attend school?" Fiona implored.

"We are finished, Mrs. Cushing," he ended, opening the door to escort her from the rectory.

"Do you know of any family where I could find a situation?"

He shook his head and held open the door for her. "Go with God."

His indifference astonished her. She caught his eyes and tried to hold them in one final attempt to sway him. But he turned away and would not watch her leave.

Fiona's feet were leaden as they fell to the pavement, first one, then the other. Family, friends—all the obvious resources had been blocked by Edna and Stanley. There was no one else.

She passed through the seedier parts of the city, horrified by the despair in the gray faces of the women and children. These were people who labored endlessly just to survive. This would be her destiny. She and Caleb and Maggie would be among these haunted souls, their expressions as empty as their bellies.

Desperate, sunken eyes stared back, looking with envy upon her finery, wondering at the perfect world she must inhabit. Little did they know she was hours away from joining them.

Fiona recognized their faces. They were her mother, her brothers, her father, and her sisters, alive as they were before the great hunger had taken them. She saw her reflection in a young woman. Poverty lined the other woman's face, making her appear a decade older than Fiona. She imagined Caleb and Maggie standing among the children before her.

She knew their hunger, for it had once been hers. The hopelessness that had been a constant in her earlier years was something she did not want her children to experience. She swore to spare them this eventuality. She had to find a way.

She walked without destination, searching for some means to turn her fate. Always before, the path had been clear. Always before, someone had been there to guide her, to tell her what to do. First it was her brother and then her husband and his family. Now she was on her own. She felt utterly lost.

It was late in the afternoon when she came upon a simple notice nailed to a post. Its invitation to join a wagon train spoke directly to her. *Go West! Free Land! New World!* She noted the address on the paper and hastened to investigate the claims in the advertisement.

A scene of exuberant efficiency greeted her. Dozens of families were milling about a supply warehouse that outfitted pilgrims bound for California and Oregon. The optimism that blanketed the people was palpable. Old and young, large families and single travelers—they were on equal footing to begin their adventures.

Fiona's excitement grew as she observed the activity. She watched for nearly an hour, her fascination burgeoning as an idea took hold. Could the answer lie in this drastic measure? Her mind made up, she strode into the first outfitter's shop she saw.

"How can I help you, madam?" the proprietor greeted her.

"I would like to go west," she said in a delicate Cushing timbre, which was barely audible in her current environment. The man stared at her as if he had lost patience with her.

"I want to go west," she said again, her tone that of another person, Fiona Lenihan, of County Leitrim, her home in Ireland.

"Where in the West?"

"All the way west."

The merchant studied her black taffeta mourning dress and the sparkle of jet beads that decorated her ears and throat. She could hardly have appeared more out of place. "Your husband will be traveling with you?"

"My husband is dead."

"Strong sons?" he asked.

"I have an eight-year-old son and a daughter who will be four in July."

"It's not a simple buggy ride. You will never make it without a strong man," he said flatly.

"Please tell me what it would cost to purchase the minimum necessary to make the journey."

"I could not in good conscience do business with you."

Fiona struggled to maintain her composure. "I would like to know what it would cost to make the journey."

"Surely you have a brother or cousin who could travel with you?"

Fiona had nothing left. The day's ordeals had pushed her to the brink, and she had maintained her poise and demeanor throughout. Now, her last hope was unraveling. It was more than she could bear. "Please."

The merchant saw tears well in her eyes. He heard the quiver in her voice and recognized her frustration. With a sigh, he gave in.

"It's late in the season to begin this journey, especially alone with two young children. If you have a mind to do this, then take the train to the end of the line, to Wheeling, West Virginia. That will save you more than thirty days' travel by wagon. My brother is a merchant in Wheeling. Give him this note," he instructed as he scribbled something on a blank bill of sale. "He will outfit you for the journey."

Fiona glanced at what he had written. Jacob Getty.

There was an address and cursory directions from the train station.

"Where should we go after we reach Wheeling?"

"My brother is well-acquainted with trail bosses and can recommend a traveling party. You'll follow the Cumberland Road. It will get you most of the way to St. Louis. Then take a ferry upriver to St. Joseph or even Council Bluffs, if you can make it that far. If not, follow the river until you reach one of those jumping-off points. By then you should have fallen in with other people headed west and can travel with them."

"Thank you," she said with an uncertain smile that gradually changed to relieved laughter. "You don't know what your kindness means. What will it cost to buy what we need for the journey?"

"I usually tell folks to plan on fifteen hundred dollars to outfit a wagon, buy supplies, and tide you over until your fields begin to produce."

"Fifteen hundred dollars," Fiona repeated, wanting to be sure she heard him correctly.

The merchant scratched some figures on a piece of craft paper and handed it to her. "The first column assumes you will bring certain items with you. The second assumes you will need to purchase everything."

Fiona thanked him again and turned to leave. Fifteen hundred dollars, she thought to herself once she stepped into the street. She turned for home, her mind swimming with ideas.

A clock tower struck the five o'clock hour. Its ominous tone gave her pause. Fiona looked up at the church. A Catholic church. Something drew her to climb the steps and enter its sanctuary. It was the first time she had crossed such a threshold in more than a decade.

Doves flew from the rafters as she entered. She was seized by a tremendous unburdening that forced her to her knees: despair, betrayal. Hope.

Surrendering to emotion, she gasped at the overwhelming sense of weightlessness. In it, she experienced a profound sense of being, perhaps for the first time. She could feel the arms of many around her, holding her, loving her—her brothers, her mother and sisters, her father, her wee nephew. They had been but spirits for many years.

The sun passed behind the stained glass rose window, bathing her in multi-colored light. She felt warmed through, as if the hand of God had reached out to offer encouragement.

Leaving the church, she walked on winged feet. A whole world of possibilities had revealed themselves to her. Buoyed with confidence and a new belief in her ability to provide the life she wanted for her children, she returned to her home in Philadelphia.

****

"Sit with me," she invited, gathering Caleb and Maggie on the chaise in the front room. They nestled against her like puppies.

"When your father died, he owed a lot of money to a lot of people. He did not have the chance to pay them all back." She paused, studying them as she chose her words.

"You always did your father proud. Now that he's gone, I'm going to do my best to give you all he had intended. But we will need to leave our home to find these things. Have you ever wondered what America looks like beyond the edges of Philadelphia?"

"The America of Lewis and Clark, you mean?" Caleb asked, his eyes growing bright.

"Yes!" Fiona exclaimed, sharing his excitement. She realized how fortuitous it was that Caleb had only recently studied those explorers in school.

"And mountains that disappear into the clouds? And Daniel Boone and Davy Crockett?"

"All those things and more. Would you like to go there?" she asked, testing the waters.

"When would we come back home?" Maggie asked.

"We would not be coming back," Fiona explained gently. "It would be our new home."

Caleb studied her as if knowing there was more to the story. "I would like to go there," he said, his words lacking the conviction Fiona had wished, but then she didn't want to raise their hopes only to dash them tomorrow. Her plan was in its infancy.

"So would I," she nodded, intending her enthusiasm to be catching.

"Me too!" Maggie agreed.

Fiona laughed aloud for the first time in weeks. It was settled, then. They were going west. Now it was up to the Cushings to make it possible.

Alone in the bedroom she had shared with Simon, after she had tucked her children in for the night, she felt a sense of calm. Leaving this life was one thing; bringing ruin to her children's lives was another. She hoped she was making the right decision.

Arching her back awkwardly, she began to undress. She gasped when she pulled the dress off her shoulders, the stiff fabric scraping one of the last wounds Simon had given her. Ugly bootprints scarred her back. Cigar burns dotted her shoulder. She had a brief vision of cowering in a corner while Simon kicked and pounded, trying to reach her face. A deep cut marred the nape of her neck where his gold signet ring had torn her skin.

She shuddered. Simon Cushing was no more. Soon Fiona Cushing would be no more as well.

"Did Father do that to you?"

Caleb's voice startled her. She pulled on a robe and turned to face her son.

"What are you doing out of bed?" she chided, kneeling and opening her arms to him.

"You tried to hide it from us, but I always knew," he confessed, laying his cheek against her shoulder.

"Hush now," she said. "Those days are behind us."

"Why are we going away?" he asked.

He needed a satisfactory answer. "Long before your father and I were married, your Uncle Seamus and I came across the sea to America. We had no money for our journey but were able to work for your Grandfather Cushing in exchange for our passage. When we came to Philadelphia, we owed Grandfather three years of labor.

"I worked only one year before I married your father. Your grandfather has reminded me that I still owe him two years of service unless I can find a way to pay him a sum adequate for my service."

"We could live in a smaller house. We could sell our toys," he said hopefully.

"What a wonderful thing to offer. But even if we sold our house and everything in it, it would not be enough. When your father died, he owed a lot of money to a lot people. That, even more than my debt, makes it difficult.

"I wish I could find a better alternative. Leaving

this place is the only way I know to give you the life I want you to have. I grew up in the fields. There was no reading, no learning, no arithmetic or geography or art. Now that I know what is possible, I will stop at nothing for you and Maggie to have it."

"How will we get there?"

"In a wagon pulled by oxen, which we will buy in West Virginia after taking a train there tomorrow. A better adventure you'll never have."

"We're leaving tomorrow?" Caleb asked with surprise.

"On the midday train. If all goes according to plan, in two days we will make camp with others who are traveling west. Now you must go to sleep."

She kissed his forehead. He was a model eldest child, serious and obedient, a good student, and delightful company. But there was a pain in her heart, knowing he had already seen too much in his eight years. She was confident she had made the right decision. If she could buy back some of Caleb's childhood, it would be worth any sacrifice.

Alone, she wandered through her home. What had been hers was hers no longer. She stood in the center of the drawing room and looked around her, the trappings of her life fading to an inventory of possessions.

There were so many things: books and vases, humidors and nut dishes. A doll of Maggie's that had fallen behind a lamp stand. She had fashioned with care this home for her family, recalling with regret and more than a twinge of sadness the acquisition and thoughtful placement of each item.

There was a silver tray the church ladies' group had given her to honor her work opening the first of many soup kitchens. The following year she had organized groups to visit the sick. Although she had started these programs, Edna had arranged for her other daughters-in-law to get the credit for their success.

A set of crystal aperitif glasses shimmered in the lamplight. She and Simon had purchased them while on their honeymoon in New York City. Happiness was the order of the day when Simon had them wrapped up and charged to the hotel bill he would leave unpaid for his father to settle, another in a life of indiscretions.

Soon it would all be gone.

Nothing meant so much to Fiona as the piano. It had been her voice when Edna had ordered her not to speak lest the family be shamed by her accent. Fiona caressed the instrument, not daring to touch the ebony and ivory. It would be better to leave her sadness and frustration locked in the keys. Perhaps one day she would have a piano in her new home. For now, her love of music would lie dormant, as hidden as her sentiments.

****

Morning followed a hollow blackness. Fiona greeted the day, certain of her decision. She dressed carefully in her mourning dress, checking herself in a full-length mirror. A pale, drawn woman stared back at her. She examined the disconsolate features and watched as wisps of fear became glimmers of confidence. Her green eyes caught fire.

Fiona tied a bow under her chin to secure her bonnet and stood in the doorway of the nursery watching Caleb and Maggie play. He was teaching her the game of jacks. The extent of her son's patience and relative lack of her daughter's brought a smile to

Fiona's lips.

She walked the seven blocks to the Cushing mansion. The jet beads on her velvet handbag clattered together with each footfall, marking her pace. The sound of her heels on the cobblestones was as steady as a metronome, projecting a confidence her soul did not possess.

The day was cool, but her torso was awash in sweat. Her hands were damp inside her gloves. Perspiration snaked across her scalp.

Fresh green shoots had broken through the surface of the hard ground. Tulips. They signaled the close to the season of the dormant and the dead. It was stirring, a taste of new life springing forth.

The cupola on the house came into view as she neared her destination. The silhouette of the house was daunting. Its seven mismatched chimneys were dark brick, stained with soot. A latticework of ivy snaked across the outer walls, the buds of new leaves sitting next to old leaves that refused to fall. Vines that had not yet reawakened cluttered the wrought iron fence surrounding the grounds.

Her shoulder and hip smarted from Simon's kicks the morning of his death. The lingering wounds left no doubt. With renewed spirit, Fiona entered the Cushing home.

She felt faint as she passed through the leaded-glass doors. Her palms left stains on her skirt where they touched. Her mouth was too dry to swallow. There was hesitation in her step.

Her audience included Stanley and the three attorneys she recognized by the way they peered down their noses at her. The meeting had been choreographed so that Fiona's chair sat opposite the attorneys, with Stanley sitting at the head of the table. Fiona felt like a prisoner before a firing squad.

"Shall we count on your presence in the fields Monday morning?" Stanley asked to call the meeting to order.

"No," she replied, her voice firm. She swallowed and rose from the table. A rush of emotion made her limbs tremble. "No," she said again, her tone and officiousness startling everyone gathered.

"I have come today with a proposal that will remove Caleb, Maggie, and me from your lives forever, and bar us and our descendants from any future claims on the Cushing name."

She would relinquish her claim on the Cushing name, as well as her children's claims, in exchange for the forgiveness of Simon's debt and enough money to outfit a wagon in which she and her children would head west, never again to see or contact the Cushings. Their former servant and her children would be out of their lives forever.

Fiona entered the meeting a Cushing and exited a Lenihan. Her knees were unsteady when she stepped into the blinding sunshine with fifteen hundred dollars in her purse. She kept walking, certain she felt Edna's eyes bore through her as she exited the front gate.

"This may have ended better than you had hoped," one of the attorneys assured Edna as they watched Fiona disappear from view. "She'll never make it to California. If the storms and Indians don't finish her off, starvation will. She has no idea what sort of pact she has made."

****

22

The conditions dictated by the trio of Cushing attorneys rang in Fiona's ears as she pulled the trunks from the attic: "You shall each be given one trunk into which you may pack as many standard household items, books, and clothing as the trunk can hold. In addition, you may take one additional trunk into which you may pack one coat and blankets for each of you. You are forbidden to take any jewelry other than what you have worn while in mourning, any decorative arts, ornaments, or all other items frivolous to your travels. All monogrammed items and objects bearing the Cushing name must remain. The minimum necessary for survival is all you have been granted. Any attempt to circumvent these terms shall nullify the agreement in full."

Edna sent three of her most trusted servants to supervise Fiona's packing and ensure neither Fiona nor her children took more than they were allowed. When she reached the house, Fiona's staff had already been dismissed. In the time it had taken Stanley to assemble the funds, Fiona's home had reverted to the custody of the Cushings.

Fiona filled the children's trunks with clothing while Caleb and Maggie sorted through their toys and books. In her trunk she packed one nightgown, a second mourning dress, a spare black bonnet, two silk day dresses, and a second set of undergarments. In the fourth trunk she packed blankets, muffs, shawls, and coats for her children, her winter cloak, and seventeen books. She had to sit on that trunk to get it to close.

At last the four trunks were stacked by the front door, waiting for the ride to the train station.

"It's time," the Cushings' groom said to her. Fiona

nodded. She called the children away from the nursery, where they were playing with their forbidden toys one last time. The groom loaded the trunks in the carriage and Fiona shepherded her children into their seats.

As Caleb and Maggie settled in for the ride, Fiona looked with defeat at her house where she had built a life for her family. She felt saddened to have been denied the opportunity to take leave of her staff. Her housekeeper had been kind to her, especially when Simon had not.

With that, the former Cushings departed. Fiona did not look back, but Caleb and Maggie watched their house longingly until it faded from view.

"Are you ready to see America?" Fiona asked.

Both of them appeared bewildered.

"There's something very important we have to keep in mind on our journey. When we leave Philadelphia, we'll no longer be Cushings, but Lenihans, like your Grandm'ar and Grandf'ar before you, like uncles Seamus and Colm, and your aunts Maeve and Katie. Now you are Caleb and Maggie Lenihan. And I am Fiona Lenihan, the name I was given when I was born. We must never again say the Cushing name. Now, who are we?" she asked, practicing with her children.

"The Lenihans," they said in unison.

"Who?"

"The Lenihans!" they cried.

The final luxury of being a Cushing came when the groom unloaded the four trunks and put them in the care of the railroad's porters. With a wink, he tipped the bellman. Fiona thanked him and he left, his departure closing the chapter on her life as a Cushing.

With her children at her side, Fiona purchased three one-way tickets to Wheeling, West Virginia. When the porter opened the door to their compartment, the children bounded into the window seats and smashed their noses against the glass, watching the activity on the platform.

Fiona sat quietly, waiting for the train to move. She prayed Edna had not ordered a late complication to derail the plan. Fiona shut her eyes and felt the vibrations of people boarding the train.

She listened to the muffled goodbyes of departing passengers leaving loved ones. She smelled the stale air generated by the hundreds of passengers who had occupied the cabin before them. She smoothed the adequate padding in her seat and guessed it would feel wholly inadequate by the time they reached West Virginia.

Her nerves began to fray. She opened her eyes to watch her children's fascination with the experience of being on a train. Finally, she allowed herself to believe in the possible when the conductor shouted, "All aboard!" and the train lurched forward.

Chapter 2

Fiona was ready to trust the reality of their freedom only after the train had left the station. Unaware of their mother's fears, Caleb and Maggie maintained an animated narrative of what was to them an adventure. They were amazed by the experience of riding a train and watching neighborhoods pass at a quickening pace.

Once the train had reached full speed, Fiona breathed freely, charmed by her children's delight. They were intrigued by each changing scene outside their window, from parks and cemeteries to factories and farms.

Fiona watched them enjoying themselves but gradually looked beyond them, gazing into the past. As she left Philadelphia, she remembered what it was like to arrive in Philadelphia a decade before, when Stanley Cushing's ship had docked on a wintry day in February 1847.

She recalled the young woman looking ahead to a new life in America, wondering where it would lead, forsaking all thoughts of hardship, and embracing the wonderful possibilities of the unknown.

Age and experience had taught her to see the future through a wary lens. She would need to reach deep within to find the same sense of wonder in a future unrevealed to make a successful crossing of America. Her children's lives depended on it.

But her heart was weary. Life with Simon had battered her spirit. Part of her did not want to make this journey. Part of her did not believe she could. She had sworn off the land because of all it had taken from her over the years, every one of the Lenihans. Now she had committed herself to a future spent living off the land. Somehow, she had gotten them this far. She prayed she would have the strength to see the journey through.

It began to rain. As the train rocked her children to sleep, a haze settled over the Pennsylvania countryside. Fiona gazed into the mist, seeing the shadowed farms with their idle plows and draft animals. That was to have been her future with Seamus. Once their service to the Cushings was finished, they had planned to start a farm in the Pennsylvania countryside. One of these farms could have been theirs. She reflected on a past when that dream was all that mattered.

The Ireland they'd left offered nothing but death. Their trek through the barren countryside was a walk past hundreds who lay dead from illness and hunger. Some had frozen to death, too weak to take another step.

Stanley Cushing's Irish immigrants spent the winter working in his foundry and the growing season in his fields. A sudden absence in the Cushings' household staff brought Fiona into their home, where she learned to serve and clear meals, pour tea, roast meat, use imperfect vegetables to make stock for soups and stews, bake pastries, and serve gentlemen brandy and cigars after dinner.

Caleb's snore brought Fiona to the present. He stirred beside her. She wrapped her arms around him and kissed his forehead.

The train chugged toward West Virginia, making stops along the way to drop off passengers and cargo and take on more of the same. She measured time by which child was asleep in her arms, the many games they played and the songs they sang, and the simple meals they ate in the dining car. Fiona frequently double-checked to be sure she still had all her money.

She watched the farmland beyond the train window. This was the dream she had shared with Seamus, a dream that was never to be. Now, she was following a new dream.

"Mama," Maggie asked sleepily. "When will we get there?"

"Soon," Fiona replied, smoothing Maggie's skirts.

"No. When will we get to California?"

"Sometime in September or October, I imagine."

"How long is that?" Maggie asked, dividing her attention between her mother and the green fields passing the window.

"Six months or so."

"How long is a month?" she asked after a brief pause.

"Thirty or so days."

"Why does it take so long?" Maggie asked with exasperation.

"Because we have so much ground to cover. There will be other children for you to play with on our journey. And so much to see." Fiona lifted her into her lap to hold her close.

"Like what?"

"Oh," Fiona responded, guessing, "lakes and rivers, and fields and flowers—lots and lots of flowers for you to collect."

28

"Will it be warm or cold?"

"Probably a little of both," she laughed, marveling at her daughter's incessant questions.

"What's California like?" Maggie asked, playing with Fiona's jet bracelet.

"A good place to start a farm."

"What will we eat?"

"In California? Probably much the same as we eat all the time."

"On the way to California," Maggie corrected her.

"I don't know, darling. We'll find out when we get to West Virginia." Fiona kissed the top of Maggie's head and looked out the window.

"I miss eating at Grandmother and Grandfather Cushings' house."

"We won't be eating there anymore. Besides, we can't call them your grandparents anymore. Now we have just your Grandm'ar and Grandf'ar Lenihan from County Leitrim in Ireland."

When she was unable to sleep, Fiona's mind returned to the past. Haunted by thoughts she had not visited in years, she gave in to them with the hope they would plague her no more, especially once they were on the trail to California.

William Lenihan, like his father before him, had scratched a living off the land. The Lenihans had lived in County Leitrim for generations, all of them memorialized by simple stones in the local church cemetery. The Lenihans were blessed with fine sons every generation. William had been no exception with Seamus and Colm.

William had three fine daughters, too. The next generation promised more of the same when Maeve had taken a strong husband and borne a healthy son.

Life continued for the Lenihans as it always had, a struggle to stay ahead of the elements, fueled by meals made of potatoes. Like all country farmers in their time, the potato had been the staple of the Lenihans' pantry. Most days there was potato stew or potato pie.

And then the fungus had come on the wind from the Continent, causing a blight that had ruined the foundation of the Irish diet. Starvation and disease followed, killing one million. Another one and a half million emigrated from Ireland, many to America, Australia, or Canada. Fiona had been among the young and able who had left Ireland, depriving the country of its next generation, scarring the land as deeply as the blackened crops.

Overwhelmed by memories, Fiona's eyes grew heavy with sleep.

And then she awakened with a start. They had reached Wheeling.

When they stepped off the train, the Lenihans and their possessions had landed in the heart of chaos. Astounded, they stood together, their eyes wide. The world around them was a rush of people, animals, and equipment. Everyone was in a hurry. No two traveled in the same direction.

Fiona breathed deeply. She needed to act on her determination and be more committed to making this endeavor work than she had been to anything else in her life. She studied the bewildered expression in Caleb's and Maggie's eyes. It reminded her of how she felt the day she had boarded Stanley Cushing's ship.

She hated herself for putting her children through this. They were far younger than she when her life had come to pieces.

Fiona realized they couldn't have been standing in a worse place. Although the requisite financial investment limited the emigrants to the middle class or above, the spectacle of all that money changing hands was a magnet for undesirables. Thieves lurked everywhere, waiting for an opportunity to exploit the naive travelers. Fiona and her children's refined appearance made them easy marks. Caleb stood as tall as he could in his new role as man of the family.

She saw a relatively unobtrusive spot next to some animal pens about fifty yards in the distance. The problem was relocating her family and their four trunks without losing either child or possessions.

Startling her children with her show of physical strength, Fiona built a tower out of three trunks and sat Caleb on top of them. "Don't let anyone touch you or these trunks," she ordered sternly. "I'll take Maggie over by that fence and be right back for you."

Caleb nodded, astonished by the sight of his mother performing manual labor. Her realm had been watercolors and teas, music and fashion. The skill with which she lifted and dragged, planned and organized was something that seemed out of character. It cast her in an entirely new light.

"Keep hold of your doll and my skirt," she ordered Maggie. Straining so that the veins in her neck and forehead protruded like tree roots, Fiona dragged the heaviest of the trunks across the dusty thoroughfare, grunting as she did so. Her pulse made her temples vibrate. She cursed her love of books, knowing her family's small library was housed in that trunk.

"Excuse me, ma'am," a young man's voice called

from above her. The wild expression in Fiona's eyes startled him. "You look like you could use a hand."

"My children and I are fine, thank you," she replied coolly, noticing how handsome her Good Samaritan was. His whole face smiled when he smiled. Even the corners of his eyes were upturned. His boyish charm was winning.

"Name's Billy Noble, ma'am," he said, the sun warming his golden hair as he nodded with respect. "I mean you no harm. I'm happy to give you a hand. Are those three trunks and the boy on top yours too?" He glanced toward Caleb, who was doing his best to appear invincible but succeeded only in appearing very small against their new reality. "Here, let me help you with this first, and then I'll help you with the others. Where are you headed?"

"West."

"I mean with these trunks, ma'am."

Fiona smiled, breaking the uncertain tension. She extended her hand to him. "Fiona Lenihan. This is my daughter, Maggie. My son, Caleb, is over there. I need to find a merchant named Jacob Getty, where I can purchase a wagon and team. Then I need to point my family west."

"I'm acquainted with Mr. Getty, ma'am. I'll take you to him. I can introduce you to a wagon master or two. At sunup tomorrow, I'm heading out with a company, but we're full up. I'll find another for you to join. Your husband, ma'am?"

Fiona shook her head, surprised such an obvious inquiry had caught her off guard.

"My apologies. Let's get you fixed up."

Fiona hoped she wasn't being foolish in trusting

this stranger, but she felt that any help, even bad help, would be better than none.

It didn't take long for Fiona to discover how fortunate she was to have made the acquaintance of Billy Noble. The thought of money changing and negotiating with merchants terrified her. She had never been responsible for more than the meager allowance Simon had allowed her each week for household incidentals. Purchasing one-way train tickets was the most complex transaction she had undertaken.

She felt lightheaded when more than three-quarters of the money Stanley Cushing had given her was gone in less than two hours.

Billy maneuvered her through the acquisition of a covered wagon and two yoke of oxen. Fiona purchased a goat and a cow for milk. Caleb and Maggie's mouths were agape watching their mother's ease at handling livestock: a woman dressed in black silk taffeta, her velvet handbag hanging in the crook of her arm, lifting the animals' feet to check their hooves for chips and pulling aside flaps of skin to check their teeth and tongues.

The children named the oxen Balthazar, Daisy, Elijah, and Rosie. Maggie called the cow Blossom, while Caleb named the goat Rufus.

"You'll need to help your ma take real good care of these animals, you hear?" Billy said to Caleb. "They'll need to get you all the way to California, and there won't be a chance to get new ones along the way if anything happens to these ones."

"Is this really our last chance?" Fiona asked Billy.

"No, but almost. When you meet up with a company in Independence or St. Joseph, that will pretty much be your last chance. Your wagon is light, so you're doing them a favor already. Just treat 'em real nice and they're sure to get you to your new home."

Fiona procured a Dutch oven for baking bread, tin dishes and cooking utensils that could withstand several months in the wilderness, and barrels of flour, sugar, coffee, rice, oats, two types of beans, and bacon packed in a barrel of cornmeal.

Billy found a company for her to join and made the necessary arrangements. The travel schedule he arranged allowed for a full day to settle into her wagon and purchase additional items she discovered she would need, such as a butter churn.

The Lenihans would join a small wagon train bound for St. Louis, the easternmost jumping-off point for the Oregon Trail. The wagon master, Clive Owens, was traveling west with his extended family. They were headed only as far as St. Louis, where they planned to capitalize on the westward expansion by setting up a trading post. Mr. Owens promised Fiona she would have her choice of wagon masters when she arrived in St. Louis. That is, if she desired to leave St. Louis. The growing city might offer a widow with young children the type of new start she craved.

Hands were shaken and the Lenihan wagon became the eighth wagon to come under the protection of Clive and his three sons. The seventh wagon belonged to a doctor and his wife who were headed to California.

Fiona was relieved to have found the Owens family to be a kind but unremarkable band of travelers. None of them seemed particularly interested in her situation, which suited her.

Once they were settled, Fiona offered Billy money,

which he refused twice before taking. "Please join us for supper," she invited. "You've been so kind to my children and me. I could never repay you."

She made a meal of savory stew and fresh biscuits, while Billy enchanted Fiona and the children with his story.

He was leaving at dawn with a small, fast-moving wagon train bound for Independence, Missouri, where he had signed on as a teamster for a wagon master leading a large company to California.

"How did you come into wagon mastering as a vocation?" Fiona asked, ladling him a second helping of stew.

"I had went to New York City to look for work and met a fellow who said he had a job for me if I could get to Independence by the first of May," Billy replied, digging into the stew with gusto.

"A wagon master?" Fiona asked, offering him another biscuit.

"Oh, more than that, ma'am. He's lived with Injuns, been around the world, and crossed to the Pacific Ocean more than a hundred times."

"He certainly sounds like he would appeal to your sense of adventure."

"Folks say he's the best tracker, best shot, and best guide of our time, ma'am. He cut his teeth with Jim Bridger—the mountain man and fur trader," he continued, seeing Fiona's lack of recognition.

"Did he know Daniel Boone?" Caleb asked with excitement.

"He might at that," Billy replied.

"And Davy Crocket?" Caleb almost squealed.

"He just might."

"He sounds like a man of fiction to me," Fiona chided.

"Oh, he's real enough, ma'am," Billy continued, his eyes bright with the thought of being in the company of such a man.

Fiona and her children listened to Billy, intrigued by his zest for the new life that awaited him. He told tales of rich farmlands, sunshine, even gold in California. It infected the Lenihans, making them hunger for all that awaited them in the West. Their meeting could not have been more fortuitous, coming at a time when Fiona's confidence was tentative.

"You're a good man, Billy," Fiona said when he rose to say goodnight. "We were indeed fortunate to have crossed paths with you. All good wishes for a safe journey."

Billy returned her firm handshake. "Good luck out there, ma'am. Maybe I'll see you all in California."

"May we be so fortunate."

"Especially for more of your fine cookin', ma'am," he said, grinning broadly.

After her children had drifted to sleep, Fiona busied herself sewing the bulk of her money into her petticoats. She had never taken needle to thread, so her efforts were crude. Now that she had a sense of what things cost, she kept handy only what she would need for food and other supplies. Surrounded by strangers, Fiona feared treachery and decided the best place to keep her money was on her person.

That night when Fiona hit her knees, she bowed her head in thanksgiving for the turn of events at the start of their journey. Billy Noble. The Owens family. She prayed their good fortune would continue.

The next day she purchased all she could carry of dried vegetables, cinnamon, vanilla, and pepper. By comparison, her pantry was exotic. Neither the Owens family nor most of the strangers around them had ever imagined the food she had first learned to cook and then grown accustomed to eating. Her impulse purchases included a bag of peppermints and packages of vegetable seeds to plant a garden.

At the end of the day, Fiona closed the rear flap of her wagon and sat with her children. "Do you know how much I love you?"

"Yes," Caleb replied, wiser than his years.

"Tomorrow we are going to begin a grand adventure. Now we must pray that all will go well for us."

"Do you think we'll meet Mr. Noble again?" Caleb asked.

"Maybe one day."

After a shower of kisses, she tucked them in and blew out the lantern.

While sleep came easily to Caleb and Maggie, it eluded Fiona. Doubt crept into her thoughts. Would this journey be their salvation or their doom? What if sickness or injury claimed one of her children? What if it took her life? How would her children survive? Fiona shifted and turned, trying to drive away demons.

Instead, she traveled to County Leitrim, where the thwap-thwap of a tree branch on the canopy of her wagon became the beat of a bodhran. Tears stained her pillow as the Lenihans danced and sang at a ceili, where Seamus whirled with a joy she could hardly recall him possessing.

They were happy then, the five Lenihan children

and their kinsmen. She sank into the comfort of her long-dead mother's embrace, the smell of baking bread perfuming the memory.

So as not to wake the children, she climbed from her wagon and stood under the full moon, shaking her fist at the faeries who made her relive the past. Now she must be about the future. She wiped her eyes and returned to bed, crying herself to sleep to the sound of a distant fiddle.

Chapter 3

"What a fine family you have." A silver-haired gentleman paused to compliment Fiona on Caleb and Maggie as they broke camp the next morning. He was taken aback by how startled Fiona seemed at his remarks. "Earl Pickering, at your service. My wife and I will be traveling with you. I see you have been touched with sadness," he said, nodding to Fiona's black dress.

"My husband. I am Fiona Lenihan, and these are my children, Caleb and Maggie. Lenihan," she said, almost as an afterthought. "We're pleased to make your acquaintance. You are from Philadelphia?"

"New York City."

Fiona felt oddly relieved by his reply.

"One of the most exciting places in the world," she said, her smile broadening.

"A bit too exciting for old folks. You know it?"

"My husband..." she said hesitantly, because of the odd sound of that word in her ears and because she feared she may have been foolish in beginning a conversation with this stranger. "My husband and I spent a week there for the opening of opera season."

"Splendid. My son tells me San Francisco boasts similar pleasures. You must join my wife and me. I'm surprised to find an opera aficionado among our number."

"You flatter me, Mr. Pickering, but as with so

many things, I am a novice."

"Your wagon and ours are the only two non-Owens wagons in this company. Please let me know if you need anything. My condolences to you all."

"Thank you. But I believe I am mistaken, *Doctor* Pickering," she said, correcting her address. "You must be the physician who is traveling with us."

"And my wife, Libby, my nurse."

"I will be as pleased to meet her as I am you, Doctor Pickering."

"'Doc' is formal enough," he said with a small bow.

"All right, Doc Pickering. If I may ask, why are you and Mrs. Pickering making the journey west?"

"With two of our children and their families already settled in California, and the undeniable benefits of the climate, it seemed sensible to join them in our final years. And you? What brings you west?"

"In search of a new beginning."

"To travel so far to find one?" he inquired.

"One does what one can, if for no reasons other than the two in my wagon."

"Ah, yes," he agreed. "Libby and I will be pleased to have your company on the journey."

Fiona smiled politely. Her life as a Cushing had made her accustomed to interacting with men like him: elegant, educated, wealthy.

"Say, might your son have an interest in helping an old, arthritic physician? These hands don't roll bandages like they used to."

"Of course," Fiona said. "Anytime you like."

"I hope you will join Libby and me for dinner this evening," he said, displaying his social graces.

"Thank you. We would be pleased." She was thrilled to have made a new acquaintance, and especially so as Fiona Lenihan.

Doc had offered his services gratis to his traveling companions. All he needed was another driver to guide a second wagon filled with medical supplies. One of the Owens boys agreed to drive it to Missouri. Fiona found this collaboration between strangers to be one of the most surprising aspects of the journey. She was intrigued by the ready trust the travelers put in one another.

When Fiona brought Caleb to Doc to help him roll bandages, they were astonished by the sheer volume of supplies. The wagon was packed nearly to the canvas ceiling with bags and crates.

"California is a long way from here," Doc explained.

"What's in all those?" Caleb asked, wide-eyed.

"Laudanum, bandages, alcohol—a whole inventory of healing aids."

"So many," Fiona said, absentmindedly.

"From what I've heard, I'm afraid by the time we reach California it may be too few."

When Doc saw Fiona's expression of mild horror, he continued.

"With so many travelers, things are bound to happen: accidents, infection, disease. Folks tell me the weather conditions can be extreme. And then there are the Indians."

"Indians!" Caleb exclaimed, his face alight.

"Yes," Doc said. "Not all are friendly. We can hope to avoid the unfriendly ones, but the Indians are nomadic, so there are no guarantees."

"Why are they unfriendly?" Caleb asked.

"Because we're in their territory. Or because other folks met them in conflict, so the Indians will not be as accommodating to the next white folk they meet."

As Fiona listened to Doc, her confidence waned. Perhaps she had undertaken too risky a journey. Maybe she should reconsider when they reached St. Louis or Independence. There could be work that would allow her to send Caleb and Maggie to school. She soothed her anxiety by telling herself there would be plenty of opportunities to make such a decision.

Doc was intimidating despite his unimpressive stature. He stood closer to five feet than to six, but he had a booming voice that lent him immediate authority. A shock of stick-straight white hair fell in a bold cowlick across his forehead. But for the pomade, it might have moved when he talked. He was remarkably good-humored and quick to laugh, especially at his own remarks.

When Fiona met Libby Pickering, Doc grew more colorful in her eyes. Libby was placid and reserved. Against the bland sweetness of his wife, Doc appeared vivid. But if Libby wasn't memorable for her engaging presence, she was for the sincere kindness she exhibited to everyone. Fiona began to suspect the woman with the perpetual smile never let a cross thought invade her mind.

Libby faded to the background. She was the perfect foil for her avuncular mate. His role was curer and hero, saving lives and making them right again. Libby was her husband's helpmate. Where his cure ended, her work began.

Fiona observed Doc's ease with young people. She

watched him teach Caleb and the Owens children. Before long, Caleb had become Doc's assistant, organizing supply boxes in exchange for pearls of wisdom regarding physiology and medicine. Fiona could not put a price on this experience.

When she studied the Pickerings, Fiona saw a great love between them, particularly of Doc for Libby. It was in the way he looked at her, the way he relied on her, the way his confidence shone when he was in her presence. Doc cherished his wife. It brought a smile to Fiona's lips.

The company set out from Wheeling and was ferried across the Ohio River, one wagon at a time. Their traveling party included more than forty Owens family members divided among six wagons, plus three Pickering and Lenihan wagons. It took nearly a full day for everyone to cross the river. With a sigh, Fiona realized it was going to be a long journey.

The way they made camp the first night set the pattern for the next six weeks. The Owens family kept largely to themselves, leaving the Lenihans and Pickerings together most of the time.

The company took meals as a group. It did not take long for Fiona's skills to earn her the position of senior cook. Libby and the Owens women took lessons from Fiona, learning new ways to season food with herbs and grasses she taught them to gather, such as sorrel, spicebush, thyme, and mint.

They ate fresh fish, boar, geese, and wild turkeys when the Owens men could find them. When the meat supply was running low, lunch and dinner were often soup and bread with stewed fruit. One night, Clive Owens handed Fiona three freshly killed squirrels.

"Squirrels?" she asked, with a mixture of incredulity and disgust.

"Good eatin', ma'am. Especially the brains. Meat makes a nice stew. Just have to watch for bones."

"Squirrels," she repeated, wearing a false smile. It had never occurred to her that a squirrel was good for anything more than harassing dogs.

Fiona could make magic out of a pot of slop, wrangle livestock, tend to gardens and fields, and tease ecstasy from a keyboard. One thing she could not do was sew. Her older sisters had been the Lenihans' tailors; Fiona had spent her early life hunched over row upon row of potato leaves. As a Cushing servant, she had learned how to cook, polish silver, and make guests feel welcome.

As a Cushing woman, a house staff of three had tended to her every need. Her sumptuous dresses had been tailored for her. The closest she had come to a needle and thread were occasional attempts at embroidery. Evenings were spent at concerts, lectures, and a dizzying calendar of parties; Sunday dinners at the elder Cushings' home were required.

Fiona's life now could hardly have been more different. Every challenge was on a grander scale. In her twenty-eight years, Fiona had lived four lives. First was her life in Ireland, followed by her life as a Cushing immigrant and field hand, and then her life as a servant in the Cushings' home. Fourth was her life as a Cushing daughter-in-law. Now, she would be a single mother living on the frontier, the most daunting of all.

One morning she awakened before the other travelers. Sunrise beckoned, and she climbed from her wagon to watch. The fog lifted around her as the sky brightened from a pale lavender to a warm shade of orange.

The flowers were heavy with dew, the air sweet with springtime's tender buds. It occurred to Fiona she had not been visited by memories of her past for several days. As she had hoped, the daily tasks had occupied her fully, leaving her untroubled by ghosts.

The company paid a toll in Ohio to travel the Cumberland Road. Along the way, Fiona noticed mothers and children gathering clay from the soil to make pottery. She saw men mining coal. In between were endless fields with families working them. Everywhere the land was providing for the people who lived on it.

She was struck by the bounty of the land. Unlike in Ireland, land was a place for sustaining life in a multitude of ways, from its rich harvests to its plentiful game and supply of fish in the rivers and streams. If all of America were this rich with abundance, their journey promised to be easy.

One day was largely like the next but for variances in the weather. Rainy days were harder on man and beast, with the mud and the damp. Fortunately, the company was blessed with more sunshine than rain, which made their forty days of travel pass more quickly. When conditions were good, they could put ten to fifteen miles behind them each day.

Fiona taught Caleb how to gather cow chips and dry wood to start a fire, and how to milk the cow. It didn't go smoothly at first, but in time he could fill a pail as well as any farm boy. Fiona churned the butter because Caleb wasn't quite strong enough. Maggie played beside her when she worked, amusing herself with dolls made from twigs and grasses. Caleb played with the Owens boys, wading in creeks and making mud pies.

Fiona liked the sense of community that formed each night when the wagons were circled to corral the livestock and protect the travelers from wild animals and other unwelcome visitors. No one was permitted to leave the safety of the enclosure but for those who kept watch.

The campfire was the hub of the moveable community. It glowed in the center of camp, used first for cooking and then for warmth and companionship.

Fiona and some of the Owens men sat in silence by the fire one evening, watching the waning flames. The Owens men smoked their pipes, too weary to maintain conversation. Camped beneath a canopy of trees, the setting had an intimate feel, safe and protected. Flowers, grasses, and clover freshened the air.

She stoked the fire and watched a storm of cinders rise against the night sky, like faeries dispersed over the countryside. In all, she had managed to bring her children some seven hundred miles. The remaining two hundred would be easier still in the growing warmth of late spring into summer, when they would reach St. Louis. After that they would travel within the security of a larger company.

She could do this, she reasoned. It was possible.

****

The Cumberland Road was a popular thoroughfare with heavy traffic in both directions. It had macadamized pavement in sections, which made for easy travel even when it rained. It was a toll road, which meant that each time they crossed into a new state Fiona needed to reach into the hem of her petticoat.

She watched people along the road with curiosity, wondering who they were, where they were going, and where they had been. They traveled single file most of the way through Ohio, Indiana, Illinois, and finally Missouri. It was a civilized experience, not far removed from taking a spin in the country with horse and buggy.

Fiona marveled at seeing travelers who were nothing like Philadelphia society or the Cushing Irish and realized how insulated her world had been as servant and served.

One day they came upon a man and his family returning to the East. In exchange for a cup of coffee he was willing to share his story. Fiona thought it odd that his family stayed by their wagon and did not look at him when he crossed to the Owens party.

"The way west is filled with danger," he began, nursing his cup. He was bursting with stories of wild beasts, storms of Biblical proportions, and savage Indians. Two of the Owens boys shook their heads and left those gathered around the storyteller. But Fiona listened intently, her concern growing by the minute. Just when she had been feeling good about their progress, this stranger arrived to deflate her expectations.

"You should turn back now," he warned. "What's out there is worse than anything you could have left behind."

After he had returned to his family, Doc spoke. "Do not let what this man said deter you. He exaggerates the dangers and says little of the benefits. I have read about these men who fail on the journey and make outlandish excuses to cover their incompetence. You noticed his family's regard for him, did you not?"

Fiona nodded.

"We'll have the benefit of traveling west under the expert guidance of a seasoned wagon master. Many men make the journey on their own. Many succeed. But you have seen the cost to one man. Folks call it 'seeing the elephant,' a gentle way of saying this man packed up his family and took them who knows how far across the country. One day he decided to turn back. He'd 'seen the elephant,' which was good enough for him. Now he could return home, as if seeing this mythical pachyderm was all his journey was about, never mind settling his family in the West."

Doc gave her a reassuring pat on her shoulder. Still, Fiona was troubled by what she had heard. She hoped that before six months passed, she would have done more than tease her children with a mere glimpse of some lost zoo animal.

The farther west they traveled, the more taxing the journey became. Everyone in the company had chores but for Maggie, who hung at her mother's skirts. Caleb helped his mother hitch and unhitch their team of oxen. He and the Owens boys drew water each night when they made camp, making several trips to the nearby river to collect all that was needed for cooking or cleaning. Fiona gradually warmed to this division of labor. Beyond the necessity, it fostered a sense of community where everyone had a stake in the company's success.

Every night her body was wracked with pain, especially the places where Simon had most recently left his mark on her. Each time she strained a muscle that had not yet healed from Simon's touch, it felt like a fresh assault.

Her shoulders and thighs were sore from raising the heavy yoke to the oxen; her hands were raw from holding the reins and tying the necessary knots. Her arms ached from wrestling livestock and tending cooking fires. She relied on the poultice a Cushing Irishwoman had taught her to make and kept a container of butter-based cream at the ready. She recalled fondly her bunkmate in the Cushing field hands' quarters, who taught her the healing benefits of roots and bark.

Some nights Fiona lost sleep, questioning her judgment, especially when she watched her children. Most nights sleep came quickly. She rose with the sun, a stiffened mess of sinew, ready to take on another day.

The routine became less exhausting as the emigrants were strengthened by chores. By the time they had traveled ten days and 135 miles and put Columbus, Ohio, behind them, Fiona found herself feeling better than she had in months.

Soon, she had energy to spare. Her dress began to fit her differently. Where her body had been weak, now it felt strong. At night she continued to sleep heavily, not stirring once.

She cherished bedtime because it meant stillness and stories. The lantern cast long shadows on the wagon's canvas ceiling. Caleb and Maggie became listeners rather than curious travelers who questioned much of what they saw.

It was an opportunity for Fiona to acquaint her children with her side of the family, on whom she had been silent during their years as Cushings. She told them what it was like to grow up in Ireland and the fun she had with her siblings running across fields and walking along stone walls. Caleb was taken with every detail. Maggie was less interested in stories of people she could not imagine.

"What happened to them?" Caleb asked.

"There was a terrible hunger. There was no food and it was wintertime."

"Why didn't you buy food?"

"Because we had no money to buy food. Our lives were very different from the life you and Maggie have known," she said, changing the subject. "You rest now. Tomorrow will be a full day." She kissed them each on the cheek and rose to turn down the lamp.

"What about Uncle Seamus?" Caleb's voice rang in the darkness.

"What about him?" Fiona answered warily.

"He worked at Grandfather Cushing's with you. What happened to him?"

"There was an accident," she replied, hoping he would ask no more.

"Did he die?"

"Yes," she said after a pause. "Your Uncle Seamus died working in the fields."

"How?" he persisted, planting his elbows on the floorboards and his chin in his hands.

"It makes me sad to think about it," she said. "I'll tell you another time. But I will tell you a tale of Finn MacCool, the way your Uncle Seamus used to tell me about Finn MacCool."

"Who's Finn MacCool?"

"Some say he was a giant, others say he was just a man, but a very good man, one of the most generous and trusted of all. He was the leader of the Fianna, an army of invincible soldiers who served the High King Cormac. It was the duty of the Fianna to uphold the principles of justice and order in Ireland.

"Now, Finn MacCool was among the smartest men in all Ireland. He gained his wisdom from the Salmon of Knowledge, who was caught by the great druid Finegas."

"What's a druid?" Caleb asked.

"What's a salmon?" Maggie asked.

"A fish. A druid is a holy man who practices magic and offers wisdom," Fiona continued without losing her pace. "Finn touched the great fish while it was cooking, and it burned his thumb. Finn sucked his thumb to ease the pain and discovered that by sucking his thumb he could see into the future. With that, Finn learned his thumb was his source of wisdom. Whenever he needed insight, he simply sucked his thumb. Now goodnight."

"So I can get smart by touching a fish?" Caleb asked.

"In your case, by eating one. The next time we cook fish I want you to remember that."

****

One of the pleasantries of the journey to St. Louis was the growing blanket of wildflowers—nature's patchwork quilt. They made cheery traveling companions with their bursts of color.

Maggie collected wildflowers whenever they made camp. It was Fiona's job to find a container for them and keep the blossoms alive until the next day when her daughter would present a fresh bouquet. Fiona supported Maggie's passion because she could pursue it within fifteen feet of wherever Fiona worked.

"What's this one?" Maggie asked Fiona one afternoon when they were at the river's edge doing the wash.

"That's a pink one," Fiona said authoritatively, pausing a moment from her scrubbing to look at what Maggie had in her hand.

"What's this one?" Maggie asked, holding up a different pink flower.

"That's a very pretty pink flower," Fiona replied, returning to the grass stains in Caleb's shirt.

"What's this one?" Maggie asked.

"A very big, very pretty, pink flower," Fiona said with a sidelong glance.

"This one?"

"A yellow and pink flower."

"Perhaps I can be of assistance," Libby offered, leaving her wash to soak as she knelt by Maggie. "I was a member of the garden society. Why don't you show me what you have," she invited.

Maggie handed her the flowers.

"This one looks like a buttercup," Libby began. "And this one is a prairie rose, I think. These are violets," she said, pointing to a cluster of purple flowers. "These are black-eyed Susans, and this looks like a kind of gentian."

Fiona watched Maggie's determined focus on Libby's every word and smiled her thanks.

"I like flowers too," Libby explained to Maggie. "I had a flower garden outside my home in New York and am proud to say award-winning roses by the front porch. The first thing I'm going to do in California is plant a flower garden."

"Did you bring seeds with you?" Fiona asked.

"Oh yes. All my favorites. Flowers have always given me such joy."

"They suit you."

"As they suit Maggie," Libby said.

One afternoon as they were winding down their travel day, Fiona sang quietly. It was an old Irish folk song whose rhythm matched the oxen's gait. Her soprano was like a flute; her trills clear and bell-like. Maggie learned the refrain and joined her mother in song.

"How did you learn to sing?" Caleb asked.

"We Lenihans were a musical family. Your Aunt Maeve could play the fiddle as if her life depended on it. Uncle Colm had a lovely tenor that blended perfectly with your grandm'ar's alto. And Aunt Katie could dance. She was the finest in all Ballinaglera. We used to gather at home with our cousins, aunts, and uncles," she said, her smile fading to memory.

That night when Fiona tucked her children into bed, Caleb asked her to tell him more about Finn MacCool.

"Not only was Finn MacCool a giant, but he was the strongest man in all Ireland. Word of his great strength reached across the Irish Sea to Scotland, where a Scottish giant vowed to challenge Finn in a test of strength. Finn and his men built a great stone bridge to Scotland for the Scottish giant to cross. But when the bridge, called Giant's Causeway, got close to Scotland and Finn could see the immense size of his rival, he stopped building the bridge."

"Did you ever see it?" Caleb asked.

"No."

"Why?"

"Because I never traveled that far from my home," Fiona replied.

"Did Finn fight the Scottish giant?"

"Yes, but I'll tell you about that another time. Sleep now, for dawn will arrive before you know it," she said, kissing him goodnight.

Fiona sat up after the rest of the camp had grown quiet. She stared into the dying campfire, seeing not flames but something dark and secret. Shadows distorted her face with the ash of memories—memories of her Finn MacCool, Seamus Lenihan.

His sacrifice had brought her to America. He could have found work anywhere, unencumbered by a promise to work for three years in exchange for his passage on Stanley Cushing's ship. But he had come back for his family, only to find all of them dead but for Fiona and their younger brother, Colm.

When they arrived in America, the dream that had sustained Seamus was owning a farm in Pennsylvania, working the land without owing anyone anything. On the day he died, kicked in the head by an unruly draft horse, Fiona had vowed she would never again rely on the land to make a living. The land had taken everyone she loved from her.

A log snapped, breaking her reverie. Tears rimmed her eyes but did not fall. She had never let them fall since that day. The land had claimed her brothers and sisters, her father and aunts, uncles, and cousins. Her wee nephew. Yet here she was, nearing the border of Indiana, on a journey to a place where she and her children were to break her vow and work the land.

It seemed an odd catastrophe had happened when God looked away for a moment. Surely this was not what He had planned for her family. Surely it was all a mistake. This was not how it was supposed to be, that she was the one who had been left behind to find her way in a world without them.

As she sat by the fire, tangled in thoughts, she came to see her situation as an affirmation of the dream she and Seamus had shared. She would not build a farm with her brother, but with her brother's niece and nephew. She would do it to honor his sacrifice. In that way she could carry on for the Lenihans. The dream of Seamus Lenihan was still alive.

****

A wagon train's existence hung in a peculiar balance, with disaster a constant threat. But so many things that could have gone wrong did not. They had beautiful spring weather for nearly their entire journey. They made good time.

During a rainy spell, a wheel fell off one of the Owens's wagons. Each broken wheel cost the company a half day of travel. While not an unusual occurrence, it was never welcome.

In the idle time, Fiona busied herself with meal preparation. She peeled potatoes, striking away the skin with each stroke, like flint to stone. She sliced them lengthwise, then crosswise, the blade of her knife a blur in her hands. With the edge of the knife she swept the pieces into a pot of broth, missing not one. Carrots followed, then onions.

"Mrs. Lenihan!" Doc's urgent call interrupted her rhythm. She wiped her hands on her apron as she ran, following his voice. A chorus of children's voices echoed his plea.

The broken-down wagon had fallen on Harold

Owens, Clive Owens's oldest son, who was in the process of changing the wheel when several hundred pounds collapsed on his leg. His wife was too hysterical to be of help, and Libby had gone with the older children to draw water.

A gruesome sight greeted Fiona. The lower half of Harold Owens's body was concealed beneath the wagon. He stared emptily at the sky. Ashen and still, he looked dead to her, except that he blinked his eyes every so often. A pool of blood seeped into the earth.

Fiona knelt at Harold's side, holding his hand to comfort him while Doc instructed her.

Her first job was to distract the young man while Doc worked to place a tourniquet around the uppermost part of Harold's thigh. "When we lift this wagon, he'll bleed to death if we don't shut down this artery," Doc explained.

On a count of three, the other Owens men lifted the wagon. Once free, Fiona helped Doc move Harold away from the wagon. She could see his thigh had been reduced to a shamble, like a tureen smashed against a tile floor. His torn pant leg was shiny with blood.

Doc used a knife to rip open the pant leg from its seam. Fiona turned away, unable to look at what remained of Harold's leg.

"We're going to have to take it off about two inches above the knee," Doc explained, his tone grave.

"Not my boy's leg!" Clive shouted.

Harold's wife screamed and ran to push Doc away from her husband. Some of the Owens boys restrained her.

"His bones are too broken to mend, and his artery is torn. There's no repairing this, even in a hospital. I'm sorry, Clive. He'll die if we don't do this. I'll need you or one of your sons to stay with us but would suggest that most of you leave and take her with you," he said quietly, gesturing toward Harold's wife.

"Can you do this?" he asked Fiona.

She nodded, as much to assure herself as to assure him.

Doc instructed Fiona and Clive on their roles. Fiona would assist with instruments while Clive would hold his son in the event he became conscious. Doc laid out his tools in the order he needed them.

Fiona gulped when she eyed what Doc would use for the amputation. It was a saw that looked little different from one that hung in the tool shed on the Cushing estate.

Although Harold hardly seemed conscious, Doc placed a rag soaked with ether over his face. Fiona watched the young man's eyes flutter then close. Doc went to work, cleaning the skin around the wound to identify the best place to make the cut. His goal was to preserve as much of Harold's leg as possible, even though it would be reduced to a stump.

Doc worked quickly to remove the ruined leg, stitch the gaping vessels, and bandage what remained. Then he removed the tourniquet.

Clive Owens cried silently as Doc Pickering maimed his son to save his life.

Fiona knew until the day she died she would never forget the sound of the saw as it cut through Harold's leg, through a young man's muscle and tendon and bone. Or the expression on Harold's face, even through a medicinal haze.

Libby arrived just as Doc had finished his work.

She placed her hand on Fiona's shoulder for support. Quietly, she showed Fiona how to tidy the operating arena, such as it was, and make the patient presentable to family members.

Doc and Clive disappeared with the medical tools and ruined lower leg. Libby explained to Fiona how they would bury the flesh, and how Doc would clean his instruments.

Libby instructed Fiona on how to make the patient comfortable, building a bed for him out of blankets. Then they sat by his side and waited for him to awaken.

"We should get his wife," Libby said. "It will be important for her to be here when he opens his eyes."

"She was distraught."

"Many are. If she is unable to sit with him, you and I can, in shifts, if you have the time."

Fiona nodded.

"I'll watch your children while you sit with him. This is the most difficult of procedures, I think," she said after a silence. "At first, the value of their lives pales in comparison to the value they place on their limbs."

Fiona was struck by the division of labor: where Doc's job ended, Libby's began. There was overlap when Doc stopped by to check on Harold, and as first Fiona and then Libby had assisted with the surgical procedure. It was an interesting blend of curing and healing. Perhaps that was why they called it an art.

Fiona sat with Harold, waiting for him to awaken. But in each of her hour-long shifts he remained asleep. She was relieved that he awakened during Libby's shift, for she was not certain she would have had the proper words. From across the camp she heard Harold's lament and knew of his despair at discovering his leg was gone.

"You impress me with your capacity to give," Doc said from behind her as Fiona sat by the fire. Although she held a book, she had not been reading. Her mind was filled with too many things stirred by her care for Harold.

She smiled her thanks. "It's the one thing I'm good at, I think."

"You are practiced at it," he said, sitting on a nearby log and lighting a pipe.

"I used to do charitable work through our church," Fiona said.

"Important work," Doc acknowledged, exhaling a smoke ring. It brought a smile to Fiona's lips.

"I find comfort in helping people. It's easy to kiss a child's wound to make it better, satisfying to give food to those who are hungry, to hold the hands of those recovering from illness. What will happen to Harold?"

"He should heal. He's a merchant, not a farmer, so that is a blessing. Trust in the power of nature. It's in God's hands now."

****

One evening Doc came upon Fiona and Caleb sitting together by the campfire. Caleb was reading aloud. Doc smiled when he realized the boy was reading from Meriwether Lewis and William Clark's journals. Fiona invited Doc to sit with them.

"Libby and I have been speaking about the future," he began, studying the faces of his audience. "I don't know what plans you have made, but Libby and I are to find a man named Kieran Moran when we arrive in Independence. He's leading a wagon train from there.

Our children know him. They say he is the best."

Fiona glanced at Caleb, who looked at her trustingly. "You and Mrs. Pickering have been so kind to us. Seeing the opera in San Francisco with anyone else would not be as meaningful. Thank you. We would very much like to come with you."

Doc bid them goodnight.

Fiona gazed beyond her son, beyond the shadow of the doctor, to the full moon that hung in the sky. She had been trusting God and the spirits to see her and her children through this ordeal. Since her dealings with the Cushings she had been hesitant to trust in anyone. Now she had been blessed with Earl and Libby Pickering, and soon with Kieran Moran.

For the first time in a long time she had a sense of real hope for the future, rather than the shaky faith in herself she had been relying on to bring them this far. Truly someone was looking out for them.

The company reached the end of the Cumberland Road and pulled into St. Louis at dusk. Exhausted from a physically taxing day of travel, they were in want of food and rest. But Fiona and the Pickerings had a more important thing on their minds: Kieran Moran. They were but one outpost away from the man who would lead them home.

Chapter 4

"Your daughter looks like you," said a smoky voice with an unmistakable Irish lilt.

Fiona turned to see its owner, a handsome older woman who wore her hair in a long gray braid. She had a lived-in face and crystal blue eyes that looked warmly toward Fiona. Smile lines were permanently embedded in skin baked brown by the sun.

When the woman extended her hand to make Fiona's acquaintance, her eye was drawn to the large silver bracelet that decorated the woman's wrist. She wore a cuff made of five bands of silver on her other wrist. A large sterling ring with a turquoise stone adorned her index finger. A necklace of silver and turquoise stones the size of plums covered her chest inside the open collar of her blouse.

The handiwork was like nothing Fiona had ever seen. Made of tooled sterling, the craftsmanship reminded her of ancient Celtic designs. But the turquoise stones were new to her. A bold echo of the sky.

The woman's handshake was firm, almost masculine. Her hands were broad and creased, like those of a laborer. Fiona knew at once they suited her. Her self-confidence put Fiona at ease.

Her name was Clare Moran.

"Moran, did you say?" Fiona asked.

"Yes. Clare Moran. My husband, Gideon, is just over there." Her voice was warm and rich, like toasted almonds.

"We've been traveling with people who are looking to join a company led by a man named Kieran Moran once we reach Independence."

"That would be our son. In that case I am indeed pleased to meet you, for we will be traveling companions."

Fiona's receptive expression bid her continue.

"Where are you from?"

"Philadelphia."

"Not where you've been, where you're from," the older woman clarified.

"County Leitrim," Fiona replied, understanding the deeper meaning of the question.

"I should have guessed. I would have said Monaghan. County Meath was my home until I was about your son's age. Gideon, this lovely girl is from Leitrim," she said to her husband as he approached.

Gideon Moran nodded his greeting but spoke not a word. He had a regal bearing, one that Fiona supposed was not indigenous for it appeared habitual rather than natural. He seemed at once distracted or bored, taking in everything around him. Silent, his manner struck Fiona as arrogant. The kind of man who was unable to focus on anyone because nothing around him merited his attention. She sensed he was difficult to please.

"We've been traveling with Earl and Libby Pickering, who are eager to meet your son," Fiona said. "Their children have told them about him."

"Really?" Clare laughed, beaming with a mother's pride.

"Where is your son now?"

"Somewhere in the mountains, doing work for the government. He doesn't stay in one place for too long. Would you like some tea? I was just getting ready to sit down for a cup. If you can spare the time, I would enjoy your company."

"I would like that," Fiona replied, looking to where her children were playing beside their wagon.

Fiona was surprised when Clare handed her a delicate, hand-painted cup and saucer.

"My attempt to civilize an experience that will prove quite the contrary, I am sure. Sugar?"

"Thank you, no. It hasn't been so difficult. The roads are good. I didn't know what to expect, but we've made it this far, and it's been almost pleasant. Now that we've finished with the Cumberland Road, I'm wondering what the road will be like for the next part of our journey."

Clare stared at her oddly. "Where we're going there are no roads."

"How will we find our way?" Fiona asked, unaware of how naive her comment sounded. It had never occurred to her there would not be groomed roads all the way across America. She had never been in a place with no roads.

"My son will show us, and we will follow, bringing culture with us." She raised her teacup in a toast.

"So out West isn't civilized?" Fiona said, wanting to be sure she understood Clare.

"You haven't met my son," she smiled fondly, sipping her tea.

"There's Libby," Fiona said, waving her over. "I know she'll want to meet you."

Libby stopped short when she saw Clare, who wore her eccentricity with abandon.

"Tea?" Clare offered in a fussy teacup, and a friendship was born.

****

St. Louis was a busy crossroads. Fiona estimated she saw hundreds of different travelers each day headed for different jumping-off points.

Some rafted along the river. Traveling parties floating on barges were a common sight. Others hired rafts to ferry them across the broad, flat river. Fiona saw wagons crossing at several points, oxen and men on horseback leading the way. So many people, she thought. So many were heading west. She and her children were but three of them.

The Lenihans and Pickerings joined the Morans and five other extended families who had heard about Kieran Moran and wanted to join his company. In all, forty-seven people traveled together the two hundred fifty miles to Independence, camping along the banks of the Missouri River. The going was more difficult, for now they journeyed over uneven paths trampled in the prairie grasses. There were more flies, more sunshine, and more humidity. But the river was lined with trees, so shade was plentiful.

Fiona's mourning dress was growing uncomfortable. She developed a rash where the streams of perspiration were trapped against her delicate skin. As her body swelled in the late spring warmth, her corset became unbearably restrictive. She tried going without it, but the buttons on her dress would not close. As with other elements of their journey, she hoped this would resolve itself. It was not yet summer; the worst of the heat lay ahead.

Over the course of their twenty-three days' travel to Independence, Clare described her son as a maverick who had attended the United States Military Academy at West Point but dropped out, spent a few years at sea, and followed that time as a guide and trapper in the West. He owned an empty house in California where his parents would live.

This conjured an image of an unsatisfied wanderer who lacked the patience to craft a home out of what Fiona envisioned was a lonely, small frame house on a humble plot of land with no roads leading to it.

In their old age, Clare and Gideon had decided to retire to Kieran's house. They were attracted by the climate, but Clare said it was the opportunity to spend time with their son that had attracted her more.

"He is our only child. In the last fifteen years we've seen him infrequently. When he was at sea he came to New York from time to time. I know in California we will see more of him, even though I understand he treats his house there as a sort of port."

"I hope you will see more of him," Fiona said. "I could not imagine living so far apart from my children."

"Nor could have I."

"Are you going to furnish your son's house with your things?" Fiona asked, sifting flour into a bowl.

"Yes. They are in storage now and will travel by ship to reach us after we arrive. We could have accompanied them, but the thought of living aboard ship terrified me. Moreover, Kieran told me it isn't safe. The sea route can be dangerous. Gideon objected, knowing what he knows about the dangers on land between here and California. But then no journey is without risk, is it?"

Clare and Gideon took to Fiona and her children instantly, becoming as adoptive parents and grandparents. They watched Caleb and Maggie when Fiona's talents were needed elsewhere to cook or nurse. While Clare told stories, Gideon whittled toys for the children.

Fiona began to realize Gideon was not what he seemed. At first, she had thought him remote. He spoke very little and maintained an air of disinterest. Given his strong presence, it never occurred to her that he may have been guarded and circumspect, even shy.

As with the Pickerings, Fiona saw Clare and Gideon were a good fit, with complementary strengths. When Gideon thought no one was looking, he was affectionate to Clare. Often, he took her face in his hands before kissing her forehead. Clare typically responded with a gentle pat. It made Fiona smile to watch them together, for seeing a good marriage gave her hope.

Caleb and Maggie adored the Morans. On their first day together, Maggie dubbed them "Mr. and Mrs. M," names that stuck throughout their journey despite Fiona's best efforts to encourage her daughter to address them properly. Gideon had bushy gray eyebrows that protruded well beyond his face. The caterpillar-like tufts of hair intrigued Maggie, who had pulled on one when they first met.

Clare was demonstrative, cuddling Maggie in her lap and listening patiently to Caleb's boyish dreams, including his retelling of Finn MacCool stories. It was a new experience for the children, who had never known such love from Stanley and Edna Cushing. The

Pickerings were kind to the children, but the Morans adored them.

The Lenihans, Morans, and Pickerings spent most of their free time together. The women took tea after they had made camp, while dinner cooked over the fire. They did their wash side by side at the river's edge, sharing feminine insights and talking about the future. They made an interesting trio, the earthy older woman at ease with her freedom, the docile physician's wife, and the young widow.

Women have a way of understanding one another. So it was with Clare and Libby on the matter of Kieran Moran.

"Tell us more about your son," Libby asked, opening their discussion over tea one sleepy afternoon. She fanned herself in the spring air thick with growing humidity. Clare glanced toward Fiona, wanting to make sure she had the young woman's attention before embarking on a topic on which they had been strangely silent since their first meeting.

"Someone once told him he was half-beast. His instincts are uncanny and guide his work crisscrossing land and sea," Clare began, putting brush to canvas as she began to reveal the portrait of her son.

In the following days Fiona learned much about Kieran. Libby fired a steady stream of questions at Clare. To the women's delight, Fiona proved an attentive listener.

Clare and Gideon had always wanted more children but had been blessed with only one child. "And even he did not want to be born," Clare said, her mouth smiling but her eyes sad. "He wriggled and pounded me from within. The doctor did not have to strike him to make him cry, for he was born howling. It was a pity we were unable to have more children. Had there been another to realize Gideon's dreams, Gideon and Kieran, two very different men, would not have clashed so horribly."

She described Gideon as a West Point man who had wanted his son to follow in his footsteps. But Kieran had suffered from wanderlust and was unable to commit to anything as structured as college. His nature conflicted with authority, and he had a yen for travel and adventure.

"While the father battled the Mexicans in eighteen forty-eight, the son battled his demons everywhere but in Mexico. Gideon earned three medals of valor during that war," Clare said proudly. "It's sad to think how father and son never managed to forge a mutual respect. If they were not father and son, I know they would be friends."

Fiona felt the depth of Clare's sadness.

"I understand your son has a reputation for his work," Libby continued, "and that many have heard of his talents and have sought him out to lead them west."

"Yes, but not in recent years. He's leading our company as a kindness to his father and me. He said he would lead us if we traveled cross-country rather than by sea. He is unwilling to promise our belongings will make it around Cape Horn intact."

"How did he come to lead people west?" asked Fiona.

"Nearly a decade ago he led some of the early wagon trains, the first settlers in California and Oregon. But he grew bored. He said the character of the emigrants made it difficult because they were so unprepared for the rigors of the journey. In recent years most of his travels have been of a government or commercial nature."

"We shall avoid trying his patience, then," offered Libby.

"Yes," added Fiona, not certain she was looking forward to meeting Kieran Moran. The more she heard about him, the more he sounded like the sort of man only a mother could love.

****

The Morans' wagon was filled with heirlooms and decorative furnishings Clare had deemed too valuable to send by sea. In contrast, the Lenihans' load was sparse. Everything was brand new. There was no furniture among their possessions and few personal treasures. Yet the Lenihans appeared as upper-class people. They had the manners of the very well-bred. They wore expensive clothing, especially Fiona's hand-beaded mourning dress. Clare and Gideon had lived comfortably in New York City but had never been near the opulence Fiona's dress projected.

"I'm sure you miss your father," Clare said to Caleb one day when he had asked to ride in the Morans' wagon.

"No," he replied. Then to Clare's surprise, he continued. "He was a bad man. He used to hurt my mother."

"Oh?" she said, exchanging glances with Gideon, who walked beside them.

"He used to hit her and make her bleed. She pretended it didn't happen. But I knew. I saw him hit her. I saw him knock her to the floor and kick her the day he died."

"How sad for you all," Clare said, wrapping her arm around his small shoulders. "What a dreadful thing. How did your father die?"

"I shouldn't say," Caleb replied, growing mute, knowing he had already said too much.

"I should not have asked."

****

"It's lovely to hear you tell your children the old stories," Clare commented one night as they sat drinking tea and watching fog settle in the valleys.

"Old stories?" Fiona asked.

"Finn MacCool and the Irish legends. Your heritage must be very important to you," Clare said probingly.

"Not as important as it should be. When we came to America, our heritage was far more important to my brother than to me. As I watch Caleb and Maggie grow older, I want them to understand as much as they can of the family they never knew. Caleb loves stories of Daniel Boone. Finn MacCool seemed a good Irish equivalent."

"And a good example of the wit and wisdom of Irish women," she said.

Fiona agreed.

That night she told her children the story of Finn MacCool's brave and clever wife.

"When Finn MacCool crossed Giant's Causeway to Scotland and saw how much larger his rival was, Finn went back to Ireland. He picked up a handful of dirt to throw at the Scottish giant—"

"You shouldn't throw dirt," said Maggie.

"Yes," said Fiona. "But Finn MacCool threw this dirt at the giant, who was called Fergus. It fell short and landed in the sea, forming the Isle of Man. The hole where he picked up the dirt filled up with water and became the lake called Lough Neagh, the largest in Ireland.

"Finn went home to his wife, Oonagh, who knew exactly what to do. She had Finn dress as a baby and climb into a cradle and pretend to be the not-so-wee baby of Finn and Oonagh. When Fergus came to the house, Oonagh offered him a drink from a pail, calling it Finn's wee cup. She offered him scones into which she had baked iron pots, so his teeth fell out when he bit into them. She showed how Finn's baby, who was really Finn, could eat the same scones with no trouble, for she did not give Finn any scones containing iron pots. Fergus grew terrified of Finn when he saw how strong Finn's baby was.

"Now, all of Fergus's strength was in his first finger, which was made of gold. The baby Finn bit off Fergus's magic finger, and Fergus lost all his strength. Finn climbed out of the cradle and pushed Fergus into the sea, thus establishing Finn MacCool as the mightiest of all men. And it would not be so, were it not for his brave and clever wife. Now goodnight," she said, kissing her children before they could object to parts of the story. "Sweet dreams of Finn and Oonagh MacCool."

****

On an evening in mid-June the trail-weary travelers pulled into Independence, one of the last outposts before the frontier. Beyond its humble borders lay the wilderness. Said to be named for President Andrew Jackson's strongest trait, Independence had the recklessness of a border town. It had been established as a supply depot and was a place for travelers to stock up on provisions they would need for their journey.

Independence had once been the premier jumping-off point for the trail, but that distinction now belonged to St. Joseph, Missouri, or Council Bluffs, Iowa. Kieran preferred Independence because it was not as popular, so it was a simpler place to do business. Starting west from Independence gave more opportunities to purchase supplies along the trail.

The Morans, Pickerings, and Lenihans were eager to arrive in the company of Kieran. The endless talk about him among this group and others who had decided to join them had biased Fiona against him. She wondered at all the excitement over a man who was going to be doing a relatively simple thing in leading a company of eager pioneers across the country. After all, she reasoned, they would be doing all the work. And it wasn't as if hundreds of others wouldn't be making the same journey, many without a guide. Moreover, she and Seamus had crossed an ocean. Would it be so different to cross a continent? They were already halfway across the country.

She understood from Clare there were no more roads to follow. But with the heavy traffic of western emigrants, would a path not have been carved to the West? Because the Pickerings and Morans were so keen to travel with Kieran, she decided she had little choice in the matter. She resigned herself to thinking that as long as they got to California in good health, it mattered little who would have led them there.

Chapter 5

Kieran Moran was a hard man, shaped by years of hard living. Lean and muscular, he radiated authority. His crystalline eyes squinted against the sun, dust sticking in the worn creases. He was sharp and quick, like his mind, which was busy taking in the details of the scene before him during his first encounter with the people he would be leading west.

He compiled a mental inventory of the characters scattered around him, categorizing each by useful function: good shot, good cook, good scout, good leader, good follower, potential problem, dead weight.

Fiona came around the corner beside him and stopped short, watching him as he catalogued the entire wagon party in seconds flat. "American diaspora," he muttered under his breath. "Bunch of greenhorns." He spat a wad of chewing tobacco at the ground an astonishing distance away from him.

Fiona raised her left brow in a combination of astonishment and disgust. With an appraising eye, she took in all six-foot-three of his confidence. Her gaze traveled from his boots and deerskin leggings to his worn felt hat, which he removed with one hand while he wiped the sweat from his hairline with the other. Her heart sped when she realized he had become aware of her presence.

He turned to look at her with his mother's blue

eyes. She was struck by his unkempt appearance. Three days' growth colored his jaw, making him appear dark and brooding.

He wasn't handsome in a classic sense, yet there was an almost peculiar beauty about the construction of his face. It was chiseled and leathery and worn like the land. From his pronounced cheekbones to his cleft chin, his features approximated mountains with their jagged peaks and granite valleys. His black hair was tied unevenly behind him with a scrap of rawhide. His enormous hands were scarred and calloused.

Something came alive in her, a mere flicker of the way she had felt years ago when she was young, and the future was a vision of hope awash in idealism. When she and her brothers had cheated death and boarded the ship for America. When her employer's son had cast a desirous eye toward her.

Nearly all of it had become lost over the years, snuffed out in the Cushing household, withering under Simon's blows.

Kieran smiled, and her inhibitions fell away. His sudden attention disarmed her. She swallowed to regain her composure.

"Fiona Lenihan, I presume." He tipped his hat to her.

She could see the resemblance now: Gideon's natural sense of authority, Clare's light of wisdom. "It's a pleasure to meet you, Mr. Moran. I've heard a great deal about you," she said with practiced diction.

His eyes narrowed.

Feeling immediately ill at ease under his scrutiny, her composure wavered. He seemed to take in every detail about her without breaking eye contact.

"Do you have any concept of what you have signed on for, Mrs. Lenihan?"

"Traveling cross-country, you mean?"

"Why are you doing this, if I may ask?"

"The same reason the others are, I suppose. The belief that whatever lies where we are going is better than what we have left behind," she said confidently.

"And that's it. That's all you have to sustain you?" he said, his tone less than reassuring.

"That and my children."

"Then I encourage you to think of them when you consider the hardships of the trail."

As much as she had wanted to like the Morans' son, Fiona did not. The speed of her reaction surprised her. "We've come this far. I don't see that what lies ahead poses such a difficulty. I have very clear expectations of what awaits us in the West, Mr. Moran. I spent my childhood in the fields. I know what it is to plant and harvest."

"The first part of the journey is the easiest. Our greatest fears are the fantastic storms we may encounter when crossing the plains. The second part brings difficult topography, mountains, and gulleys. The final portion of the journey is spent battling failing draft animals and equipment and crossing first a desert and then the Sierra Nevada, hoping to avoid the early storms the Donner party encountered ten years ago. Cholera, dysentery, scurvy, heat, cold, starvation, and unfriendly Indians will be constant threats."

"I will not be deterred from making this journey."

He made no reply other than to look her over from head to toe. He stepped a bit too close to her. Their proximity made her nervous.

"That's a beautiful dress you're wearing."

Fiona blushed. "Thank you," she replied, her response guarded, wary of the turn in conversation.

"You aren't planning to wear that on the trail, are you?" His words cut.

"I'm in mourning, Mr. Moran. I really haven't anything else."

"Then wear a black armband. I can't have you fainting from the heat," he said dismissively.

"But Mr. Moran, it wouldn't be proper."

"Mourn all you want when we get to California. Until then, I insist you are outfitted for the trail."

"Please tell me where I can find a dressmaker in Independence." She pressed him for information despite his growing irritation.

"There's fabric at the general store."

"I can't sew."

She regretted her response immediately.

A cloud of judgment passed his eyes. His dismissal left no question of how he had categorized her.

"Then barter." He tipped his hat to her and was gone, leaving a chill in his wake.

Fiona seethed. How dare he prejudice himself against her over such a simple matter. She sensed in him a man devoid of compassion and felt the elder Morans' disappointment in their only child.

Caleb and Maggie had spent too much time cooped up together. They needed to be separated before someone drew blood. Fiona donned her crisp, lesser-worn mourning dress and bonnet and took Caleb with her to the general store. Mother and son stepped into the streets of Independence, a scene that overwhelmed them once they were on the main artery. Fiona heard herself gasp. The chaos of Wheeling was insignificant by comparison. Mother and son clasped hands by instinct.

Fiona had not fully appreciated the reality of Independence until she left the cloister of the wagon community and was swallowed up by the dusty streets. It approximated Fiona's recollection of the docks in Philadelphia when she and Seamus had come to America. Such a collection of unsavory characters and desperation Caleb had never seen.

Skullduggery lurked everywhere. Rough men and hard women stared at the elegant widow and boy, the hunger in their eyes unnerving Fiona as she felt the covetous leers directed toward her handbag. She and her son were obvious marks that escaped no one's eye.

What Fiona wished to make them understand was that they were not so far apart, that what they shared was their look to the West as their last hope. Instead, she felt like prey. Fiona glanced anxiously over her shoulder and realized they were being followed by a pair of men who seemed to delight in her fear. She urged Caleb down the street, quickening their pace toward the retail establishments.

She resented Kieran for sending her out of the camp without accompaniment, or at least a proper warning. The lawlessness that surrounded them was terrifying.

"Let's hurry," she said, feeling self-conscious in her extravagant dress with its layers of petticoats. Her jet earbobs and bonnet glittered in the sunlight, adding to her rich beauty. She breathed an audible sigh of relief when they reached a general store.

"How can I help you?" the proprietress greeted her,

taking in the widow's finery. "Your dress is exquisite. I've never seen anything like it."

"I need to trade it for another dress." Before the woman could object, Fiona continued. "I need a simple dress to wear on the trail."

"We don't sell finished clothing, only bolts of fabric."

"I see," Fiona nodded, her composure failing. All this for yet another problem. A bolt of fabric and notions were of little use to her in the immediate future. She dreaded facing Kieran again wearing her mourning dress.

The proprietress watched Fiona's reaction and hatched a plan. She called her voluptuous daughter over to the counter and ordered her to take off her dress.

"But Mother, it's brand-new!" the teenager wailed.

"You can have her dress," she gestured to Fiona's garment, not once meeting her eyes. The proprietress was nearly salivating at the value of all that silk and lace and the one-of-a-kind undergarments. Fiona's dress was worth far more than the simple calico frock the girl wore. In fact, carefully disassembled, Fiona's dress could make a tidy profit when sold for its trimmings.

Fiona followed the sulking teen into a back room where their dresses were exchanged. She gladly surrendered all but the under layer of petticoats to the girl. The bulk of Fiona's coins were stitched into that petticoat.

The calico dress hung on Fiona, for she did not possess the same assets as the girl. The dress emphasized Fiona's thin figure that had been concealed by the mourning dress. She was secretly pleased to be rid of the cumbersome garment and all it represented.

Fiona removed the fashionable black bonnet from her head and set it on the counter. "Please take this, too." Its fluted silk, lace, and jet beads were a work of art. The proprietress suggested a large-brimmed straw hat to protect Fiona's fair skin and a pair of thick work gloves to protect her hands.

Determined to learn to sew, and anticipating free time on the trail, Fiona stopped at a rack that held an array of fabrics. The children were growing fast and would need new clothing. She selected a bolt of chambray. The thought of matching patterns at seams struck her as too great a challenge for a novice seamstress.

Giddy from her profit, the proprietress filled a bag with peppermints for Fiona's children and wished her well. Fiona paused in the doorway before returning to the teeming streets of Independence. She noticed they did not attract the same attention now that she wore a simple dress and hat, similar to other women. She breathed easily and set out in the direction of their camp. Caleb insisted on carrying the bolt of fabric.

Fiona rounded the corner looking like a breath of spring. A breeze lifted the wide brim of her hat, and she reached up to hold its crown.

"You look beautiful, Mother."

The dress made Fiona look younger. Its cornflower shade restored the roses in her cheeks, which the somber black dress had stolen. Its scooped neckline accentuated her long neck and revealed her graceful clavicle and bone structure, hinting at her modest bosom in the way her high-collared mourning dress had not. Without realizing it, her image had changed from that of a pious and repressed widow to that of an attractive woman.

Buoyed by their successful shopping trip, mother and son laughed and chatted, taking in the adventure of Independence. The simple dress garnered barely a nod from passersby, and the threat had been lifted from their initial foray into the streets. They passed the pair of men who had followed them to the general store and to Fiona's relief did not catch their attention.

Now Fiona and Caleb appeared as they were, two of hundreds of travelers. An air of confidence slipped into Fiona's walk.

When Kieran Moran was on the street, people got out of his way. He was not menacing, but something about him demanded respect that people granted without question.

He walked toward Fiona and Caleb, not recognizing them at first. As a seasoned admirer of the gentler sex, the lithe woman and her young charge caught his eye. An enormous straw hat concealed her identity, but he recognized the boy as the one who had been sitting near Clare earlier that day.

It was an epiphany. He watched them approach, unaware of his presence. He watched her in particular.

Fiona had been transformed. Stripped of her layers of garments, she was young and beautiful in the simple dress.

Fiona's gaze moved from one side of the street to the other, alternately discovering things to point out to her son and looking at what he had found for her to see. As she turned her head, the hat exposed and concealed portraits of her face, showing them a little at a time, then suddenly not at all. And then she looked up and saw him watching them, watching her. He greeted her with a subtle curve of his lips. She smiled an obligatory greeting of recognition. Although the smile belonged to Kieran, she was glad to see a familiar face.

"Mr. Moran," she said when they had reached one another.

"Kier."

"Mr. Moran," she said firmly. "Meet my son Caleb, Caleb Lenihan." She watched him crouch to her son's level, a gesture that struck her as demonstrating an odd degree of sensitivity for such a man. "Caleb, this is Mr. Moran. He's going to lead us across America."

"You shouldn't have ventured out alone, Mrs. Lenihan. These streets are not safe for unaccompanied ladies."

"My son is with me."

He chose not to respond, but she knew they had reached an understanding. The tension that had grown out of their first meeting returned. Fiona decided she liked him even less. How dare he send her out to barter her clothing without so much as a word of guidance.

"We should return to our preparations, Mr. Moran," she said.

"Kier."

"I have no wish to address you in the familiar, Mr. Moran."

"It's unfortunate how such a high-handed woman can so easily pretend to assume the role of servant."

"What do you know of my life?" she said sharply.

"I know what I see. Your pretension is unbecoming. It will not serve you well out here."

"How two such agreeable parents could have produced such a disagreeable man," she thought aloud

81

before she could bite her tongue.

"That is the question," he said coolly. "You'd best get on with your preparations. When I am next past, I expect your wagon to be properly outfitted."

Chapter 6

Kier never had to ask for silence. Everyone gathered hushed when he began to speak. "Name's Kier Moran," he said, addressing the crowd that ringed the wagon bed that served as his stage. "I'll be your guide to California. We pull out tomorrow after breakfast.

"You can expect we'll be in California around the middle of October, about four months from now. We'll track the Missouri River to the Platte and North Platte, which we'll follow for several hundred miles before reaching the Sweetwater River. Then we'll head overland through the Hastings Cutoff to the Great Salt Lake. We'll follow the Humboldt and Truckee Rivers as we get closer to California. Along the way we'll restock supplies in St. Joseph, Council Bluffs, Fort Kearney, Fort Laramie, Fort Bridger, Salt Lake City, and at smaller trading posts after that."

His commanding presence kept all eyes riveted to him.

Fiona watched him from her position several feet away. He exuded an arrogance that made him seem unapproachable. Something about him left people almost afraid to give him anything less than their full attention. Folks wouldn't say they warmed to Kier, but they would agree he demanded their respect.

Momentarily distracted from Kier's address by a young woman wearing what Fiona knew was the latest fashion from Paris, Fiona missed Kier's introduction of a trio of young men who would be traveling with the company. She admired the canary yellow gown and matching parasol. Edna Cushing and two of her daughters-in-law had ordered similar ensembles to wear on Easter.

Fiona returned her attention to Kier describing the young men assisting him in exchange for their passage, a horse, and a lump sum to give them a start in California. His assistants were expected to drive the supply wagon, patrol the length of the wagon train as it progressed, and lead the night watch.

"We are a company of sixty-eight wagons, three hundred twenty travelers, and two hundred fifty head of cattle. Today you will elect a body of three men to represent your interests. All your concerns will be brought directly to them rather than to me.

"We'll set up a cattle guard and night watch. Every morning at oh-four-hundred, the night watch will fire their rifles to start the day. At oh-seven-hundred, the bugle will sound, and we roll wagons. When Brent, Sam, and Billy come around to see you after this meeting, you need to give them the number of able-bodied men traveling with you."

"Why so long?" asked a man in the audience. "I heard this part of the journey takes three months, not four."

"We are a large company," Kier said. "Smaller companies can travel at a faster pace. Fewer wagons and fewer people mean fewer things to slow you up. The time is now for you to join a smaller company."

Some members of the company asked questions. In the lull, Fiona turned to look at those gathered, her traveling companions for the next four months.

A broad cross section of people was represented: those of great wealth, those who had invested their last penny in the journey, young families, older couples, and large groups with multiple wagons. Some wore expressions of hope, others of concern. Many appeared ambivalent. What they had in common was the willingness to embark on Kier Moran's itinerary, to follow his lead, and to trust in his ability to deliver them to their new homes.

Fiona noticed a dashing man who was looking her way, a gentleman with impeccable grooming and a smile to match. He wore a suit of clothes that included an ascot, a brocade vest, and a gold pocket watch. His refinement was a welcome sight.

He could have been a figure from her life as a Cushing. Once she might have offered him a cigar or brandy. In later years she might have played the piano at a dinner he attended. He might have kept company with Simon. The man's admiring glances made her blush. She turned away when she realized he was making his way across the crowd toward her.

Kier watched their interaction from afar, missing no detail of the man's gambit and Fiona's response, even as he managed to continue answering people's questions.

"Jake Farragut," the man said, extending his hand and bringing her comparatively delicate fingers to his lips.

"Fiona Lenihan," she breathed, taking in his pure good looks. He was smooth all over, from the feel of his hand to the comb of his hair and the silky resonance of his voice.

"These are my children, Caleb and Maggie."

He gave them a dismissive nod before continuing. "Quite a fellow we have running our company. Folks say he's near a red man and that he's rather handy with rifle and tomahawk. I hope he has what it takes to guide us cross-country without giving in to his primitive urges."

"Primitive urges?"

"A man doesn't—how shall I put it to a lady— develop notoriety with such articles of violence by making infrequent use of them. I intend to lead that governing body, so I can deal with him directly."

Fiona was inclined to agree with him.

"A man like that needs rules, and I plan to keep him under tight watch. From where do you hail, Mrs. Lenihan?"

"Philadelphia," she replied.

"A recent widow?"

"Yes, two months."

"I see," he said, looking pointedly at her blue dress.

"And you, Mr. Farragut?" she asked, shifting uncomfortably under his appraisal.

"Jake, please. Boston and New York are my former cities. San Francisco shall be my new one. I plan to settle there in a grand home with a gentlewoman whose acquaintance I hope to make along the way. Ah!" he said, beckoning to a well-dressed couple. "Have you had the pleasure of meeting the Reverend Josiah Pride, his lovely wife Evangeline, and her sister, Caroline Gillespie?"

Fiona greeted the trio with a near curtsy.

"Charmed," Caroline said, twirling her canary-yellow parasol. Fiona was reminded of her least favorite sisters-in-law and other brittle women of the upper class. Caroline's perfect bone structure was matched only by the artistry of her silk dress and crocheted gloves.

"I'm going to San Francisco to open a school for young ladies," she said, with an emphasis on the "I" as if knowing her mission in life would outclass Fiona's.

"How admirable. I understand there are quite a number of women out West in need of refinement," Fiona responded.

Their interlude was broken by Kier's call to elect the governing board.

"Wish me luck," Jake said in parting, kissing first Fiona's hand and then Caroline's before crossing to where Kier stood.

Fiona's eyes followed Jake until they were distracted by Kier's magnetism. He gave her a hard look before Jake drew his attention. Fiona straightened her posture in defiance.

A hostile undercurrent ran between Fiona and Kier. Although they had not had another private conversation since the afternoon of their meeting, their initial feelings resurfaced with subsequent encounters. Jake's comments had only served to cement Fiona's views of Kier.

As Jake had predicted, he was elected to the board, receiving the most support of the three men who now represented the company's interests.

A consummate politician, Jake was a fast favorite of the company. He moved through the emigrants with ease, assuming the roles of friend and patriarch. Upstanding and personable, his shadow darkened Kier's persona. Jake ingratiated many, particularly those whose favor others sought to curry, including the Reverend Pride and his wife.

In contrast, few could say they liked Kier. Intense and abrupt, his manner put off most and kept others on edge. He hollered commands and growled orders. His normal speaking voice was a string of clipped words. He seemed intentionally unapproachable and limited his contact to a select few, his mother among them. Most of his time was spent outside the boundaries of the moveable community.

"If you have questions or concerns, bring them up when one of my men stops by each of your wagons to confirm you are properly outfitted for the journey. After that, bring them to Jake Farragut and the others you have elected to represent you, Tom Thorpe and Hiram Parker. We leave after breakfast. Good luck."

"Mother," Caleb asked as they headed back to their wagon. "Do you like that man, Mr. Farragut?"

"Of course. He's going to be an important part of our lives these next few months."

"He reminds me of Father," Caleb said bluntly.

"Because he's a gentleman. We haven't seen many since we left Philadelphia."

"I like Mr. Moran."

"Yes. He and Mrs. Moran have been very kind to us."

"No, the other Mr. Moran," he insisted.

"Oh?" she asked, her left brow arching in surprise.

"He talks to me."

"Why, you've only just met both men. Many gentlemen believe children should be seen and not heard. I'm sure that's the reason Mr. Farragut didn't talk with you. Where did you speak with Mr. Moran?"

"At Mrs. Moran's wagon."

"There you are," Clare called to them. "One of Kieran's men is waiting at your wagon."

Fiona and Caleb hastened to meet him.

"Billy Noble!" Fiona exclaimed when the two came face to face outside her wagon. "What are you doing here?"

"My job, ma'am. The wagon train I told you about. Howdy, Caleb and Maggie," he said, tipping his hat to her children when he saw them.

The children grinned with affection, while their mother regarded him with incredulity.

"You've been takin' good care of your animals like I told you, right?" he asked Caleb.

Caleb nodded enthusiastically.

"You work for Kier Moran?" Fiona said, aghast.

"Yes, ma'am."

"So, he's your man of fiction," she said, a bit too quickly.

"Oh, he's the best, ma'am. Better than fiction," he exclaimed, unable to contain his enthusiasm.

"I see," she replied, trying to remain sincere.

"We should turn to business, ma'am. Mr. Moran gave us a tall order in visiting every wagon and fixin' any problems before supper. Let's take a look inside your wagon."

Billy confirmed Fiona had a full inventory of Kier's required supplies: extra timber for the heavy rains ahead, to keep the wheels from sinking in the mud; a tarp that could serve as a shelter for people and animals; and enough food items to feed her family alone or in combination with others who may have wanted to prepare meals for a larger group.

As Billy worked, he described the company's supply wagon, which he would drive on some days. It contained barrels of jerky and other foodstuffs to use as emergency rations, tools and spare parts for wagons, gunpowder and other munitions, medical supplies, rope, timber, pots and pans, and an assortment of other dry goods that would be replenished at the forts where the company would make camp along the trail.

"I'm so pleased we're traveling together," Fiona said at the close of their meeting, shaking Billy's hand. "Please stop by whenever you have time. You're always welcome to sit with us. The children and I would love to hear of your adventure thus far."

"Yes, ma'am," he grinned before moving to the next wagon.

****

On a warm spring morning ripe with promise, the wagon train pulled out of Independence. The wagons traveled in a single column of emigrants filled with fresh dreams and fresh supplies. A team of older children drove the cattle behind the last wagon.

They traveled northwest along the banks of the Missouri River, along the western border of Missouri, the western edge of civilization.

Brent Starr sounded the bugle, and members of the company assumed their positions as drivers, riders, or walkers.

"Roll wagons!" Kier shouted. The teamster in the lead wagon cracked the whip to put his team in motion.

Once they were underway, Kier rode the length of the column from front to back. When he passed Fiona's wagon, he tipped his hat to her.

She was so surprised she leaned over the side of

her wagon to see if he did the same to anyone else.
He did not.

Chapter 7

Their first day on the trail was much the same as the second and third, and for several days after that. The women cooked breakfast; the men harnessed the teams. Everyone broke camp. They traveled at a steady pace, stopped to rest during the heat of the day, and continued until late afternoon when the morning rituals were repeated in reverse: the wagons were circled, the men tended to the animals, and the women prepared supper.

The process was exhausting. Its repetition was exhausting, which meant a quiet camp shortly after dark when the travelers had turned in for the night.

Kier walked the perimeter of the camp with Billy Noble at his side. Kier showed his apprentice how to check the security of the enclosure, the watchfulness of the men on guard some ten to twenty yards away from the wagons, and the environment beyond that. "After a few patrols I'll give this responsibility to you, Brent, and Sam. I'll show you how to look for signs of danger that can befall a camp after sundown: thieves, wild animals, hostile Indians."

Billy responded with an affirming nod, already scanning for potential threats.

The company made good time for the first few days. Kier pushed them, but not too hard, breaking them in gradually to the rigors of the trail. By the beginning of the second week, they were traveling up to seventeen miles per day. The weather was with them and Kier took advantage of this easy stretch to cover as much ground as possible.

He kept the wagons moving, ensured a plentiful food supply, and dealt with daily problems such as broken axles, disputes between travelers, and failing draft animals. He reordered wagons to put slow wagons behind fast wagons to increase their pace. He showed travelers who took too long to break camp how to be more adept at harnessing a team or loading a wagon. He worked with drivers of decrepit wagons to make them trail worthy.

Kier worked hard from sunup to sundown, when he remained at a distance. His men—Billy Noble, Brent Starr, and Sam Thorne—were his public face. Their personable competence more than made up for Kier's standoffishness.

When the wagons stopped, Jake took charge. People gravitated to him because he appeared to care about them in ways Kier did not. He was a skilled conversationalist and could quote Scripture for any situation.

When seen against Jake's polished demeanor, Kier's unshaven appearance and brusque way of dealing with people made him look downright feral. There was no question in the minds of those with limited imagination which man the company should have preferred; which man Fiona should have preferred.

Jake had befriended some of the more respected travelers, including the Reverend and Evangeline Pride, Caroline Gillespie, and Fiona, whose reputation as a cook and as one of Doc's nurses preceded her. Jake had also become friendly with Doc and Libby.

"Hey, mountain man," Jake taunted his rival one evening when they were out of earshot of the company. Kier looked up from his work to see Jake and the other two elected officials, Tom Thorpe and Hiram Parker, approaching. Cowards never attacked alone.

"I wonder," Jake said to his companions without breaking eye contact with Kier, "why is it we need to pay this savage to lead us cross country? It's a scam if I ever saw one. I could lead this company and would do so without cost."

"What's a scam?" Caleb asked, stepping out from behind a horse where he had been watching Kier work.

Jake was startled to see the boy.

"A scam is a lie told to cheat people out of their money," Kier said. "You should go back to your mother," he nodded reassuringly toward Caleb. "You too, boys," he said, ushering Caleb and three of his friends away from the scene.

When they were out of earshot, Kier turned to address Jake and his men. "The money is spent on supplies for the company and on wages for Billy, Brent, and Sam. Now if you'll excuse me, there is work to be done."

"What are you doing with our young?" Jake asked, his tone accusatory. "There's nothing you can do or say that can be of benefit."

"Yeah, what were you doing out here?" the others echoed.

"Explaining how cattle are herded. They asked to be given the tasks of the older children. I told them they won't be given those responsibilities until they understand how to keep one cow in line, let alone two hundred fifty."

Annoyed by Kier's even response, Jake pursed his lips in spite. "You watch yourself, Moran," he challenged. "I'm watching you. We all are," he scowled before turning on his heels, followed by his cohorts.

****

Jake was persistent. He courted Fiona from dawn until dusk, when he turned in for the night. He was a firm believer in early mornings and early nights and made no secret of his conviction that nothing pure was accomplished after dark.

He rose earlier and earlier, wanting to best Kier by greeting the wagon master with a list of his desires for the day. Kier took Jake's orders in stride, reacting little to Jake's presentation of demands, which only encouraged Jake to make a greater effort to goad his rival.

After his morning visit to Kier, which increasingly bordered on harassment, Jake would stop by Fiona's wagon to chat while she prepared breakfast.

"You must curb your son's fascination with Moran and his men. The Devil can appear in any form to tempt the innocent."

"Jake," she chided. "The Devil in Billy Noble? Why, he's the most wholesome among us."

"Moran, then. Surely you can't say the same of that beast."

"He's been teaching the boys skills for the journey," she explained.

"The Reverend Pride can teach our young all they need to know for the journey."

"Kier knows many practical things about animals and equipment."

"Caleb and the other young people should stay

away from him," Jake objected. "Any form, remember. The Devil can appear in any form. 'Even Satan disguises himself as an angel of light,' Two Corinthians Eleven to Fourteen," he quoted. "'So, it is no surprise if his servants also disguise themselves as servants of righteousness.'"

"Jake—"

"Do you doubt my judgment?"

Fiona was overcome with a gnawing unease. "No," she replied, wanting to clear the air.

"I must check Moran's work. With that, I leave you to yours."

Fiona sliced an apple in half and peered up through her lashes to watch Jake walk away. She didn't like their conversation. Nor did she like the way Jake had stopped using Kier's first name.

"Mr. Farragut seems to have taken an interest in you," Clare said when they sat by the fire that night.

Fiona knew she was stating what had become obvious to many, so she wondered at her motive. "He's a gentleman," she said.

"He appears as one."

"He reminds me of the life I had," Fiona replied, avoiding Clare's eyes.

"If you don't mind, how did a girl from County Leitrim become a lady of society?"

Fiona laughed bitterly. "It has taken distance to realize how unusual that was, although it seemed natural at the time. I was foolish. I believed he loved me, when in fact he wed me to spite his mother.

"I was a servant in my in-laws' home. His parents tried to annul the marriage, but the scandal had progressed too far. As a newly married couple we had made a spectacle of ourselves in New York and Philadelphia. My eldest brother-in-law intervened and convinced his parents to drop the matter. And so it was that a poor Irish girl became a lady of society."

"Did you like living in that society?" Clare asked.

"It had a certain beauty," Fiona replied wistfully. "More than anything, it held such opportunities for my children. Caleb would have been able to attend university. In California I hope to give them a life that will allow for education."

"And what of you?"

"Me?" she asked, looking up at Clare with a start.

"What do you seek?"

"A better life for my children."

"So you've said," Clare replied, encouraging Fiona to reveal more than she had been willing to share.

"It's my duty as their mother."

"And Jake Farragut is part of this?"

"I don't know," Fiona said, looking away. "He speaks of living in a grand home in San Francisco with a gentlewoman at his side."

"Are you tempted?" Clare asked, sipping her tea.

"Yes."

"For your children?"

"For my children," Fiona repeated, finishing her tea in a single gulp.

****

Kier had refused to agree to the governing body's demands that every Sabbath should be observed, noting the importance of traveling on days when the weather was with them. To keep the peace, he managed to schedule travel on every day but Sunday for the first few weeks. His definition of rest included hunting, washing, and repairing, duties on which he was unwilling to compromise. In his company there was no such thing as a day of leisure.

The Reverend Pride began each Sunday with an early morning service. Most of the company stood in a wide circle around the minister, listening to his weekly teaching. Kier was never seen anywhere near this gathering.

Afterward, Kier and one of his men took a group out hunting. This group rotated each week but Kier made sure it always included a handful of good shots. For the others, he made himself available to help tune their skills with rifle and bow and arrow. The men who most needed help were the last to ask for it. The men who asked his advice wanted to improve their already adequate skills.

In weeks when their supply of fresh meat was dwindling, he took fathers and sons hunting. He did not include boys younger than ten because their squirming and loud whispers tended to scare away animals. In time, he relaxed his rules to invite some of the younger boys, since it was never too soon to learn important skills.

When the group of fathers and sons left camp one Sunday morning, Kier noticed Caleb watching him. He wore an expression of longing that was doused when Jake took him by the arm to pull him into one of his Scripture discussions.

****

Continuing the pattern they had established when traveling from St. Louis to Independence, the Lenihan wagon was always either immediately ahead or behind the Moran wagon. Caleb and Maggie sometimes rode with the Morans for variety. They had grown close in their short acquaintance, and Fiona felt more comfortable when she knew the Morans were near.

The Pickerings were positioned somewhere in the three wagons ahead. Fiona was called regularly to assist Doc with the usual occurrences of births, muscle strains, and broken bones, which gave her an opportunity to make the acquaintance of fellow travelers. Her reputation grew as a woman knowledgeable in the culinary and healing arts.

The elder Morans and Pickerings formed the core of Fiona's traveling companions. Clare and Libby were her two closest friends. Fiona worked well with Doc and enjoyed learning from him. Importantly, both the Morans and Pickerings were good to her children and had become extended family, filling the roles of their long-dead grandparents, aunts, and uncles.

Fiona saw Kier frequently in the distance, sometimes out ahead, other times riding well to one side or other of the train. He never slept in the camp, choosing to spend most of his time outside the perimeter and away from the heart of what had become a mobile community.

Every morning when Kier rode past her wagon he tipped his hat to her. It became a ritual she welcomed but never fully understood.

Over time he seemed to drift in and out of the enclosure during evening hours, chatting casually with people but never with Fiona. Occasionally she saw him sit with Clare. Her children brought her tales of Kier, although she had no interaction with him. They kept their distance, each acutely aware of the other.

Fiona began to hear people speak well of Kier.

Some even raved about his admirable qualities and talents, sounding like converts to Billy Noble's way of thinking. There was praise for his generosity, taking time to work with men and boys to refine their hunting and carpentry skills. Fiona decided Kier's decision to reveal himself gradually to everyone but her was intentional on his part.

When Jake noticed how people in the company had taken to Kier, he began to belittle him during his Scripture discussions. "Look at him," he said one evening, nodding toward Kier. Immediately a dozen heads turned. Fiona refused to join them. "Have you ever happened upon a more disagreeable man? He was expelled from West Point. That ought to tell you something about his character."

"Why does Kier's character matter to you?" Fiona asked.

Some in the group gasped.

"Because it does not matter enough to you," Jake replied. "Allowing your son to spend time with him is a grave mistake on your part."

"Not everyone in the company finds him disagreeable," she challenged.

"The people who matter most do. Those gathered here do," he said, eyeing the Reverend Pride and his wife and her sister, and a number of the wealthier members of the company.

"It troubles me that you refuse to discount him," Jake continued, almost glaring at her. "He must have done something unspeakable to have been expelled from the academy."

"Perhaps he did something remarkable to get in."

The flash of anger in Jake's expression startled her.

"Jake," she pleaded, knowing she had struck a nerve. "Let's not waste a good meal on subjects that trouble you so," she said, helping him save face. "What passage should we discuss this evening?" she asked, opening her Bible.

"He's an uneducated, Indian-loving heathen. You're of a certain society. You've heard the finest performers in the finest venues, dined with civic leaders, and attended balls with giants of industry. You belong in that sphere with men of position and honor. Moran is not worthy of your company."

****

One morning Fiona was teaching a group of women how to prepare breakfast for a crowd. Among them was Caroline Gillespie, the Reverend Pride's sister-in-law, who was having considerable difficulty using a knife. Evangeline Pride worked beside her and tried to calm her sister's nerves. After a time, Caroline began to complain, insisting that learning to be handy in the kitchen was a waste of her time because she intended to hire a staff when she reached San Francisco.

"Perhaps Mrs. Lenihan would like a position at my school?" she asked, a bit too sweetly.

Fiona merely smiled, but not very sweetly. She regarded Caroline as a test of her patience and distracted herself by looking up to check on her children. Maggie was playing quietly with her dolls. Caleb had disappeared.

"Where's Caleb?" she asked Maggie.

Maggie shrugged.

Fiona scanned the camp but saw no sign of her son.

Caleb and his trio of friends had gone exploring a few yards outside the enclosure. They came upon a moldering carcass of a cow at the edge of a watering hole. One of the boys kicked its bloated belly. To his delight, it sprang back like the membrane of a drum. Amidst giggles, all the boys kicked the carcass, each one taking a greater running start to benefit from the bounce. It was better than jumping on a bed.

It became a competition to see who could run the farthest and the fastest at the cow, and who could gain the biggest bounce.

When it was Caleb's turn, he had the best running start of all. But when he hit the cow's distended belly, instead of bouncing, his head broke through. He disappeared into the muck up to his shoulders.

The boys screamed. Caleb's arms and legs flailed.

"Get him out!" one of the boys yelled.

Fiona heard their cries. "Stay here," she instructed Maggie as she ran toward the commotion.

She arrived to see Caleb sputtering, his head and shoulders covered with rotting guts and dung. The smell was overpowering. Caleb blinked, his startled eyes bright.

Fiona pulled him into the watering hole. She sat him down hard and began scouring him with her bare hands. It was a rigorous exercise for mother and son.

"Spit," she ordered, wanting him to clear his mouth of the horrid mess.

A bystander handed Fiona a cake of lye soap. She scrubbed her son, furiously washing away the muck from every orifice. She removed his shirt and abraded it, her anger showing in the rough way she wrung the garment.

No one said a word.

Caleb stared at her, his eyes wide. It was the

cleanest he had been in weeks.

Another woman took her cow-bouncing son by the ear and led him into the watering hole, washing away the splatters of grime. Without exchanging either word or glance, Fiona handed her the soap. Two other mothers followed suit, and soon the pack of explorers had been reduced to four little boys scrubbed raw in front of a growing crowd of onlookers.

Fiona finished with Caleb's shirt and handed it to him. "Now go to the wagon and stay there until I say you can come out." He nodded and made a beeline for the wagon.

Fiona regarded the thin layer of slime on her dress, apron, and forearms. She sighed with frustration and relief.

"Mrs. Lenihan!" Caroline called across the patch of land that separated them. "Mrs. Lenihan. The food is burning."

Fiona looked at Clare.

"You can laugh now," the older woman said with a twinkle.

Fiona reached up to wipe her brow with the only clean spot on her arm.

The group of women burst into laughter. Fiona saw Kier on horseback in the distance, taking in the scene. She felt him watching her.

As the company was harnessing the animals and preparing to travel, Kier rode past Fiona's wagon. Caleb was sitting inside the back of the wagon, leaning over the closed tailgate.

"How's the cow?" Kier asked, his serious demeanor becoming a crooked smile. When Caleb knew he wasn't being reprimanded, he smiled back.

"You'll never kick a dead cow again," Kier said over his shoulder.

The boy grinned.

****

The company was now following the Platte River. They had passed into the frontier, leaving the state of Missouri and entering vast plains filled with prairie grasses as far as the eye could see. Trees had given way to open space that went all the way to the horizon.

During a midday break, called "nooning," Fiona and her children stepped from their wagon while the animals were being watered. Enchanted, she stared across the endless landscape.

She waded into the waist-high grass, her hands outstretched to allow the flounced-top stalks to tickle her palms. The grass swayed in unison with the wind. Monarch butterflies punctuated the ocean of gold and green, their brilliant colors turning them into mobile wildflowers. Grasshoppers leaped from where Fiona stepped. Cicada maintained a steady hum.

Maggie and Caleb followed her. Maggie was lost in the tall grass, unable to see anything but blue sky above her. Fiona lifted her to her hip.

"There's nothing here," Maggie remarked, squinting against the sun.

"There's everything here," Caleb said, correcting her as he struggled to walk through the grass. "It goes on forever."

"I've never seen anything like this place," Fiona said to Clare, who had joined them. "Think of all the potatoes that could grow here."

Clare began to laugh and looked at Fiona to share the joke. Her smile faded when she saw the remark was not meant in jest.

"Kieran tells me it only gets better," Clare said.

"It seems my son has developed quite an admiration for your son. I've heard many things about him in recent days, few of them from his mother."

"What would you like to know?"

"He spends a lot of time outside of camp, but I've noticed him venturing among us some evenings."

"It takes a bit for him to warm to people."

"Was he always this way?" Fiona asked.

"I suppose."

"What's it like to be his mother?"

"He's my son and I love him," Clare said proudly. "Someone once told me, 'Where there is no love, put love, and there it will grow.' Over the years I have persisted in my love for my son. He is difficult. But there has been progress."

Fiona nodded her understanding. "Have you found love where you put it?"

"Oh, yes. A fine heart beats in that man. A pity so few ever see it, among them his father. In my autumn years some hopes still burn brightly, that he will find peace and stop chasing himself to the far corners of the earth. And that he and Gideon will make amends."

"Do you think it possible?"

"A mother believes her son can do anything."

Chapter 8

Caleb was fascinated by Kier and found the likes of him, Billy Noble, and Brent Starr to be in the same league as Daniel Boone. Caleb studied them from afar and spent as much time as an eight-year-old could in the presence of these men.

One evening Fiona found Caleb talking to Kier and Billy where they were working in the makeshift corral. The wind carried Caleb's childlike voice. He was firing questions at the two men with the speed of a marksman.

"Kildare," Fiona heard Kier reply to her son's inquiry.

"Your horse is named Kildare?" Caleb asked, his eyes bright at the suggestion of violence.

"He is," Kier replied, teasing a smile. "I like riding an animal whose name carries an implied threat," he quipped, then laughed to show Caleb it was a joke.

Billy grinned with good humor and waved his greeting to Fiona when he saw her approaching.

Caleb laughed harder when he understood the joke. Kier glanced beyond Caleb's shoulder to Fiona, who was not laughing.

"Mrs. Lenihan," he greeted, his smile still fresh from his exchange with her son.

"Come, Caleb and the rest of you," she said when she saw three of Caleb's friends. "We need to leave Billy and Mr. Moran to their work."

"Aw, it's okay, Mrs. Lenihan," said Billy. "We've spent the whole day in near-silence on horseback. Talkin' is golden."

"Actually, Kildare was named for the county in Ireland known for its horses. You should ask your mother to tell you about it. Do you know the derivation of your name?" Kier asked Caleb, then met Fiona's eyes before returning them to her son's. "Caleb was one of twelve men Moses sent to spy in the land of Canaan. He entered the Promised Land with Joshua. It means 'bold.' It suits you."

"What does 'Kieran' mean?" Caleb asked, relishing the topic of discussion. He was not about to obey his mother and leave in the middle of such an exchange.

Fiona stood in silence, watching her son and these men enjoy each other's company. She was an outsider but knew Kier's aim was to draw her into their conversation.

"Black."

"Black?" Caleb giggled.

"They say when I was born, I had the blackest hair and the blackest eyes anyone had ever seen. Some say I still have the blackest heart anyone has ever seen." Kier looked up at Fiona, who appeared unmoved.

"Naw," Caleb giggled again.

"On the other hand, the name Fiona suits your mother," Kier said, watching her.

She shifted uncomfortably under his attention. "It's time for bed, Caleb."

"Pure and white."

She grew flustered, her eyes wandering but always returning to his.

"And light. Your mother is rather serious for a Fiona," he continued, teasing mother and son, coaxing the hint of a smile out of Fiona. "She should smile more often. Maybe even laugh." His eyes danced.

Fiona reddened. His unexpected charm was beguiling. It was a liberating moment, and she found herself laughing, perplexed as much by her reaction as by Kier's previously unrevealed warmth. Up to that moment, she would have surmised that if anyone needed to smile or laugh more it would have been Kier.

"Goodnight, Caleb, Jimmy, Bobby, Frank," Kier said, smiling affectionately at the boys. "Mrs. Lenihan," he continued, shifting his focus to her. Something in the way he said her name quickened her heart.

"Mr. Moran, Billy," she replied with a nod to each. She put her arm around Caleb, and they headed back to their wagon, Caleb's friends following like ducklings. She paused to shepherd the group of boys ahead of her and turned to look back at Kier. His eyes had never left her. She rewarded him with a smile.

Billy watched their exchange with a broad grin. "That's a fine woman," he offered. "And she sure can cook."

Kier cast him a warning glance before returning to his work.

****

Late one night Kier saw an opportunity to speak with Fiona. The camp was quiet. It seemed they were the only two restless souls in the company. She sat at a campfire, immersed in a book, her limbs drawn against her body to preserve warmth.

Uninvited, he stepped into the firelight. He appeared to ignore her as he established himself on a rock, opened his book, and reached inside his pocket. The foray produced spectacles that he hooked around his ears and settled on his nose with the facility of an habitual wearer.

She wondered what Jake would have thought, for the presence of the book and spectacles went against everything Jake said about Kier.

"Mr. Moran," she greeted, thinking she may have seen the shadow of a smile cross his face.

"Mrs. Lenihan," he returned, giving her his full attention. "We did not get off to a good start."

"It was an honest start," she offered, her expression suggesting a willingness to pursue the conversation. "But I believe in fresh starts."

"A pleasure, Mrs. Lenihan," he began as if meeting her for the first time. "I hope you will call me Kier. I'm not my father."

"A pleasure indeed, Kier Moran."

"Mrs. Lenihan."

"Fiona," she responded. "Although now I hardly know how to relate to you, as the son of your parents or the idol of my son, or as the man in our employ to guide us across the country."

"It isn't worth the hassle," he said with a dismissive gesture.

"But you are being paid a handsome sum."

"I'm being paid a sum to do my parents a kindness. That I am leading you and hundreds more is incidental."

"Jake said—"

"Jake said." He guffawed, then paused as if to stop himself from pursuing that line of talk. "Do you have any sense of the difficulties of this so-called job? I tried to dissuade you and others from making the trip. Very few have a clear idea of what the next few months will hold. It's not an easy journey. When the people become disillusioned—and they will—my job becomes that much more difficult.

"At this stage I'm doing a lot of instructing. Observe how that changes. That's why I urged you to elect a representative body. I don't have time to tend to the individual needs of three hundred twenty people. The sum I'm being paid is not worth the trouble. What is worth the trouble is the chance to set things right with my parents. What are you reading?" he asked with a winsome glint, his change of subject accompanied by a change in tone.

"Lewis and Clark," she responded, turning the spine of her book toward him.

"Seeing it firsthand isn't enough?"

"I've already read what I brought," she said, closing the book.

"I can offer you Emerson or Whitman."

"Thank you. I'll read anything."

"You strike me as a woman of discriminating tastes."

"Perhaps because you don't know me," she said, her eyes dancing with amusement. "I like to read everything—books, journals, newspapers. It gives me something to think about. Traveling cross-country leaves a great deal of time for reflection. Some days, after the eleventh mile, there is nothing to do but sort things out. What are you reading?"

"The Bard. *Julius Caesar*."

"Hmm," she purred, not sure how to interpret his response.

"Damning with faint praise?"

"Not at all," she laughed, their tension dissipating. Her eyes twinkled. "I was thinking aloud. I never thought of Julius Caesar as a bard."

"*Julius Caesar*, by the Bard, William Shakespeare."

"I see," she replied awkwardly, embarrassed at having revealed her ignorance. "I'm humbled by how little I know."

"The same could be said for all of us," he said to ease her discomfort.

"I confess I'm not familiar with Mr. Shakespeare."

"His sonnets are his finest work, I think. When we reach California, I'll give you a book."

"Thank you, but I wouldn't want to take one of your books," she said, subconsciously caressing the cover of her book.

"I've committed my favorites to memory."

"Oh?" she said, realizing she liked the sound of his voice.

"When, in disgrace with Fortune and men's eyes,
I all alone beweep my outcast state,
And trouble deaf heaven with my bootless cries,
And look upon myself and curse my fate,
Wishing me like to one more rich in hope,
Featur'd like him, like him with friends possess'd,
Desiring this man's art, and that man's scope,
With what I most enjoy contented least;
Yet in these thoughts myself almost despising,
Haply I think on thee, and then my state
Like to the lark at break of day arising
From sullen earth, sings hymns at heaven's gate,
For thy sweet love rememb'red such wealth brings,

That I scorn to change my state with kings."

She suddenly found herself ill at ease but could not decide whether it was the words or their delivery that had rendered her so. "It's beautiful, but melancholy."

"Compared to some of the others, I suppose," Kier agreed.

"Life can be dreary. I like to think of art as uplifting. That someone out there has found joy to write about," Fiona said, a sadness settling over her.

"But there is joy. Thoughts of his beloved make him not want to change places with kings. Is there no joy in your life?"

"My children are my joy."

"Other than that?" he asked, the subtle inclination of his head requesting a response.

"What more can a mother want?" she deflected.

"Hoping to find it out West, are you?"

"I am. I don't want their lives to be like mine. Look where I've drawn our conversation." She laughed uneasily, knowing she had revealed too much. "Well," she continued after a pause. "Goodnight, Kier."

She rose to leave when a spirited mutt ran past them with a golden-haired toddler in pursuit. Kier reached out and snared the child, raising the giggling boy above his head.

"Doggie!" he said, pointing excitedly beyond Kier's shoulder.

"You can't be running through my camp late at night dressed like this, little one," Kier admonished gently, straightening the two-year-old's nightshirt. "You could get hurt, and then Mrs. Lenihan would have to patch you up," he teased, settling the little boy on his knee.

"I'm sorry," his mother said, arriving breathlessly at the campfire. "He's learned how to climb out of the wagon. It's become a problem at night when we're asleep," she explained as Kier handed the boy to a woman Fiona judged to be a teenager.

"I'll stop by tomorrow and show you a couple of tricks," he offered. "Do you know one another?" He introduced Fiona Lenihan to Hope Whittaker and her son, Jeremy.

"Lenihan," Hope repeated. "Like Lend-a-hand."

Fiona smiled easily as Hope and Jeremy bid them goodnight.

"It's time I checked on my children. Goodnight, Kier."

They held one another's gaze before Fiona disappeared into the night.

****

Caleb read aloud from Lewis and Clark's journals while Fiona and Maggie sorted through dried beans. His cadence was halting, like a young reader struggling with material beyond his level. As automatically as her fingers worked with the beans, Fiona corrected his pronunciation.

"Mrs. Lenihan, Jake Farragut would like to know if you'll hold another cooking class tomorrow," said Brent, stopping by Fiona's wagon.

"Jake is the kind of man who would kick a dog, then shoot it to cover his crime," Caleb remarked.

Brent stifled a laugh.

Fiona looked at Caleb. "What did you say?"

"Jake is the kind of man who would kick a dog, then shoot it to cover his crime," he repeated.

"Who told you that?"

"Mr. Moran told it to Billy Noble."

"He did, did he? What have we said about saying bad things about other people? Mr. Moran was wrong to have said that about Mr. Farragut." Fiona's posture became erect. "Thank you, Brent. Please tell Mr. Farragut I will be pleased to hold another class tomorrow."

He tipped his hat and left, continuing to stifle a laugh.

"Mother, what if the bad things people say about other people are true?"

Fiona hesitated. Perhaps Jake was right. Kier was beginning to have a noticeable influence on her son. She sighed, not knowing how to sort out her mixed feelings for both men.

"It's not polite to talk about other people, good or bad. Read some more to us."

Fiona's work with the beans became another woman's task when Fiona was needed to assist Doc with a dislocated shoulder and broken leg.

As they worked on the injured man, Fiona began to rehearse her discussion with Kier. She held onto one patient from behind while Doc pulled his arm to reset his shoulder. She was deaf to the man's cries. Her mind sorted through every curse, looking for the perfect gambit. She held the other patient's hand while Doc reset the leg. As the man's tension and discomfort rose, so did hers. By the time the man was resting quietly, Fiona was ready to take on Kier.

She strode purposefully through camp and found him among the horses. He was crouched beside a paint that had gone lame. Fiona stooped on the other side of the horse and peered at him from beneath the horse's belly.

Kier was binding the horse's leg and was so focused on his work he was only vaguely aware of her presence.

"Do you know anything about child rearing?" she said firmly to open their conversation.

"I'm guessing I'll know more in the next minute or so than I do now."

Fiona's anger withered under Kier's nonchalant humor. The corners of his mouth rose in a show of amusement.

"What good does it do to try to teach my son right from wrong when one of his idols can undo in a moment what I have worked his whole life to instill?"

"What debauchery am I guilty of perpetrating on your son?"

"It's easy to snipe at others' weaknesses, to want to speak unkindly of another's shortcomings, real or otherwise."

"This wouldn't have anything to do with some ill-placed comment about kicking a dog that Caleb may have overheard?"

"It would," she replied, lifting her chin, an action that only provoked more of a smile from Kier, given the unusual logistics of their conversation.

"You've brought up your children well. I have no intention of undermining you. Nor do I have any intention of casting some people in a more favorable light than they deserve. I will reserve such observations in the presence of Caleb, but if he asks me a direct question, I will give him a direct answer."

"Thank you," she said, unsure of how to react after Kier deflated her anger.

The horse stomped impatiently, tossing its head.

"It's settled, then," she said.

"'Tis."

"Good," she said, stumbling in the unexpected silence, claiming the last word.

As suddenly as Fiona had appeared, she disappeared, leaving Kier to his work. A smile softened his lips.

****

"Do you sleep?" Kier asked late that evening, joining her at the campfire.

"When you sleep, you dream. I don't like to dream," she replied, closing her book on her index finger to mark her place.

"Why?"

"Experiences long past come alive in dreams. It can take five or ten miles or even several days of travel to leave a dream behind. If I don't sleep much, then neither do you. I don't believe I've ever risen before you, and you're always prowling long after I've turned in for the night."

"Prowling?" he said, his expression bordering on impish.

"I don't know what else you'd call it, wandering around in the dark."

"Keeping watch on me?"

Fiona opened her mouth to speak but realized she didn't have an adequate response. It seemed the better she got to know Kier, the worse she was at keeping up her end of their conversation.

"Don't let me interrupt you." He pulled his spectacles and book from a pocket and thumbed through the pages to find his place.

She studied him as he sat, firelight bronzing his skin. He looked almost handsome, with his face in rugged shadow. The rough-hewn peaks and valleys were a roadmap to his adventures. He met her gaze when he realized she was attempting to read him rather than her book.

"How did you come to be a lover of books? In Ireland?" he asked, his curiosity evident.

"There was no learning in Ireland. At least not in my Ireland. My father-in-law had a substantial library."

"Where did you begin?"

"Quite honestly, with the children's readers that belonged to my nieces and nephews. From there, I read things I heard people talk about. I moved on from old newspapers and journals to what intrigued me in my father-in-law's library, from Austen to Dickens."

"You seem to favor a lot of English tales for an Irishman," he teased.

"I'm not an Irishman. I'm an American."

"You can't forget the better part of your life."

"What is there to remember but heartache and death?" she said, her expression shifting with memory.

"Someday it may have greater importance to you. So, you've taught yourself the classics?" he asked, steering their conversation.

"I like books. I don't know enough to appreciate them fully, their historical context and all. The more I learn, the more I want to know about people, about life," she said, gauging his response.

"We self-taught are a difficult breed. We have a peculiar view of the world because it is our own. No teacher put it there."

"I don't know whether that has been the case for

me," she offered. "I learned a great deal as a housemaid. Every guest was a teacher. My ears were wide open to the gentlemen's after-dinner discourse over brandy and cigars. I listened as I worked. Each night those ideas swirled in my mind, making it difficult to fall asleep: philosophy, the stock market, hybrid crops, the price of land in Pennsylvania.

"All I know is what I was able to absorb and share with my brother. Those smoke-filled nights in the parlor opened my eyes to the world beyond my employer's home. I wish I had a formal education. Caleb is fortunate to have had schooling."

"It's not all it seems. Even I attended college," Kier said.

"Did you?" she exclaimed, her eyes dancing. She was curious to hear his explanation.

"Bowing to paternal pressure, I attended West Point for a year. But then I went to sea and the world became my classroom."

"Where did you sail?"

"Everywhere," he said, smiling broadly.

"Where is your favorite place?"

"Right here. Much of the world has been discovered. The American West is one of the few remaining frontiers."

"What were you searching for, to have traveled so far?"

"A greater awareness. Ironic how I managed to find it here in the West after all these years," he said, stoking the fire until a column of cinders swirled skyward.

"Do you think you'll ever stop traveling?"

"Hard to say," he said with a shrug. "I can't

imagine staying in one place for more than a few days." His voice drifted to a companionable silence. "Well, goodnight." His tone became officious. "I've got to get back to my prowling."

"You're mocking me."

"And you're smiling," he said flirtatiously.

"You seem to have that effect."

"Then I'll not soon be persuaded to change my ways," he said, leaving her to her book.

Their common interests fostered a genuine affection that grew over subsequent evenings spent talking by firelight. Their duties often kept them from the luxury of such informal meetings. Some nights her children may not have slept soundly, or she was needed at Doc's side. Or Kier needed to address livestock problems, cattle thievery, drunken travelers, or discussions with the elected officials.

Sometimes their only contact for days was Kier's tip of his hat when he rode past her wagon, or a public encounter where he was careful not to single her out lest rumors begin. They came to cherish their visits, never running out of topics, only time in which to share them. Enjoying each other's company became one of the pleasures of the trail.

Without realizing it, they had become friends.

When they were together, Fiona felt the corners of her mouth rise in a reflexive smile, indicative of her delight at simply being in his presence. The way he engaged her in conversation drew her nearer to him in spirit, even though they had never touched.

There came a time when Fiona wanted to touch him. She had watched him from afar when he had touched her children with affection, patting Caleb on his shoulder reassuringly and lifting Maggie high above his head, her torrent of laughter dancing through the air.

Fiona wanted to share Kier's warmth. She longed to feel his touch on her cheek, her hand, the small of her back. But she was afraid. He had ignited a cornucopia of feelings, some of which left her more than a little off balance. Despite this, she wanted to spend more time with him and feel the weight of his crystal-blue eyes upon her.

"My mother has no doubt told you of the relationship between my father and me?" he said one evening.

"Hinted, but not explained."

"I feel you should know what has passed between us. My parents have grown fond of you, as I have come to enjoy your company," he said.

She closed her book to give him her full attention.

"My father and I have long been at odds. He was the model West Point cadet, his military career testament to his promise. There was no doubt I was expected to follow his path.

"When I walked away from West Point, Gideon Moran, the colonel and the man, told me I was damned to a life of mediocrity and that I would never do anything of consequence unless it were to sully the Moran name. I cannot say he has come to accept me, but we have come to an uneasy peace. Our relationship is civil these days, which pleases Mother."

The closeness of the moment was broken by the squeals of little Jeremy, who had run away from his parents' wagon, only to be gathered into his father's arms and hauled back inside to bed.

"Now there's a besotted father," Kier observed,

watching Silas Whittaker.

Fiona agreed. When Kier turned to his book rather than continue discussing his relationship with Gideon, she closed their conversation. "Goodnight, Kier," she said after a silence.

"Fiona," he said warmly.

She turned to peek at him over her shoulder and was pleased to find him watching her walk away from him.

****

Jake was not about to let Kier's progress with Fiona go unmatched. He was aware of Fiona and Kier's firelight encounters held under the guise of sharing the light for reading. He decided to become Fiona's morning suitor as Kier was her evening suitor.

"What are your plans when you reach California?" Jake asked, watching Fiona prepare a kettle of oatmeal with stewed fruit.

"I'd like to start a farm."

"You would rather live in the country than in San Francisco?" he asked, aghast.

"I've decided the best way to provide for my children is by living on a farm," Fiona said while chopping apples.

"The country is lacking in civility. Surely a cultured woman must see that."

"I do. But these next years are not mine. They are for my children." She stirred the pot, tasted the concoction, and added more cinnamon.

"What about living as a gentlewoman in San Francisco?"

"Perhaps. What made you want to be a gentleman in San Francisco?" she asked.

"An agreement with my business partner in Boston. With the westward expansion, there is growing need for luxury items. As I am unwed, it is easier for me to open a San Francisco office for our import company."

Fiona wondered if he puffed out his chest when he talked, or if she only imagined it when he thumbed his suspenders.

"What sorts of things do you import?"

"Silk and tapestry, Turkish rugs, vases from the Orient, spices, antiques."

"It sounds lovely," she said, tasting the fruit and deciding it was appropriately seasoned.

"You seem like a woman who appreciates fine things."

"There is an elegance to a lifestyle where those objects are essential," she agreed.

"With me, you shall have it," he said smugly.

"How do you like your coffee?" she asked, pouring him a cup.

Chapter 9

"I don't believe in guns," Fiona replied when Kier asked if Caleb could join a group of fathers and sons hunting small game near camp.

"Guns are a part of your life whether you like it or not. You need them for food and protection."

That Kier had offered to act in place of Caleb's father was nearly lost on Fiona.

"Give Caleb the chance to hunt. I'll watch him while assessing the quality of our marksmen. We'll soon travel through territory that could hold encounters with unfriendly tribes, and I need to know the level of skill in the company."

Fiona relented and kissed her son goodbye. The look she gave Kier told him all he needed to know. She had entrusted her child to his care and would not rest until he had returned the boy to her safely.

As the men and boys rode out of camp, Fiona was touched by the way Caleb looked first to her, then to Kier, and back to her again. He could not have been in more capable hands, but she worried all the same.

Jake stoked her concern. "Why do you let your child spend time with the savage? It's irresponsible."

By mid-afternoon, she had a headache. She did not like feeling caught between Kier and Jake. When the men and boys returned to camp, Caleb was grinning broadly.

The camp had grown quiet for the night. After tucking her son into bed, Fiona sat alone on a fallen log, trying to read by firelight. In truth, her mind wandered from the words on the page. She considered the significance of Kier's taking Caleb on the hunting trip.

As if on cue, Kier joined her.

"Thank you for taking Caleb with you."

"He's a natural hunter."

"There is much I do not know," she said by way of apology.

"You'll learn, as will Caleb, as will Maggie."

"It seems you made quite an impression," she said admiringly. "As he was drifting to sleep, Caleb spoke nonstop of the day. He tried to teach me how to hold my breath to steady my aim, and how to scan the hunting ground to discover what lies concealed in plain view. He's filled with metaphors of the earth, put there by you," she said with a glimmer of flirtation.

"Nature is a sensual feast. To survive out here, you must make peace with nature. Make it your ally. You need to become aware of the subtleties of your environment."

"How do I do that?" she asked.

"Concentrate on your surroundings. Look carefully at everything around you." He watched her gaze leave his, tentatively at first, to examine the area around them. "Close your eyes," he said, his tone gaining her trust. "What do you see?"

"A campfire, stones, you, trees, and the moon."

"What do you hear?"

"The crackling of the fire, the rustle of night breezes in the tall grass, voices in nearby wagons," she replied.

"What do you feel?" Kier asked, studying her.

"Warmth from the fire, coolness from the breeze."

"What do you smell?" he asked, his gaze continuing to penetrate.

"Wood smoke, coffee, tripe, clover."

"What do you taste?"

"Wood smoke," she said, opening her eyes. "What do you taste?" she asked, beginning to take him through the same exercise.

"Ask me in the order I gave you. Begin with the simplest."

"What do you see?" she asked.

"Three wagons to your left and two to your right, a spider spinning a web in the low branch over your shoulder, a crescent moon, a woman whose face shines earnestly in the glow of firelight, and a marmot watching us from the shadows. Its eyes reflect the light."

Fiona began to see the environment as Kier saw it.

"What do you hear?" she asked, hoping she had fared better on this point.

"The Thompsons arguing, the Olsons making up, Joseph Clark snoring, the sound of your toe tapping against the dirt, the neighing of horses, the whimper of a dog, the hum of crickets." Kier did not take his eyes off hers.

She grew increasingly amazed at the extent of his perception. Once he pointed things out, she heard and saw them, too.

"What do you feel?"

The space between them grew uneasy. A flicker of tension passed like a flame blown in the wind.

"Warmth from the fire, coolness from the breezes,"

he said, using her words.

"What do you smell?"

"A hint of lavender, talcum powder, peppermint."

Fiona lowered her gaze when she realized he was describing her scent. "What do you taste?" she asked breathlessly. Their faces had grown very close. She could almost taste his kiss.

His lips were but a whisper from hers when she turned her cheek, breaking the spell. He backed away from her.

Simon was the only man who had kissed her. His regard for her had nearly killed her. She had no desire to let any man get close to her until she had discovered how to avoid such a situation again.

"I see there is much to learn," she said.

"You will, in time."

She felt his meaning.

Fiona watched him as he spoke, mesmerized by the way he described the West. In his own way he was dashing, if you looked beyond his leathery skin and demeanor—or perhaps despite his leathery skin and demeanor. His high cheekbones and distinctive cleft chin gave his face character, as did an uneven set of dimples and a strong jaw. And his eyes. She was defenseless against those eyes. And then there was his crooked smile.

"Learn to experience each moment fully," he said, "or someday you may regret missing all it has to offer. Learn to rely on your senses to help determine whether a situation is safe. Practice this exercise. Teach it to your children. It will occupy them for a few miles."

"I'll do that," she said. "Thank you," she said after a pause. She didn't know what else to say, given what had passed, or nearly passed, between them.

"Goodnight, Fee," he said, leaving her.

Fee. No one had called her that in years. She liked the way his voice sounded when he said it.

****

Two days had passed, and Fiona's heart still fluttered when she thought of her lesson on the senses. It was early in the morning, shortly before sunrise. The coffee was brewing. She and Clare were in the early stages of breakfast preparation. A man of his schedule, Jake wasn't due to stop by for another fifteen minutes.

Kier strode past where Fiona and Clare were stoking the cooking fire. He greeted them in passing.

Clare looked from Fiona to Kier and bowed her head to hide her amusement. It was unusual for Kier to stop by at this hour of the day.

"What do you see, Mr. Moran?" Maggie asked him.

Kier and Fiona exchanged glances. She nodded to affirm his suspicions. His mouth turned upward as he crouched beside Maggie to play the game.

"I see your mother and mine, the morning sun, a cooking fire, a coffeepot, and a prairie dog who's just stuck his head out of his hole to take a good look at you."

"Where?" she exclaimed, turning to look behind her.

Fiona smiled at Kier and handed him a cup of coffee. "As you predicted, your exercise has become a favorite."

He made no effort to conceal his pleasure at how his take on the world around them compared with that of a precocious three-year-old.

"I'll see you in eight miles," he said, taking his leave of the women.

"Interesting, my son here at this hour," Clare said, watching him walk away.

Fiona revealed nothing.

****

It had been a demanding day in the stale air of the prairie. Kier had pushed them for a solid fifteen miles in humidity choked with dust. Everyone in the company could fairly claim exhaustion. The camp grew quiet early. Fiona and the children were asleep, nursing sunburns and mild cases of heatstroke, lulled by the sound of katydids.

Kier made the rounds to check in with those on watch. The untended campfires within the circled wagons faded to glowing embers.

Buoyed by his freedom, Jeremy Whittaker climbed from his parents' wagon. He followed the bark of a dog. On uncertain footing he made his way across camp, pleased with the progress of his solo adventure.

His bare feet stumbled into a dying fire, bringing tears to his eyes. The cloying perfume of burning flesh hung in the air. He fell forward, singeing the palms of his dimpled hands. His nightshirt caught a spark and smoldered until the hem became a circle of fire. He shrieked, too young to understand what was happening. His cries grew to howls as his nightshirt went up in flames.

By the time Kier reached him, he was lost. Kier tackled the burning child, smothering the blaze with a saddle blanket. "Get the Pickerings. And Mrs. Lenihan. And run!" he ordered the first person he saw.

Hope's screams roused the camp, stirring even

Fiona from her dead sleep.

"Mrs. Lenihan! Mrs. Lenihan! Come quickly!" a woman implored.

"Stay here," Fiona ordered her children, climbing over the tailgate and running toward the center of confusion. The acrid smell of burned flesh poisoned the air. A wave of nausea swept through her. It was an odor she knew well from the times Simon had burned her with his expensive cigars.

Silas and Libby were huddled together with Hope, who was in shock. Kier and Doc were crouched over the burned toddler. Fiona swallowed tears of disbelief.

Jake arrived at the scene, demanding to know what had happened and wanting to take charge of the situation.

"Come, Mrs. Lenihan," Doc ordered quietly. "Bring butter and bandages."

"Wait," Kier interrupted. "There's some aloe in my wagon. It's better for burns than butter. Releases the heat."

"The doctor requested butter," Jake snapped, rebuffing Kier.

Doc nodded impatiently to Kier, ignoring Jake. "Fine. Hurry. We're losing time."

Doc and Fiona worked to Hope's agonized wails, a terrible sound Fiona hoped never again to hear. It took both Silas and Libby to restrain her.

Kier kept onlookers at a distance.

Jeremy's cries became a whimper as he surrendered to the pain. Aware only of the child who watched her through swollen red eyes, Fiona began to sing, trying to comfort him with an Irish lullaby as she smoothed aloe over his charred skin. Behind her,

Hope's sobs abated as the healing magic of Fiona's voice took hold.

Doc listened to the small boy's heartbeat through his stethoscope. His face was grave when he rose to speak with the parents. Hope wanted no part of the doctor's pronouncements and ran immediately to Jeremy's side.

Fiona's heart wept as the little boy looked up at his mother with fear. Fiona wished she could be of greater comfort but recognized the limitations of her service. When her song was finished, she rose to leave.

"Please stay," Hope whispered, her voice hoarse from crying.

Fiona nodded and began another song. Silas knelt to join them. Behind her, she was aware of Kier urging everyone to return to their wagons. Not wishing to be outdone, Jake took over the role of ushering people away from the scene.

Fiona's pure tones cut through the stifling air like a bell, bringing clarity to an evening shattered by the unthinkable.

Libby spelled Fiona, urging her to take a break.

"Will he live?" Fiona asked Doc.

"Trust in the power of nature. It's in God's hands now."

"What more can I do?"

"There is little to be done. His heartbeat is faint." Doc patted Fiona on the shoulder and returned to Silas and Hope.

Chilled by the cool air that had broken the heat, Fiona crossed to the remaining fire. She wanted to be near its warmth, staring into the flames that stole life. The light in her eyes faded to memory.

She had seen and experienced much she had tried to forget. Often, she had wondered where those dark images went. Now she knew they ringed her in shadow, ever present, threatening to douse the light she fought to keep burning at the center of her being.

She stood at the shore of an abyss. It dwelled within her, a simmering cauldron overflowing with betrayals and broken dreams. The lost spirits of loved ones. Images of the burned child swirled with more than two decades of heartaches that threatened to pull her into the netherworld.

At last she realized Kier was standing beside her. He was taken aback by the haunted look in her eyes, a bereavement that masked deeper injury.

"Mrs. Lenihan," he said, clearing his throat to gain her attention. His salutation had no effect. "Fiona," he began again. "Fee."

His keen observation noted the film of tears that dampened her eyes as they regained focus, moisture that was immediately blinked away and hidden with the balance of her secret sadness. Her recovery was practiced, which lent additional insight to the complex woman he was coming to know one revelation at a time.

He reached out to take her face in his hand, their initial touch startling them both. He turned her face toward him and stared into her luminous green eyes, watching their expression evolve from despair to relief.

"I'm going to kiss my children," she said, pulling her shawl around her, at last realizing she wore only a nightgown. She touched her hair, embarrassed to have been seen in such a state, her black curls hanging loosely about her shoulders. "Then I think I'll sit with them a while," she continued, looking toward the young couple.

A stiff breeze stirred her curls, making her shiver.

"It's going to rain," Kier stated. "I'll help them back to their wagon."

Thunder rumbled in the distance.

"Please tell Hope and Silas I'll be with them soon."

He watched her take leave of him, the outline of her slender body silhouetted beneath her nightgown in a flash of lightning as she disappeared into the night.

The funeral was held at dawn under a steady downpour. Fiona was there, and Doc and Libby, and Kier and Jake, among others. Many stayed inside, wishing to avoid the deluge and the sadness of a child's burial.

Fiona and Kier stood on opposite sides of the circle that ringed the tiny grave. He watched her intensely, studying her face and the way it looked beneath the generous brim of a black silk bonnet she had worn because it shielded her face from the elements. Raindrops bounced off its stiff visor as if it were an umbrella.

She felt the weight of his stare and returned it. They held one another in an even gaze.

Hope and Silas thanked Fiona for her kindness. She embraced them both. Hope did not want to let go of her.

Fiona crossed slowly to her wagon but was intercepted by Jake.

"If no one has admonished you for your behavior last evening, then I must do so now."

"What do you mean?"

"The company saw you half-clad, your hair falling across your body in a show of vanity. You must be more attentive to your appearance."

"My appearance was not foremost in my mind last evening," she said crisply.

"Your appearance must be foremost in your mind at all times. You have a reputation to consider." His words were thick with warning.

"Thank you for your guidance," she said to end their exchange.

Chapter 10

A good day on the trail had a rhythm, a pulsating beat like the pounding of a bodhran. A good day was a fifteen-mile monotony of dust and sweat, framed by hot meals at morning and evening, punctuated by nooning to water the animals. Some days they neared the twenty-mile mark; others they made no progress at all. Injury, illness, or a broken wagon meant the entire company came to a halt. They traveled at the pace of the least among them.

A good day was mind-numbing by the third mile, the steady gait of laboring oxen a guarantee of slow progress. Riding in a wagon was hard on bodies as it bounced over the trail, absorbing every rut and rock. Walking beside the wagon was hard on feet, wearing the soles of boots with the constant crush of dust and stone.

When travel was done, the women's work began. After an exhausting day the women needed to bring order to the camp, feed people, and settle them for the night. The men made minor repairs, but in general they rested, smoked cigarettes, and revisited the day's progress.

Traditionally, husbands drove and repaired the wagons, checked the wheels for loose rims, tended to the livestock, hunted for game, and stood watch at night. Wives cared for children, prepared meals, tidied the wagon, laundered and mended clothing, and maintained peace in the family.

Fiona filled both roles. Above that, she was a nurse for Doc and a cook for the company, not to mention a regular participant in Jake's Scripture discussions. The demands were constant.

At times she felt the strain of being many things to many people. She sought refuge in her fireside talks with Kier.

During daylight hours she admired him from afar, noticing the steady control he took of a situation. When an animal stumbled in one of the rodent holes that dotted the prairie, Kier would put the animal out if its misery and devise a measure for the family to continue despite the loss. Replacement animals were uncommon, which necessitated a certain amount of charitable negotiation.

On one occasion, Kier arranged for a stricken family to offer their eleven-year-old son's labor and a half-barrel of flour in return for the use of another family's ox. A different family rebuilt their broken wagon into a cart that carried less than half their possessions, while Kier arranged for their necessities to be carried in three families' wagons.

Other times, the day's frustrations ranged to the amusing, when teams of oxen and mules broke free, wreaking havoc on the order of the company. Kier's dealings with such debacles were equally as smooth as with the wretchedly emotional. He was a study of concern, his ability to round up runaway animals as natural as making peace among squabbling neighbors arguing over weevils in the flour.

Surely Gideon had noticed this, Fiona wondered. If

Gideon's fear was that his son would not amount to anything, he must have formed an opinion to the contrary by now. But neither Clare nor Gideon discussed the matter. Under the circumstances, Fiona was afraid to ask.

As the company's elected leader, Jake was supposed to adjudicate quarrels. But he became flummoxed with others' conflicts. There was an awkwardness about Jake that he covered with bluster. Fiona watched him struggle with minor tasks and noticed how he managed to excuse himself from activities that required any real skill.

Mishaps that delayed the company's progress left Jake irritable. To Kier they were but anticipated inconveniences he had factored into the travel plan.

One day the company came to a halt at the third mile after a toddler fell out of her wagon and was crushed by its wheel. She was the youngest of six children, but her parents' grief matched that of Silas and Hope. As with the Whittakers, Fiona sat with them until the child's injuries stilled her breath. The company made camp on the spot and left the next morning, a small grave concealed in the dust behind them.

Part of another day's travel was lost when a wild animal mauled a young boy after dinner. The men in the company were prepared to hunt a wolf but Kier told them the culprit was likely a rabid dog. Burial was at sunrise and the company got underway after what would have been their nooning.

On both occasions Jake had been testy about why they had not broken camp immediately after the burial and continued in the sunny weather. Kier's decision stood, and the company paid their respects to the families. Fiona overheard some grumbling about Jake among the company, which gave her pause. Opinions were changing about the elected leader, and not for the better.

****

"May I ride with you?" Hope asked Fiona one morning when she was cleaning up breakfast.

It was the first of many days Hope sat on the bench with Fiona. Although Hope was nearly a decade younger, she reminded Fiona of her sisters, Katie and Maeve. There was something sisterly that grew out of their relationship. Their conversations hinged on different subjects from those Fiona shared with Clare or Libby, who sometimes rode with her.

Where the older women and Fiona were comfortable with the silences that fell between them, Hope was not. At times she talked to fill the space. She spoke of how her family lived on neighboring farms in Tennessee, and what it was to leave her kin and follow her husband, who was determined to go west. Hope had not wanted to move away, for it meant she would never again see her sisters.

"It was hard to go," Hope said. "My mama and all my sisters and aunts sobbed and fell on our wagon. Jeremy was but a few weeks old, and he cried too. Before his passing, leaving my family had been the worst thing in my life.

"Part of me is still angry with Silas. Jeremy would still be alive if we had not left Tennessee. But Silas is a good man. I have to keep believing in him and his dream, because it's all we have."

Fiona reached over to embrace her.

Where at first Fiona thought Hope had little in

common with her or with Clare or Libby, in time she came to believe they were not so different, especially when she began to join them on the riverbank.

"These men," Libby muttered under her breath one evening as she knelt at water's edge and began to scrub her laundry against her washboard. Her anger amplified the strength of her arm. "Why did we women bother to come along on this godforsaken journey?"

"To civilize the wilderness," Clare replied sagely.

"To create something out of nothing," Fiona offered. "Much as we do every day. Never in all my life have I been met with so many mouths to feed and so little-known resources. With all the grasses and shrubs we gather, it's a wonder we haven't poisoned anyone yet."

"Can you really imagine these men out here without us? They wouldn't have made it very far. Filthy and starving, they'd be buzzard pickings," said Clare.

Hope laughed, marveling at the humor of the older women.

****

Nebraska Territory was known for spectacular thunderstorms that could last for hours. They were preceded by brilliant electrical displays that led to Biblical downpours. Flooding was a regular concern. Whenever the skies began to darken, Kier turned the company toward high ground.

To the travelers, these storms meant wagons lost in swollen streams, mud up to the hubs, broken axles, and possible drownings. While the additional strain was hard on the men, it was hard on the women as well, leaving them little time to tend to their work. Stormy days were among the most difficult.

For Kier it had been an exhausting week, getting his company through three such storms. If there weren't the accidents, there was the fear the flour and gunpowder could be ruined. On stormy days he charged all three of his men with the safe passage of the supply wagon. Keeping watch on the company he reserved for himself.

On the first sunny day, he pushed the company fourteen miles farther across the plains. They had lost time due to the storms, and this was the best opportunity to make it up.

Mosquitoes came with rain and hot weather. They feasted on Maggie's sweet skin, covering her body with raised welts that she scratched bloody. Miserable, she whimpered in her sleep, leaving Fiona unable to comfort her.

Miniature predators found Fiona's fair skin irresistible. She battled rashes and hives. She slept with her feet elevated to manage the swelling in her ankles from the vermin who gnawed at her exposed flesh beneath the hem of her skirt and the tops of her boots.

"Kier," Fiona called to him one night as he made his rounds. For the better part of an hour Fiona had tried in vain to quiet Maggie. Her wails were making it difficult for other travelers to sleep. Caleb was badgering her to stop crying, which only made matters worse.

Fiona's face was drawn. "I don't know what to do," she confessed. "People have asked me to quiet her, but I can't. Should we sleep outside of camp?"

Clare stopped by Fiona's wagon when she heard voices. She returned with Doc.

"I'll take her," Kier said, reaching for the

sunburned, bug-eaten child. He and Doc headed toward the river.

"You go," Clare said quietly. "I'll stay with Caleb."

When Fiona reached the river's edge, Kier and Doc were crouched beside Maggie, who mewled forlornly.

Kier reached into the riverbed and slathered the girl's limbs with clay.

"Stay with her," he instructed Fiona and Doc.

Fiona covered Maggie with her shawl to keep her warm and curled up beside her to make her feel safe on the bank of the dark river.

"Sing to me," her small voice requested.

Fiona complied, brushing stray curls out of her daughter's face.

When Kier returned, he waded into the river with Maggie and gently washed away the hardened clay. "Takes out the sting," he explained, bringing her back to shore.

At the river's edge, Doc and Fiona applied aloe to Maggie's arms and legs.

"That's for the burn," Kier said. "I brought whiskey as well."

"You're not giving my daughter any drink," Fiona objected.

"A wee taste will help her sleep," Doc assured.

Sated from her treatment, Maggie drifted to sleep.

"Now she needs blankets," Kier explained, climbing to his feet with the girl in his arms.

"It's good to know these remedies," Doc said to Kier.

In silence, the three walked back to Fiona's wagon, where Kier transferred Maggie to Fiona.

"Thank you," she said humbly. She was not accustomed to being the nursed.

The next afternoon when they had made camp, Jake stopped by her wagon to question Fiona about the incident. "There has been talk all day," he sniped.

"Maggie couldn't sleep, and neither could anyone in any of the neighboring wagons," Fiona explained. "We had to do something."

"Next time, discipline your child appropriately," he ordered.

Feeling much better from Kier's remedy and a day spent in the shade of the wagon's canopy, Maggie played quietly under its shelter as Fiona prepared dinner. Then she spotted a butterfly. She followed it around one wheel, under the wagon, and to the far side of the wagon, outside the enclosure. When she lost sight of the butterfly, she spied a cluster of wildflowers and went to pick a bouquet.

Engaged in an increasingly heated conversation with Jake, Fiona did not notice Maggie had disappeared.

"In fact, I have a better solution," Jake said, his tone condescending. "I will give up my place at the front of the column to position my wagon beside yours. That way I can keep a gentleman's watch."

"That won't be necessary."

"You reject me so easily," he criticized.

"It's not that," she explained. "There is more dust this far back in the column. You shouldn't give up your place."

"Then I'll arrange to have your wagon moved to the front of the column."

"You know I need to be near Doc."

Maggie sang to herself as she collected wildflowers in the golden light of afternoon. A gentle breeze lifted her ringlets. Bumblebees flew around her, visiting the flowers. Suddenly she stopped.

"Or is it the Morans?" Jake snapped. "Despite my warnings, you seem to have developed a liking for their son."

"Mama!" Maggie shrieked.

Fiona spun wildly. She did not know where her daughter was. Following the voice, she rounded the corner of her wagon and saw a lone bison bearing down on Maggie. The girl ran under the wagon and the 2,000-pound beast stopped. He stared down Fiona, whom he now had in his sights. The bull grunted and lowered its head. Only fifteen feet separated them.

Fiona stood perfectly still. She heard Clare and Libby approach; they had come to see the cause of Maggie's unholy sound. Fiona swallowed hard and watched the bison watch her.

"Maggie, go to Mrs. M," she instructed quietly. "Walk slowly to the fire and meet her there."

"Do something," Jake yelled to no one in particular. "Doesn't one of you have a rifle?"

Fiona could hear her daughter's frightened cries behind her and felt some relief when Maggie was safe in Clare's arms.

Fiona's pulse pounded in her ears. The bison bucked his head. Fiona swallowed again, fear creeping over her. She was no match for the enormous beast.

The bison slowly raised his tail. She wondered if she could fall to one side and get out of his way when he charged. But he was so close. She didn't know if she would have time.

The bison charged, and a single shot rang out. Fiona jumped out of its path. A second shot rang out, and the bison fell dead before her. Jake ran to her side in a show of concern.

"You all right?" Kier asked, walking past Fiona and Jake and standing over the carcass.

"Why did it take you two shots?" Jake asked. "I thought you were supposed to be a crack shot."

"How did you know?" Fiona asked, wondering how it was Kier had responded so quickly.

"Got word there was a lone bull outside the enclosure. He was probably driven out of his herd by a dominant bull," he said, looking at Jake, who continued to stand at Fiona's side.

"He could have killed Maggie," Fiona said.

"He could have killed you," Kier said.

Fiona nodded, trying to catch her breath. She felt suddenly dizzy.

"Settles the question of what to eat for supper," Kier said, trying to humor her.

That night a group of men and women skinned and carved meat from the animal. They cooked big chunks on spits over the fire and dined on steaks. The remaining meat was salted and held in reserve for stew the following day.

For her trouble, Fiona had rights to the remains. Kier showed her how to prepare the hide. He taught all who were interested how to make soup ladles from the horns, sewing needles and knives from the bones, and axes from the shoulder blades.

Fiona kept one soup ladle and shared the bison's riches with her fellow travelers. She wasn't sure she needed one axe, let alone two. And all the sewing needles from the bones of a single bison would do her little good.

****

Word spread within the company that if they met any Indians their best hope was they were Sioux, because that was the tribe with whom Kier had lived. Since he knew them, he could probably save the company trouble. However, he had no relationship with other tribes, including Crow, Pawnee, Snake, Blackfeet, or Comanche. Kier would be but any white man to them.

The farther west they traveled, the more the company's concern grew, especially when a group of Indians was sighted on a distant ridge. They came no closer, but it was a frightening experience for many in the company. Stories about Indian attacks had captured the American imagination for some time. Few in the company were willing to believe any Indians they encountered could be other than savage warriors.

With increased tension came an increased need for rest. The camp grew quiet earlier than usual. Maybe it was the oppressive heat and humidity. Maybe it was the pace at which Kier drove them. Mostly it was because the travelers grew exhausted with fear about the unknown trials that lay ahead.

Some nights, after a particularly grueling day, Fiona was so tired all she could do after dinner was crawl into her wagon. She was asleep before she was in bed. More often, she sat by the campfire. It gave her peace. It also gave her time with Kier when he could join her.

"When we first met, you said something curious. I've been wondering about it ever since: 'American dias-'," she said, stumbling over the word.

"American diaspora. Yes," he said, laughing sheepishly. "Far too easily these cross-country journeys assume an almost Biblical reverence. Folks describe them using epic prose that exaggerates the simple realities of the trip. They envision themselves as a pilgrim people bound for some far-off promised land.

"In reality, I'm left with a disenfranchised group of mismatched emigrants whose weaknesses I must turn into strengths. You've seen how our company has taken shape. It's my job to work with every man and woman to ensure the majority will make it safely to California."

"How are we doing so far?"

"All right," he said, nodding affirmatively. "But the worst part of the journey is yet to come. For the last few years I have joined relief parties in the Sierra Nevada to help late travelers to safety by the middle of November. Every year there is at least one family that has gotten lost or is too weak to make the last few miles unassisted. We started this after the Donner party. We don't find everyone, but we find many who need help finishing the journey."

"How do people end up in that state?" Fiona asked with interest.

"Poor planning, to be finishing the crossing so late in the season. Bad luck. Sickness. Injury. If you're a small family with one able-bodied man and he gets scurvy or grows lame, that family is in a sorry state. The worst part is crossing the Sierra Nevada. People are tired when they reach the eastern foothills. Oxen teams are all used up. Some of the most difficult travel is in the climbing and descending. Wagons slip. People fall."

Fiona listened, sobered by all she heard. She was

glad to have Kier on the journey. She trusted him to help them through the mountains.

A bolt of cloud-to-cloud lightning illuminated the sky. The rumble of thunder followed.

"You've taken on quite a challenge as a woman with children too young to be of material use on the journey. Essentially, you're doing alone what entire families are doing."

"Please don't underestimate me."

"I'm not the one of us who does," he said gently.

"My father said a day's hard work is our way of repaying our Maker for the gift of another day," she said, watching the unsettled sky.

"A wise man."

"I suppose. Every child should have at least one such memory of the man who gave him life."

In silence they watched the lightning. It was difficult to breathe in the torrid air.

"Do you?" she asked.

A long time passed before he spoke. "Yes."

She bid him goodnight when she realized he was not going to tell her about Gideon Moran.

Chapter 11

"The sky is on fire," Caleb said with wonder, gazing toward the wash of clouds that hung in the dawn sky.

Fiona glanced up from the breakfast preparation and shared her son's appreciation for the unusual sunrise. A towering array of clouds, layered one upon the other, climbed toward the heavens. One cloud looked like an enormous anvil, extending toward the ceiling of the sky. Backlit by a red sun, the sky indeed appeared to be on fire.

Fiona turned away to spoon the biscuits into a baking pan and stir the pot of stewed fruit where it bubbled over the cooking fire. When she turned back, the sky had changed dramatically. Violent sprays of clouds jutted out from the sunrise, individual flames against their celestial mates. The display was a giant hearth fire complete with embers, flames, and coals.

"Look, Mr. Moran," Caleb called, excited to show him the sky.

Fiona turned to see Kier approaching. He tipped his hat to her before engaging in discussion with Caleb.

"Red sky in morning, a sailor's warning," he said, nodding toward the sunrise.

"What's that mean?" Caleb asked.

"Storm's coming."

"How near?" Caleb asked, studying the sky in an

attempt to see what Kier saw.

"We'll get wet."

"Where are we?" Fiona asked Kier, diverting her attention to the endless sea of gold and green, with hills that rolled like waves toward the horizon. "It looks nearly the same as where we were yesterday and the day before, and the day before that."

"Some call it Prairy Erth. Bounty as far as the eye can see."

A breeze swept across the tall grasses in gentle ripples. Horsetail tops waved back and forth in a lazy rhythm. Few obstacles lay in their path.

It also meant there was nowhere to hide.

Yarrow, thistle, cattails, and blue flax appeared and disappeared as they traveled within sight of the Platte River. Caleb and Maggie competed to see who could spot a new kind of flower first. Copper mallow, bee balm, locoweed, and prairie violets kept them occupied for the next mile. When Maggie realized her brother knew more than she did about the flowers, she began to ask him questions about what they were seeing. Fiona listened to Caleb too, taking a close look at the flowers for the first time.

She enjoyed listening to her children's conversation and was pleased with their friendship. Watching Caleb and Maggie reminded her of Seamus. The five-year age difference between them was the same.

As the day wore on, a stifling dampness settled over them, infusing the atmosphere with a sunlit haze. The air was thick as buttermilk. On and on they marched through the oppressive mugginess, Fiona's head aching more with every minute.

Kier and Brent were out front, leading the scouting party. The pair stopped on a ridge and Kier surveyed the sky in all directions, his expression oddly pensive. He studied the cloud formations. "I don't like the sky."

"We can handle a little rain," Brent replied with a shrug.

"Describe the air to me," Kier said.

"Just another airless summer day. It's miserably hot and it isn't even noontime," said Brent.

"Do you notice that musty smell?"

"Now that you mention it."

"Keep moving. If we're lucky, it won't form until we've traveled beyond it. Let's pick up the pace," he said nodding toward the company. "I'll ride back to check on Billy and the children driving the cattle. We'll delay nooning until we ride clear of this storm."

There was some complaint when Kier postponed stopping, but people's tempers settled when they saw the sky. Giant thunderheads were building around them, wads of cotton multiplying like rabbits. They were beautiful, a pristine cathedral of vapor. But Kier knew the destruction they could breed.

It was a massive system, extending for miles into the atmosphere. The blue sky turned an unnatural greenish-yellow as a haze settled over them. Blinding white clouds became infused with violet. The sun disappeared.

The first breeze of the day seemed to bear false relief. The clouds tumbled to a low ceiling, their majesty lost in an ominous witch's brew. They began to churn, wispy fingers twisting from the cauldron in the sky.

It grew strangely quiet. The breeze stopped. Flies

and grasshoppers disappeared. The drone of the cicada faded. Oxen, horses, and dogs hushed. The travelers glanced nervously at the heavens. The gentle breeze returned, becoming a gale. Forks of lightning snaked toward the ground, followed by the rumble of thunder.

Kier rode the length of the company, encouraging them to circle the wagons and take shelter beneath them. Sam and Brent met him midway up the column.

A bolt of lightning struck the ground less than a mile away. The resulting thunder vibrated through their bodies.

"Put the wagons close together, nearly touching. I want a solid wall around our people," Kier ordered.

Brent and Sam nodded and tore off across the prairie, riding low in the saddle.

Day became night as the storm continued to bear down on them. Rain began to fall. With it, all sound returned. The animals brayed nervously, their eyes blazing with fear.

Death descended from the ominous skies. The curling streak of pioneers had only a mile's warning before it hit, shattering everything in its path.

They watched in horror as the enormous tornado approached.

Kier galloped around the perimeter, warning everyone to take cover under their wagons.

Fiona grabbed her children and threw her body across them. She looked up to gain some sense of the terror around her. To her astonishment, a prolonged blue-white bolt of lightning turned the sky brighter than day, its spark illuminating the cyclone.

She watched in awe through strobes of lightning as the dark chimney sucked up water from the river. The funnel cloud uprooted a dozen large trees like an impudent child ripping flowers out of a garden. Wreckage was tossed everywhere, especially toward the company of wagons.

Fiona heard screams from her fellow travelers and thought she saw a person blow past her until an ox flew by and she knew it was real. Their goat, Rufus, was vacuumed up by the wind, guide rope and all. A terrible crash was followed by the upending of wagons, some of them blown across the prairie like tumbleweeds, occupants and possessions spilling over the ground.

Other wagons were blown apart by the storm's fury. Individual planks impaled livestock and battered people. Leaves blown off trees were left sticking out of wagon wheels like porcupine quills. Fiona heard the canvas of her wagon start to tear.

Then it was over.

The tornado changed course and moved away from the company, disappearing in a wisp of air. Debris held aloft by the storm crashed to the earth. The lunatic winds stopped, leaving torrents of rain in their aftermath. Hail followed, pelting them with chunks of ice the size of silver dollars, shredding canopies.

Fiona knew Doc would need her. She climbed from under her wagon and joined her fellow travelers to survey the damage. Each was overwhelmed by the scope of destruction.

A dead man stared at the sky, run through with a board. An ox had been pulled in two, his innards scattered in the twenty feet that separated his front end from his hind end. A wagon was broken against a tree trunk stripped of its branches. Limp bodies hung from the ruins.

"Go back to the wagon," Fiona ordered Caleb. Her voice was shaking.

"But Mother," he argued.

"Now," she said, the tension in her voice escalating. "Climb inside and stay there with Maggie so I know you're safe." She did not want him to see but knew he had.

She turned to check on the Morans and Pickerings. Gideon met her halfway. "You women are needed elsewhere. I'll stay with the children."

"Clare is all right?"

He nodded. "She went to find Kieran."

Fiona reached up to embrace the old man.

Her mouth fell open at the storm's path of destruction a thousand feet wide. As far as she could see, not a petal or leaf remained. What had been verdant and rich with life only minutes before was now dead.

Trees had become airborne battering rams aimed at wagons. In places, the river had been reduced to a morass. Broken prairie grasses lay in a tangle on the disfigured earth. Shards of man and beast were indistinguishable on mud stained with their commingled blood. As haunting as the images of all she had seen in Ireland, they did not compare with the violence of what surrounded her.

Fiona realized they had been at the front edge of the storm where it had veered away from a straight line of destruction. Had Kier not pushed them and made camp anywhere before where they had stopped, they would have been in the direct path of the tornado, where nothing at all remained, not even topsoil. The land was barren, scorched by wind as if it had been destroyed by fire.

Sobbing quietly, Evangeline took Fiona's hand. They locked arms and together they walked through the ruins, separating to check for wounded among the dead. Fiona gasped to contain her emotions, postponing grief as she had so often in her life.

"Look!" a man cried.

It was a full rainbow. Portions of a second rainbow arched above the first.

Kier and his men catalogued the damage. Nine were killed: two when their wagon toppled over and crushed them; three by flying debris. A father and his eldest son were killed with a tree fell on their wagon. Two who had been spat out from the heart of the storm were unrecognizable.

Forty-one people were injured, nine of them gravely.

An even dozen draft animals were dead or missing. Seven cattle were gone, as was Fiona's goat. Thirteen wagons were destroyed; an equal number would need extensive repairs before the company could travel.

Billy led a group of men to dig nine graves. Before they were finished, they would need two more.

The settlers' naivete was lost in that storm, stolen by the winds that carried away lives and possessions. Accidents were a tragic but expected part of the journey. Indian attacks were a risk of which they were aware.

It was the monstrosities of nature that left them feeling outmatched, knowing they were defenseless in the face of such power. A somber spirit took hold.

****

Like many, Caleb had reached the limits of tolerance.

"I want to go home," he sobbed, creating a scene. "I want to go home!"

Around the camp, Caleb's cries gave several travelers pause. He expressed what many felt. Collective morale was at a low.

Fiona tried to steer him toward the privacy of their wagon, but he dug his heels into the ground and refused to move. "Why did you make us leave our home? Why did you bring us out here? I want to go home!" he yelled, arching his back in a temper tantrum like he had not thrown in years.

Fiona knelt to embrace him, holding him to soothe his frustration. At that moment, her empathies were more closely aligned than she could admit. "Hush," she whispered in his ear, rocking him gently.

Once he had grown quiet, she lifted his face and held it in her hands, drying the remnants of his tears. "I have an idea," she said, her tone an elixir. "You are the most observant Lenihan. Someday after you and Maggie and I are settled in our new home, we'll need a way to remember all that's happened to us, good and bad. Why don't you spend some time every day putting our story on paper?"

"In words?" he asked, his eyes growing wide. "Like a book?"

"In words or pictures, you decide. It's your book. You have a gift for noticing things. Keep a record so we will remember. How does that sound?"

He nodded eagerly.

"Now hurry to bed. It's been a very long day."

Fiona rubbed her face. She was tired and had nothing more to give. She had been sucked dry.

"Fiona," Kier's voice called. He materialized at her

side. "Doc has asked for you. A woman has gone into labor and it's not going well. My mother will keep watch over your children."

She stepped into the uneasy night.

****

The company did not break camp for several days, choosing instead to make the necessary repairs to the wagons, hunt for fresh game, and allow the wounded to heal. It was the first decision on which Kier and Jake had agreed.

The next morning Fiona prepared Jake's coffee with cream and sugar, just as he liked it, and handed it to him with a smile.

"Moran did a good job with God's wrath. He kept the company calmer than any man felt."

Fiona nodded.

"I will concede he has some useful qualities," he said, taking his first sip of coffee.

"It would seem so."

"You make the best coffee in the company. I'll stop by for another cup later."

"I'll see you then," she said with a polite smile.

****

Fiona, Clare, and Hope were knee-deep in a pool of water, doing the wash. As they scrubbed items against washer boards, bubbles from the lye cakes hung on the surface like sea foam.

"I'm going to have a baby," Hope announced, not missing a step in the rhythm she had established.

"That's wonderful news!" Fiona smiled broadly, turning to embrace her.

"Is it?" she asked without looking up.

"Of course, it is. Think of the joy Jeremy brought

to your lives."

"And the pain of his passing. What if something happens to this child? How would I go on?"

"As you are now," Fiona said. "Life continues. People die. Babies are born. We go on for their sake. So many died yesterday, yet a beautiful child came into the center of our grief last night. He is a miracle, as your child is a miracle."

"Many have shared your tragedy, yet we endure," Clare said tenderly.

"Our first son was taken by influenza," Libby said, staring into the past. "He was three years old. Not a day passes that I don't think of him. But God blessed us with other children. And grandchildren, too." Her eyes glistened with tears.

"Kieran has a sister in heaven," Clare said, "one of five lost to us. We called her Grainne Moran. She lived but four days. Grainne and Kieran were the only of our children to be born living." A mist darkened her eyes.

"Caleb and Maggie have a sister, too," Fiona said. "She was born dead. In my heart I named her Kathleen, after my mother. I think of her often and wonder what she would have been like. Her birthday was last week. She would have been a year old."

"I'm sorry," Hope said quietly. "I didn't know. Why does God give us children only to take them away? The pain is unbearable."

Their answers came in succession:

"To make us appreciate what we have."

"To show us that what we have is never really ours but God's."

"To teach us to love."

"To give us hope."

"You will survive this sadness of Jeremy's passing," Fiona said, taking Hope's hands in hers. "We will welcome your child into our lives."

"Promise me you'll not forget me when we reach California," Hope said, looking urgently at the women.

"Never." Fiona smiled, her affection shared by Clare and Libby.

"And you'll come see the baby? I want my baby to know each of you. I've been so blessed to have known you. I'll miss your kindness and wisdom when we go to our separate homes."

****

The following morning, eleven wagons left camp pointed east, filled with those who had decided it was better to go back than go forward on this journey.

As Fiona prepared her wagon for the day, she watched Kier meet with the travelers. There were twenty-four in all, among them many who had been injured in the storm. He gestured toward the east and showed them a map. At one point they looked toward the sky, where Kier seemed to trace the path of the sun. He handed them some documents and what appeared to be a purse, Fiona assumed filled with money. Then he shook the hands of the men and boys. He embraced a widow, who seemed unwilling to let him go. Fiona noticed the widow did not look back once their wagons were underway.

Chapter 12

Caleb watched the young buck down the barrel of a rifle, his eyes as unmoving as the deer's. Kier lay on his belly beside him in the thicket, coaching the boy in what he hoped would be his first kill.

He had given the boy a tall order for the hunt, instructing him to take the shot when he was ready. Kier was testing his instincts, wanting to determine the boy's aptitude. Kier had decided to take it upon himself to train Caleb in the art of the hunt. He was an eager student who had beamed with pride at Kier's invitation.

Fiona had hesitated but did not object. He was good to her children and gave Caleb a much-needed role model. Kier had taught him things she never could have passed on to him, important things about animals, the land, and people, things he would need to know when building a future in the West.

The shot was perfect; Kier would have taken it. But he wanted to give Caleb the chance to judge the situation. The boy was unmoving, his finger poised on the trigger. Kier was trying to sense fear or hesitancy in the boy when the shot rang out, missing the target. A second hunter brought down the deer, a measure of insurance Kier had installed. He was willing to be a patient teacher, but not so willing as to lose a valuable kill. Caleb's eyes fell to the ground in defeat.

"Good job, son," Kier complimented the boy on his

focus, concentration and steady aim. What the boy lacked was confidence. He was too cautious. Next time he would tell the boy when to take the shot.

By dusk the air was thick with mosquitoes, but there was no sign of the hunting party. Fiona's nerves made her irritable. Billy assured her they would return.

"Look, Mama." With pride, Maggie showed off a doll's bed she had made from prairie grasses and clover. "Sally is sleeping."

Jake cleared his throat. "I have come to request the pleasure of your company for an evening walk."

"Come, Maggie," Fiona said, taking Jake's arm and extending her other hand to her daughter.

"It's growing dark. Little girls might lose their footing," Jake said.

"I want to sleep by Sally," Maggie wailed, objecting to the idea of a walk. Fiona realized the idea of a walk didn't hold much appeal for her either.

"Why don't you join us here?" she invited.

"Bear in mind my offer of a private conversation. Night is falling. What have you to say regarding the whereabouts of your son?"

"The hunting party is due back soon."

"According to whom, one of that Indian lover's supplicants? I continue to be surprised by your cavalier maternal instincts. Quite frankly, I am appalled by your willingness to put any stock in that sinner and the way you encourage your children to do the same. A poorer role model than Moran cannot be found in this company."

"He has more to offer than you are willing to acknowledge."

"Do I hear you defending this man?" he said

incredulously.

"Come, Maggie, it's time for you and Sally to go to bed." Fiona rose, signaling to Jake their conversation was over.

"You astonish me with your willfulness. Mark my words," Jake called after her as she led Maggie to their wagon. "Your association with Moran will ruin you and your children."

It was dark when Fiona climbed out of her wagon after tucking Maggie in for the night. She saw Billy across the circle of wagons, strumming a guitar.

"Tell me about Kier," she asked, taking a seat across from him.

"He said they would be back," he replied, smiling with confidence, not losing his place.

"You signed on with Kier to go west. Has it been what you expected?"

"More," he said fondly. "Kier is the best man I have ever known. He is everything folks said he would be, the best tracker, best shot, best man in a bad situation, the best man to cross America with. He's fair and decent too. Caleb is in the best of hands."

Fiona nodded, relieved to hear him validate her beliefs.

"Do you play?" he asked after noticing the way she studied his hands on the strings.

"No. I like music, though. I'm enjoying listening to you."

She grinned with delight as he played a rendition of "Amazing Grace" that turned the traditional hymn on its ear.

A disturbance at the far end of camp interrupted his song. The hunting party had returned.

"He said they would be back," Billy repeated, his smile wide.

Fiona and Billy joined the growing numbers welcoming the hunting party. She broke into a run, eager to see her son and hear of his adventure.

"How was it?" she asked, sweeping him into her arms.

Caleb was giddy. "The best day ever! Mr. Moran is better than Finn MacCool!" he exclaimed, spit threatening to fly out of his mouth. His words came in a single sentence, broken in odd places where he needed to stop for breath.

Fiona could see it had been an incredible experience. He was brimming with excitement. Although he had made no kills, he was honestly credited in several when the party had the good fortune to encounter buffalo.

"Buffalo?" she exclaimed, thrilled about the full scope of her son's adventure.

"Yes! They were real loud. They ran right past us. Mr. Moran told us how to follow one by looking down the barrel and then aiming just past its head, so the bullet will hit it at the right time."

"I see," she replied with mixed feelings at the gruesome images pouring from her son's mouth.

"And then he showed us how to field dress the animal."

Kier was greeted as a returning hero, for the scope of the kill was immense: twenty buffalo, thirteen deer, and fifteen rabbits—as much as the hunting party could carry home. It would give them food and other supplies for days to come. Kier was showered with praise but was quick to give credit to other members of the party.

He used the occasion to bolster the confidence of the men and their skills.

Across the crowd, Fiona smiled her thanks to Kier.

He organized teams of men and women to skin the animals and prepare the meat. It was an activity that lasted the night. Portions were set on spits to roast, while pieces were cut in strips for jerky. He instructed people how to work the skins into blankets and harvest tallow from the fat to make candles, soap, and lubricants for wheels.

Music and dancing were in order as the company enjoyed a break from travel. Some dozed after a full day of hunting and a full night spent processing the carcasses. Others chatted amiably in a show of goodwill that ran throughout the company. Children played along the edge of the Platte River. Maggie gathered an enormous bouquet of wildflowers that Fiona arranged in a tin pitcher.

In the distance Fiona saw a stream of wagons pressing west, a reminder that tomorrow they would do the same.

Jake had insinuated himself as the leader of the celebration. He made speeches praising the hunting party and those who had prepared the feast. It struck Fiona as odd that he made such a public display of himself at an event in which he had played no role. She knew he had been asleep in his wagon during the full night of skinning the animals and preparing the meat and hides.

That evening Fiona stood at the edges of what served as the wagon train's mobile town square, discussing the bountiful food supply and trading local gossip with a handful of women. All around them was music and dancing, and the sounds of nearly three hundred contented souls. The swirl of women's skirts and the glow of lanterns gave the event the air of a holiday celebration.

Something made her shoulders stiffen. It drew her attention across the town square.

He was a magnet for her gaze. He watched her through the fires, through the dancers and families and crowds of people, his intensity unfailing. And then he smiled faintly, an expression meant for her alone. Again, she returned his gaze and turned away, unable to meet his eyes with the sensual force with which he held hers. When she looked up, he was gone.

Reaching the place where he had been standing, she inquired after him. Some shook their heads; others directed her away from the fire.

The music and voices faded. On the outskirts of camp, a man pointed her to a rock formation beyond the edge of the enclosure. The rise of granite served as a natural lookout.

He stood in the distance, his tall frame silhouetted against the prairie moon, his rifle slung over his shoulder. It was just like him to stand alone outside the boundaries of camp, apart from civilization. There was more strength in his solitude than in the company of a hundred of her traveling companions.

She hesitated before crossing the dark field. Looking back to the firelit festivities as if to change her mind, she turned away and stepped into the night. A cool wind blew across the plains. She drew her shawl around her shoulders.

She called his name when she was within range. "Kier," she said from the base of the outcropping, looking up to where he stood.

He looked down at her, his expression inviting. When he offered his hand, she took it. Their touch lingered as he pulled her to his level. Cast in a spell of their making, their hands were clasped longer than necessary before parting.

"I wanted to thank you for all you've done for Caleb," she began, her gaze steady. "You've made quite an impression. He can't stop talking about the hunt and all you taught him. He describes the stampeding buffalo in such vivid terms."

"It's a thrilling experience. Perhaps one day you will see it."

"One buffalo was enough." She laughed. "Thank you for being so kind to Caleb and Maggie."

"They're a pleasure."

She smiled her thanks. Their conversation hit an impasse, and she decided that to say anything would be a mistake. Sustaining an awkward silence, she turned to leave. "Well, goodnight, then."

"Finn MacCool."

"What about Finn MacCool"? she asked, her mouth turning upward in a smile that matched the one he wore.

"Caleb is rather taken with him."

"He said you were better than Finn MacCool," she said gamely.

"Did he?"

Fiona did not know how to respond, so she said nothing. A fresh tension settled between them.

He returned his gaze to the stars. "I've often wondered whether man will come to navigate the skies now that he has mastered the seas."

"It would take quite a ship, I imagine," she replied, elevating her eyes to the place that held his attention.

"Yes. But oh, to sail around the staff of Bootes, the tail of Scorpius, and all of Cassiopeia."

"You know how to read the night sky?" she asked in wonder, turning to watch him look heavenward.

"That one is Leo, the lion, setting in the west," he explained, showing her the constellation. "And Scorpius, the scorpion, to the south, about to set. The bright star at its heart is called Antares." She watched and listened as he pointed out the North Star and told her of its navigational significance, and Ursa Major and Ursa Minor, the Big and Little Dippers. He explained how the stars rose and set, like the moon and sun.

"Mastering the night sky could take a lifetime," she observed.

"Its science and myth provide endless fascination. And a map when you're at sea. Just as the stars have their place, so does everything in nature. Together we are nature's constellations." He lowered his face and turned to meet her eyes.

"Have you found your place in the 'constellation of nature'?" she asked.

"No."

"Perhaps you are meant to be a wanderer, weaving the threads of people's lives together with yours."

"Perhaps." An easy silence followed. "I've always been drawn to the stars. So many nights I've lain awake, studying them, hoping to learn from them, their sense of order. I've grown fond of sleeping under them. They have been my one steady companion."

Kier's fingers turned her face toward his. She felt the full weight of his gaze. His eyes twinkled as they held hers. He lowered his face and kissed her, taking a sip of her before tasting her fully.

His demeanor was more characteristic of the tranquility of the moment than of the personality of the man she was coming to know. Their lips parted and Kier drew away to regard her. He seemed amused by her reaction, as if it were the first time anyone had ever kissed her.

His hand continued to explore her face, caressing its planes before reaching to where a pair of jet-encrusted combs held her curls in a sensible knot.

She shivered when his fingertips brushed the nape of her neck, electrifying the surface of her skin. His hands came to rest on her upper arms, where he held her in earnest. She opened her eyes to regard him, the depth of her affection nourishing him in a way she could not imagine.

His overture complete, he stepped into her and parted her lips with his tongue to taste her sweetness. Tentatively at first, her arms moved to hold him as he held her. She kissed him back, savoring the feel of him in her mouth.

A coyote howled in the distance. "I should go." She stumbled away from him on uncertain knees, her fingers raised to her lips. Desire raged in her eyes.

Climbing from the outcropping she ran from him, luxuriating in the taste of his kisses.

She could not determine whether to embrace these feelings. No one had taken such liberties with her but Simon. By the time she reached her wagon, her composure intact, she concluded that whatever she was experiencing was wrong. She was a widow. It simply wasn't proper to develop affection for another man with her husband in his grave only three months.

Kier's affections beckoned her mind to wander beyond their encounter, to wonder about sharing more than just a kiss, to consider what it would be like to lie with him, as lovers, as his wife.

"I've been looking for you." Jake's voice startled her. "Why did you leave the circle?"

"I took a walk," she said.

"You followed Moran."

"I wanted to thank him for taking Caleb hunting." She swallowed nervously, realizing he was closing on her.

"You forget so easily our discussion of only last night? You're trembling, Mrs. Lenihan. What did he do to you?"

She shut her eyes as he towered over her. His size made her feel small and vulnerable in a way that Kier's larger physique did not. He was right. She was trembling.

"Did he do this?" he asked, gripping her by her upper arms and forcing her torso back. She gasped, surprised by his unexpected aggression.

"You're hurting me."

"How about this?"

An involuntary scream crossed her lips when he forced his mouth over hers, nearly destroying the beauty of Kier's kiss. Her hands became fists; he caught them before she could strike him.

"Stop," she protested, visions of Simon filling her mind.

The sound of a match striking the bark of a tree caught their attention. Shielding the flame with his hand, Kier brought its glow toward his mouth to light a cigarette.

Jake whirled to face him.

"Leave the lady alone," Kier said. A silvery cloud of exhaled smoke rose above him.

Fiona eyed both men nervously.

"I could say the same of you. As a gentlewoman, she needs to keep company with her betters, not with the likes of you."

"I told you I wanted to thank him for taking Caleb on the hunt," Fiona interjected.

"And it took you how long to do this? I watched you leave camp. I know how long you have been away."

"Why don't you take the lady at her word?" Kier suggested.

"Why don't you stay out of matters between ladies and gentlemen?" Jake retorted.

"Go to your wagon," Kier told Fiona.

"Stay," Jake countered. "I want you to see just how a businessman attempts to converse with a boor."

"Stop it, both of you," she pleaded. "Goodnight," Fiona said haltingly, turning to leave. If she made an exit, perhaps they would follow her lead.

Clare wondered at Fiona's pensive mood when she thanked her for keeping an eye on Maggie and Caleb and led her drowsy children to bed. Fiona seemed oddly distracted and a bit too eager to turn in for the evening. Clare's chance meeting with her equally distracted son allowed her to piece it together. Something had finally happened between them. Her cheeks grew round with an enormous smile.

Fiona lay awake for hours, languishing in sensations that were maddening to where she felt she must have done something wrong. She had never felt this way before. Kier's embrace had touched a distant part of her where no man had trod. She had been damaged by love and feared the repetition of history.

Yet, she wanted to shout; she wanted to scream and laugh and dance. She yearned for him as she had for no other, but she feared where these feelings might lead. She felt his presence as if it were his child growing inside her, draining and revitalizing her. She knew it was wrong to imagine holding him inside her, to engage in fantasies while in mourning. She was a widow with two young children. They were her priority.

Come dawn, she had reached a decision. Kier was a luxury she must do without.

As was his custom, Kier tipped his hat to her the next morning. She looked quickly at him and as quickly away, remembering her decision. For her children's sake, she could not give in to temptation.

To their mutual chagrin, Fiona and Kier's personal relationship faded after their moonlit encounter. Her motive became avoidance. In turn, he avoided her.

Jake made an elaborate apology for his actions. She believed him to be a decent man but knew his words were hollow. He did not possess the same depth of character as Kier.

It was a difficult position, trapped between the unwelcome advances of one man and the banished embrace of another. She owed Kier an explanation but doubted she could articulate her feelings well enough to make him understand her untenable circumstances.

The company made excellent time over the next several days. Morale was high, but their collective energy grew low. Kier found a place to set camp, making good on a promise of much-needed rest and hunting to replenish food supplies.

The distance Fiona had created with Kier earned her a new perspective on the attractiveness of the man. She had not noticed before, but there were several women in the company who had designs on him. Fiona observed his practiced management of their ongoing flirtations. She found herself jealous of these women, but relieved by Kier's good-natured rebuttal of their affections. For the moment she seemed the only woman in whom he had any real interest. And she knew it was her fault she was no longer enjoying his attentions.

She missed their fireside talks, his daily greeting, and the unexpected encounters when he happened by her cooking fire or she went to retrieve her son, who by now knew when to cut short his visits with Kier and come back to their wagon for the evening.

The night before they broke camp, the company feasted on venison scored by the hunting party. There was music and dancing. A community celebration.

Kier's and Fiona's eyes met over the heads of a trio of adoring women who made their way over to him. But still she avoided him. She traveled on dangerous ground if she were to give in to her feelings for that man.

She danced with Jake. It was one of the man's true skills. As she spun around and around, she watched Kier watching her, and her desire for him grew. She had no control over her feelings for him.

No, she told herself. She belonged with a trustworthy man like Jake, whose business sense in the East would serve him well in the West. As much as she was prepared to scratch a living out of the earth for herself and her children, the desire to live the life of a Cushing was strong. Jake Farragut could offer her that life.

In her mind, she extolled Jake's virtues. He was a good Christian who always attended Sunday services. He was admired as the leader of the company, and he had a good head for business. He was an enjoyable dinner companion. Moreover, he had been very attentive to her. But she could not add to the list. She was unwilling to make a similar list of his less attractive qualities.

Her mind turned to Kier, and she had to stop before she had a list twice as long of his admirable qualities. She could not help herself. Although she was in the arms of one man, her mind was filled with thoughts of another.

Chapter 13

Fort Kearny was located where trails from several jumping-off points converged and where the Platte River split into north and south forks. Built by the government to aid travelers, it was an active center filled with emigrants who were pleased to have come so far while planning the next leg of their journey.

It was also a military installation and supply depot where the travelers could purchase cheese, fresh butter, and milk. The next supply depot was three hundred miles west, in Fort Laramie.

People were dusty, tired, and hungry for a meal not eaten on the move. A few days without rain had turned the trail to a choking powder that all but those traveling in the lead wagons were forced to eat.

Kier led the company into the enclosure. Several men in uniform greeted him with an invitation to join the commanding officer. In his absence, Billy and Brent were to settle the company for the night.

Fiona had expected Kier to make rounds but saw only his assistants. She did not have the nerve to ask for Kier. Clare did, making sure Fiona was within earshot when she did so. "Have you seen my son?"

"He's having dinner with the officers," Billy explained.

Clare exchanged glances with Fiona.

"Brent told me they're old friends," he continued,

addressing the women's surprise.

With access to fresh provisions, Fiona set about making an especially tasty meal. Her frustrations with Kier were played out in the exquisite feast. There was pork roast with gravy, green beans, potatoes with shallots, cheese dumplings, and biscuits flavored with dried fruit.

Doc Pickering opened one of four bottles of Château Lafite Rothschild he had brought and shared it with Fiona, the elder Morans, and Hope and Silas. The other bottles were to be opened on special occasions along the trail, including their last night together as a company.

"That was quite a meal," Libby complimented. "I'm sorry a certain wagon master missed it."

"Thank you," Fiona replied.

They were just beginning to relax when Maggie was awakened by nightmares about the tornado. "Hush," Fiona soothed, drawing her to her breast, and realizing how the storm's toll had left an impression. Fiona carried her out of the wagon to keep Caleb's peace.

She walked and rocked Maggie, humming a gentle melody as she moved away from the wagons. Climbing a rise, she turned and realized she had a clear view inside the commanding officer's home. The lanterns were blazing. Seven men and one woman were gathered around the table.

A fresh-shaven Kier was seated at the commanding officer's right. The guest of honor. What place did a wagon master have among these decorated men?

With Maggie whimpering on her shoulder, Fiona swayed back and forth, watching Kier. He was a different person than the one she had known, a callused outrider with an affable side. As she watched him among men of rank, laughing and chatting with everyone present including the commanding officer's wife, she realized Kier's surliness might have been a persona.

Who was the real Kier Moran?

Kier was the center of attention. His audience was rapt by what seemed to be his lively story telling. He was grinning more than she imagined possible. Flexing dimples she had never noticed, he looked young and carefree, almost boyish, in a way he did not appear on the trail.

It was then that Fiona realized some of the craggy grooves in his face were smile lines, in little evidence during the company's day-to-day travel.

Fiona watched the men in uniform treat Kier as their equal. Not what she would have expected.

The commander's wife signaled the attendants to clear the table. When that task was finished, they brought brandy and cigars. Fiona longed to be part of their lively conversation, even as an attendant. She recalled how much she had learned when waiting on the Cushings and their guests.

She felt inexplicably saddened to be left out of Kier's world. Although they had become friends, she realized she had never been part of his world, given what she witnessed that evening.

It was her fault. She had avoided him. Now he was at ease in a world without her, all because she had feared where another kiss might lead. Had she been foolish? Choosing Jake seemed safer. But was she denying herself something far greater? Was she denying her children?

Kier lacked permanence, so there would be nothing to hope for when they reached California. Jake would settle in the grand home he envisioned in San Francisco. Was the choice not clear?

The following evening, July 4, members of the company organized a dance to celebrate the country's eighty-first birthday. They invited members of smaller companies camped at Fort Kearny as well as those who were stationed there.

Large boards were laid out on the ground to make a dance floor. A band was cobbled together from musicians in different companies. There were three fiddles, a banjo, a mouth harpist, a string bass, two guitars, drummers, a penny whistle, and a jug.

The wooden dance floor lent itself to showcasing the better dancers, Silas among them. Fiona watched from the crowd, her toe tapping to the beat.

"Come on!" Silas yelled to her.

"Please, Mama," Maggie urged, yanking on her arm. Fiona gave in. She led Maggie to the dance floor and moved to the beat with her daughter, twirling her the way her father used to twirl her at ceilis back home.

Most of the fun for Fiona was watching Maggie enjoy herself, particularly when Silas cut in. Laughing and clapping to the rhythm, Fiona stepped off the dance floor to stand with Hope, who loved to watch dancing but loathed participating.

Fiona looked to see where Caleb was. He and his friends were collecting fireflies in bell jars.

Then Silas pulled Fiona into the dance. The music became a competition, one musician challenging another. Most of the dancers left the floor to watch

Fiona and Silas, whose dueling footwork complemented the ad-libbing musicians.

She tapped a step dance from Ireland in response to Silas's Tennessee mountain sequence. It ended as an earthy, passionate dance of the Cushing Irish, the community of immigrants indentured to Stanley Cushing. The crowd cheered the dancers and musicians.

It was the most fun Fiona had in a long time. She caught a glimpse of Jake's stormy expression and knew she would have to answer to him for it.

She did not see Kier, who watched from afar.

Then everyone took to the dance floor again. The fiddle-led music grew faster and more daring, moving from the genteel to the impassioned. The fireflies danced. Silas swung Fiona around. The fireflies whirled. Fiona swung Maggie around and laughed when Silas at last coaxed Hope to dance with him.

Fiona's face bloomed with delight. The roses in her cheeks blazed.

One time when she spun, she saw Kier. And again, then again. Or she thought she saw Kier, for when she turned again, he was not there. Her quick scan of the crowd told her he was not among them.

The lead violin held a high note, then an even higher note. Then the string broke, promptly ending the music. The crowd roared their appreciation. It was the perfect finish to a memorable evening.

As expected, Jake caught up with Fiona when the revelers returned to their wagons. He scolded her for what he regarded as low-class behavior. "What was that?"

"Dancing," she said proudly.

"Some might call it that. Unbefitting is what it is. I

am appalled you allowed your daughter to participate in such a spectacle."

"I enjoyed it and so did Maggie, thank you," she said, turning to face him. "You forget where I was born. Tonight was a celebration of memory. I want my daughter to know the joy of her people in music and dance."

"Then teach her the parlor dances of young ladies."

"Jake, I had a wonderful time tonight, and I don't want to lose that feeling. Where we're going in California, we won't have these opportunities. There are likely far more parlor dances in our future than ceilis. I want Maggie to know the beauty of both. Thank you for your concern. Goodnight."

Fiona found no rest. She tossed and turned between her children. Rather than disturb their sleep, she climbed out of the wagon and into the moonlight.

The evening air chilled her. Goosebumps rose on her flesh beneath her nightgown. She tightened her shawl around her shoulders.

The dance had affected her. She hadn't let go like that since her days as a Cushing Irishman, in the community of field hands, before she became Fiona Cushing. It was the last honest period of her life, she thought. Until now.

She felt stronger than she had in a long time. Her joy at dancing had freed her to take pride in traveling this far, standing up to the Cushings, and leading her children on this odyssey.

The next day was Maggie's fourth birthday. On their last day of camp in the safety of Fort Kearny, Fiona baked a cake with chokecherries and decorated it with wildflowers.

The elder Morans, Pickerings, and Whittakers gathered around the little girl, whose face shone with glee. Caleb gave her ribbons for her hair that Fiona had found at the general store. Gideon presented her with a doll he had whittled for her, and Hope with a set of doll dresses she had sewn from fabric scraps. Maggie was overjoyed.

Chapter 14

Gideon Moran was relentlessly silent. Fiona had wondered whether it was because he didn't have anything to say, had more to say than his daily audience would appreciate, or that he had grown accustomed to his wife doing the talking for both of them.

If it were true that every child is a reflection of both parents, then Fiona knew what of Kier was his mother. The balance of Kier—the stormy and unreachable part—had to be Gideon. Although the interaction between Gideon and his son could best be described as civil, the long-standing tension between them was palpable.

Fiona turned these circumstances over in her mind while loading the wagon. She could not imagine the Morans' sorrow at their life with Kier. She felt a mother's pride at Caleb's developing character and recalled her father's joy at sons Seamus and Colm. She could only wonder at Gideon's private disappointment. She hoped one day to know him directly rather than through the filter of Clare. Was there a great hidden depth to his character? Or was he a simpler man than Kier?

The company set out on a perfect day, with light breezes and a cloudless sky. Fields of gold and a canopy of blue stretched endlessly in all directions, meeting at the horizon. The air smelled of clover and sunshine. Dragonflies frolicked in the prairie grasses. The sun was just shy of hot.

Beside her, Maggie sang an Irish song and played with her dolls. Caleb was reading inside the wagon and periodically spelled out words, requesting Fiona's guidance for pronunciation and meaning. Fiona alternately focused on her children and allowed her mind to wander as she breathed in the simple freshness of the wind.

The miles crept by in an uninterrupted stream, like butter melting in the winter sun. It was easy to find peace in this experience, Fiona thought. She studied the landscape and realized their journey across Nebraska Territory had taken them from lush, rolling hills that had gradually given way to an endless vista of prairie. Broad, flat expanses met the sky beyond where she could see.

Fiona listened to what Caleb was reading. "'This morning at eight o'clock, an Indian called from the other side, and informed that he had something of consequence to communicate. We sent a pi-ro-gue—' What's a pi-ro-gue?"

"Mr. Moran said it's a kind of canoe."

"'—for him, and he informed us as follows: Five men of the Mandan nation, out hunting in a S.W. direction about eight leagues, were surprised by a large party of Sioux and Pawnees. One man was killed and two wounded with arrows and nine horses taken; four of the Wetersoon nation were missing, and they expected to be attacked by the Sioux.'"

Indians. Fiona wondered if they had been fortunate to have so little contact with Indians, or if it was normal to have seen so few. From what Caleb had read in recent days, it seemed Lewis and Clark had far more contact with members of different tribes than had the company.

Kier would know. But since she had put a damper on their friendship, she had seen little of him.

"Mother?" Caleb asked.

"Yes?"

"Do you think we'll see Indians one day soon?"

"I don't know," Fiona replied, scanning the vista off either side of the wagon.

"Mother?" Caleb asked again.

"Yes?"

"Can we get a dog?"

A quarter-mile beyond the company, Kier had ridden ahead to scout with Billy and a handful of men, Jake among them. It had been a contentious gathering, peppered with an exchange of snide remarks between Jake and his cronies about what they believed was their slow progress.

"You wind and turn these wagons like there's some hidden art to it," Jake disparaged. "Why don't you just point us due west and lead us in a straight line? Even I could do that. Even that simpleton, Whit Smith's boy, could do that."

"Maybe he winds about because he's lost and is trying to find the way," snickered Hiram Parker, one of Jake's cohorts.

"We're following the contour of the land," Kier explained evenly. "It's easier on man and beast than going up and down hills in a straight line."

"Says you," Hiram chortled. "I wonder what a real guide would have to say about that."

Billy looked to Kier for a response.

Sensing something his companions could not, Kier raised his hand to halt the party. His eyes narrowed to a squint. He removed his spyglass from his saddlebag and scanned the horizon but saw nothing out of the ordinary. Yet, there was an odd tension in the air.

"Circle the wagons," he ordered the men.

Billy turned his horse but stopped when the others did not follow.

"What are you doing?" Jake asked. Meeting Kier's cold eyes, he appeared to back down. But he disliked Kier and wasn't about to let the rangy outdoorsman show him up.

"Circle the wagons," Kier said again, the urgency in his voice growing.

"We press on," Jake countered.

"Billy," Kier ordered, instructing his man to act.

Jake drew his pistol and aimed it at Billy's back. "I say we press on. I'm the chosen leader of this group. You're just the hired help."

"You can press on, but for the safety of the company, we're making camp now," Kier growled.

Jake fired a warning shot over Billy's shoulder. Kier tackled him, leaping from Kildare's back and knocking Jake to the ground. "Go," he hollered after Billy, wrestling with his opponent.

"Jake," Tom Thorpe hollered, seeing the danger Kier had sensed.

The two bloodied men stopped fighting and followed their companion's gaze. A full complement of war-painted Indians was bearing down on them at a gallop. Pawnee.

"This will be fierce," Kier said, mounting Kildare and pulling his rifle from its saddle holster.

"Here's your chance to put that pistol to good use," he told Jake.

Kier turned in his saddle and fired at the approaching warriors. Both shots hit their marks.

Flaming arrows tore into the canvases of wagons before Kier reached the first wagon in the column. The family screamed, wanting to save their possessions. Kier knew the wagon would be a total loss. "Leave it. Take cover!" he hollered at them as he rode past.

Kildare's speed was magnificent. Kier had traveled nearly half the length of the column before Jake and his men had taken refuge below their wagons.

From his vantage point, Kier could see hysteria snake the length of the company as mothers and children climbed from their wagons. Husbands and fathers knelt to defend them, rifles drawn. He raced and shouted commands, trying to impose some order to avoid a wholesale slaughter. He managed to shepherd most of the travelers into a gully on the other side of the column. Many were reluctant to leave their belongings and stayed inside their wagons. It would be their undoing.

Pawnee warriors invaded the company, killing indiscriminately and taking what they could of the travelers' animals and possessions—blankets, jewelry, and anything for trading. They also took scalps as trophies of the hunt. They celebrated their success in high-pitched screeches that were more terrifying to the travelers than the specter of the attack.

Kier dismounted and yanked Kildare to the ground to use him as cover, pulling his spare rifle from its scabbard as he did so. He fired and reloaded repeatedly. Kildare flinched. Kier smoothed his hand over the steed's neck and shoulder to calm him.

Nearby, Brent and Silas had turned the Whittakers' wagon on its side and were firing from behind their wall of cover. When Kier ran out of ammunition, he drew his pistol and joined them there, slapping Kildare on his haunches to send him from the battlefield. Gideon took his place beside his son, the barrel of his rifle lining up beside Kier's pistol. The two men had a moment to acknowledge their kinship before the shooting began.

Fiona and her children dove under their wagon. She shielded them with her body. Terrified, she watched the slaughter of man and beast, her face grimacing with every death wail that polluted the air around her. Shrieks were accompanied by acrid smoke from burning wagons and shouted dialogue in a language Fiona did not understand.

Caleb's curious head bobbed up to see all he could of the bloodshed, and Fiona found herself fighting with him as much as with her fear. He was too young to witness these things, despite his boyish intrigue with the gruesome. When a tomahawk split the skull of a man standing not five feet before her, she buried her face in her children's hair, unable to watch any longer.

Jake was unskilled with firearms. He cowered beside Sam, envying the ease with which he aimed, fired, hit his target, and reloaded, all in perfect rhythm. Three warriors rushed Jake and Sam's position. If Jake had even attempted to fire, that would have helped. But they were too many for Sam. Outnumbered, he fought valiantly in a contest that ended his life.

Across the way, Jake could see Kier fighting side-by side with Gideon, two expert warriors trained by different schools of experience. Their faces were steely with concentration, hardly flinching as their pistols cracked with each precisely aimed round. When the bullets were gone, Kier ran headlong into the chaos, drawing knife and tomahawk. Gideon covered him, clearing his son's path of danger until he became lost in a fog of smoke.

The battle had turned in the company's favor. The Pawnee were retreating when Kier went down. Lowering his defenses as he watched the enemy withdraw, he failed to notice his approaching assailant.

The blade of a tomahawk landed in Kier's shoulder, bringing him to his knees. Out of ammunition, the Pawnee warrior used his rifle like a club, swinging it toward Kier's bowed head. Before he could strike, Kier rolled away, yanking the embedded tomahawk free. Leaping to his feet he swung the weapon like an axe, taking out his opponent as the rifle struck his upper torso, cracking three ribs in the process. He fell forward, barely able to breathe. The dying brave cut a gash across Kier's torso with his hunting knife. Brent and Silas reached Kier as he stumbled to the ground. He was covered with blood.

Fiona held onto her children until well after the sounds of those around her confirmed the attack was over. Once released, Caleb hopped out from their place of refuge, wanting to get a better look at the dead man lying beside their wagon.

Fiona frantically lifted her children into their wagon, wanting to do everything she could to protect them yet knowing she was powerless to shield them from violence. She did not want her son to see a man struck down, did not want to have such an image enter her daughter's mind. Fiona was determined to keep them from life's tragedies for as long as she could. She realized her hands were shaking.

"You will not leave this wagon until I say you can come out," she told them. The tone of her voice compelled them to obey.

"Come," Clare's voice soothed from behind her. "We are needed elsewhere."

"I'll stay with them." Gideon offered, the barrel of his rifle still warm in his hand.

Clare and Fiona made their way toward the worst of the carnage, following the sound of Doc's voice. They walked through the destruction in silence, the magnitude of the horror rendering them mute. Around them rang the sobs of the living, the moans of the wounded, and the wails of those discovering their lives had been changed forever.

The work of tending the wounded separated Fiona and Clare when they knelt to check the fallen. The first two people Fiona touched were growing cold. A third died before her eyes, a woman whose blood poured out of the place where a hatchet was embedded in her neck.

It grew quiet around them, the nearer they drew to the epicenter of the attack. There, no one mourned, for entire families had been killed. The magnitude of the horror stopped Fiona where she stood. She had seen this before, families lying dead on the ground. Then it was a bloodless death, a slow violence of starvation and disease. Now it was the opposite, a ravenous violence of hatred and misunderstanding.

Tears pooled in her eyes, tumbling down her cheeks as the images of past and present collided. She sank to her knees beside a broken child. How she wanted to run from this chaos and cling to her children, seeking an affirmation of life in the face of death.

Fiona rose numbly, her walk becoming a stagger as her heart sank with every step she took over the dead to reach the dying. She was overcome by the scene of the dead and half-dead around her, of the bodies that littered the bloody grasses. Heads deformed by scalping shone gruesomely in the sunlight.

She was reminded of the hopelessness of Ireland. There were too many to care for. She could not comfort them all.

"Fiona, praise the Lord you are untouched," Jake bellowed, running to her side. "Come away from this desolation. This is no sight for a lady's eyes."

"Doc needs me."

"Let others do the work."

"No," she said, walking away from him. She did not like being forced to speak in what had become a cemetery. She wanted to be silent to honor the dead.

"I'm asking you, Fiona."

"I will find you later," she said, continuing away from him, the truth of her words fading in her ears. She did not understand his behavior or how he could consider stepping aside when so many were in need. As the company's leader he should have been marshaling the remaining resources to bring order to the camp.

When she drew near where Doc was treating patients, the cries of survivors crescendoed around her, rising from a single sob to a deafening wail.

The air smelled of blood. It tasted of death.

She heard Billy taking charge of the healthy and unbroken, organizing them to restore order. It occurred to her she had not heard Kier's voice.

She found the place where Doc and Libby were at work. It was an awful scene of dying men, many of them calling for their mothers. She had not seen such an expanse of agony since her walk through the Irish countryside on her way to Stanley Cushing's ship. The human toll from the tornado had not been as extensive.

An irrational fear simmered within her. Where was Kier?

"Start over there," Doc ordered her, indicating an area some distance from where he was working.

She looked at him to acknowledge his instruction.

Then she saw him. Rather, she realized the bloody mess Doc and Libby were working on was Kier.

Fiona cried out. "Sweet Jesus," she said, moving toward him.

"No, Mrs. Lenihan." The firmness in Doc's voice halted her step. "You are needed elsewhere. Libby and I will take care of him. Start with the woman in the far corner. Mrs. Hammond needs you."

Fiona took a long look at the wounded giant, pale and still. He appeared dead to her, as dead as Seamus when she saw him laid out on the table in the field hands' quarters.

She gasped, forcing herself to suppress all that she wanted to unleash. Pinching her eyes closed to stop the tears, she was successful in preventing all but one from dampening her lashes. It took all her years of practiced recoveries to allow her to perform as required.

At that moment, Kier regained consciousness and howled in pain. His cries stabbed at Fiona. He thrashed and fought Doc and Libby, cursing them in their struggle to hold him down.

"We need to stop the bleeding," Doc told him as

Libby handed him a threaded needle.

"Burn it!" Kier hollered.

"There is no need," Doc responded calmly.

"Burn it or I'll do it myself."

In the distance Fiona could hear Evangeline singing a hymn.

****

At nightfall, Fiona was tending to rows of wounded. She had been so focused on her nursing she had lost track of Kier's whereabouts. As she lifted a cup of water to a man's lips, she had no idea that Kier lay directly behind her.

"Ma?" Kier asked the female form kneeling beside him. Fiona turned and the lantern illuminated both their faces.

"I'll find her," she offered simply.

"Don't," he said, grabbing her wrist. "How many?"

She could not bring herself to look at him. "Twenty-three. Thirty-seven more are wounded."

"Thirty-six. I'll be on horseback tomorrow to lead us out of here."

"But you're hurt."

"This is a bad place to make camp. They attacked once; they'll do it again." An uncomfortable silence hung between them. "Your family?"

"They're well. Hope is with them."

"Billy?"

"The camp is quiet due to his and Brent's efforts," Fiona assured him.

"Sam?"

"He's among the dead. I'm sorry."

Their conversation ceased. Kier released his hold on her wrist and slid her hand into his.

"Stay with me a while," he said at last. "I have missed your company."

She looked at him. He was in shock and not quite himself. Laudanum had left him tipsy. Once he knew she would not leave him, he gazed up at the night sky. "Do they have stars like this in Ireland?"

"Yes."

"Tell me about Ireland."

She grimaced at the suffering she read in his face.

The hold on her hand tightened, then released.

"Tell me about when you were young," he nearly grunted between clenched teeth.

She winced when he tried to speak. Unconsciously caressing his hand, she told him of the Emerald Isle until he slept. He held her firmly, not wanting to let her go.

"I was born in a small house on the shores of Lough Allen near Ballinaglera in County Leitrim. It was a rather unremarkable place. But it was the only home I knew for most of my life. Although I did not see it then, I see it now as beautiful, a sea of green fields and blue lakes, one for every day of the year. And trees to climb and ruins to discover from people who lived long ago. My family was there. My mother, brothers, sisters, and their husbands and children. My father."

"Tell me about them," he said, closing his eyes to the pain while tightening his hold on her hand.

Fiona winced.

"I had two brothers, Seamus and Colm, and sisters, Maeve and Katie, and a wee nephew, Sean, whose father died before he was born." She described her family in brief before turning the conversation to the land, for she did not want to discuss her family at length, especially not now and maybe not ever.

"On the west coast of Ireland, the sun is at once gold and pink. The most beautiful play of light I shall ever see was the way the sun shone on County Sligo the day we sailed away."

"You and your brother."

"Brothers. There were three of us."

He relaxed his grip on her hand. Fiona watched him manage the pain, almost as if it were a mental battle that had begun to turn in his favor. She held his eyes, wanting him to know she was there for him.

She reached for a basin of water. In silence, she wrung out a cloth and stroked his face to quiet his fever. Even more, to comfort him. She wanted to absorb his pain and make him whole again.

"What do you miss about Ireland?"

"Running wild through the fields of heather. They seemed endless, stretching for miles beyond where I could see."

"Like the plains we travel now."

"In ways," she said, her smile turning dreamy.

"Why don't you run wild in these plains?" Kier asked with what Fiona interpreted as a drugged man's attempt at flirtation.

As he drifted to sleep, something deeply felt passed between them. She wondered at his thoughts and his reaction to them when a curious expression passed his eyes before they closed in sleep. Fiona lowered her cheek to his hand.

She was aware of his distinctive scent: leather, horses, and sweat. She wiped the droplets of perspiration from his brow with her fingers, prolonging their contact and pondering him in sleep. How she had missed him these past weeks.

She took the cloth and tenderly brushed his face with it, tracing the bridge of his nose, the curve of his cheekbone, the softness of his lips. The cleft in his chin. The strength of his jaw line. He was unlike anyone she had ever known.

Perhaps she had been foolish to let his demonstrative gesture affect her. It would have been a lie to insist she harbored no similar feelings for him. All the same, she was afraid. Out here on the plains she felt bound by his authority, a situation not unlike her life with Simon, when she was prey to his wealth and power.

With the challenges that lay before her, she needed to keep a clear head. Her children depended on her. She had brought them this far; she could not focus on her desires until her children lay safely asleep in their beds in their new home.

Fiona trudged back to her wagon, drained from the day. A familiar-sounding cough caught her attention. She followed the sound until she came upon Doc leaning against the far side of his wagon, a bottle of whiskey in his hand. From the looks of him, he had consumed the better part of the bottle.

Fiona was stunned. "Doc."

"Mrs. Lenihan."

"What are you doing?"

"Some drink to remember. I drink to forget." He took another swig. "Do you know how much suffering a physician sees in a lifetime? More than anyone who's not a healer can ever imagine. Today alone I closed the eyes of more than a dozen whom my best efforts could not help. I cut away the ruined parts of two men's legs and a little girl's arm. If infection does not set in, not a day will go by when they do not curse the name of Earl Pickering."

"That's not so. Their loved ones will speak fondly of you for saving their sons and husbands and daughters."

He took a long drink from the bottle. "They'll never know the pain of the patients."

"You did all you could."

"Sometimes it is not enough. You should leave me, Mrs. Lenihan," he ordered her, his words slurring together. "There are better ways to bide your time than with this decrepit wreck of a man. I mean to finish this bottle and sleep the sleep of Socrates. More death awaits us on the morrow."

Fiona found Clare sitting outside her wagon. She clutched a rosary, its worn beads testament to their use. Fiona sat beside her.

"I cleaned him today after he fell," Clare began, needing to speak of the experience. "I haven't washed him in years. His scars are terrible for a mother to see. There did not seem to be a part of him that has not seen injury of some sort. I knew my nightly prayers have been answered when I saw the remnants of more than one wound that should have been mortal.

"It's startling to believe I could have given birth to such a man. As difficult as it may be for us to see him in this state, with his wounds freshly stitched and burned, I believe this to be a relatively mild setback for him. Watch him lead us out of here tomorrow," she said, chuckling bitterly, absentmindedly toying with the rosary beads.

"He said he would."

Chapter 15

Dawn came early to a chilly gray morning tinged with melancholy. Fog hung low over the plains, reminding Fiona of Ireland.

True to his word, Kier was in the saddle, ready to lead the wagon train forward. As if nothing was out of the ordinary, he tipped his hat to her when he rode past. She knew the terrible pain he must have felt. Riding a horse with a lame arm was one thing; it was another thing entirely to ride with a shoulder wound and broken ribs.

Progress that day was arduous. The train was halted more than once to tend to the wounded, when the jarring motion of wagons bouncing over uneven ground tore open stitches and hammered at broken limbs. At one stopping point, those whose wounds proved too much for them were buried.

Kier struck a compromise between progress and comfort, all the while scanning the horizon for a return party of Pawnee. The company was vulnerable, disorganized in its readiness of able-bodied males who were healthy enough to defend it. They would not withstand another fight.

That night Kier was a topic of conversation during dinner preparation. Word had spread of his serious wounds and how he had demanded Doc burn them with a hot poker. "You know how that must have hurt," said one of the women who witnessed the procedure. "Smoke rose from his shoulder as the flesh blistered. He made not a sound."

"He is the most resilient man I have ever known," said another.

"Such bravery," added a third.

Fiona shuddered at the words and chopped potatoes all the faster. She checked to see where her children were—exactly where they were three minutes earlier.

After dinner, Fiona tucked her children in for the night and walked to the makeshift infirmary to begin her shift.

Doc was his usual capable self, all effects of the alcohol worn off. He greeted her warmly. Fiona wondered if he had indeed forgotten.

Most of the sick and wounded needed a change of dressing or cold compress to soothe their fevers. Fiona held one man's hand until he passed. Unconsciously, she hummed Gaelic folk songs, trying to deliver him to peace.

She could not help but think of her brother Colm and his fever aboard ship. She had been by his side until the end. She recalled how she had closed his eyes and laid her head against his chest, feeling the emptiness of his quiet heart. Colm had died on a dark night in the middle of a dark sea, his body cast overboard with a prayer of thanksgiving for his release.

"This man has died," she reported to Doc across the tent of ailing men.

Doc nodded to a pair of teenaged boys to remove the body. He saw her tears glisten in the lantern light. "Why don't you rest a spell."

"I'm fine," she said, smoothing her skirt.

He nodded with a sympathetic smile and motioned to the woman at the door for the next patient to be admitted. It was Kier.

Fiona and Kier's gaze gave them pause, an experience that was not lost on Doc. "Come in, Mr. Moran. Mrs. Lenihan will take care of you. His dressing needs changing," he instructed Fiona. "Be careful of his arm as you remove his shirt."

Kier sat on the table, facing her. He watched her hands begin to tremble as they reached for the hem of his shirt.

"I keep telling Doc my dressing is fine, but he insisted," he called over his shoulder to the physician, to distract Fiona's nerves.

She gasped when she saw his bare chest. Clare was correct in her description of his scarred body. The freshly cauterized wounds stared back at her in a gnarled mass of blistered tissue.

"You see?" Kier teased, his eyes dancing. "This is nothing."

"Change his dressing, and he'll be on his way," Doc urged good-naturedly. "The sight of his scarred body makes even me nervous."

Fiona reached around Kier to unwrap the soiled dressing. He glanced down to watch her handiwork. At the same moment she looked up as if to speak. Their lips nearly met by chance. She turned away quickly.

Doc's brow arched in amusement.

"I got this one from a tiger in Burma," Kier said, pointing to the angry scar on his undamaged shoulder. "And this one from the poisoned arrow of an unfriendly native on a Pacific island."

Uncertain of what to say, she smiled softly and

dipped her sponge in alcohol to cleanse his wounds. She felt him wince when the alcohol made contact. As if he were her child, she had the sudden urge to hold him to her until the burn subsided. Her fingertips brushed the surface of his skin and grew damp with his sweat.

"That was from some poorly loaded ammunition that misfired during exercises at West Point," he said, describing the origins of a large scar on his washboard abdomen, just above the cauterized stab wound.

"His words are terrible music to a doctor's ears," Doc said, interrupting Kier's litany. "Mrs. Lenihan has a bewitching voice. If you stop regaling her with your gruesome tales, she might sing to you."

"I—I seem to have lost my voice," she apologized hastily.

"All right, then," Doc said. "When you're finished with him, why don't you take a few minutes to get some air."

She nodded, agreeing to what seemed like a good idea. She was flushed and felt the sudden perspiration under her arms and along her back. She knew Kier was watching her, and that Doc was watching Kier watching her, which made her even more self-conscious. She would indeed need to clear her head after this.

"That should do," she smiled tightly, meeting Kier's eyes after helping him pull the buckskin shirt over his head.

"Nicely, in fact. Thank you, Fiona, Doc." Kier departed the tent with a nod of thanks.

There were no other patients waiting to be seen. Fiona had begun to organize the bandages when Doc insisted she rest.

Fiona stood in the doorway of the tent and pulled a shawl around her shoulders to ward off the night breezes. The fresh air had a cleansing effect.

Once she had taken a few steps, Kier materialized from the shadows.

"Walk with me," he requested, falling into step beside her. She did not object.

"When I came into the tent, there were tears in your eyes."

"A man had just passed."

Kier listened.

"It wasn't so much his passing as that it reminded me—" She stopped, unable to continue. Her throat was clogged with emotion.

"Of?" he pressed after a silence.

She shook her head fearfully, her eyes focused on a faraway place.

"Come, Fee," he urged, his words a tonic. He led her by the hand into the trees, away from prying eyes, guiding her along the treacherous ground until they had reached a clearing by a stream. He released her, and she stood, unmoving, her eyes downcast.

A lone tear slipped between her lashes and glistened in the moonlight. He wiped it away with a tender brush of his thumb and closed the distance between them with an embrace. She felt the power of his arms around her, the completeness of his shield and comfort.

"My brother Colm. We lost him on our voyage to America. As with this man, I held his hand until he died, singing songs from our childhood until he was gone." Tears coursed down her cheeks.

"We were born the same year, Colm and I. He was

198

my best friend."

"What of your other brother?" Kier asked gently.

"Seamus was the eldest. A good man. He died in the fields in Pennsylvania."

"Why did you leave Ireland?"

"My brothers and I wanted to come to America."

"Why did you and your brothers choose to make the crossing to America?" he asked, his hold tightening on her.

Kier braced himself for what was to come. When she did speak, it was like a mountain stream during spring runoff. Ferocious. Unforgiving.

Her words rushed together in a single sentence. She vomited agonies and vivid images from every kind of hell, of her family dying from starvation and fever, their teeth stained green from eating grass. Sobbing, she recalled the countless dead along the roads. She was haunted by a stray dog feasting on corpses, its belly fattened unnaturally.

Kier was jarred by what had gone unspoken for years. He heard her wretched sadness and felt her guilt over having survived when so many others had perished.

Suddenly her tumble of words stopped. Fiona cried fresh tears for her loss, the first real tears she had allowed herself to shed. Accompanied by wrenching sobs, she heaved against him. "They are all dead, but for me."

Kier drew her closer to him and rested his cheek against her head.

She was nearly limp from the experience. The night became still around them. Her attention shifted to the arms that held her.

"Why did you make me do this?" she asked, wiping her tears.

"Because you needed to be bled of the poisons within you."

"Some things are better left unremembered."

"You must never forget."

"I don't know why I'm the one left living. I don't have Seamus's strength or Colm's kindness. I don't have either of my sisters' gifts of storytelling or good humor. They were good people. Far better than I. Of all of us, I don't know why I'm the one."

"None of us knows why we're here, what it is we're meant to do. You are the only one left of your people. Their hopes and dreams are alive in you. You are the custodian of their spirits."

She drew away from him to read his expression. Her eyes glittered like emeralds, rendering her ever more luscious.

"Look. I've stained your shirt with my tears," she apologized, running her hand along the darkened patches of suede that covered his chest.

"Oh, to be bathed in your tears."

"Your dressing," she gasped, concerned she had ruined the bandages on his wounds.

"Untouched," he said, smiling reassuringly. He took her hand and placed it over his heart. "I am very well, thanks to you. Don't think me cruel. I've sensed your need to speak of these things, and I wanted to be there for you when—"

The look in her eyes silenced him. He was suddenly very real to her. No one had ever been as patient and kind. No one had allowed her a voice, a chance to speak, in the way he had offered. She felt overwhelmed. Kier was more wonderful than she had imagined.

He traced the curve of her face with his fingers and brushed tear-dampened curls from her eyes. He smiled until he had provoked the same in her, and then he bent to kiss her. She turned away from him and he kissed her cheek with all the passion he had intended to kiss her mouth.

He waited a moment, unsure of how to take her turned cheek.

Tentatively at first, but with conviction, she wrapped her arms around him and tightened her hold, wanting to make certain he knew her meaning.

He smiled to himself and drew her near to him, kissing the crown of her head.

"I shouldn't let myself do things like this," she whispered.

"Why?"

"My husband is but three months dead."

"You're on the frontier now. You answer to no custom by which you were bound."

"All the same," she replied, hesitating and drawing away from him to see his face. Unable to complete her sentence, she knew if she didn't walk away from him the entire night would be lost. "I should get back." The corner of her mouth turned upward.

Kier let go of her hand, finger by finger. He made no move to stop her.

Chapter 16

It was a day for self-pity. Maggie banged her head falling out of the wagon and cried for nearly an hour, even after Doc assured Fiona it was a minor injury. The Whittakers' wagon broke an axle. And Fiona's hemline caught fire in the ashes of a cooking blaze, singeing her petticoats and some of the family's money. All this and it was only 0700.

And it was raining.

"Mother, just think," Caleb said from inside the wagon. "When we get to California, we won't have to worry about cooking fires, broken axles, and falling out of wagons anymore."

Her son's attempt to brighten her spirits had some of its desired effect. She let go of her frustration even though it was still a bad day.

Despite their rough start, the company made good time, which for the optimistic meant they had traveled more than thirteen miles closer to their new homes. For the trail-weary, it meant yet another monotonous day of progress in an unchanging landscape but for the rain, which finally stopped around the eleventh mile.

They had begun to see something new along the trail: dead oxen and crippled cattle. It was the first sign of the toll the journey would take on draft animals. A few enterprising men tried to salvage the lame cattle, but most were not worth saving, even for the meat. An animal worked to death would be nothing but gristle.

The company was nearing its fourteenth mile when Kier saw something in the distance. He studied it with his spyglass. The expression he wore was one Billy had come to dread.

"What is it?" Billy asked.

"What's left of a wagon train," Kier said grimly.

"Indians?"

"No. Take the wagons along the side of that rise," he said, indicating a travel path some hundred yards away. "I want a wide berth between what's left of that company and ours." He spurred Kildare to a gallop and waved at Brent to follow.

The sorry-looking cluster of wagons occupied a small part of the prairie and were nearly lost in the expanse. Like an animal carcass decomposing in the sun, the earth had begun to claim what was once a vital organism in the wagons and their occupants. It would have been easy to miss, but Kier seldom missed anything. It was the smell he noticed first.

Kier and Brent found the wagons in varying stages of disrepair. A handful had broken wheels. Others had torn canopies. There were sixteen in all, parked haphazardly, seemingly abandoned like a ghost town. Dead animals lay where they had fallen, some rotting in their harnesses. Kier could see where predators had made a meal of easy prey. Hundreds of flies ravaged the place, their incessant buzz adding to the grotesque scene.

"Hello there," Kier called out.

Brent regarded Kier with skepticism that turned to surprise when a weak cry rose from the gloom.

"How did you know?" Brent asked.

"Emigrants are scavengers. No one has touched these wagons. Hundreds of people passed by here and let good animals die. There's a reason for it. Raise your kerchief," Kier ordered as they rode toward the pitiful sounds.

"Help," sobbed a feeble voice.

Kier cut open the canopy of the first wagon and found a middle-aged man lying beside what appeared to be the bodies of his wife and child, covered with blankets.

The smell was overpowering.

Kier lifted the man from the wagon and placed him in its shadow on the ground.

"I'm Horace Evans," the man said in a near whisper. "I don't know who is left."

"We'll find them," Kier assured.

"What is it?" Brent asked Kier.

"Cholera, from the looks of it. We won't be joining our company tonight," he said, wanting to contain the infection.

The disease had nearly wiped out the travelers. The dead were decaying in wagons that had become their caskets. Eight of the seventeen wagons contained survivors, or at least those who weren't dead yet. The living lay among the dead; it was left to Kier and Brent to separate them.

"How did they avoid wild animals?" Brent asked.

"Carrion. They tied their canvases shut, which helped a bit."

Kier rode out to meet Billy. Speaking from what Kier judged to be a safe distance, he instructed Billy to make camp for the night several yards upwind from the remains of Horace Evans' company.

It did not take long for Jake and some of his cronies to investigate what Kier was doing and why he had ordered Billy to set camp before their normal travel day had ended.

"Stay back," Kier warned, finally raising his gun to enforce a safe distance.

"What's all this about?" Jake demanded.

"Lending a hand," Kier replied.

"Why are you wasting time here? Can't you see they'll all be dead soon?" Jake sniped.

"They need help we can give."

"Press on, Moran," Jake challenged.

"We will not leave these people here."

"They're doomed. Can't you see? We're losing time arguing."

"They have no food or water. They need Doc," Kier said, standing his ground.

"Another company will find them," Jake argued.

"This is a good place to make camp. Game is plentiful, and several wagons need repairs. We've been driving hard. Our company could use the rest."

"Kier is right," Tom Thorpe opined in a low voice. "We can't just leave these people here. And we could use the chance to hunt and rest our families and animals."

Jake said nothing but turned his mount toward the company, glaring at his cohort all the while. He returned to find Fiona gathering supplies to join Doc and Libby and the Prides in caring for members of Horace Evans' company.

"Let the others go," Jake said. "I will not have you endangering your life for those people, all of whom are going to die anyway."

"She'll be fine," Doc said to assure him. "We'll most likely return on the morrow. You're welcome to join us."

Jake was startled by the offer. "The company needs me here," he retorted. "I would rather Mrs. Lenihan be here to cook and care for our own travelers who may fall sick. What's more, she should not leave her children."

"I'll watch the children," Clare offered.

"As will I," Hope said.

Unsure which was the right decision, Fiona kissed her children and joined the others. She trusted Doc.

Jake trusted the Prides to keep an eye on Kier and distract him from Fiona.

Laden with food, blankets, and medical supplies, the Pickerings, Prides, Fiona, and six other young women crossed the divide between the two companies.

In the shadow of Horace Evans' wagon, Kier and Brent had laid the twenty-three bodies of the living. Kier stopped Fiona after the others had passed. "You should go back," he said privately. "You could fall sick."

"Mrs. Lenihan!" Doc called for her. She looked at Kier, hesitated, and ran forward to help the physician.

Fiona was appalled by the wretched state of the human beings who lay before her. There was an emaciated boy around Caleb's age. Lost and disoriented, his eyes were unable to focus. He could no longer speak. She had not seen the likes of this hunger in America. She drew him to her and gave him a sip of fresh water. The boy choked and gagged before finally swallowing it. Once he was quiet, she fed him a few bites of cold porridge. She did not want to wait for the fire to warm it, so fragile his thread of life. She sang to him until he slept in her arms.

Her next patient was a teenaged girl who spoke in disjointed phrases about the animals that crept about their camp at night. As with the boy, Fiona fed and comforted her.

Kier, Brent, and Reverend Pride went about the grim task of burying the dead. The Reverend led them in prayer before they shoveled dirt over the bodies.

To Fiona's chagrin, Doc set a quarantine of three full days. If those who had come to care for the sick remained free of signs or symptoms of cholera in three days' time, they would be safe to rejoin their company and bring the surviving members of Horace's company with them.

She had not counted on being away from her children for one night, let alone three. Pangs of regret at helping these people wrestled with guilt. Maybe Jake was right. Why should they sacrifice themselves for these strangers? Maybe Kier was right. She should have turned back when she had the chance.

Kier watched Fiona bid her children goodnight from across the divide. Caleb and Maggie waved to their mother from where they stood beside Hope and Clare.

Jake watched Fiona, resentful of Kier's access to her. He watched Kier watch Fiona's interaction with her children and cast his rival a sharp stare.

"All twenty-three are still living," Fiona said with as much cheer as she could muster when they turned back toward their campfires. "To save twenty-three lives is worth the risk."

"I hope it is," Kier said, smiling cordially before

walking away from camp. He had no intention of sleeping in either camp that night, but away from them both, where he could keep them in equal perspective.

Jake's expression softened when he saw Kier wander into the darkness alone.

****

The next morning Kier stepped into the divide that separated the two camps and ordered Billy to suggest Jake lead a hunting party. Although the need for fresh meat was not urgent, it was wise to keep a reasonable surplus on hand in the form of jerky. What's more, there was no telling how many new mouths to feed there would be from Horace's company. Mouths belonging to the infirm who would not be able to contribute for several days at least.

Kier's underlying motive was to keep Jake from moving the company without them. Despite the fact several key people in their company—Jake's friends among them—had come to the aid of Horace's company, Kier could not be sure. He relaxed a bit when he saw the hunting party leave camp, Jake riding abreast of Billy.

Fiona, Doc, and the others worked tirelessly. Two died before midday, a young man and an older woman. Three more died before sunset.

Kier and Brent spent their days caring for the animals and salvaging what they could in the way of supplies. They emptied the wagons and removed their canvases, hoping sunshine and fresh air would help decontaminate the equipment.

The survivors would need to be absorbed into the company. Nine wagons were worth saving. Since none of the sick could drive their own wagons for a few days,

Kier would need to arrange for others to help.

Two of the children had been orphaned and would need to rely on the generosity of other families. One was the young boy, Isaiah, whom Fiona had nursed and taken a special liking to. When the other patients did not need her care, she spent extra time with the boy. His pallid face brightened visibly whenever Fiona was near. But Isaiah was not going to live. She knew it. Doc knew it.

"I must say how pleased I am to have come to see Kier Moran in a new light," Evangeline said, joining Fiona and Libby for a cup of coffee in a rare break from duty. "Given my recent experiences with him, and what others have said about him, I believe I've held an inaccurate opinion of our wagon master."

"Jake may have done Kier a disservice in lobbying so effectively against him at the beginning of our journey," Fiona replied.

"Jake is a good Christian. I'm sure he said what he did out of concern for our protection. One must admit, Kier has done little in the public forum to counter Jake's opinion. The Reverend has been impressed by Kier's strong work ethic and determined approach to taking the proper course of action. These people owe their lives to Kier Moran."

At that moment the three women overheard a conversation between Kier and Reverend Pride, who walked past them.

"You come upon a wounded animal, you kill it," Kier said to the minister. "You come upon a wounded man, you give him life."

Libby cast Fiona a sidelong glance.

Reverend Pride nodded in agreement. He studied

the wagon master when he strode into the divide between the two camps to speak with those who were minding the company while the hunting party was away.

Fiona could see from the minister's expression how surprised he was to discover Kier to be different from the man he expected.

Fiona cried when Isaiah passed. Losing a battle for life into which she had invested so much of her heart weighed on her. Overwhelmed by the sum of her experiences at Horace's camp, Fiona wandered to the far perimeter and stood with her back to the sorrow. She didn't want to be there any longer. She wanted to be with Caleb and Maggie, moving west, away from this place.

She stood with her arms folded tightly around her in an embrace, for there was no one to comfort her. Closing her eyes, she let her head fall back and her body sway like prairie grasses in the breeze.

Her eyes opened to a glorious, ever-changing watercolor in the sky. Sunset. The undersides of thunderheads were chameleons in the dying light, reflecting first coral then gold and violet, a final pulse of color as darkness settled over the land.

Fiona was awed by the beauty around her, feeling as if she was discovering it for the first time, when in fact, she had lived beneath the sky all her life. How had it taken so long for her to embrace it?

Kier Moran. It was Kier who had taught her to see anew the world around her and embrace the subtleties through sight and sound and feel and smell and taste.

The call sounded in the other camp to settle in for the night. She joined the others at the divide.

As she had the night before, she blew kisses and waved to her children and to Hope, Clare, and Gideon. Tears glistened in her eyes when Clare and Hope ushered her children away from view.

Fiona was restless the second night away from them. Long after the others were asleep, she remained with Kier by the fire. Exhausted, they sat side by side, leaning against a wagon wheel.

Fiona was numbed by all the misery. She knew why Doc drank. To forget would be a relief.

"How do you do it?" she asked Kier while staring into the flames. Her voice broke with emotion. "How do you face all this death and appear so unaffected? I want to cry and scream and beat my chest for all the pain we have seen on our journey. I am numbed by the suffering," she said, her voice choked to a whisper. "Four people died in my arms today. One death blurs with another, and soon the dignity of each life is lost. How do you do it?"

"Sometimes I go for a long, hard ride. It's like anything else. In time, one gets almost used to it, less affected by each individual passing. I have seen a lot of death in my years."

"Is this the worst you've seen?"

"No. The frontier has its risks. Every one of the people who has traveled away from civilization—including you and I—does so knowing we face injury and death. These people do not die alone. We travel as a company, an extended family, to support one another until we reach our destinations.

"Some of the harder deaths are of men alone in the wilderness. They set out with empty packs and dreams of returning laden with pelts, and Indian wives who are more than companions. I lost three friends in two years. We found two of their bodies the next spring; the other is still out there. One froze to death. The other was mauled by a bear but died after crawling a ways on his belly. Both died alone. To me that is the more difficult death."

"You were alone out there," she said, meeting his gaze.

"I'm accustomed to being alone," he replied, shifting uncomfortably.

"Did you think of taking an Indian wife?"

"I'm not a marrying man."

Kier put another log on the fire, which cracked and snapped. The act ended their conversation. Fiona watched Kier stoke the fire with a branch until she noticed his eyes glaze, his actions reflexive as his mind wandered from the present.

She drew her knees to her and wrapped her arms around her legs. "Do you think we will encounter more Indians?"

"Yes."

"Pawnee?" she asked with a shade of worry.

"Other tribes," he replied absentmindedly.

"How do you tell them apart?"

"They share traditions unique to their tribes. Some wear distinctive skins, feathers, and paint. We're now in the territory of the Plains Indians, who follow the buffalo. The tribes travel a great distance every year."

"How do you know the friendly Indians from those who mean us harm?" Fiona asked.

"Most are friendly. But too many travelers have heard exaggerations, half-truths, and outright lies, so they'll shoot anyone they see, assuming any Indian is unfriendly. When one of their own is killed, the tribe seeks revenge.

"The Pawnee keep ceding their land to the United States. Later this year they'll probably be forced onto a reservation. Drawing imaginary lines on the land doesn't fit their way. Under the circumstances, almost anyone would take up arms. We just happened to pass by on a day they were looking for trouble."

"Will it happen again with other tribes?" she asked, concerned about future encounters.

"The reservations?"

"The attacks."

"Hard to say," he shrugged.

"It's difficult to have walls imposed on your world," she said, thinking of the Cushing estate. "It robs men of hope. In recent days I've looked into the eyes of so many without hope. Have you ever been without hope?"

When he didn't respond she continued, thinking he may have assumed it was a rhetorical question.

"My children give me hope. In my darkest hour I know I cannot give in to despair, because of my children. Even when I do not believe in myself, they continue to believe in me. To give in to despair would be to betray them. There is nothing more disheartening to a child than to see a parent give up. I'm ashamed to admit that one of my children has seen that in me."

"Caleb."

"Caleb," she said, her words heavy with shame. "But I finally learned something Seamus had tried to teach me. To despair, to lose hope, is my decision. When we walked across Ireland, Seamus told us we could do it, just a few more steps. Nothing is insurmountable if reduced to a few more steps, a few more minutes. A few more steps and we can rest, a few more minutes and dawn will come, a few more miles and we are that much closer to California. I'll say it any way I can to keep from losing hope."

She returned her attention to the fire. Its warmth and rhythm brought peace, like the heartbeats of her children, calm and even as they slept.

"I've been wanting to thank you for your kindness in listening to me speak of my family. I cannot bear to think about them, yet I never want to forget them. It's curious how a death so unrelated to my life can have such an unexpected effect, how anyone can withstand grief and keep it hidden. Then suddenly it all comes rushing out, brought on by the death of a stranger."

Unbeknownst to either of them, Evangeline had awakened and lay silent, listening to their discussion.

"Grief is like a poison unless it's accompanied by hope," Kier explained. "It sometimes requires a great purging to see the hope."

Fiona had no response.

"I favor independence perhaps more than any other American quality," Kier said. "But it's not a quality in the natural order. We speak of independence and freedom, of the ability to control our lives. In truth we have so little control, so little freedom and independence. Death can be sudden and unexpected. We have a short time to live. Too few choose to savor life in its glorious brevity."

"Sometimes responsibilities stand in the way of our enjoyment of life," Fiona replied. "I fear leaving my children alone with no one to care for them."

"Yet you left them to come over here and nurse the

sick at the risk of contracting disease."

"Yes. I've grown to trust you and Doc. I believed you would not have put me in danger, knowing what it would mean for my children."

"I told you to turn back," Kier said.

"You did," she acknowledged.

"Do you fear death?"

"Do you?" she answered with a question.

"It's a butterfly. A caterpillar attaches itself to the underside of a leaf and forms a cocoon, becoming first a chrysalis and then a butterfly. The caterpillar dies unto itself to rise again as the butterfly. It sacrifices its very being to pass through to its next life."

Fiona let Kier's words wash over her.

An amiable silence settled over them. After a time Kier turned to look at Fiona and realized she was asleep. He regarded her thoughtfully and covered her with a blanket.

****

The second full day brought a cloudless sky and more work. Efforts were rewarded when fevers broke, and the survivors gained strength.

The hunting party returned triumphantly. Across the divide that separated the camps, Jake showed off their success. Kier nodded with approval; there would be enough meat to last for the next two weeks.

Kier watched Fiona's interaction with the group and felt her loneliness at not being able to share in her children's joy at the bounty. He watched Fiona's greeting to Jake, which was by comparison cordial.

The sounds of celebration wafted through the air as Doc and his crew tended to the seventeen survivors. Merrymaking was good for morale and provided a distraction from the bleakness in Horace's company. It also assured Kier that Jake was in no hurry to move the company before Kier and the others returned. He knew one of the deciding factors was that Fiona was in Horace's camp. Were she in the main camp, the outcome might have been very different.

It was a long day. More died. The good news was that Horace had regained his strength and was able to talk with Kier about how his company had come to be in dire straits.

Traveling from Virginia, they had a remarkably easy journey until they took sick, Horace guessed from contaminated water. Disease spread quickly. With no one to care for them, they began to perish. All would have died without Kier's intervention.

Sleep on the cold, hard ground was slow in coming that night. It seemed she had no sooner found rest when Doc awakened her to tend to a dying woman.

Fiona groggily assumed her place at the woman's side. She rinsed an old cloth in water and sponged the woman's brow.

"Don't leave me," the woman whispered, her voice broken from dehydration.

"I'm here," Fiona replied, taking her hand.

"I've done terrible things in my life," she began, crying tears that would not flow. "I never loved my husband. I never wanted any of my children. And now they're all gone. I've watched each of them die before me. Do you think this is penance enough? For me to die knowing I never cared for any of them as I should?"

"I'm sure you loved them more than you realize."

"No," she shook her head with her waning strength. "And now I'm to die without making amends.

I'll be in Hell for sure, before tomorrow."

Fiona spoke without knowing the proper response. "You mustn't believe that. I can see in your eyes you loved them all. You would not speak of it now if you did not believe it."

"I'm sorry," the woman said, her eyes turning to glass. "So sorry. Forgive—"

"You are forgiven," Fiona said, unsure whether the woman heard her before she passed.

Fiona sat with her a moment before closing the woman's eyes and pulling a blanket over her face. "How are the others?" she asked Doc.

"They'll make it until morning. You should rest."

Fiona left the glow of lanterns that illuminated the scene. She walked away from the sleeping patients and their sleeping caregivers and stared toward the horizon, wishing the sun would rise so the sick would indeed last until morning.

The breeze chilled her. When she shivered, she realized her shawl lay where she had been sleeping.

She had grown weary of the dead, exhausted by the futility of caring for so many of them. How she longed to experience joy and for those around her to revel in the same. She did not know how many more deaths she could witness. It was difficult to focus on the hopefulness of the living in the face of so many dead.

Kier joined her. A chorus of animals howled in the distance.

"Coyotes?" she asked.

"Wolves."

"How can you tell?"

"Too much time spent in their company."

Fiona listened to the wolf cries, wondering if the

beasts were as mournful as they sounded.

"The moon is beautiful tonight."

"'Tis," he replied, his gaze joining hers where it focused on the enormous globe.

The rays of the gibbous moon turned clouds to puffs of sterling. Fiona admired how it made the landscape shimmer, transforming the river and every pond to glistening pools of silver. It shed a peaceful light and hinted at the magic in the world around them, making the ordinary extraordinary.

Kier tore a piece of bread off the loaf he was eating and offered it to her. She shook her head.

"You have to eat something." He extended it to her until she accepted.

"Do you know the meaning of the Latin word 'panus'? It means bread. 'Cum' means with. So, one who breaks bread with you is your companion," he said, chewing on another mouthful.

He studied her until her eyes met his, the message settling between them like a loaf of fresh bread. She put a morsel in her mouth. The flavor warmed her through.

The sun rose on the living who had survived the night. Later that day, Doc lifted quarantine, and Horace and his thirteen fellow survivors joined Kier's company bound for California.

Chapter 17

Much of Kier's work went unnoticed by his company, including his devotion to assuring an easy day of travel for the emigrants in his care. Some days that meant riding ahead to find the smoothest route. Other days it meant finding the best place to make camp, near a water source with ample game. On this day it meant avoiding the unspeakable by negotiating safe passage.

Blood was on the wind. Riding ahead with Billy, they came upon the site of a massacre. The Indians had left none alive in the fifteen wagons. The settlers had been surprised, outgunned, and ill prepared for a fight. Kier recognized the way the arrowheads were bound to the shafts. Sioux. He looked up to see a dozen Sioux warriors riding along a ridgeline, watching him.

"Stay here," he warned Billy. "Don't make sudden moves, and keep your weapons holstered."

Lifting his arms above his head to show them he would not reach for one of his many weapons, Kier rode out to meet the warriors. He slowed as they approached and greeted them in Siouan. "Ahau!"

From his vantage point, Billy watched Kier talk with the men. At first several of them had their bows drawn, ready to strike him down. After a few moments of conversation, the warriors sheathed their arrows. Kier gestured to where the company was traveling.

Then he gestured toward Billy. Kier raised his arm in a movement Billy did not understand. Then Kier and the warriors parted company and Kier rode back down the hill.

"What's happening?" Billy asked.

"A few of us are going to pay them a visit," Kier replied with a distracted air.

"Who?" Billy asked.

"I'll decide by the time we reach the company."

"Who are those Indians?" Billy said to clarify his original question.

"Oglala Sioux. I know them," Kier said.

They rode with haste until Kier spoke again.

"When we get back, I need you to set camp quickly and quietly. Place a double watch for the rest of the day and night. I will deal with Jake, but you need to keep a close watch on him. If he does anything foolish, we may pay for it with our lives. Brent will lead a group to tend to the dead from the other company."

"What is the meaning of this?" Jake demanded when he saw Kier speak with the man driving the lead wagon and Billy guide the wagon to set camp.

"Unfriendly Indians," Kier replied, stopping beside Jake's wagon. "They killed everyone in a smaller company and mean to do the same to us. I've asked to see their chief to negotiate our safe passage."

"Fine. You see the chief, but we're not stopping," Jake said authoritatively.

"They probably have arrows trained on us right now. If we don't stop, we die," Kier stated.

Jake sighed loudly.

"You'll need to work with Billy to quiet the company and keep everyone calm. One false move and we'll end up like the other company. I'm sending Brent and some additional hands to tend to the dead."

Billy rode up to join them. "What should we tell them?" he asked. "They're scared."

"They need to be," Kier replied, looking at Billy and Jake.

"When will you return?" Jake asked.

"With luck, after nightfall. If we're not back by tomorrow morning, move the company as early as you can. We'll catch up."

"Who's 'we'?" Jake asked, his eyes narrowing.

"Not sure yet. We need to bring blankets and other goods to trade. I'll handle that. You and Billy stay here and keep watch."

Kier galloped away without listening to their response.

"What do you see?" Fiona asked Caleb, starting a new round of what had become one of the Lenihans' favorite games.

"Sunshine, a few clouds on the horizon that may mean rain, a cluster of trees in the distance, a small stream—" Caleb replied.

"I see an Indian," Maggie said, interrupting him. "I see lots of Indians."

Fiona and Caleb stared at the ridge above them. Maggie was right. There were several men on horses atop the ridge, spaced at equal intervals, watching the emigrants. Their gaze was unsettling.

Their bodies were painted and decorated with feathers in an exquisite fashion. It occurred to Fiona she hadn't seen Kier for a while.

Word was camp was being set. Fiona shivered, wondering at Kier's thinking. She was surprised to see

Kier gallop past her, his expression serious. Billy followed on his heels, ordering the frightened settlers to make camp quickly and quietly, and to limit conversation. No one was to show a weapon of any sort.

Fiona didn't like the situation. The Indians watched the settlers set camp. The smell of fear soaked the air like spilled whiskey. Everyone yearned for Kier's reassurances.

"Fiona Lenihan."

Kier's breathless voice startled her. He had stolen up behind her unnoticed. She turned to face him and was taken aback by his stern efficiency. "Bring Caleb and meet me at the rear of the train. Maggie will stay with my parents," he managed a stiff smile of encouragement at the little girl, whose face searched his for an explanation. "You must come now, Fee," he ordered, his eyes hard. "Others will set camp for you." And then he was gone.

"You be good for Mr. and Mrs. M," she instructed Maggie. "We'll return soon." She took her daughter's concerned face in her hands and kissed her before turning to leave, knowing that "soon" was relative.

Maggie started to cry.

"Hush," Fiona said, holding her daughter's small body to her. She cradled her head in the palm of her hand and rocked her until the tears stopped. "Mrs. M will take good care of you," she promised, entrusting her to Clare.

The two women exchanged uncertain glances before Fiona walked the length of the column, Caleb keeping pace beside her.

The Sioux continued to watch the settlers. Fiona

felt their eyes upon her as she and Caleb hastened to meet Kier. She shepherded her son, wanting to insulate him from the warriors' chilly gaze and from whatever danger lay ahead.

Kier materialized from a cloud of dust kicked up by the horses. His smile of greeting hinted at encouragement, but she sensed his unease, marked by flinty efficiency. She had not felt so distant from him since the day they had met.

"What do you smell in the wind?" Kier asked Fiona and Caleb and others who were gathered with them: Horace Evans, Brent Starr, Jake's crony Tom Thorpe, and two other men whom Fiona did not know well, Tobias Jones and Joseph Clark. She was the only woman; Caleb was the only child.

"What you smell is death," Kier said. "Not far beyond our camp lie the remains of an entire wagon train, massacred two days ago by the men who watch us now. They wear full war paint. They have a taste for blood, and we are ready targets.

"They are the Oglala Sioux. Seven years ago, I spent a season with them. I became blood brothers with the honored son of the chief and visited them many times in recent years. The chief and his son were good men. That chief has since died, as has his fine son. His second son now wears the mantle of his forefathers. He is not of the same quality as his brother or father before him.

"We'll visit him in his camp and bring blankets and other items for trade that Billy is gathering. I will meet with the chief to secure safe passage through these lands. Brent will lead a group to the other camp to tend to the dead."

"Why do they want to fight?" asked Tom.

"They've been wronged by past parties of travelers, and they seek vengeance for the violence done against them," Kier explained.

Billy and Silas arrived with piles of blankets. Three other men followed carrying barrels of jerky and gunpowder, which they loaded into a small wagon.

"We're going with you?" Horace asked.

Kier nodded.

"Why have you chosen us to accompany you?" asked Tom.

"Because you represent our party well. I need your trust. Do exactly as I say. Discuss nothing while we are in camp; we can rehash every detail when we return. The purpose of this outing is to assure safe passage through this territory."

Kier spoke briefly to Billy, whom he was leaving in charge of the company. No one heard their exchange. He patted the younger man on the shoulder, and Billy left them with a subtle nod.

"Leave all weapons behind," Kier said, returning his attention to those gathered. "Even the smallest knife may compromise our safety."

Horace helped Fiona and Caleb climb to the bench of the wagon. He handed her the reins. Fiona watched Kier finish a private conversation with Brent, who left quickly to do his work. Then they were off, making the one-mile journey to the Sioux camp.

The men walked beside the wagon, which Fiona drove at a moderate pace. They traveled in a tense silence.

When they neared the camp, Kier gave them additional instructions. The men were to offer everything in the wagon for trade. Fiona and Caleb were to stand behind Kier. Everyone was to remain silent.

"How will we know what to do?" Caleb asked.

"I'll tell you. Follow my lead but say nothing, even if you do not understand what is happening. I'll explain everything when we return to camp. Keep hold of your mother's hand," Kier said, offering a measure of fortitude to the boy, whose eyes were wide with anticipation.

Fiona saw the camp before they reached it. Crossed poles that formed supports for teepees rose above the trees. Smoke from cooking fires wafted into the air. It smelled delicious, roasted meat and something warm and earthy.

Kier walked ahead of their party. Unsure of what to do, Horace, Tom, and the other men walked near Fiona. She slowed to a stop when a dozen painted men came from the camp to meet Kier. He walked with a confident swagger. Significantly taller than the other men, he used that height to his advantage. He raised his arms and one of the men checked him for weapons.

Kier spoke to them in a Siouan dialect. Like him, some of the Sioux men wore deerskin breeches. Others wore loincloths. Where Kier wore heavy boots, the other men wore moccasins. Their torsos were covered with ornamental jewelry and various weapons, but they wore no shirts. Feathers and beads were woven into their braided hair.

A party of women, children, and old men had gathered to watch the spectacle. The Sioux stared at the visitors, Fiona in particular. She realized she was probably hurting Caleb's hand by holding it so tightly.

Fiona watched in amazement as the Sioux men gradually accepted Kier. By the end of their exchange, they were laughing. Waves of nerves swept through her when she realized he was referring to their party. Perspiration ran from her cleavage and pooled in the hollow of her navel.

It was at this point that Kier returned to his companions. He met Fiona with clipped determination and offered his hand to steady her as she climbed from the wagon.

"Unload everything in the wagon and follow me," Kier said, lifting the barrel of gunpowder.

Fiona and Caleb carried as many blankets as they could hold. Caleb walked closely beside her, standing tall, trying to appear as confident as the men in their party.

Kier stepped forward to greet the chief, renewing an old friendship. Fiona thought the chief seemed pleased to see him, despite Kier's description that had led her to believe the man might not have been so welcoming.

The trading began and soon Fiona realized it was not a trade in the formal sense, but an offering. Kier had brought a wagon full of supplies that he presented to the chief. He wanted nothing in return but assurances his wagon train could pass through Sioux territory unharmed.

As Kier was conducting this transaction, a woman who had been standing near the chief walked to Fiona. She said something Fiona could not begin to understand then pointed at her and turned to look at the chief.

Kier said something in reply, which brought laughter to Kier and the men. The eyes of dozens were upon her, laughing at her, sharing in some joke. Kier smiled at Fiona and she smiled back. She kept smiling, despite the shrill hysteria she felt climbing her spine as the laughter continued. Her cheeks grew warm. Beads of sweat crossed the small of her back.

The woman returned her attention to Fiona and stepped forward, pointing to Fiona's jet hair combs. She hadn't realized she was wearing them, for she wore them every day. Fiona granted what she assumed were the woman's wishes and removed the combs, her curls falling free as she handed them to their admirer. In return, the woman offered her a beaded bracelet. Fiona accepted it graciously, hoping her nervousness was not apparent.

She trained her eyes on Kier, hoping for a sign. But he revealed nothing.

Another woman stepped forward and pointed to Fiona's wedding band. She reached for it.

"No, Fee," Kier ordered her through clenched teeth behind an easy smile.

There was more discussion among the Sioux and Kier, and more laughter aimed at Fiona. She looked at Kier, unblinking, and tried to feel less self-conscious.

It was as if Caleb and the men were invisible. Fiona was the only person of interest to the Sioux men and women. She wasn't sure whether this was good or bad.

Then the mood shifted. Kier spoke to the chief and seemed to conclude the proceedings. They shook hands and Kier walked toward them. Fiona was relieved. Although she reasoned she would later look back on the experience and find it interesting, she was ready to return to the company and move as far away from this place as possible.

But something unexpected happened. Kier sent Caleb, Joseph, and Tobias back to the company. Horace, Tom, and Fiona stayed behind. She moved to object.

"Don't fight me on this," he nearly hissed at her, his face uncomfortably close to hers. His hands grasped her shoulders. "Don't say a word. Do exactly what I tell you. Lower your eyes and assume a posture of humility. Stay close, and we may live through this."

Kier gave Joseph and Tobias a quick set of instructions before crouching to Caleb's level. Fiona watched with fearful interest as he rested his hands on her son's shoulders and told him something that only made Caleb's serious expression deepen. He nodded earnestly.

They appeared as father and son. When Kier was finished speaking with Caleb, both looked toward Fiona. She smiled affectionately at the pair before she realized she might not be appearing humble enough to suit Kier. He patted the boy on the shoulder and stood, the cue for the two men and Caleb to head back to camp.

Fiona was screaming inside. What was happening? What was Kier doing? She wanted to yell but maintained a serene veneer. Her eyes followed him, waiting for him to give her direction. Sometimes she watched those watching her, but always returned her gaze to Kier, mindful of how something so simple as looking at another person could get her into trouble. The Sioux had cultural mores of which she was unaware.

When Kier stole glances at her, his eyes seemed

reassuring, but she wondered. She tried to see beyond his crystal blue gaze and found nothing but determination. She was not his priority but a part of his scheme.

Kier, Horace, and Tom went into a teepee with the chief and several other men. As a woman, Fiona was barred from entering. She sat alone on the ground outside the tent, wondering what the next few minutes would hold.

Women and children passed her, looking at her with curiosity. She felt like a criminal on public display. It took effort to maintain calm. She wanted to be in her own camp so badly she could taste it. She longed for afternoon tea with Clare and Libby. Whatever Kier was up to, she no longer wanted to be part of it. The chief had seemed content with the offerings they had brought. What more did Kier need to do to guarantee their safe passage?

Initially afraid to respond to the gawkers, an unusually winsome child smiled at her and she could not help but return the gesture. The little boy of about two stepped forward and touched her curls, then backed away when they sprang from his hand. Emboldened, he reached forward again and grabbed a fistful. Another child stepped forward and touched her fair skin. They stared at her green eyes.

Most talked openly about her and shared humor that was lost on Fiona. She discovered that if she treated them with kindness, they returned the warmth. Taking her lead from the child, she began to smile at the women and children who passed. They smiled back.

The men emerged from the teepee an hour later. Horace stumbled in the cloud of smoke that accompanied them.

"Walk behind me," Kier said quickly.

Fiona took her place between Kier and Horace. She wondered if they were going back to their camp.

Where the women and children's stares were those of curiosity, the way the Sioux men regarded her was more threatening. She clasped her hands and walked immediately behind Kier, casting her gaze to the ground.

To her dismay they were not leaving camp but staying for dinner.

"Watch me, but do as these women do," Kier instructed under his breath, gesturing to a group of Sioux women who stood apart from the rest.

The community gathered in a large central area and sat in a ring, men on one side and women on the other. Fiona sat outside the main circle with the separate group of women. She was situated nearly straight across from Kier. Taking her cues, she sat when the women sat, and sat as they sat, cross-legged on the ground.

Through it all, she watched Kier. Through it all, he was with her. Now that she could see him, she felt his unwavering support. It was enough to sustain her. He sat to one side of the chief. Horace and Tom sat a few men away from Kier. The chief scrutinized Fiona and discussed her with Kier. Alternately lowering her eyes and watching Kier, she was aware of how Kier and the chief laughed and talked about her. She knew Kier to be subtler. Unsure what was next, she had no choice but to trust him.

When it was time to eat, people went to a central kettle and served themselves bison meat and organ stew. There was pickled venison and dark bread made of dried acorns, chokecherries, and crickets. Looking at the food made Fiona's stomach churn. To be polite, she would need to sample it all. The idea of eating something with insect legs sticking out of it went beyond the exotic.

As dinner progressed, she managed to control her fear enough to peek at those around her. She saw a mother singing a lullaby to her baby, an old man carving a twig into a shape while a small boy watched, and a teenaged boy and girl engaged in a subtle flirtation. There was a woman imparting wisdom to her grown daughter, and a man teaching his son how to tie an arrowhead to a shaft. Two girls played a game of dice using a basket and game pieces made of beaver teeth. A group of boys around Caleb's age enacted a hunt beyond the circle of adults.

In short, Fiona saw a community that was not so different from hers. There were men and women, parents and grandparents, aunts and uncles, and children of all ages. She felt a strong sense of family among them, and a strong sense of warmth and belonging. This gave her new insight into Kier. She watched him across the circle until his eyes met hers, and she knew at once he had seen all that she had seen.

The chief shared a long pipe with the men in the circle. It was filled with sage, but Horace and Tom had no tolerance for anything other than tobacco. It left them seemingly drunk. They were taking in every pleasure and seemed to have forgotten about the woman who was with them.

Kier took a long drag from the pipe before passing it to the next man. All tension left him. His eyes grew revealing, especially when they took in Fiona. He grew reckless and a bit too honest, seeming openly desirous of her. Here, away from prying eyes, his stare could penetrate without the risk of inciting gossip.

Meanwhile, Fiona was becoming progressively disturbed about another problem, one of a female nature. Her menstrual cloth was saturated. She was afraid to stand when the dancing had finished because she dreaded revealing the stain on her skirt. She'd had no idea they would be away from their camp for this long.

The stream was nearby. She wanted an opportunity to wash herself but was afraid of what it might mean to Kier and the others if she left the circle. She was playing a role. Their lives depended on its apparent authenticity.

After dinner, the Sioux danced in a beautiful ritual done by firelight. The women performed first. It was a night chant filled with graceful movements to the beat of small drums, tambourines, and rattles made of hooves. Theirs was a simple, peaceful song. Fiona wondered what the lyrics meant.

With a wild yell the men leaped into the center of the ring. Utterly naked, theirs was a dance of virility. The drums pounded like the heartbeat of a racing animal. The raw energy of the dance conjured a heady sensuality that seemed to pulsate between Fiona and Kier as the men danced between them. As the flames of the campfire danced between them.

His touch seemed to reach across the space between them. She was disconcerted by his lusty stares as he smoked a cigarette. Mindful of his instructions to appear humble, she cast her eyes down when the intensity of his attentions made her blush. However, she confessed the yearning between them was mutual. She longed to be near him. She wanted to be with him and feel his touch, his breath on her skin, his heartbeat through her chest. She craved the feel of his hand on her cheek and his caress on her bare shoulder.

Closing her eyes, she tried unsuccessfully to cast out these thoughts. No one had ever made her feel the way Kier made her feel, and certainly not from across a distance that included a group of naked dancing men who were singing about something that had to do with their genitalia.

It was all too much. Concerned about the blood and disquieted by Kier's behavior, her tension ratcheted. His unwavering attentions made her heart race. She was afraid of his demonstrative behavior in front of all these people.

After the dancing had finished, people set about quieting the camp for the night. Fiona's heart was in her throat when Kier strode purposefully across the circle, headed for her. At that moment she realized her wish might be coming true.

He stood above her in a show of pure virility. She would have done anything he asked.

"Come," he ordered, offering her his hand and pulling her to her feet. Their bodies were very close, but only for a moment. It was an intimacy that alluded to secrets. His body brushed against hers, and she nearly gasped when he entered her space. He held her upper arms and lowered his face to hers. "I'll explain everything later," he whispered in her ear. "Keep doing what you're doing."

By design, he planned their exchange to appear as

a stolen moment, not intended to be witnessed by anyone. He was a shrewd man and knew how to make his every gesture one of impact. But the atmosphere made him careless, and he lingered more than he should have. He planted her hands at his lower back and took her face in his to kiss her forehead, nose, and mouth.

Her arms crept around him, holding him to her. She did not want to let him go.

"I'll see you at dawn," he said, leaving her.

Her back was up as they parted. He knew it and had anticipated it but hoped to defuse her anger long enough to maintain the illusion. He backed from her and smiled affectionately, a hint of boyish charm turning his smile to a grin that showed his elusive dimples. Despite her growing anger, she sensed it was in their interest to pretend to return the affection.

To Fiona's surprise, she was shepherded away from camp with the group of women she had been sitting among all night. Her head was spinning. She followed them to the stream and tried to wash herself, thankful for the opportunity.

Fortunately, not all her petticoats had been stained. Trying to ignore the laughs of the women at her predicament, she rinsed out her soiled cloth and tore off part of her petticoat to make a new one.

She was angry with Kier. His taste was still in her mouth, a delicious, warm flavor that spoke of sage and fine tobacco. She craved more of it, feeling her desire for him grow. Nevertheless, she spit it out and rinsed her mouth with water, wanting to cleanse him from her. How dare he put her and her son through this.

She noticed none of the other women washed. She followed them to where they were admitted to a dome-shaped structure outside the camp. She looked to the women for cues and was surprised to see the blood stains in the dirt where the women had simply bled into the soil.

Each woman knelt to prepare a bed for herself. Fiona followed, then rolled on her side with her back to the other women, who stared at her and continued to talk about her, even after the fire had grown dim.

Crying silently, she felt the blood ruin the makeshift cloth. What a mess. The whole day had been more than she imagined, and she had come to imagine a lot on the trail. She hiked up her skirt so she could use it to cover her soiled petticoats in the morning.

It was hard to sleep on the uneven ground. Whatever was burning in the teepee gave her a raging headache.

It also caused her to dream.

She closed her eyes and opened them to an old barn. Ground fog hung in the air, dissipating when it rose toward sunlight that seeped between wooden slats. She walked through the haze, taking in the detail to determine where she was. Ireland? The Cushing estate?

Doves flew from the rafters. For a moment she stood in a church on a side street in Philadelphia, her future growing clear as the doves became mist. The memory faded when she turned to see him standing at the far end of the barn, his lean form hard and strong. She felt her heart beat as if for the first time.

He strode toward her, his gait slow and easy. In a single gesture, he removed his hat and took her in his arms. Her lips fell against his chest, parted by a gasp as her dress fell away and she stood naked against him. He lowered her onto a bed of straw and eased himself over her, ravishing her with his lips, caressing her from the small of her back to her shoulder blades, pulling her to him as they made love.

She would remember the way Kier rose and fell above her, his face golden in the light, the stiffening of his body when he came inside her, the euphoria of her quickening as her toes curled in delight, the warmth of his body perfectly spooned against hers. The way he whispered his love for her as their hands clasped at her breast, the peace as their eyes closed to sleep.

Fiona awakened alone, lying on her side in the spooned position she had lain only moments before with Kier. But he was not beside her, only the sleeping Sioux women. A fresh surge of menstrual blood ran between Fiona's legs. She closed her eyes to the present, wanting to resurrect the dream.

She felt as though every detail had occurred. She was ravenous for Kier. She tasted his kisses, yearning to feel his hands moving across her skin as they had in the dream.

At last it was dawn. She rose, soiled and sticky, with dried and fresh blood saturating her undergarments. She had been wise to protect her skirt. It would hide everything as long as she did not sit. She kicked dirt over the soiled earthen floor of the hut.

Their eyes met when she was ushered into the enclave. His shone with appreciation. He was oddly affectionate and touched her possessively, more as he had in the dream than in life. "You are—" he whispered in her ear, his last word lost to haste when he drew away from her. She wondered what he had meant to tell her.

She stood beside him, flustered by the dream, even

though she kept telling herself it was only a dream. And she was filthy. Casting her eyes down required little effort. She felt nothing but confusion and anger and shame.

Horace and Tom did their best to contain their good spirits. She wondered at the kind of night they'd had that left them so happy early in the morning.

Their departure from the Sioux camp was similar to their arrival in the way the men insisted on discussing Fiona with Kier and laughing at her expense. She was relieved when their conversation appeared to move to more serious matters, her presence all but forgotten.

At last, Kier bid the Sioux farewell. He gestured to Fiona, then to Horace and Tom, who nodded in thanks. Fiona merely did her best to disappear. The four of them left the Sioux camp, walking in brisk silence.

Once they were well clear of the camp, Kier's demeanor changed. "Let's step up the pace. We need to make good time before they change their minds."

Horace and Tom were energized, feeling the effects of having won the match and with it their safe passage. Fiona was oddly quiet, her comportment sullen.

"What did they say?" Horace asked.

"I'll explain everything later," Kier told them. "Just know you were perfect."

He reached for Fiona's hand, but she pulled it away.

"Faster," he said in frustration, ordering them to a run, his response to her rejection of his affections.

A fresh coat of blood ran down her legs, the warm fluid further staining her already ruined underpinnings.

The pounding of her feet on the hard earth encouraged the deluge, drowning her pride. Her eyes flooded with tears that she stubbornly refused to let fall. She hated Kier in that moment.

They arrived breathlessly at what should have been camp. But the wagons had already moved out and were now only a cloud of dust in the morning sun. Bewildered, she turned to Kier for an explanation.

"Come on," he urged his companions, wearing a mask of victory.

Fiona's strength dissolved. The hope of finding refuge in her wagon had been the only thing that kept her moving on the one-mile run from the Sioux camp. Now it was gone, who knew how far ahead. She was completely wrung out by the extremes of being Kier's beloved on the one hand and a mere cog in his plan on the other. She wanted to turn on him and lash out with the full force of her emotion. But more than that, she wanted a bath and a few moments' peace to regain her composure. She realized she would have the opportunity for neither.

"I need to stop," Fiona said, her words a demand that would have put a wrench in Kier's plans.

"No time," he replied, breathing hard. "Get to your wagon."

Billy emerged from the cyclone of dust, galloping toward them with Kildare and two other horses in tow.

"Good to see you all this morning," he greeted them with a broad smile as much for the fact the four were alive as for the success of the plan.

"The sun's up and all's well in the world?" Kier asked him cryptically.

Billy responded with a laugh as Kier mounted his

black steed.

"I'll take you to your wagon," he said, offering Fiona his hand.

"I'll run, thank you," she replied coolly, continuing after the wagons.

Kier and Billy exchanged glances.

Tom was glad for the ride, but Horace offered to stay with Fiona.

Convinced he could do no more, Kier spurred his mount to a trot. He circled behind the herd of cattle that followed at the end of the train, alternately watching Fiona and Horace running in the distance and scouring the landscape behind him for any sign of the Sioux.

As she ran, Fiona was haunted by images of her dream. She tried in vain to place her thoughts elsewhere but was unable to divorce herself from them. They replayed themselves in her mind, over and over. Frustrated desire, guilt, and anger warred within her, making the distance pass quickly. She had a reckoning with Kier Moran, and it was going to be that night.

Chapter 18

The camp turned in early, quieted by exhaustion. Fiona had managed to put up an excellent front and deflect people's questions to the next day. She was too tired to share matters that were too raw for her to articulate, even to herself. She needed time to consider all that had happened before discussing it with anyone.

Unsettled by her thoughts, she broke Kier's rule and walked beyond the perimeter of camp to the pool she had seen before sunset. Having cheated death once that day, she felt a bit reckless. But she did not care. She had been pushed too far. Moreover, violating one of Kier's rules fit nicely with the anger she harbored toward him.

Stepping beyond the edge of civilization left her feeling strangely independent, emboldened by her emotions regarding the man with whom she wanted neither to see nor speak.

She vigorously washed her soiled garments, then dove into the pool to bathe, immersing herself in the peace of still water at night.

Deeper and deeper she swam, drawn under by her obsession to be cleansed of blood and soil and of her want for him. Out of breath, she broke the surface, gasping for air. Again, she went under, the currents sweeping past her nakedness like a thousand hands. Like his hands. She burst into the night, attempting to free herself from images that would not release her: wild, passionate, sinful.

She dove again to wash them away but could not. He was deeply embedded in her spirit. Every time she closed her eyes he was there, making love to her, moving with her, filling her with desire.

Weary of fighting her longing for Kier, she lay back on the water to float on its surface. She watched the moon as it was obscured by an approaching storm. Something about the rain made it impossible to purge him from her mind. She felt him as if he were in the water with her, bringing her dreams to life.

He strode through the tall grasses, penetrating the night, as driven as the hard rain that had begun to fall. She had skirted his protection by wandering beyond his established boundaries. Clare had told him she was bathing.

Rain pelted them, the seeker and the sought, a torrent that would have driven lesser mortals to shelter. Fiona arched back and lifted her arms toward the sky, welcoming the rush, letting it wash over her face and body. Kier fingered the brim of his hat and kept walking, undeterred. Lightning turned the sky blue-white.

Fiona stepped into the tall grasses, dressed, and set out for her wagon cleansed of all but her thoughts of Kier.

Introspection turned to frustration at her inability to free herself from him. He had put her and her son in danger. He had teased her with his affections. Her pride was bruised by the emotional extremes, the way he lured her with his smiles and stares, but never delivered on what his empty flirtations had seemed to promise.

With her every step, her anger grew; with his every step, his desire to ensure her well-being increased. It was at that moment they met, a collision of tension and relief illuminated by the storm that raged overhead. He appeared before her as the man in her dream, a potent silhouette against the storm's electricity. That he made no move toward her only confirmed her anger in the real Kier, a man who did not finish what he began. Her eyes fell in disappointment.

Without a word she moved past him, her cool greeting speaking for her.

He snared her arm as she passed. "Let's go inside."

He felt her stiffen.

"I don't want to be anywhere near you," she said coldly.

The air between them was moist, the rain turning to steam as it fell around them.

"There's nothing you can say that I wish to hear. Let me pass."

"No," he said firmly. "I need to talk to you."

She spun away from him, tearing her arm out of his hand. "It's always what you need, isn't it? Well, you have taken from my children and me more than I care to give. How dare you come into our lives and use my children for your gain. You maneuvered your way into our affections, then betrayed us when it suited you."

She stared at him defiantly. The pain in her eyes caused him to wince.

"We trusted you. Caleb has gone his entire life without believing in the integrity of men, until you came into our lives. He cares more for you than for his own father. I will never forgive you for betraying him, for the hurt you have caused a child who has already seen too much. You were so willing to throw it away. And on what?

"There was no need to put him in danger by taking him with us. He could have stayed with Maggie. You could have orphaned Maggie if your plan had gone awry. And me? What was I supposed to be, some paramour you could humiliate to show how important a man you are? From this time on, I don't want you near my family. You are not the man I thought you were."

Kier stood in silence as she voiced her anger.

She was struck by his demeanor, his remarkable skill at reacting the opposite way she thought he should in a crisis. The more hysterical the situation, the calmer he became. She had seen it before, when they were attacked by the Pawnee. It was a curious gift. It infuriated her.

The rain fell in a deluge, roaring as it pelted the ground. Those in wagons parked nearest to where Fiona and Kier stood arguing peered out to see the commotion.

It was quite a sight, the vision of two people hurling their passions at one another, one in a shout, the other in a whisper, illuminated by irregular shocks of lightning.

Fiona stopped. As suddenly as her outburst came, her embarrassment followed. And the shame. Knowing she had said too much, she turned away.

On the surface, she appeared to be overreacting. But this stormy conversation masked another conversation in which she did not wish to engage.

When Kier spoke, he was circumspect. "You're right. We could have died out there today."

"Then why did you take Caleb and me with you?"

"If we had died, then everyone in this company would have faced the same fate."

She trembled with the gradual realization he had taken her with him in part because if he were to die, he wanted to die with her. Or was that what he meant? She was unsure.

"Let's get out of the rain so we can talk," he invited.

"There's nothing you have to say that I want to hear."

"I owe you an explanation. I want you to understand what happened to us. You must trust me, Fee."

"There is no more trust between us," she said, her lips quivering.

"I've brought you this far. We made it through the last hours."

"No. I no longer want to keep company with someone who has so little regard for my children and me that you would destroy everything between us in a day," she finished, her voice fading to a whisper, emotion robbing it of strength.

"I need you to hear me out. You owe it to all that has passed between us."

With tortured eyes she looked at him, all that went unspoken bubbling to the surface. She was furious with him for bewitching her in her dream, for the reality of him not matching her dream, for his willingness to use her affections to his advantage, and for his unwillingness to follow through on them. Most of all, she hated the doubt that when he took her in his arms it was Fiona Lenihan he kissed or the woman she was only pretending to be.

She began to cry, her tears lost in the rain. But Kier saw them.

After what they had endured, they had an inexplicable need to be together, to assure one another they had survived the ordeal, and to share the experience. He offered her his hand and left it extended.

She turned away from him to hide her vulnerability. He reached for her, placing his hand on her shoulder and squeezing it gently.

"Let's get out of this rain. I can offer you a cup of bad coffee."

"I shouldn't. My children—"

"Mother knows I went after you. And the dozen or so people who witnessed our exchange from behind their wagon flaps will find you if needed, I'm sure."

Fiona glared at him and softened when she met his droll expression. When they reached the supply wagon, he held open the flap for her to enter.

They were soaked through. He handed her a blanket. Its bright stripes of red, yellow, green, and black brought an unexpected smile to her lips. She had never thought of him as owning anything of such extravagance. He was a man of simple tastes: deerskin, chambray, and one red wool flannel shirt he wore from time to time.

"I've had it for years," he explained when he saw her study it. "Traded four points for it—four beaver pelts. You can sit on the barrel," he said, indicating an upended barrel.

Wrapping herself in his blanket, she settled on the barrel, wondering if she was sitting on a keg of gunpowder. He handed her a cup of lukewarm coffee. Shivering, she held it in her hands for warmth.

"Why don't you put on some dry clothes? You can return these to me tomorrow," he said, offering her a shirt and breeches. She shook her head.

"It's not an offer, but an order."

"I'm fine," she smiled wanly at him, trying to hide her shivers. "With this blanket around me I feel warmer already."

"Have you always been this stubborn?" he said, attempting to humor her.

He walked to the end of the wagon and removed his wet shirt, revealing the same well-defined back and shoulders she had dressed with bandages after the Pawnee attack. The same back and shoulders she had caressed in the dream. Scarred though he was, his physique was magnificent, muscles braided throughout.

A shudder went through her that had nothing to do with being cold. Before she could stop herself, she began to imagine running her hands over his scarred flesh, over the strong muscles in his back and shoulders, his firm midriff and torso.

He reached for a dry shirt and turned to face her. His abdomen gleamed in the lantern light.

Fiona raked his body with her gaze, the same body she had caressed in the dream. Hunger parched her mouth. She drew her attention reluctantly from Kier's torso to his face, where he snared her eyes.

"I should go." She could hardly breathe.

"Stay."

A restive silence thickened the air between them.

"You haven't finished your coffee yet," he said with amusement meant to dissolve the tension. He buttoned his shirt and tucked it into his breeches before sitting on a barrel beside her and taking his mug of coffee in hand. He sipped the inky black fluid. She watched him closely and knew he was savoring more than the coffee. He watched her good-naturedly, a smile tempting his lips.

"Are you warm enough?"

Fiona nodded, trying not to shiver. But she could hide little from him.

He reached over to pull the blanket above her shoulders and brushed a damp curl away from her cheek, tucking it behind her ear. Returning his attention to his coffee, they sat together in a silence that would have been awkward under other circumstances.

She sipped the coffee but didn't swallow. Trying to conceal her disgust, she suppressed a gag.

"I told you it was a cup of bad coffee." He laughed, offering her a spittoon.

As a lady, she was in a bad spot: undrinkable coffee or unacceptable behavior.

She could not bring herself to spit, even in front of Kier, so she swallowed the vile liquid. Its bitter taste burned all the way down to her stomach. Coughing and sputtering, she began to laugh.

"Nothing like frontier coffee." He smiled. "So thick you could stand a fork in it."

Fiona laughed harder, an absurd reaction she could not contain. Kier was amused to the point of laughter, and they shared a belly roar that would have given any onlooker the impression that something other than coffee had been in their mugs. As they laughed, their bodies touched, expressing an easy affection.

Fiona realized it was the first time she had seen Kier crack more than a hasty grin outside Fort Kearny. It occurred to her she was seeing something rare indeed,

Kier as a happy man. Even his eyes were shining; their coolness warmed to an inviting blue. As he laughed, joy shone in his face, expressed in his full set of dimples.

They were as two good friends enjoying a moment of release that drew them closer. That was the true prize of their shared experience at the Sioux camp. More than their freedom, it was a deepening of affection their hours together had won them.

"How about some Scotch?" he offered, his laughter dying. "It should warm you up," he said when he saw her hesitate.

She nodded, and he rose to dig the prized bottle of twenty-year-old Islay whiskey out of the bottom of a steamer trunk, along with an inelegant pair of glasses made from ground-down old liquor bottles.

Kier grew serious as he poured their drinks and placed hers into waiting hands. He clanked his glass against hers. She followed his lead, not once taking her eyes from his. The soft glow from the lanterns gave his hair a russet sheen.

"Sláinte," she said with a twinkle, raising her glass in an Irish toast. The smooth bitterness of the whiskey eased down her throat, tasting of caramel and smoke.

"I choose to be honest with you because I believe you can handle the truth," he said.

She nodded, warding off a shiver as she swilled the amber liquid.

"I asked you and Caleb to come with me because I figured the best chance of making any kind of appeal was through my family. Chief White Thunder's father and brother before him had an extraordinary sense of family. Introducing him to my own family would create an opening for discussion. Introducing you and Caleb as my wife and son was—" he hesitated, studying her unwavering focus.

"Why not Maggie?"

"Too young. And too precocious in her observations. I couldn't have her treat me as anything less than her father. Any doubts would have been amplified, given our own uncertain dynamic. Caleb was perfect. He's ideally wide-eyed and perceptive. We had to appear convincingly as husband and wife, father and son. You were our best chance."

She took another sip of whiskey. "That doesn't change the fact I'm still angry at you for using us, for using my son."

"I did use you and Caleb. And I would do it again for the same gain."

She stiffened.

"What were they saying when they asked you about—our family?"

"That you're too thin. You'd be a beautiful woman if you had a little more meat on you," he said with a crooked smile.

"And you agreed?"

"Impolite not to agree with the chief's wife."

She stopped, unsure if she should have been angry or grateful.

"What else did they say?" she asked.

"Naw." He grinned, a burst of dimples flexing. "Nothing of consequence."

"Then why are you blushing?" she challenged.

"I don't blush."

"Perhaps it's the Scotch."

"Among other things, they said we have a fine son."

"Maybe someday you'll tell me the other things," she said, giving him a sidelong glance.

"It was a gamble, but it worked, thanks to you. I know it wasn't easy, and I wish I could have had a moment to let you know what was happening. But I knew you would understand the importance of what transpired and your role in bringing it about. Thank you for playing along so well."

"Why did you bring Horace?" she asked after absorbing his last comment.

"Gravitas."

"Tom Thorpe?" she asked, taking another sip.

"Jake's eyewitness."

"The others? Joseph and Tobias?"

"They were in the last two wagons," he shrugged.

"So, how was it, my husband, that when we retired for the evening we went to different tents?" she asked, curious about that turn of events.

"Sioux men don't lie with menstruating women."

He watched as her understanding grew with her embarrassment. She turned away from him, her cheeks ruddy.

"There's little I don't know about you—or anyone traveling, for that matter. Part of my job is to read people and discern situations. I see you every day. I watch you every day. I knew you were bleeding and that it would save us from having to appear intimate as husband and wife. I also knew it would save me from having to bow to a custom of hospitality where I would have been obligated to offer you to the chief or a man of his choosing last night."

"You wouldn't."

"If you were not bleeding, I would not have taken

you with me or claimed you as my wife."

"Oh?" she said, not following his logic.

"If you were mine, I would not share you with anyone."

Fiona had no response, so she stared into her glass of Scotch. She took another sip.

"The Sioux believe menstrual blood to be a powerful substance that is harmful to men. That's why menstruating women stay outside the household and the camp. That's why you took dinner last and sat outside the circle, then were isolated in a separate hut with the other menstruating women."

"That view gives women a curious amount of power."

"Perhaps. The Sioux also believe that intimate relations are detrimental to a man's power. The woman is viewed as a temptress. A man's restraint is a mark of his bravery. Couples who have too many children are considered irresponsible. If you must know, I was complimented for fathering only two children in nine years of marriage, particularly given your—beauty," he concluded.

Fiona felt the color rise in her cheeks again and immediately changed the subject. "Why did they kill the people traveling ahead of us?"

"Retaliation. The white man went back on his word. In eighteen fifty-one a treaty was signed, the Treaty of Fort Laramie. It was supposed to assure tracts of land for the Sioux, Cheyenne, Arapaho, Crow, Arikara, Assiniboine, Hidatsa, and Mandan peoples in exchange for safe passage for immigrants. In return, the U.S. government promised to compensate the tribes for damages done by the settlers and to make annual payments for their loss of land. The treaty promised the Indian lands would be theirs forever.

"It didn't take long for these promises to be broken. On the one hand, I can't say I blame them for fighting back. The sun is setting on their way of life."

"Will there be a day when people no longer live in fear of each other?"

"Some tribes are more accepting of the white man; others have the prescience to see the coming of the white man as the beginning of the end of their way of life."

"Do you believe that?"

"Yes. It's the misconceptions about Indians that will do them in," Kier said sadly.

"You know a lot about Indians."

"Hoping to help find a reasonable peace," he replied before finishing his Scotch.

After a silence, Fiona spoke. "I wish I could relive the last two days absent the fear."

"What made you afraid?"

"The uncertainty of what was happening and what was to happen. Other than that, I saw beauty and mystery. I saw families. I saw women and children, art and music, and dance."

"You did indeed see dance," Kier grinned, refilling his glass. "It's a shame you missed some of the more sedate, traditional dances, many of them danced by women. The finale was something reserved for—well—the Sioux equate a lack of self-control between a man and a woman with the behavior of dogs. When the men danced, what they were shouting was that their genitals were 'of dogs.' Another memorable chapter to add to your trail experience."

Kier smiled at her to the point of laughter, and she returned the gesture.

"What was it they called you?"

"My Sioux name. It means Moon Over Water. In the Sioux tradition, names are associated with your clan. Mine was the moon. Chief Gray Moon brought me into the clan, so I took his clan's name. Before Chief White Thunder changed his name, he was known as White Moon."

"Moon Over Water," she repeated. It evoked an image from long ago of moonshine on the sea. "I love moonlight on water," she said suddenly. "It was one of my favorite images, perhaps the only positive one, from our voyage to America."

She took a sip of whiskey in the awkward silence and felt Kier's gaze upon her. He smiled for her benefit, but his eyes didn't smile at all. They churned with something darker. Emboldened by the alcohol, she held them, refusing to release him while not allowing him to release her. She felt her chest rise and fall more quickly with each moment. The growing heaviness of the space between them made it difficult to breathe.

He was so near, their bodies so close she could see every detail of the blue in his eyes, smell his musky scent, feel their imminent surrender. Her heart raced as her body prepared to make the dream reality. Kier saw the fine beads of perspiration begin to glisten on her brow and brushed them away. He took her face in his hands.

She anticipated his kiss and all that would follow as their lips drew near. His breath caressed her face and neck. And then they drank one another in, her lips parting when Kier's met hers. They lingered in the long, delicious interlude of their embrace until he drew away to meet her eyes. He smiled at her and she returned his affection.

His kiss had a curious power over her, intoxicating to where she had no memory of how she came to be sitting in his lap on the floor of the wagon, the four-point blanket wrapped around his shoulders instead of hers. He held her in his arms, sharing the warmth of the blanket.

All she could recall was the taste of his kiss, its smoky flavor with a hint of peat. Whenever she breathed, he was there, eliminating the space between them. He finally broke to kiss her eyelids, temples, ears, and throat. Wrapping one arm around his back, with the other she brushed his cheek, first with her palm, then with the back of her hand.

"You beguile me in a way no one ever has," he said, his voice a languid whisper.

They sat together, unmoving, simply luxuriating in the beauty of their intimacy. They had shared a great deal in recent hours, and somehow this exchange was what they needed. It put a finish on a series of events for which finding the words proved nearly impossible, especially to anyone other than those who were there.

Kier lifted her chin with his fingers. Pausing a moment to explore her eyes, he lowered his mouth to hers. Their kisses were rich and easy, without urgency. They celebrated their thanksgiving for surviving their ordeal. They kissed for a long time, like young lovers perfecting their technique.

Fiona took his face in her hands and held it above her, caressing its curves and planes. Her fingertips lingered in the dimples that formed as his smile broadened. She studied his face, her eyes bright with the epiphany that Kier was the most unexpected gift in her life. He was her mentor, friend, and companion, she thought, drawing him to her, a concept that seemed at once shocking and obvious.

His kisses wandered beyond her face, to her neck and the edge of her dress. She lifted her chin to expose more of her to his touch. He anointed her using first his fingers and then his tongue, tantalizing the skin beneath her neckline.

With a sharp intake of breath, she gathered his shirt in his hands. Pulling it from his waistband, she reached beneath it to touch his flesh. Her hands ran up his back, exploring his muscles and bones. His skin. His warmth. They lingered on his scars. He was as magnificent as he had been in her dream.

His hand slid beneath her camisole and caressed her breast. Fiona gasped, her arousal reaching heights she had never experienced.

She sighed when she felt his hand travel beneath her skirt and up her inner thigh. The low, primal sounds that came from her lips shocked her. Kier had introduced her to sensations Simon had never cared to explore. Rapturous from the storm of new feelings and emotions, she reached for the buttons on Kier's shirt, suddenly wanting to feel his flesh against her flesh.

She eased her legs apart to invite him to lie between them.

"Kier?"

A voice called through the rain.

"Billy," Kier whispered.

"Kier?" Billy called from outside the wagon. "Kier?" he said again, announcing his presence before opening the flap and bounding into the wagon. Kier and Fiona separated to greet him. They were sitting casually on the floor of the wagon by the time Billy entered. The four-point blanket, restored around her shoulders, hid the evidence of their embrace. She discreetly buttoned her clothes, her attention on the two men, not missing a beat.

Billy knew he had interrupted them. Their faces were flush, their hair unkempt. He took his cue from them and did not acknowledge what all of them knew.

The awkwardness passed, and Kier and Fiona welcomed his company. Together they sat and talked, sharing companionship and tales from the Sioux camp. Kier told the story of watching Fiona watch the naked men dance. It got the expected reaction from Billy, and all shared a hearty laugh.

As the conversation bounced from Kier to Billy and back again, Fiona watched Kier. She felt warm and safe, and no longer shivered. She could not have imagined such an evening would follow the horrors of the previous day and night. She was content, which enabled her to grasp a new understanding of the man.

She enjoyed relaxing with Kier and Billy over a nightcap of Scotch. She had a deep affection for both men, although of an entirely different nature. She wanted more of what she and Kier had shared and suspected he did as well. But she was pleased with the opportunity for casual conversation among friends. She hadn't laughed that much in a long time.

"It's late," Kier said, aware of the hour. "It will be another early morning, if this rain stops. I want us to be as far away from the Oglala Sioux unrest as possible. We'll be to Fort Laramie in a few days. We can rest there."

"I should get back," Fiona said. Kier rose and offered his hand to help her to her feet. She accepted it and rewarded him with a private smile.

As she walked across the camp, she realized Kier was indeed the man in her dream, as much as he was the man who had been her husband in the Sioux camp. She closed her eyes and let the rain wash over her, feeling in its touch the caress of her beloved.

****

When Kier toured the perimeter at dawn, he happened upon Fiona, who was watching the sunrise. She was so lost in her thoughts she was unaware of his presence. She felt better about many things than she had in a long time. The most painful memories of Simon were gone. Now she could think of him in a distant place, far from her heart.

"Good morning," Kier said, dismounting. He took her in his arms and gave her a kiss reminiscent of their time together, now only hours old.

"The sky is so vast," she said, turning toward the sunrise. "Look at the colors of dawn: lavender, rose, marigold, heather. It's like a magnificent garden. So beautiful. I can see why you like it out here. How about a cup of real coffee?" she offered. "It should be ready by now."

She left his embrace to pour him a cup.

"Now, that's not coffee," he said with a twinkle.

"It's the best Fort Kearny had to offer."

"You've tasted my kind of coffee."

"You've been away from civilization too long," she teased, taking the mug from him as he turned to mount Kildare. He kissed her again before leaving.

"I'll see you later." He grinned, showing his dimples as he tipped his hat to her in the usual way.

Smiling to herself, she resumed the breakfast preparation. She cut the dried fruit rhythmically, the blade slicing through the succulent flesh. First apricots, then figs and prunes.

Jake's hand slammed the knife to the cutting board. The blade nearly cut off her fingertip.

Fiona jumped and looked up in horror at the perpetrator. Jake's action reminded her of something Simon would have done. Of things he did.

"I want to know what happened between you and Moran in the Sioux camp."

"Nothing happened," she said quietly, realizing two of her fingers were lacerated. Her blood had begun to stain the fruit.

"Why don't I believe you?" he asked mockingly.

"Because you're unwilling. You find it too easy to presume that something passed between us because it would give you cause to hate him more."

"He has clearly influenced the way you address one who questions the events of the past hours for your own good. Need I remind you that a lady has to follow a certain code of behavior?" He released his hold on her hands.

She wrapped her wounded fingers in her apron. "What if something did pass between us? You have no claims on me."

"None that I have announced. I understand there was a disturbance in camp last night, one caused by you and the person with whom you claim nothing passed."

"Kier told them I was his wife. I was angry with him for putting me in danger, for putting Caleb at risk."

"That's what I needed to know," he said triumphantly. He pulled her hand from her bloodstained apron to inspect the damage. "It's only a scratch," he said, shoving her hand back toward her.

Fiona raised her fingers to her lips and sucked on them until they stopped bleeding.

Chapter 19

Fiona never knew going downhill in a wagon could be a technical challenge until the company reached the summit of Windlass Hill. It was the steepest part of the trail so far. Hundreds of wagons had been ruined on its slopes, over the years, when they lost control and smashed into the valley below. Pieces of those wagons littered the countryside and had become an inventory of spare parts.

The safest way to get a fully loaded wagon down the long, sloping hill was to brake the wheels, chain them in place, and slide the wagon down the steep incline with teams of draft animals and men. It was a tedious process. Caleb watched with fascination as Kier supervised the work. It took up to a dozen men and sometimes a mule or two to pull back on these wagons, controlling the speed of their descent, while the teams of oxen pulled forward.

The reward for making this harrowing descent was a scenic meadow filled with ash trees that surrounded a freshwater spring. Ash Hollow was one of the most popular campsites on the trail.

Three days later the settlers came upon the first real topography they had seen in weeks.

"What's that, Mama?" Maggie asked, seeing a narrow spire in the distance.

"That's Chimney Rock," Caleb answered eagerly.

He went on to explain how one of his friend's fathers told him to watch for it. "Jimmy's dad said the men call it Elk Penis, but the ladies call it Chimney Rock. He said Mr. Moran said the Indians call it Elk Penis. He said we have to call it Chimney Rock, so we don't offend the ladies."

"He did, did he?" Fiona said, turning around to look at her son, who was hanging over the back of the bench, looking smug after delivering this nugget of knowledge.

"What's an elk penis?" Maggie asked.

"It's a rock shaped like a chimney," Fiona said, casting her son a warning glance.

They camped with Chimney Rock in silhouette against the sunset and spent the next two days watching it loom 475 feet above them as they approached and passed it. A series of individual mesas dotted the landscape beyond Chimney Rock. Behind them ran a hundred-mile bluff that ended in another landmark, Scotts Bluff.

Tales of the tragic death of the fur trapper Hiram Scott, for which it was named, spread through camp. Word was he had been too sick to travel, so his fellow trappers left him to die. The next spring his skeleton was found at the bluff, one hundred miles from where his companions had left him. The vivid story made the stark drama of the landscape even more compelling.

While the travelers were intrigued by the individual landforms, it was the series of them that gave the travelers the sense they were making progress toward California.

"When are we going to stop?" Caleb sighed, weary after several miles of travel. They had made good time since Kier had bartered for their safe passage, but it was taking a toll on the backs and limbs of man and beast.

"We're moving quickly so we can put as much country behind us as we can before the travel becomes difficult. It's bumpy and dusty on these flats, but we reached twenty miles yesterday," Fiona said to encourage him.

They set camp for the night. She waited for Kier by the fire, reading a book but not comprehending, distracted by her desire to be with him.

"Walk with me," he said from the darkness beyond the firelight. They strolled in silence, Fiona sensing his discomfort.

"I'm not a good enough man for you," he said bluntly.

She stopped walking.

"You are young and beautiful and have fine children," he said, facing her. "You deserve a man who will marry you and build a life by your side and wake up with you every morning. I'm not that man."

"Why are you saying this?" she asked in disbelief.

"Because I will walk away when we reach California. You will stay and I will go. I can't do that to you without your understanding there is no hope with me for the life you deserve."

"But you said after—"

"I'm a selfish man. I'm drawn to you. I would lie with you every night for the rest of our time together, but that would ruin your chances for a life with a better man. I cannot do that to you, to Caleb and Maggie. I'm sorry, Fee. I'm sorry I'm not that man."

He took her hands in his and kissed them before placing them together and walking away.

Moonlight shone in her tears. She stood alone, emotions colliding and combusting, threatening to explode in a wail of agony. She gasped, trying to still her shock. At some level she knew he was right, but she wanted more from him, not less.

She pressed her hands against her face and squeezed in a vain attempt to force her tears back into their ducts, her devastation back into her wounded heart.

After that, she stopped looking for him. The initial sadness passed, leaving a lingering melancholy in its wake, which she did her best to conceal.

Sensing the void, Jake became persistent to the point of staying up past his habitual bedtime to sit with her by the fire. But she cut those occasions short, feeling empty when sharing that experience with anyone but Kier. She and Jake didn't have enough to talk about to warrant spending any length of time together. All the same, she tried to give Jake a chance. At least he was the type of man with whom she had the possibility of a future.

"Teach me about Shakespeare," she asked Jake one evening, trying a new line of conversation. She hoped to talk about anything other than Scripture. And Kier.

"What do you want to know about William Shakespeare?"

"Anything you think I should know. I understand Mr. Shakespeare wrote plays and sonnets."

"The sonnets are a bunch of romantic nonsense. But his plays have some merit. He wrote one about warring families whose children fell in love. It was a foolish choice on both their parts. Led to their doom."

"How so?" she asked, wanting to know.

"She pretended to kill herself and he believed she did, so he killed himself to be with her. When she awakened, she killed herself to be with him."

"Oh," she said, taken aback by his explanation.

"It's difficult to read. Lacks clarity. His writing style leaves something to be desired," Jake critiqued.

"If you're not fond of Mr. Shakespeare, who is your favorite author?"

"There are so many," he said, sounding pretentious.

"Such as?"

"Why do you press me on learned matters?" Jake said testily. "You are no scholar."

"You're right," she said, folding her hands neatly in her lap. "How about the Psalms, then? Tell me about Psalm Eighty-Eight."

****

Kier paused at the crest of a hill, studying the company's next obstacle. Frustration stretched before him in an explosion of flame and smoke that towered in the sky, fueling a choking haze. The rain-starved brush lands were on fire, tens of thousands of acres raging in an impenetrable wall that cut off the trail. There was nothing but scorched earth between them and the inferno.

The fire burned away from them in the direction they needed to travel. The North Platte River disappeared in the smoke, its steady calm a contrast to the power of nature around it. Kier decided on a new route and returned to the company to discuss it with Jake and the other elected leaders.

"We need to stop at Fort Laramie," Jake said. "You know we're running short on supplies."

"We can't get to Fort Laramie. We can sit here and wait for the fire to burn itself out or for a good rain to put it out, and risk attacks by unfriendly Indians or the full wrath of that fire if the winds change. If we head south toward Fort Bridger, we can travel around the fire."

"What are the risks of this route?" asked Tom Thorpe.

"Water. If we go several days without rain, we could have trouble finding adequate water. We'll travel among smaller water sources—the Laramie River, Medicine Bow River, a fork of the North Platte River—and move between them rather than along them. We can fill our casks here and ration our supply. That should get us most of the way to the Green River, where we can camp before crossing it and making the three or four days' travel to Fort Bridger."

"How well do you know this route?" asked Tom.

"Well. I've traveled it many times."

"And you think we can make it to Fort Bridger all right?" Tom continued.

"It's our best option. Bathing and laundry will suffer, so we'll need to prepare the women."

"I can think of more than a few children who won't object," Tom said with a laugh.

The company took its nooning on the spot. Kier and Jake addressed the travelers, explaining the change in course and the procedure everyone was to follow with respect to filling casks with water and rationing it over the next 330 miles, or about twenty days. Kier's announcement elicited grumbles from the crowd.

Fiona did not look at Kier while he spoke. Instead, she watched Maggie play with a pair of birds in flight that Gideon had carved for her. She raised and lowered them, making them circle the air around her, like two creatures whose fate had bonded them for life. They were two of a kind, halves of a whole. They belonged together.

The sound of Kier's voice mauled her heart. She could almost hear him say her name.

"Look!" Hope Whittaker cried, pointing to the northwest. An angry cloud of smoke had begun to obscure the blue sky over a far ridge.

In the excitement Fiona looked up at Kier, then glanced as quickly away when she met his eyes. Regardless of the new terrain, she decided these next weeks of travel were going to be very difficult, as if beholding a scrumptious feast and being forbidden from partaking. It was easier to stay out of the dining room, far away from the temptation, than to be anywhere near it.

She needed a diversion. Sewing. She had been meaning to learn to sew. It would occupy not only her mind but her hands as well. Now seemed like as good a time as any to develop a new skill. The children were growing. They would need new clothes.

"Hope," she said, hurrying to find her friend after the meeting had ended. "I have a favor to ask."

The company had left behind the humidity of the plains for cooler, cleaner air as they traveled west with a snow-capped range of mountains in continuous view to their south. The days were sunny and warm but not hot, and best of all not sticky.

Waves of gold and green had given way to more sharply demarcated hills the color of straw, with little green in sight. There were fewer trees and smaller water sources, mainly creeks and streams that ran at the bottom of gullies. It was rougher country than they had traveled. Here, the sky was a startling shade of blue, especially where it met the pale earth.

Hope worked daily with Fiona to help her make a new dress for Maggie. Caleb needed a new shirt more urgently. Since it was more difficult to make a shirt than a simple jumper, Hope demonstrated and constructed the shirt while Fiona tried to follow Hope's lead and apply the instruction to her work on Maggie's dress. With their every meeting, Fiona made progress. Soon she could produce an entire line of tiny, uniform stitches that made an even seam, free of puckers. Once she understood the basics, she took to sewing as she had to cooking. The two skills had in common the satisfaction of a useful finished product.

The going was steady in the sunny weather, so Kier pushed the company more than seventeen miles a day. Twice they neared twenty miles. There was no rain, but they managed to find enough water for drinking and resting the animals. Cottony white clouds built up in the sky each afternoon but never did more than blot out some of the clear blue. One day they saw a distant thunderstorm near the mountains to the south, but that was the closest they came to any rain.

Fiona noticed Kier had gradually begun to reappear in camp, but he never looked for her. While her heart ached, it did so more for her children, who did not understand why Kier had grown distant. He spent less time with his mother as well, leaving a sadness Fiona could read on Clare's face.

Kier was distracted by the escalating difficulties of the journey. There were disputes between travelers and domestic issues where Kier did his best to calm abusive husbands and fathers. There were animals with little work left in them. There were broken wagons and runaway cattle. And there were two women and two children who looked his way with a terrible sadness.

Fiona and her children traveled in silence across the broad valley. Tall grasses slapped against the spokes of the wheels, *thap*, *thap*, *thap*. They set camp at the edge of a lazy stream, dismayed by its shallowness.

It was a golden evening. The sky blended seamlessly with the earth at the horizon. Long shadows fell across the prairie. Caleb was playing with his friends at one of the other boy's wagons. Maggie was sitting on the bench, singing and playing with her carved birds.

Fiona was bone weary. Her skin glistened with perspiration. She sat on the tailgate and closed her eyes to the fragrance of sweet clover as a gentle breeze stirred her stray curls. Barking dogs, laughing children, and the conversations of many were but fragmented sounds. A fiddler tuned his strings and began to play. Oxen bellowed. Somewhere, a baby cried. The rays of the late-day sun had a soporific effect, their warm fingers caressing her skin. She felt more relaxed than she had in days.

A shadow crossed her, blocking out the magnificent light.

"Fee."

She almost believed it a dream, for she had not heard him say her name in days. Opening her eyes, she stared up at him, registering no emotion.

Many a time Fiona had been on the receiving end of Edna Cushing's withering glower. Now she turned it on Kier, projecting all the truculence she could muster. She wanted to punish him, to make him feel the way she felt at his avoidance.

She let the silence that followed work on him until she saw his torment dim the crystal blue of his eyes.

The tensions that raged within him ignited her guilt. "Sit with me a while," she invited. "The sun is so beautiful. So healing."

Kier joined her on the tailgate to watch the early stages of sunset. "Fee—"

She quieted him mercifully with a whisper. "You'll miss the best part of the sunset."

Watching the sky blaze from coral and gold to periwinkle, pink, and lavender, they sat together, feeling the weight of their companionship.

"You owe me no explanations," she said. "I have no claims on you."

"You and Caleb and Maggie have a lifetime ahead of you. I am but a character along the way."

"An important one," she said. She turned toward him to make her point. "I can think of a boy who longs for an invitation to go hunting and a little girl who needs to be lifted high above your head now and again."

"And a woman who sits alone by the fire who could use some company. Now and again," he said, watching her ardently.

"Now and again."

Maggie's little-girl voice took flight in a Gaelic folk song her mother had taught her. Fiona covered Kier's hand with hers.

****

Each hour brought the travelers to higher ground as

sweeping grasslands gave way to outcroppings of granite that interrupted the golden hills. Mountains loomed dramatically to the south. As they seemed to grow larger, Kier reassured everyone they would not be crossing them.

Fiona and her children watched the changing land formations with interest, reaching for additional wraps and blankets when the sun was no longer there to warm them. The days were hot and breezy; the nights cool and crisp. Deciduous trees gave way to pine trees and slender, delicate trees that rustled in the wind.

Kier ended the day's travel in the shadow of a vast garden of granite sculptures, gigantic boulders balanced one upon another and tossed about like wooden blocks in a child's nursery. The settlers were agog.

"What is this place?" Fiona asked Kier when he rode past as she was unhitching her team.

"The Arapaho call it Vedauwoo, which means 'Land of the Earthborn Spirit.'"

His response was warm but remote. Fiona sighed. If he could do this, so could she.

Dinner was on the fire. Caleb was off with his friends, sketching some of the unusual rock formations in his journal, and Maggie was helping Fiona mend a hole in the canvas wagon cover.

"Come," Kier invited quietly, surprising mother and daughter. "There's something I want to show you."

He led them into a grove of trees whose green leaves made music as they danced in the wind.

"They sound like running water," Fiona marveled.

"Quaking aspen. In the autumn they turn blazing gold. Against the dark green of the pine trees, it's quite a sight. You'll see for yourself when we reach the High

Sierra in September."

Fiona stopped to listen to the aspen.

Maggie smiled up at her when she had identified the sound. "Like water," she agreed.

They continued to listen as they walked through the woods. Fiona was struck by the vibrant green of the aspen leaves against the light of the evening sun.

"Stop here," Kier directed, positioning Fiona and Maggie where they could see a giant rock formation above the trees. It was topped with a rock that resembled a tongue.

Maggie giggled, recognizing the shape.

Kier swung Maggie around his shoulder to carry her piggyback style. "Hang on," he instructed, breaking into a trot, which elicited giggles.

"Do you have time to bring Caleb here?" Fiona asked when he lowered Maggie to the ground. "I'd like for him to see them."

Kier nodded. "I'll do you one better and bring the whole band," he said, referring to Caleb and his three close friends.

"Thank you for sharing this with us. How did you come to find this place?"

"I've camped here often, right over there," he said, indicating an ideal campsite near the base of another rock formation that was sheltered from the wind by a giant pile of granite boulders.

Fiona tried to imagine him there, alone by his campfire, wrapped in his four-point blanket and making a pot of bad coffee. She nearly jumped when she felt his hand at the small of her back. She had missed his touch.

"Let's head back," he said, steering Fiona toward camp.

They walked quietly through aspen trees scented from a nearby grove of spruce trees. Kier took Fiona's hand to help her step over petrified logs and the remains of fallen trees. She didn't want to let go, but soon they were within range of camp.

They parted company outside of camp, leaving Fiona and Maggie to return to their work repairing the canvas.

****

The following day of travel was largely downhill. The winding pass opened to a broad mountain valley ringed on three sides by mountains. It was seventy miles across, but the company could see tall mountain peaks Kier said were one hundred miles away. Its beauty enchanted the travelers. The wide-open space had grandeur unlike anything they had seen on their journey.

Kier led the company to the floor of the valley, where they made camp at the side of a lively stream. Pleasantly situated, there were beautiful views in all directions. It was so flat they could see where they would be traveling for the next few days. Unlike travel in the plains, it was easy to mark their progress in ground filled with landmarks.

"We've now traveled one-third of the way to California," Kier began his address to the group as the sun set on their first day in the valley. "The most difficult two-thirds of the journey lie ahead of us. We've made good time until now, traveling fifteen or so miles daily across open prairie. Now, the farther west we go, our best efforts will bring us slower travel days. It's important that we continue the good work we have undertaken. Reverend Pride." Kier gestured to the minister, turning the floor over to him.

"Let us pray," the minister began. The travelers bowed their heads. "May God continue to bless us on our journey, bless our families, bless our friends, and bless our leaders. Bless our animals and wagons that they remain strong and steady for our journey. Bless the food we eat, that it will be as bountiful as the feast we share this evening. Amen."

The company was settling into camp one afternoon when a growing rumbling startled everyone, causing the travelers to stare fearfully in the direction of the sound. Charging buffalo? A cattle stampede?

A herd of wild horses galloped toward camp, then veered to the north around the wagons. A cloud of dust followed the dozens of horses like the tail of a comet. The ground shook beneath their pounding hooves.

There were horses of black and gold, russet and white. There were roans and grays, paints, and a palomino stallion with a long white tail. Feral and ungroomed, their manes were long and flowing, and hung in their eyes. Their hides glistened in the late-day sun, casting long shadows across the sagebrush. Snorting and neighing, their communication seemed to intensify the urgency of their flight. It was a majestic vision, this herd of racing beasts.

Initially frightened, Maggie clung to her mother, but turned to watch the beauty of the magnificent creatures as they raced past.

Another day of travel brought the company to the western edge of the desert. The water they had rationed had not been enough for some beasts, who succumbed to their thirst. A few travelers were not far behind. Kier urged those who had a store of water to share it with their fellow travelers.

"Look, Mama," Maggie said, pointing toward a bank of thunderheads.

"I see," she replied with a smile. "But they're probably like all the rest. No rain."

Perhaps it was Maggie's instinct; perhaps it was Fiona's growing sense of pessimism. In either case, the clouds Maggie had noticed brought the company the first rain it had seen in more than two weeks. It was a simple gift, an answer to countless prayers.

The rain gave life to wilted plants and people. Travelers who had lain weakly in the beds of their wagons stepped into the rain and raised their hands to heaven. Gentle drops coursed down faces and wagon canopies. Draft animals bowed forward to lick the drops from the sunbaked earth.

People embraced, thankful for nature's deliverance.

Fiona and her children clasped hands and danced, clapping and playing in the rain, all nightly chores forgotten.

Others joined them and soon more danced than stood still—mothers, fathers, children, old, and young. Even dogs bounded among them. It was part of the unexpected poetry of the trail, the sudden romance that could make a simple event indelible.

Drenched, Fiona stepped out of the group. The dust had turned to mud beneath her feet. Kier stood on the perimeter of the circle, a full-dimpled grin lighting his face when their eyes met. She lifted her outstretched hands, arched her face in gratitude, and returned her attention to Kier.

Giddy from the company's good fortune, she laughed with abandon. He held her face in his hands

before their arms held one another, for they knew the
joy of rain.

Chapter 20

A blood-curdling scream, followed moments later by a single gunshot, broke the dusty peace of nooning. A rattlesnake had bitten Caroline Gillespie above her knee. Fiona arrived just as Kier had begun to suck the venom out of Caroline's leg.

It was an unusual sight, the gentlewoman lying sprawled on the ground, her petticoats tossed haphazardly above her waist and Kier lying between her legs, his lips and hands on her inner thigh. The offending snake lay dead just beyond Caroline's outstretched hand.

Fiona turned away in embarrassment before getting her wits about her and stepping forward to help.

"What's the meaning of this?" Jake said, as taken aback by the vision before him as anyone. "Cover that woman!"

"He's drawin' out the poison," Billy said. "He cain't talk till he's finished."

"How do you know what he's doing?" Jake snapped at him.

"Dead snake. Rattle on its tail. Man suckin' out poison," he replied with deadpan.

Sympathetic to Caroline's predicament, Fiona knelt to rearrange her petticoats. Caroline stared at the sky, paralyzed with fear.

Kier spit three times, each time returning to suck

more poison from Caroline's wound. He rocked back to his heels and took a bottle of whiskey from an onlooker, drank a swig, washed out his mouth, and spat the contents on the ground along with the remnants of the poison.

"Don't touch her," he said to Fiona. "She needs to lie still. Get Doc and bring some blankets."

"All right, everybody," she heard Kier say. "Give Miss Gillespie her privacy."

Jake ushered the crowd away from the spectacle.

"Am I going to die?" Caroline asked Kier.

"Not if I can help it."

"I feel as if I'm floating to Heaven," she said, sounding far away.

"Snake bites can do that," Kier reassured her.

"I'm cold. My leg feels strange," she said, hysteria rising.

"Doc is on his way."

"Am I going to die?"

"No," he said again. "The snake won't get you, but how your body takes the wound might. I'm going to carry you to your wagon so you can rest," he explained. "When I lift you, don't put your arm around me. You need to keep still."

"Oh, why is this happening to me?" Caroline wailed. "To me!"

"You stepped on the snake, and he bit back."

Caroline merely burst into tears.

When Fiona and the Pickerings arrived, Kier was settling Caroline into her wagon with the help of a pair of women who fashioned a bed atop the many steamer trunks that lined the floor. He stepped aside to let Doc and Libby take charge.

"Will you stay with me?" she asked Kier.

"You're in good hands," he said. "Mrs. Lenihan will stay with you."

Fiona looked up at him sharply from where she was helping Libby cover Caroline with blankets.

"Oh, my darling," Evangeline said, arriving breathlessly at her sister's wagon. "Will she be all right?" she asked Doc.

"Should be, thanks to Kier's efforts. She'll be feeling poorly for a few days. Her leg will hurt and swell a bit, but there should be no permanent damage."

With all the goings-on, the company never broke camp after nooning. This allowed extra preparation time for a happy event, the marriage of two of the company's teenagers.

"Do you think Doc will let me go to Ted and Anna's wedding tonight?" Caroline asked Fiona when she had taken over for Libby. "Anna asked me to stand up for her. I hate to miss a wedding," she said sweetly.

"I'll ask Doc," Fiona said, checking her for a fever. "You do seem a little warm."

Fiona had called it correctly: Doc confined Caroline to bed rest. Anna would need to find a stand-in for her maid of honor.

With one plan thwarted, Caroline moved quickly to another. "Would you plump my pillows? I want to look my best when Kier comes to check on me. He's very attentive to needy ladies, or so I've heard."

"Lean forward," Fiona instructed, then beat each one of Caroline's pillows. Each blow was a little harder than the last.

"You know, we thought so ill of Mr. Moran when we began our journey, but my sister's opinion of him has changed. He's actually quite handsome, don't you think?" she said, looking up at Fiona as she lay back on her mountain of pillows. "He's never been married. I've never been married. That could change."

Fiona assumed her finest Cushing affectation and watched Caroline with a forced smile. She wasn't sure whether Caroline was baiting her or if word of Fiona and Kier's affection had not reached her bejeweled ears.

"Would you be a dear and ask when he's going to stop by? I don't want to be asleep and miss him," she said with a giggle.

Fiona nodded. She decided Caroline had a noxious laugh.

"Oh, and one more thing. In all this excitement, I've not had a thing to eat. Do you have anything on the fire? I'd prefer to eat from your pot. Not everyone is as handy with animal parts and prairie grasses as you."

Without realizing it, Fiona's gait carried an annoyed stomp, so much so that when she rounded a corner in search of Kier, she collided with him, stepping on his foot.

"Mrs. Lenihan," he said with a crooked smile.

"I—I was just looking for you."

"Oh?"

"On behalf of Caroline. She asked me to plump her pillows, so she'll look her best when you look in on her," she blurted out, then immediately regretted doing so. "I'm on my way to bring her something to eat," she said, changing her tone and taking off in the direction of the campfire.

Kier caught her hand. "You're jealous," he said with amusement, easing her around to face him.

"I'm not," she replied, straightening herself as if to give the appearance of being above petty emotions.

"Something I haven't seen in you," he teased, tipping his hat and leaving her to her work.

"Needy," she muttered under her breath. "Animal parts," she said, ladling a bowl of stew for Caroline and delivering it to her with a flaky biscuit.

Anna, the bride-to-be, was sitting with Caroline, so Fiona was relieved of small talk.

The frontier wedding was lovely. As planned, at sunset the young couple exchanged vows in front of everyone but Caroline and the men who were guarding the perimeter. Reverend Pride officiated, and Evangeline led the company in song.

"Mama, can a snake bite me?" Maggie asked.

"A snake can bite anyone. That's why we need to look for them where we walk," she was saying when she stopped at Caroline's wagon. She glanced up to see Kier visiting with the snakebite victim. As Caroline had described, he was indeed attentive.

"Let's go find Caleb," she said, walking away. "Brent was going to show the boys how to repair a loose rim on a wheel."

"What was your wedding like?" Maggie asked. "Was it like Ted and Anna's?"

"A little," Fiona said after a long pause. "We got married in a courthouse rather than in the middle of a wagon train."

"Did you carry flowers?" Maggie asked.

"Pink roses."

"Are those your favorites?"

"No. My favorites are any flowers picked by you," she said, rubbing noses with her.

As Fiona's eyes grew heavy that night, Caleb offered a detailed explanation. "Brent said we have to heat up the iron rim of the wheel so it will fit over a wooden wheel and cool to a perfect fit. Once the rim is fitted around the wheel, the whole thing is dipped in the river to cool. If the iron is too hot, it could burn the wooden wheel. Too cold, and it won't fit around the wheel."

His narration faded to a night of dreams about wagon wheels, weddings, and snakes.

****

The Green River. It was the first real water the travelers had seen in weeks. Rich in trout, waterfowl, and game that grazed along its banks, it meant not only full casks of water, but a hearty meal served riverside. In the West, where there is water, there are trees. Fiona saw more trees lining the Green River than she had seen since they had left the banks of the North Platte more than three weeks earlier.

To people who had long since passed the point of smelling gamy, it meant clean clothes and baths for all who wanted them. The women drew water upriver from the animals, who drank upriver from the laundresses, who washed upriver from the bathers. It was a busy site, where the cool water served many purposes.

"I'll find us a good spot for laundry," Fiona said to her friends, carrying her final load of fresh water to her wagon.

With a full basket in her arms and a fresh cake of soap in her pocket, Fiona searched the banks for a spot that would be comfortable for Clare and Libby's aging joints and Hope's expanding belly.

As she sorted her wash, a yellow ribbon floating in

the water caught her eye. It looked out of place, streaming from where it was caught on something under a cluster of willows. Fiona pulled on the ribbon and stumbled back on the bank. She began to shake. Her breath came in jerky gasps as a sob rose in her chest. At last she screamed, a wretch of horror.

"What is it?" Hope asked fearfully as she approached Fiona's chosen spot.

"Get Kier," she said.

Billy appeared as Hope hastened to find Kier.

"What is it?" he asked, kneeling to comfort her.

"A little girl. There's a little girl in the water. She has yellow ribbons in her hair."

Billy stepped into the river to free the child from the tangle of branches at water's edge. She had dark, curly hair and was about Maggie's age. She had been dead for a few days, but the cool water had preserved her face.

A crowd had gathered by the time Billy laid the dead child on the bank. She was doll-like, her small face porcelain white and her bowed lips dark against her skin.

"Indians?" Jake asked Kier as they stood over the child.

"Drowned."

"How do you know?" Jake challenged.

"No injuries. Get someone to dig a grave," Kier ordered Billy.

"I'll do it," he said quietly.

"You all right?" Kier said, crouching by where Fiona sat under Clare's protective arm.

"She has yellow ribbons in her hair," Fiona said, choking on tears. "How could a mother leave this place knowing her daughter wasn't with her?"

"She may have run off, or there may have been an Indian attack where she was lost in the confusion, or she may have been carried downriver by the rains. There's no way of knowing," he said quietly.

"How could you lose your child?" she said, demanding an answer she knew she would not get.

"She came from wealth," Jake commented, crouching at Fiona's other side. "She's wearing a finely made dress. If we meet up with her family in San Francisco we can tell them we laid their daughter to rest."

Fiona regarded him slowly, wearing an expression of consternation tinged with abhorrence. "She has yellow ribbons in her hair," Fiona said again, her expression distant. "I need to find Maggie," she said, hastening in search of her child.

****

Three days later, the company reached Fort Bridger. Built as a fur trading post by mountain man Jim Bridger, it was now operated by the Mormons. They offered peas, turnips, rose hips, and barley for sale to travelers, as well as ferry service across the Black's Fork of the Green River. This stop was a welcome opportunity to rest, restock, and make repairs.

Fort Bridger was a vibrant place that served as a dividing point for the trail. From the fort, travelers continuing on the Oregon Trail headed north toward the Bear Valley. Other travelers went west along the Mormon Trail through Utah Territory. Kier would lead the company along the Mormon Trail because it was the most direct route to central California. In addition, the Mormon settlers had established a thriving trade in the Salt Lake Valley. Ready access to supplies would make this part of the journey easier on the company and fortify them for the weeks ahead.

Fiona sighed dreamily as she and Caleb led their team of oxen to the river's edge to drink. It felt good to make camp in what approximated civilization. The fort was situated in a scenic spot with a view of the snow-capped Uinta Mountains. An extensive network of fields, planted with an array of vegetables, surrounded the fort's main buildings.

Fiona, Clare, and Libby had made plans to visit the dry goods store not only to purchase what they needed but for the fun of browsing. It would be the first time they had been indoors since their stop at Fort Kearny a month earlier.

Wandering in a leisurely way through the aisles of foodstuffs, pots, pans, fabric, notions, furniture, and farming tools felt like an indulgence. The shopkeepers maintained an orderly store, which only enhanced the experience. To her surprise, they stocked a few finished clothes. Fiona poked through the racks of shirts and pants, camisoles and skirts, blouses and nightshirts. A green calico dress caught her eye. Trimmed with ochre eyelet, it was soft and feminine. It also looked to be her size. When she saw the price, she turned away to study the coffee grinders.

"That would look lovely on you," Clare said, joining her. "The green would bring out your eyes."

"It is pretty," Fiona said, turning to look at it. "Maybe when we get to California, I can learn to sew such a dress."

"Pretty dresses are a feminine affliction," Clare said.

"Looking at something like that makes me realize how I look," Fiona said, laughing.

"Maybe you could get a blouse," Clare offered. "Do you have enough chambray left to make a skirt?"

Fiona shook her head.

"When was the last time anyone did anything nice for you? For your birthday, I'm buying you a blouse. We'll find fabric so you can make a skirt."

"Oh, Clare, I couldn't."

"Humor me. I don't have a daughter. And Lord knows I'm well past the years of wearing pretty things. This would look lovely on you," she said, holding up a yellow gingham blouse to Fiona. It had a ruffled cuff, which seemed like an extravagance. "I'll take this," she said to the proprietor.

"Thank you," Fiona said, humbled by the gesture.

"For children, it's peppermints. For women, it's something pretty to wear."

Clare helped her select a bolt of muslin fabric that matched the blouse. Laden with provisions, they headed back to camp. The proprietor's son followed them, pulling a handcart filled with their sacks of flour, bacon, and coffee. Fiona had a bag of peppermints for her children and ginger she could use to bake sweets.

Fiona tried to sleep that night but could not. Images of yellow ribbons floating in the water, pretty calico dresses, and Jake's comments about wealth, gentlewomen, and propriety ran through her head.

She would be haunted forever by memories of the yellow ribbon floating in the Green River and of the little girl's perfect face. She grieved for the mother, knowing how her heart must ache at the loss of a beloved daughter.

Wiping tears from her face, she climbed out of her wagon and went to sit by what remained of the fire. She put her head in one hand while she drew her shawl more closely around her with the other. It was cold at night on the high plains.

"You're up late," Kier said, joining her.

She turned away from him to wipe her face clean. "Couldn't sleep. I can't stop thinking about the girl in the river. How her mother must feel."

"How she'll hope someone like you found her and laid her to rest."

"The land is unforgiving."

"In many ways. But we can embrace its beauty and its joys and sorrows while we live beneath the dome of the sky. We're entering rough country," he said, changing his tone. "Much of it downhill."

"Isn't that easy?"

"Not when it's steep, like Windlass Hill. It's hard to control the teams. We won't have an easy day until we're in the Salt Lake Valley."

When they reached her wagon, he took her in his arms. Reluctant to part from her, he pressed his forehead against hers, then drew her to him in a full embrace.

"Goodnight," he whispered in her ear, holding her close.

Chapter 21

The first day out from Fort Bridger was spent traveling southwest, winding through a series of enormous buttes carved with drainage channels that had the appearance of gnarled fingers dotted with age spots made of greasewood. As the sun arched across the sky, it cast shadows on the buttes, making them appear alternately imposing or menacing, and at times manmade, like an ancient fortification. The memory of the megalithic burial grounds in County Sligo flickered behind Fiona's eyes.

The technical challenge of traveling downhill began on the third day in a place known as Echo Canyon. Kier encouraged Caleb and Maggie to test the acoustics, and soon every child in the company was barking and howling, which seemed to inspire the draft animals to do the same. Fiona was glad she didn't have a headache, for the children never grew tired of the game. Even some of the men joined at one point, including Brent, whose bugle echoed for the better part of a minute as its sound ricocheted around the canyon.

Kier halted the company at some of the more treacherous sections and encouraged travelers who had large or heavily loaded wagons to lower them on pulleys rather than risk losing control of the wagon on the decline. It took the better part of a day to move sixty wagons in this manner.

On the afternoon of Kier's second of three promised days of downhill travel, it rained. Not only did it rain a lot for August, it rained a lot for any day. Kier found the rain to be a blessing, for the mud slowed the wagons on the steeper terrain. But it also softened the earth, rendering it unstable.

On the third day, parts of the trail had sharp drop-offs. The path had been worn into the side of a mountain and was wide enough for only one wagon.

The first forty wagons made it safely to the bottom of the hill. Their occupants spilled out into the sunshine to make repairs, play cards, or do laundry at a nearby stream. The children chased gophers around the countryside, never managing to catch them before they disappeared into one of innumerable holes, only to reappear with their heads popping out a different hole.

The narrow road near the top of the hill meant families waited inside their wagons for their turn. The tedious process made for long stretches of time for one group of people to share the same cramped space.

Kier's and Billy's shirts clung to their torsos. They had removed their hats to do the heavy work of easing the wagons down the hill because sweat kept sliding their hats too low over their eyes. Along with Brent, Silas, and Horace, they formed the core of the group of men guiding the wagons. Their bodies had begun to show it. Exhausted and suffering from any number of cuts, scratches, and muscle pulls, no one would be happier than these men when the last wagon was in the valley.

The group was tense as the men slid the medical supply wagon down the hill. Doc and Libby stood at the bottom, watching the process with concern. While no one wanted any wagon to be damaged, the items in the medical wagon were irreplaceable. The company breathed a collective sigh of relief when the wagon came to a stop in the valley.

Hunched with fatigue, the men walked back up the hill. Kier made an inventory of the remaining heavy wagons and knew they were still hours away from being finished. He looked up with a smile when he saw the next wagon in line was his parents'. Fiona's stood behind theirs. Clare regarded her son with enough pride to renew his strength.

Fiona had shushed her children for the hundredth time that afternoon when suddenly a commotion erupted in one of the wagons behind hers. The sound of rocks and earth sliding were followed by a crash.

Animals brayed. People screamed. Kier broke into a run with the other men at his heels. Fiona climbed out of her wagon and followed Kier to see what had happened. Clare and Gideon were right behind her, as were Caleb and Maggie. The commotion blossomed to hysteria.

Part of the unstable path had given way, taking a wagon with it. The yoke and harnesses had caught on newly exposed roots and boulders that protruded from the erosion site. Two of the oxen were hanging against the dirt, but the other two dangled in midair more than a hundred feet above the ravine. They kicked and bawled, shaking the imperiled wagon as they moved.

It was Joseph and Prudence Clark's wagon. Joseph was one of the men who had gone to the Sioux Camp.

"Take this," Kier said, handing one end of his rope to Billy as he tied the other around his waist.

Billy belayed the lines, using the base of a

mushroom-shaped granite rock, as Kier did the same using a tree before he disappeared over the edge. Brent and the others stood at the precipice with the onlookers, watching in consternation.

Kier rappelled down to the wagon and used his knife to tear open the canopy so he could enter without putting additional pressure on the wagon's unsteady balance. The family's two small children had been riding in the bay of the wagon but were now flung against the family's cargo, which was strewn against the front entrance to the wagon. The boy stared, wide-eyed with fear. He was silent, but his younger sister was crying. When she saw Kier coming toward her, she tried to stand.

"Stay there," he said gently, doing his best to calm them. "Don't move until I tell you. Joseph?" he hollered, trying to gauge the father's location. Or whether he was alive.

"Prudence and I are here," he said from beyond where Kier could see. "This won't hold much longer." His voice was thin.

Fiona could hear the woman sobbing.

"I'm going to take your children up, then come back for you. Is there any way to cut your animals loose?"

"The entire harness, but not the animals," Joseph said. "Only thing we're hanging onto is the harness." His voice began to waver.

"Billy, take up the slack," Kier yelled over his shoulder. "About ten feet." When the rope was taut, he reached for the children. He started with the boy, who was about five years old. "Hang on to me and don't let go, no matter what happens."

The boy nodded and proceeded to wrap himself so tightly around Kier that he had trouble breathing. Easing the boy's desperate hold, Kier reached for the toddler. But she was frightened, so her reaction was to move away from him. Red-faced, she screamed and hit at him.

"Come on," Kier urged, offering his hand. He didn't want to risk a temper tantrum, which could be enough movement to make the wagon fall to the bottom of the ravine.

"I need help," Billy said, straining to hold the weight of Kier and the boy. Horace and Gideon moved to add their weight to the rope.

Suddenly the wagon shifted, sliding another six inches down the hill. Silenced by her mother's screams, the girl stared at Kier. In the moment before she began to cry again, Kier snatched her.

"Now, Billy!" he yelled.

"Don't let go," he said firmly to the boy as they began their ascent. The girl fought Kier every inch of the way, kicking and squirming and hitting at him.

Brent and Silas knelt at the edge and lifted the children to safety, one at a time. Hope embraced them and led them to where Fiona stood with her arms around Caleb and Maggie. She knelt to assess the children, who seemed unharmed.

Fiona closed her eyes. How easily they could have been killed. How easily their parents could still die. And Kier—

"Send down another rope," Kier ordered as he rappelled down the uneven wall a second time. "I'm coming for you," he yelled to the Clarks. "If the wagon falls, can you hold on to anything?"

Suffocating in their harnesses, the dangling oxen had begun their death struggle. That was all the wagon needed to slide another eighteen inches down the mountain. The onlookers screamed. Fiona felt ill.

"I'm coming around the wagon," Kier said. "Need that rope," he growled loudly to those on the trail above.

There was a scramble to find another rope in one of the wagons at the top of the trail, secure it around the rock, and send it down to Kier.

The sounds of braying oxen, a howling toddler, and a traveler who kept saying, "Oh my God, oh my God," in varying volumes, echoed around the canyon. Fiona's mouth went dry with worry. She found it hard to swallow.

The second rope reached Kier as he began to step down the earthen wall beside what was once the top of the family's wagon. He stopped when he was level with the couple. When Kier met Joseph's eyes he knew something was wrong. His leg was tangled in the harness straps. It appeared broken. Kier could tell that every time the wagon slid it made the situation worse.

"If I tie a rope around you, and people above pull you up the hill, can you do it alone?" Kier asked Prudence.

"No, no, no," she sobbed. "I can't move. I can't move."

When her agitation grew, so did the animals'. The two oxen pinned against the wall bellowed and jerked their heads.

"Your children are safe at the top. They need you."

Kier watched as Joseph tried to console Prudence and win her cooperation. From where she was positioned, and the level of her fear, Kier knew she would not be able to jump to safety when the wagon fell.

He edged toward her with the rope in his hand. "I'm going to tie the rope around you," he said, trying to sound calm as the wagon began to slide. "Your husband needs my help, and then we'll all ascend the wall together." Behind him, Joseph cried out in pain. "Lie still," Kier said to Prudence. Her grip on the harness blanched her knuckles. "I'll take care of you."

Working quickly, he managed to secure the rope around her midriff. The wagon slid a discernible amount, then stopped, slid then stopped. The oxen gave up their struggle.

Kier took his hunting knife out of his sheath and cut away the straps around Joseph's leg. Kier was leaning over to be sure he had released it when the wagon slid out from under them, smashing against the rocks as it crashed to the bottom of the ravine. The growing crowd above them screamed.

Brent and Silas struggled with their rope when Prudence became dead weight.

Fiona ran to the edge and peered over, fearing the worst.

Prudence had fainted and was hanging limply. Kier was pressed against the wall, his body the only thing keeping Joseph from following his wagon into the ravine.

"Bring her up, then send the rope back, unless you can get me another one—now."

Brent and Silas strained to pull Prudence to safety. Several moved to help them, including Fiona. The tension on the rope increased sharply when Prudence came to. Like her daughter, she fought and screamed, howling all the while.

"You're going to be all right," Silas said to her, hoping to quiet her panic. When they eased the woman onto the trail, Fiona knelt to check her for injuries while a third rope reached Kier. The woman's children ran to her, and she grew still at last when she held them.

"You're almost safe," Kier said, securing the rope around Joseph. Every tendon in his body strained to keep the man pinned against the mountainside. His body shook with tension. His muscles quivered with fatigue.

"Everything we owned was in there."

"We'll walk to the bottom to see what we can salvage. You ready?"

Joseph nodded.

Kier could see he was in a lot of pain.

"Bring us up!" he yelled. "Both lines together at the same speed."

Many joined to pull Kier and Joseph to safety. Even Caleb added his strength to the line that held Kier. Gideon pulled with him.

"Thank you for saving my family," Joseph said.

"We'll get you to Doc straight away so he can tend to your leg. Your wife and children are unharmed."

Tears fell down the man's dusty cheeks.

The crowd cheered when Kier and Joseph were pulled to safety. Fiona met Kier's eyes before tending to Joseph's injured leg. They registered a sense of mutual relief.

"I need your knife," she told Kier. With it she cut open Joseph's pant leg to expose his injuries. It looked to be a clean break; there was no bone protruding from his skin. Although he was bleeding heavily from where the harness straps had cut his flesh, he was not bleeding from an artery. Fiona knew the man was a good candidate for Doc's healing.

"Does someone have a broad plank to stabilize his leg? To carry him down the hill to Doc without causing him additional pain." She applied pressure to the man's deeper wounds to quell the bleeding and secured a tourniquet.

Two men stepped forward with an old door someone had brought for their new home. Prudence and her children followed him into the valley.

Clare embraced her husband and son, holding them close. "Come," she invited, beckoning Fiona and the children to join them. All six stood with their arms locked around each other, thankful for the grace that united them. Kier took Fiona in his arms and held her meaningfully.

"Thanks for pulling with the other men," Kier said to Caleb, ruffling his hair.

The boy glowed with pride.

Jake and his cronies had climbed the hill and arrived at the scene in time to see Kier and Fiona's embrace.

"What happened here?" he barked. "Why have you stopped bringing the wagons down the hill?"

Twenty people spoke at once, telling him all that had transpired. Jake gave Kier a hard look. He didn't like it when Kier was heroic.

"The rest of the wagons are going to have to go back up the hill and find another way down," Kier said, assuming his role as wagon master.

"Why?" Jake demanded.

"Nothing left for the wagons," Kier said, pointing to the damaged trail. A man could pass beside the gaping wound in the mountainside, but a wagon could not. "Brent," he said, "start moving these wagons back up the hill. I'll meet you later to find another route into the valley."

"I don't want to divide the company," Jake said.

"No way around it. Let's get these four wagons down the hill. You all can set camp. We need fresh meat, too. You and Billy can organize a hunting party."

Kier and Fiona exchanged a glance before everyone moved to carry out their orders. Their interaction was not lost on Jake.

****

Jake had given himself the task of guarding camp while Billy led a hunting party. The men returned with assorted small game and two dozen fish. Fiona coordinated meal preparation with the other women. They set up a central fire where several pots were cooking at once, among them fried trout, rabbit stew, and soup made with the meat of an animal she could not identify. At least it wasn't squirrel.

It was strange not having Kier in camp. Billy was capable of running the company in Kier's absence, but still Fiona missed knowing Kier was nearby.

She had put the children to bed but knew Caleb was awake, reading by lantern light. She sat by the fire to be alone with her thoughts but grew distracted when she looked around the circle. It was odd to see the camp arranged this way, with so many wagons missing from the enclosure.

There was a lively game of poker being played across the camp. A few feet away, two women sat knitting in rocking chairs. Fiona considered sewing a bit more of her muslin skirt but was too tired to begin a new project before bed.

"It's been quite a day," Jake said, joining her.

"It has. The Clarks lost their wagon, but they're alive. Doc said Joseph's leg will mend."

"I want you to know I have asked another woman to be my wife," he said smugly.

Fiona turned to him with surprise. "I'm happy for you."

"I had planned to propose to you, but when I saw Moran's indiscretions with Caroline Gillespie and her pursuit of his attentions, I was forced to intervene."

"She's a beautiful gentlewoman," Fiona said, unsure how well she was concealing her relief.

"I wanted to convey this formally, so you do not mistake my lack of attention for anything more than propriety with my intended. I will no longer be seen speaking with an unwed woman who is not my wife."

"Of course," she replied.

"Well then, goodnight, Mrs. Lenihan."

When he left, she stared into the fire. This was not what she had expected.

****

It took three days for the rest of the company to find a passable route to the mountain valley where Billy and his travelers were camped. In their time spent waiting, Billy took the initiative to organize daily hunting parties. He figured the other travelers would be hungry when they arrived. And the company could never have too much fresh meat on hand.

Kier and Brent arrived midday, which allowed for time to rest and water the animals while Billy's part of the company broke camp. That afternoon Kier led them on a winding route through a series of channels cut in the earth.

The walls of the canyons were lined with pine trees, which made travel fragrant. The air felt cool and crisp. Dramatic, snow-covered peaks came into view now and then, when the pine-covered mountains allowed for a sliver of beauty. Kier called it rough country, but it was among the most beautiful Fiona had seen.

They spent their nights in cool mountain valleys before descending still farther the next day. At last they entered the Salt Lake Valley, a vast expanse that appeared when the trail flattened at the base of the mountains. Before them an enormous lake shimmered in the sunlight. The lake was on the scale of the valley; Fiona could not see the other side.

"Whoa," Caleb breathed when he took in the view. As with many points on the trail, the landscape before them was like nothing they had ever seen. "Is that the ocean?"

"No. But Mr. Moran warned us it's salty, like the sea, and that we'll need to draw water from the surrounding streams."

Kier pushed the company hard once they reached the valley, wanting to put as much ground as possible behind them before making camp. It was a long day that would have left the travelers spent and irritable, but the breathtaking mountain views held their interest.

Rising more than nine thousand feet above them to the west, the Oquirrh Mountains appeared to touch the ground where the lake began. Kier explained the Paiutes named these mountains the "oquirrh" or "shining" for their appearance. Standing behind them at nearly twelve thousand feet were the stunning Wasatch Mountains, which Kier said meant "of many waters." The range glowed red-orange in the fading sunlight.

The travelers were impressed to know they had descended into Utah Territory through the Wasatch Mountains, and even more impressed to hear they would not be crossing the Oquirrh Mountains. Their travel would take them around the southern portion of the lake, then due west across the Great Salt Lake Desert.

By now, Kier did not need to urge people to fill every container they could carry with fresh water. Fiona purchased two more casks at a trading post. She wanted to ensure adequate water for her family and be in a position to offer some to others who might be in need. If there was one thing her relatively empty wagon could offer, it was storage for extra drinking water.

"It's so beautiful here," Fiona said when Kier passed her wagon. "I don't want to go any farther. If I could wake up every morning to the sun on the Oquirrh Mountains and watch the Wasatch Mountains at sunset, I would be very blessed."

"The Mormons feel that way too," he said, easing Kildare to a stop.

"Who are the Mormons?"

"They settled this valley about ten years ago. Fled religious persecution back East."

"Do they welcome non-Mormons?" she asked, taking in the stunning view.

"If you'll consider joining them. They call us non-Mormons Gentiles. There's been trouble between the U.S. Government and the Mormons. It will come to a head one of these days. It's better if you're far away from it."

"They're fortunate to have found this valley. It's the most beautiful place I've ever seen. Is California beautiful like this?"

"Parts of it. California has a different majesty. Several of them, in fact. It depends where you want to build your farm."

"I haven't any idea."

"You'll know it when you see it." He tipped his hat and continued up the column, checking in with the settlers as they made camp.

Buoyed by their progress, the company set aside time to enjoy the evening. Doc opened another of his bottles of Château Lafite Rothschild, which he shared with Fiona, the Morans, and the Whittakers. Two bottles remained: one to enjoy along the trail and the other to consume on their final night together as a company.

There was music and dancing, several card games, a knitting circle, a quilting circle, and an old man who told a group of children ghost stories. Caleb and Maggie sat with the children, wide-eyed as they listened to a tale about a Forty-Niner who now haunted the gold mines in California. Fiona decided it was a good night to continue work on her muslin skirt.

She sewed until her fingers grew stiff. With a sigh of accomplishment, she set aside her skirt and went outside to take in some air before bed.

The full moon hung in the sky like a silver dollar, immense and orange where it sat above the horizon. It cast bright light over the land beneath it, giving brilliance to objects accustomed to shadow. A breeze stirred the air, perfuming it with the smell of salt marshes and goosefoot, hinting to the coming end of summer.

Fiona sat alone on the perimeter of camp, away from the fire. She listened to a chorus of wolves and stared into the night, sorting out her thoughts. She was tired of this journey and eager to settle in a place called home.

Plaintive cries sang in the night, arching across the sky like an aurora, first one, then the others. She wondered at their meaning, whether the wolves spoke to each other as a family, or called to one another in warning or encouragement about prey or nearby men or the beauty of the moon. Over time, she had grown accustomed to the primal song and knew she would miss it when they reached home.

Kier joined her. He cupped his hand to the wind and lit a cigarette.

"You no longer fear the wolves?" he asked. Moonlight turned his exhaled smoke to a shimmering fog.

"No. Their cry reminds me of the old music. To my ears it is a lament, a keening. But they can't be so mournful all the time."

"Not so the Irish."

"We are a melancholy lot."

"The Plains Indians view the wolf as a fellow hunter. They are fascinating creatures. And misunderstood, much like other hunters." Kier leaned forward on his knee as he spoke.

"Jake has proposed to Caroline Gillespie," she said.

"That should come as good news."

"It does," she said definitively. "They are a good

match."

He stayed with her the length of time it took him to smoke his cigarette. Together they contemplated the full moon.

"Billy did a fine job these last few days. I've been thinking of asking him to work for me when we reach California."

"Work for you?"

"On my ranch. I've got my hand in a few things," he added cryptically.

"You have a ranch?" she turned to look at him with surprise.

"Where the house is."

"What made you choose to live in California?" she asked, curious as to why a wanderer had selected that place.

"It's where life brought me."

"Have you thought of living elsewhere?" she asked, studying him.

"I live elsewhere most of the time."

The tension between them was more noticeable in the silence that followed. Kier finished his cigarette and crushed the smoldering butt with the sole of his boot.

"You could settle down," she said, looking up at him. "Make a home at your ranch."

"On the day they bury me."

Chapter 22

"Listen up," Kier said, addressing the company during what would have been their nooning had they been on the trail and not camped by the Great Salt Lake. He had scheduled the rest of the day to prepare for the desert and mountain portions of their travel, which he assured them would be difficult.

"Tomorrow we begin our desert crossing. Bring as much fresh water as you can stow. We will not see a water source of any size for two hundred miles or about two weeks. After that we cross only small creeks and streams until we reach the Humboldt River, which should more properly be named a creek.

"In the coming weeks you may be forced to leave some of your possessions—even your wagons and animals—in order to finish the journey. If there is anything in your wagon you can do without, I encourage you to discard it now.

"We will follow the Humboldt River until it fades into the desert at a place known as the Humboldt Sink in the Forty Mile Desert. This is the most desolate stretch, filled with sand, salt, and alkali flats.

"If your animals drink the water, they will die. If you drink the water, you will die. At the end of the Forty Mile Desert is the Truckee River. We'll camp there to restore our spirits and fill our bellies with fresh water and salmon."

As Fiona listened, she drew Caleb and Maggie to her. Kier's instructions made her stomach crawl with what she imagined were the creatures called lizards. Yes, surely that was a tail that swept across her belly on the inside, followed by the scrape of its tiny claws. She shuddered at the image of the desert beasts consuming her from within. But she had come this far. There was no turning back now. Seeing the elephant was out of the question.

"When we reach the western end of the desert, we begin our ascent of the Sierra Nevada. Travel in the mountains is equally rigorous. We need to cross the mountains before October fifteenth. Otherwise we'll face mountain snows."

He paused a moment to allow the group to absorb all he had told them. Hearing "desert" and "snow" in almost the same sentence seemed incomprehensible.

"This afternoon I encourage you to lay in water, feed, jerky, blankets, and other supplies. To preserve your animals, you'll want to lighten their loads. Be sure you have something to cover your feet. The desert is hot during the day but cool at night. Assess the sturdiness of your wagons. Secure more lumber and spare axles now because there won't be any available on the trail—nor will there be trees to build new ones.

"Think of your crossing the desert as an ocean crossing. You must be self-sufficient until you reach the next port, which will be the resources found in the Sierra Nevada. You cannot rely on your neighbors to offer much help on this crossing, because the rigors of the journey will spare no one. Billy, Brent, Horace, and I will be available to help you with any last-minute preparations. Good luck."

An ocean crossing. Fiona liked that image, for it was one she understood.

Exhausted from refitting her wagon for the journey, Fiona turned in early. Nerves kept her from sleep, but she decided it was better to lie in wait for sleep than linger by the fire. She had taken to heart the wisdom of walking beside her draft animals rather than driving them from the bench, to spare them unnecessary strain. Since she had ridden most of the way, walking the better part of twenty miles a day would be an adjustment. But she would adapt, just as she had to every new turn in this adventure. She had to.

****

The trail kept them within view of the lake for three days, until they lost sight of it behind a small mountain range. Non-potable though it was, there was something unsettling about leaving behind the only vision of water that wasn't a mirage.

Fiona found Kier's comparison of the desert with the sea odd but apt, for the desert was a sea of salt as surely as the ocean was a sea of water. There was nowhere to go but the distant port, and there was no stopping along the way to rest. Boots and hooves cut through the expanse of salt and alkali like the rudder of Stanley Cushing's ship had cut through the waves of the Atlantic. Where the earth was not baked solid, their footprints became their wake.

Fiona's feet burned. Every day she tried to walk a little farther than the last, walking beside Daisy and Balthazar, the lead oxen, offering encouragement in the form of gentle words and even a song now and then. Sometimes Caleb walked beside her, wanting to feel as grown up as some of the older boys who walked with their families. Maggie would not be left out, but her trek ended the same way every day, with Fiona carrying her.

It occurred to Fiona she may have made a tactical error in not purchasing a pair of flat men's boots in Salt Lake City. Her worn but dainty Cushing boots were going to be hard-pressed to carry her all the way to California.

It was the flattest stretch of the trail so far. They could see the horizon until it became lost in the heat, its dividing line blurred in a vibrating wrinkle where sand became sky. The land looked like a bowl of eggs before they had been properly blended, a tangle of yellow streaks and albumen. Visions that appeared to be hills came and went until a new mound of earth seemed to approach, growing a little larger with each mile.

The changing topography was welcome, for its steady march helped the travelers mark time. As they neared what was a small mountain range, they were surprised to see a great white stripe across the desert. Salt.

An entire field of salt. Acres of the white crystals covered the ground like snow or hail that must have fallen only minutes before they passed. It crunched like gravel beneath their feet.

The eleven-thousand-foot peaks of the Ruby Mountains held their interest for two days. Patches of snow were still visible, despite the late summer date. Or was it snow? Alkali? Barren canyons separated small mountain ranges, broken by arroyos and alkali flats miles wide.

At sunset Fiona stood outside the circle of wagons, admiring the play of light on one of the mountains. It shone pink-gold at the close of day, a pile of rock and useless soil made to look like the finest treasure when nature cast its eye upon it. She turned to see Kier approach.

"It's a beautiful view," she said, returning her attention to the sight. She didn't want to miss a moment of its fleeting glory.

"'Tis," he agreed, but he was looking at her when he said it, admiring the way the same sunlight turned her face pink-gold.

"We made it another day," she said, unaware of his ardor.

"We did."

"Are we crossing well?" she asked, shifting her focus to him.

"So far."

"When does it start?" she asked, holding his gaze.

"Soon."

"How will we know?" she pressed.

"You'll see things that people cast aside on the spot. Whole wagons with one broken wheel. Trunks and beds and chests of drawers. Books. Animal carcasses. Graves."

"I feel we are stronger than that."

"For now," he nodded, but his tone was dubious.

Fiona was having a hard time engaging him in conversation, so she cut it short. "Well, I've got to get some sewing done," she said, turning to leave.

"Sewing?" he questioned, his interest at last piqued.

"Yes," she said proudly. "Sewing."

****

"Humbug." That's what Fiona overhead one of the

travelers say when they reached the much-anticipated Humboldt River. Indeed, Humbug River was more fitting. Or even Humbug Stream. Or Puddle. Crossing it would prove a drowning hazard to none.

The tradeoff for traveling along the banks of this meager water source was travel that took them on the most convoluted route imaginable. The river wound its way elaborately through narrow canyons and grassless flats. At times the water in the river seemed to stand still, gathering alkali as it baked in the sun. It was ugly, smelly, and downright worthless. No wonder Kier had encouraged them to bring their own water and feed.

Here was where Kier's promise came true. Their progress of fifteen or more miles a day slipped to fewer than ten. Every new sunrise brought a new misfortune.

Draft animals began to fail. Fresh carcasses joined those strewn across the desert, their remaining flesh picked clean by predators and their bones bleached white by the sun. It got to where Fiona could judge how long the remains had been there by how well they blended into their environs.

When the canyons were at their narrowest, they drove through the Humboldt River. This worked until a wheel hit a rock at an awkward angle, shattering the axle and bringing the company's single-file travel to a halt. Or until the miserable water swelled the fragile wood in the wheels, causing them to break apart.

Every other day a family was forced to abandon their wagon and continue on foot or turn what was left of their wagon into a cart pulled by dying beasts or men. Frustration followed mishap. People grew weary in mind and body, with the most unforgiving part of the desert yet to come.

Fiona was walking nearly all day now. Hope was not, her ankles swelling as badly as her belly in the heat. When Fiona walked beside her team, Maggie rode with Hope. Fiona did not want to leave her to ride in their wagon because she had seen firsthand the damage a wheel could do to a small child. If she wasn't riding in the Lenihan wagon, neither was Maggie. The four-year-old was too young to leave untended, but Caleb was grown up enough to sit quietly in the bay of their wagon. On the days when his legs grew tired, he sat with a book, watching the Morans or Hope follow but never grow any closer.

Fiona did not understand how he could read while they traveled. She grew ill sitting in the back of a moving wagon if she could not see the horizon. Just like a ship, she reasoned. As there was seasickness, there was desert sickness. People vomited from heat, thirst, alkali, dust, and salt.

Gradually, the journey became too much for some. Like their animals, they fell where they stood and were buried nearly on the spot. Their consolation was that there were so many other graves along the trail. Oddly, in the middle of the desert, few died alone.

Scattered possessions followed scattered graves. There were four-posted beds and breakfronts, rocking chairs and steamer trunks. One trunk had fallen on its side. Leaves of white blew across the desert, shining like glass in the sunlight. A tattered discard blew against Fiona's shoe. It was the page of a book.

Fiona realized part of someone's library was going to waste in the desert. When they stopped for nooning, she took a walk to find it. While a few books in the broken steamer trunk had been destroyed by the elements, the majority had not. She opened the lid to find volumes by Goethe, Dickens, Molière, Voltaire, Emerson, and Thoreau. Some were worn, as they had been treasured; others were nearly new.

The spine of a book of poetry by Walt Whitman cracked when she opened it. *Leaves of Grass*. Ironic find in a desert. She wondered what fate had befallen the owner of these books and doubted he would have been parted easily from this library.

The next days she found more books discarded along the trail, already being eaten by the desert. She reclaimed what she could, including two plays by Shakespeare, one about a king called Lear and another about a Scotsman called Macbeth. A copy of *The Tempest* was caught among the greasewood. By the time the company reached the base of the Sierra Nevada, Fiona had collected more than three dozen volumes.

While books were Fiona's prized item for scavenging, others in the company sorted through abandoned furniture, tools, and wagon parts. Everything was fair game in a land where the original owners would not return to claim their possessions.

Caleb kept count and recorded in his journal that along one seemingly endless stretch of the trail lay sixty-three abandoned wagons that were beyond salvaging. More than a thousand oxen were dead or dying. As the company passed, the doomed oxen looked at them sadly, foam dripping from their parched mouths. Some of them had been whipped bloody by their masters, whose frustration was applied to beasts who could work no more. Without their oxen, if a wagon couldn't be converted to a handcart or modified for a horse to pull, it meant all the wagon's contents were lost. The finality of this juncture was difficult to accept, so far from either end of the desert.

"It feels funny, scavenging the remnants of other people's lives," Fiona confessed to Clare, who joined them with her plate of food. Behind them, Maggie intoned a hymn.

"Better a lover of books gathers them than the desert, who won't appreciate them at all."

"How's Gideon holding up?"

"He's an iron-jawed hunk of jerky. Like his son, the rigors of the desert have left him unfazed."

"And your team?"

"Straining a bit, but all right. A far cry from those poor beasts we've seen today. Makes your heart ache to see them suffer. You want to give them water, but it will only prolong the inevitable. A shotgun would do them a favor but Kier said we can't waste our ammunition with so much of the journey still ahead of us.

"Kier has encouraged me to add one trunk to the desert refuse, but I cannot. It contains a silver tea service and a set of silverware that were gifts to Gideon for his service. I cannot abandon something that represents the better part of his life. But if the team shows signs of failing, I will need to leave something behind. I hope that day never comes."

"We have room in our wagon," Fiona offered.

"Thank you. Before journey's end I may accept your offer."

At night the temperature dropped sharply. On top of their sunburns, the air gave them a chill. The skin of the buffalo that first had Maggie and then Fiona in its sights kept them toasty. Many travelers had opted to sleep on the desert floor, but Fiona wanted to keep her family as far away from desert creatures as possible. They would make do in their wagon, surrounded by their supply of water and feed that dwindled even as their library grew.

While the travelers spent their days walking through alkali dust and sand that was often inches thick, the difficulties of travel were compounded by even a few drops of rain. One day they got just that in the form of an odd little squall that blew across the desert on the heels of a dust devil. It was enough rain to turn the alkali to mud and bring white streaks of salt to the surface of the earth.

Exhausted, the teams struggled to make their way through the muck. Fiona encouraged Daisy and Balthazar, pulling on them as she strained to lift her caked boots from the stew of minerals.

All it took was a misstep here and a stumble there, and Fiona was face down in the watery slime. Even with the aid of two men to regain her feet, Fiona looked as if she had been rolling in mud like a pig. The mess covered her face and her dress, front and back.

It was quite a sight.

After that, she pulled out the lumber to give the oxen stronger footing. Others added their boards to the trail, and everyone who followed had an easier way across this stretch. At nooning, when Fiona walked back to retrieve her lumber, she nearly collided with Caroline, who stood before her in typical perfection. Her lavender silk dress was cool and crisp. The contrast between the two women could not have been more pronounced.

"What happened to you?" Caroline asked with her noxious laugh. "Mud all over your only dress," she said with a patronizing slap. "I would offer you one of mine, but as you can see, I'm far more delicate."

Fiona was surprised by her sudden urge to push Caroline into the same puddle she had crawled out of only an hour earlier. It was true. The mud was now caked on her only dress. The lone option was to let it dry, then chip off the plaster. Or don one of the elaborate dresses that sat idly in her trunk.

"Thank you all the same," Fiona replied, shifting the muddy lumber in her arms to balance the load.

"Oh, there you are, Kier!" Caroline said.

Fiona could not bear to look at him. Instead she trudged on, hoping to do so unnoticed.

Suddenly her load was lightened. She turned to see Kier lift the back end of her lumber.

"Please don't say anything," she said, hoping her ridiculous tears would not show. She had no idea where they came from.

"You need to wash that off your skin or it will burn."

She nodded.

When they reached her wagon, he tried a little humor.

"You have to admit, today your dress garnered more attention than Caroline's."

She turned to look at him with a warning that gradually turned to laughter. "I suppose I am quite a sight."

"Next time, ask for help when the passing gets rough. It wasn't nearly so bad forty wagons earlier. Stay right there," he instructed before leaning into her wagon. He emerged with a dampened cloth that he used to wash the alkali off her face and neck.

His touch was tender as he caressed the curve of her cheek and the neckline of her dress with only a cloth to separate his hand from her skin. She met his eyes and knew he felt it too. At last she looked away, fluttering her eyelashes when the cloth touched her lips.

"Give me your hands," he said, washing first one, then the other.

It was sweet torture standing this close to him, experiencing the intimacy of his touch and knowing it would not last.

"The rest I leave to you," he said, putting the cloth in her hands and closing her fingers around it.

She watched him walk away, certain she would never feel for another man what she felt for him.

A lone peal of laughter drew her attention.

"Oh, Fiona," Hope laughed, taking in the sight of her alkali-ravaged friend. She tried to speak but could only clap both hands over her mouth, trying not to laugh but succeeding only in laughing all the harder.

"Thank you so much," Fiona said with mock sarcasm.

Hope burst into an uncontrollable fit of giggles. "I'm sorry, but you should see yourself," she said, her words lost to laughter once again.

Clare arrived to see what the commotion was, then stifled laughter.

"You too?" Fiona said with a mock scold.

The three women gave in to their laughter, Fiona at last joining them. Clare stepped forward to brush away a layer of dust that had settled over the mud on Fiona's dress.

"You can't touch me unless you're wearing gloves," she said. "Kier said so. Otherwise you'll burn your hands."

"What does Kier know of brushing dust and mud off ladies?" Clare asked.

"Enough to wash my face and hands free of it," Fiona replied, surprising herself with the emotional shriek that followed, somewhere between laughter and tears.

"How's that skirt coming?" Clare asked, considering Fiona's dress a total loss.

"Let's just say I need to make this dress last a few more days." Fiona could not help it. She snorted a chuckle that became a belly laugh that Hope and finally Clare joined. Fiona had lost all control. It felt wonderful.

****

The Indians who lived along this part of the trail were not known to be hostile to travelers and liked to trade with them. But they were known to steal cattle. The company could see small groups of Piute and Shoshone from time to time, but they never came within five hundred yards of each other. Kier increased the watch around the livestock, just in case. The company's remaining two hundred and twenty head of cattle could be a temptation.

Occasionally they came upon springs in the desert, which provided a source of fresh water, although in quantities suitable only for refreshing the thirst of travelers. There was nowhere near enough to refill casks or sooth the animals' foaming mouths.

Where the trail allowed, Kier organized the company in three parallel columns to help reduce the dirt that caked the people and animals that traveled at the rear of the company. But in many places the trail was narrow and could accommodate only one wagon. That meant miserable going for the last wagons in the column.

To Fiona's wonder, in the middle of the desert they had to stop for a crossing over Emigrant Pass. As they had at other points in their journey, the heaviest wagons were dragged downhill to prevent them from losing control on the descent. The wait in the desert sun was made more tolerable by the abundant Emigrant Springs, which had enough water to reward the tired animals for their hard days' work.

On a warm September evening, they celebrated Gideon's seventieth birthday at a place called Stony Point. Fiona surprised him with a cake, of sorts, a sugary confection baked in a Dutch oven.

It brought a rare smile to his lips. Under his sunburn, he nearly blushed from all the attention. When Caleb and Maggie presented him with handmade gifts, Fiona recognized Kier's elusive dimples on Gideon's face. He graciously accepted Caleb's carved wooden lizard-like creature and Maggie's drawing framed with dried flowers as if they were the most important gifts he had ever received.

At some level, Fiona wondered if they weren't. A gift from the heart of the child has a special magic. Fiona surmised that, before Caleb and Maggie, Kier was the last child who had bestowed on him such a gift. She returned his smile when he cast her an appreciative nod. With his bushy white eyebrows and a twinkle of glee, Gideon Moran looked like a leprechaun.

Two babies were born in the middle of the desert.

Fiona admired their bleak start in a land nearly devoid of color. Their howls reminded everyone that new life could spring forth in the barrenness they traveled day on day.

Fiona assisted Doc with both deliveries. As she watched the tiny faces wrinkle with anger at the jarring reality of the world into which they had been born, it occurred to her these children were a reminder of the life that was all around them. It was there to be discovered, beneath the layers of alkali.

When they wriggled and pumped their small fists in the uncertainty of the desert air, Fiona could not help but smile. Swaddled in blankets until all that showed were their little faces, Fiona cradled them against her before nestling them in their mothers' waiting arms. Being blessed with new life was a happy contrast to the foreignness that surrounded them.

A few days later, a fast-moving wagon train gave Kier word of an Indian attack at Stony Point where five emigrants had been killed. Kier decided it would have been prudent to keep that news to himself, but Jake spread it around camp. Of course, this stirred up the company and gave them something else to worry about.

What Jake did not share was the suspicion that the so-called Indians who had attacked the settlers were not Indians at all, but a gang of white men dressed and painted as Indians, bent on thieving from passing travelers. This would have been new information to most of the company.

The going became markedly more difficult at that point. At the eastern edge of the Forty Mile Desert, the number of cases of scurvy grew by the day. Young and old were not spared its cruelty.

First came weakness and exhaustion, which everyone had in some measure, making it problematic to discern illness from health. Then came body aches and bruises, which were common ailments. Only when the afflicted began to bleed from their swollen, purple gums, at their fingertips, and from old scars, could Doc make his diagnosis.

Ascorbic acid was his cure, which he administered liberally, so liberally he realized it was one item in his inventory he had not brought enough of. He ran out just as the company was entering the portion of the desert where the Sierra Nevada first came into view. The last obstacle of their journey.

Kier assured him they were now thirty miles away from a trading post that stocked fresh oranges. Fiona wanted to cry at seeing the bruised and bleeding faces of children and old men and women, each of them suffering all the more in the relentless desert.

The mountains came into clearer view with each new mile. As if to taunt them, they loomed larger while the travelers grew more desperate. Every day was a struggle in the sun and sand. Rather than look toward the distant Truckee River, all they could do was stare at the imposing peaks.

Sheer walls of rock climbed straight up from the desert floor, forming what appeared to be an impenetrable fortress that extended for miles in either direction, beyond where the eye could see. The travelers were disheartened, knowing in some cases they had dragged themselves across the desert only to meet such a formidable barrier.

"We're crossing those?" Caleb asked Kier when he rode past where Fiona and Caleb were walking, stroking Daisy and Balthazar, trying to keep their determination strong for the last miles of desert.

"We are."

"They're so big," he said, awed by the towering faces of rock.

"Only as big as the desert we've nearly crossed."

"If Finn MacCool were here, he could carry us across in a single day."

"If you can talk him into it, I know of a number of our fellow travelers who would be the happier for it," Kier said warmly.

One of the effects of desert travel was a hard night's sleep. Most nights Fiona was already dreaming by the time she pulled herself into her wagon. The heat and the noise from the sick and restless would often awaken her, but she could return to her hard sleep with no effort. It was from such a sleep that Caleb's frightened cries awakened her.

"Mother!" he screamed.

She turned up the lantern to see blood running from both sides of his mouth, coming from gums that ached to hold his teeth. Trying not to reveal her panic, she wiped away the crimson stream. Tears threatened to fall. Her child had scurvy, and Doc had no more antidote.

"I'm so sorry," she whispered, reaching to dip a fresh cloth in water.

"Am I going to die?" he asked, tears running from the corners of his eyes into his dusty hair.

She could control her emotions no more. Her lower lip quivered when she spoke. "I'm going to find Mr. Moran to see if he has anything else we can use. We're almost through the desert. Mr. Moran said there's a trading post there where we can buy fresh oranges."

"It hurts," he said, fighting off a whimper.

"Why didn't you tell me?" she asked gently. Emotion made her eyes sparkle like jewels.

"I didn't want to scare you."

Had he even breathed of feeling unwell two days earlier she could have gotten some of the last of Doc's ascorbic acid. Now it was too late. There was nothing she could do but comfort him and hope the bleeding did not begin to show in his diarrhea.

She had seen the worst cases of scurvy in the company, heaps of palsied bones that bled from their eyes. Before they reached the Truckee River, she knew a handful of souls would be lost to complications of scurvy. She had never dreamed one of them might be her son.

Maggie sat up to watch what was unfolding in their wagon. Her eyes were wide at the show of tears on her mother's and brother's cheeks. The cloth Fiona used to pat Caleb's face was stained with blood.

Fiona took a break from soothing Caleb to gather Maggie in her arms and ease her fears. She rocked her daughter, holding her closely. Caleb watched them as a fresh stream rolled from his eyes into his hair.

"Do you think you can stay alone while I go get Doc?" she asked, awaiting each child's response. It took everything in her to keep fear from showing on her face. Her children looked to her to assure them things would be all right. In this case, her heart ached with the knowledge she could not. "I'll be right back. Promise."

Unfortunately, Doc was not as skilled at hiding the truth. He had nothing left to treat scurvy.

Libby climbed from the wagon to embrace Fiona

as she took the news. After all the people she had helped along the way, in living or dying, it seemed cruel to think her own child could be taken from her. Tears welled in her eyes, but she refused to let them fall. Caleb was going to survive this, she reasoned. He had to.

"Maybe Kier has something we haven't considered yet," Doc said. The weariness in his voice matched the weariness in his eyes.

Fiona wrapped her shawl more tightly around her and set out to find Kier. It was he who found her. Awakened by the sound of voices, he rose to investigate and met her in the center of camp. He knew by the way she was walking something was wrong. Tight and hunched with worry, she nearly burst into tears when he stepped into her path.

"Do you have anything for scurvy?" she asked, doing her best to keep her emotions in check. Her knuckles were white where her hand clasped her shawl.

"No," he said quietly, ashamed he could not help her.

"It's Caleb," she cried. "And I'm afraid Maggie has it too. She hasn't been herself."

"How bad is he?"

"He's bleeding from his nose and mouth. His tears are red."

"At first light I'll ride ahead to the trading post along the Truckee and bring what oranges I can carry."

"I hate seeing him suffer. It reminds me what I have done in bringing them out here," she said, wiping her tears.

"We can rest at the Truckee River. Now let's go take a look at Caleb."

Fiona struggled to keep her emotions at bay as Kier climbed into her wagon to visit with Caleb and Maggie. When she heard her daughter giggle, she knew Kier had done what she could not. She turned away and used her whole hand to wipe the damp streams from her face. Laughter that was a mixture of sorrow and relief followed when she heard Caleb say, "Yes, sir," to Kier.

Leaving the company in the capable hands of Billy and Brent, Kier departed early the next morning. He had wanted to bring another rider or two with him, but so many were weakened by the travel, if not scurvy, there were no grown men to accompany him. Each was needed to move the wagons west.

Conveying his promise to Fiona in a single glance, Kier sped away, riding toward the immense mountains that loomed before them. He returned with two dozen lemons and oranges. It was all the trading post had. The proprietor assured him there was a shipment due from California in the next few days. Kier prepaid for fruit from that shipment to see his people through to the end of their journey.

There was juice to give everyone afflicted a small drink—enough to keep them alive until they reached the Truckee River. Those who suffered had loose teeth hanging from their fragile gums, so drinking the juice was the only way for them to ingest the cure.

Fiona was so focused on tending her children she hardly noticed the last three days of travel, with driving winds that threatened to overturn the high-profile wagons and mounds of sand ankle-deep that slowed man and beast. When she wasn't encouraging Daisy and Balthazar to keep their step in the punishing conditions, she comforted her children with compresses and as much water as they would drink.

The night before they reached the Truckee River, Caleb took a turn for the worse. Fiona held him to her and rocked back and forth, trying to comfort a child whose every sinew ached for living. One more day and they would reach the river. One more day and there would be oranges and lemons aplenty to bring her son back.

"Mother?" Caleb said. His weakened voice cracked just above a whisper. "Do you think I've grown up? I don't cry now when I get hurt like I did when I was a little boy."

Fiona was glad her son could not see her glistening eyes. "You've become so grown up," she replied, kissing his forehead. "You're such a big boy, such a good boy. I'm so proud of you."

She stayed with him until he slept, then tucked blankets around her children before climbing outside to clear her mind of the hopelessness that threatened to consume her guilt.

The three-quarter moon looked different that night where it rose in a cloudless sky. An unusual haze hung around it like a veil, amplifying the reach of its beams and casting an almost surreal glow over the desert floor. But the reach of the silver fingers was not enough to touch Fiona, to bathe her in their serene light. She shivered, feeling impotent, knowing she had failed her children.

Kier laid his hand on her shoulder.

"What am I doing to my children?" she said forlornly. "Caleb's small body can't last much longer. I can't have brought him to this godforsaken place to die. Laboring in any field in Pennsylvania would have been better than this. I am hideous, watching them suffer because of me. And still they look to me as they always have, so trusting, waiting for me to deliver them from this. How can I face them when I have brought them such ruin?"

Kier stepped in front of her and took her hands in his. "You and Caleb and Maggie will live through this. Leave that to me. Your children need your conviction. Those who look up to you and rely on you need your conviction. I need your conviction."

She nodded her head in the darkness.

"Have you ever seen a rose window?" he asked, his gentle tone massaging her frayed nerves.

"In a church?"

Kier nodded.

"Once or twice." She thought back to the Catholic church on the side street in Philadelphia and recalled being bathed in multi-colored light when the sun passed behind the rose window. She had felt the arms of her loved ones around her, holding her, loving her. She had been warmed through, as if the hand of God had reached out to offer encouragement.

"The medieval pilgrims who traveled to Europe's great cathedrals were taught to focus on the window. It represents a well-ordered soul, with God in the center and other parts of our lives extending from this center. You are a God-fearing woman. Think on that during our last day in the desert tomorrow and on any day when the journey is difficult."

After a thoughtful silence, Fiona spoke. "Thank you. Your friendship has been the most significant in my life."

"You shall always have it."

Chapter 23

The aroma of salmon cooking over a wood fire wafted through the evening air. The cool waters from the Truckee River had a medicinal effect on the travelers, renewing them like wilted flowers touched with dew. The camp brimmed with good cheer when bellies were satiated with salmon and oranges.

"The Salmon of Knowledge," Caleb said, taking small bites of the meaty fish.

Fiona drew him to her in an embrace of relief that her son had recovered to where he was referencing folk tales.

A hunting party returned with seven deer, which made for a hearty venison supper. Fiona took the opportunity to don her self-made skirt and new yellow blouse. The warm color brought out her eyes and earned compliments from many, even Caroline. Well, maybe not a compliment.

"Where have you been hiding this sweet little dress?" she said. There was vinegar in her words. "It makes you look so—authentic," she said, finally settling on a descriptor. "I would take you to be a traveler on any street," she continued, fingering the eyelet trim on the sleeve of Fiona's blouse. There was a reiteration of an offer to work in Caroline's school for young ladies when Caroline learned Fiona had made her own skirt.

As there was salmon for dinner, there was salmon for breakfast on the day they began their ascent. One by one the wagons rumbled uphill, the desert floor growing distant below them. Negotiating switchbacks and hairpin turns, Fiona soon realized how slowly this crossing would progress.

The few heavy wagons that had made it this far were too weighty to make the first push uphill. Kier led the effort to remove the axles and wheels and hoist the laden boxes hundreds of feet up the cliff, using three separate pulleys manned by dozens of strong shoulders.

The mountain trail was rugged. Craggy and difficult in places, it made man and beast lame. Doc had his hands full stabilizing sprained ankles and bandaging bleeding shins.

In other places the trail was nothing but smooth rock. Teams of oxen slipped and fell to their knees. Their blood stained the rocks and soles of the travelers' shoes. By the end of the day, blood had been tracked everywhere until the footprints ran together in a single red stain.

Men drove their teams mercilessly, whipping them until they kept their footing. It was an abusive trek for the animals who, like the people, had already endured so much.

More belongings were discarded. All but the most infirm walked beside the wagons to minimize the load the teams had to pull. Fiona was surprised to see the number of heirlooms that littered the side of the mountain trail: wardrobes, dressers, hutches, china, even a dining room set with eight upholstered chairs.

There was a piano, now ruined by the elements. She wondered at the resignation their owners must have felt when they cast these treasures aside, having kept them during even the most unbearable of days in their desert crossings.

Fiona walked beside Balthazar, stroking the ox's face and offering words of encouragement she wasn't sure helped. But he was the alpha male on her team. She reasoned wherever Balthazar went, Daisy and the others would follow. She did not want to resort to beating her animals to urge them westward. What's more, she did not know how she would have explained such behavior to her children.

The air felt different as they climbed in elevation. Humidity soaked her thirsty skin. A cool wind blew from the high mountain passes, which remained out of view. It was a sharp contrast to the stale desert heat that had been their steady companion.

On their final turn west, Fiona looked back for the last glimpse she would have of the desert in which she had felt captive for forty days. It was as distant as the feel of the sun's burn on her neck. She was now where she had only gazed in wonder days earlier, climbing those impossibly large mountains that appeared as more than intimidating when viewed from the endless expanse of alkali.

At the end of the first steep incline, Fiona decided the mountains were not as impassable as they had appeared. But when an ox collapsed in its yoke and its companion tripped under the sudden shift in weight, breaking its leg, Fiona realized the error of her belief that the journey had become easier. It was true that people had become rejuvenated at the river's edge, but some of the animals were too worn to withstand the rigors of the mountain passes.

Men moved the dead and near-dead beasts out of the path, and a difficult decision followed for the family: what to keep. As was the custom on the desert floor, trunks, furniture, and even entire wagons were left behind when the oxen were no longer viable.

With each step Fiona and the oxen took in the mountains, it seemed Caleb and Maggie grew stronger. The color in their cheeks returned with their appetite, and soon they were gorging themselves on oranges and herb cakes Fiona baked with the same potpourri Clare was drying for her next batch of tea. They walked beside her now, Caleb leading Blossom, the milk cow, and Maggie collecting acorns.

The mountain streams teemed with fish and the woods with wildlife. Small game was plentiful and eased the travelers' hunger, the pangs of which some still felt, even though the barrenness of the desert was behind them. Fiona combined lemons with butter and mountain trout and discovered a tasty dish, especially when garnished with sweet berries and seeds from the sugar pine.

The first drops of rain were welcome. They fell like a gossamer curtain against the sun, scintillating with the sparkle of diamonds. The mountain showers came and went, making rocks and leaves glisten in the late-day sun.

It was a curious thing, the way a day could be at once sunny and rainy, warm and cool. But always it was beautiful, in the shimmer of light that grew increasingly spectacular with each new vista.

There were lakes of glass and groves of black oak and quaking aspen, some of which had turned a brilliant shade of gold. In between rain showers, the sky was a shocking blue that offset the distant snowcapped peaks and the yellows and greens that shaded the mountainsides.

The fifth day of rain was not welcome. The wagons at the front of the column had a relatively easy time of it in the soft earth, but the last wagons struggled to make any progress along a trail thick with oozing mud that swallowed wagon wheels, oxen hooves, and men's boots.

Fiona traded her new ensemble for her trail-worn blue dress and pinned up her petticoats so what money remained would not find its way through a rain-dampened hole in the thinning fabric. She ordered Maggie and Caleb to stay in the wagon, an instruction she did not need to repeat when the children saw how everyone and everything that touched the mud grew exhausted trying not to sink to their knees.

A horrific crash broke the strain. Part of the hillside gave way above a group of wagons that were no more than ten beyond them. Fiona watched in horror as an assemblage of boulders and entire trees crossed their path in an obscene sheet of mud, striking down three wagons and shoving a fourth over the side of the mountain. Trees with trunks two feet thick had been snapped in half by the force of the mudslide.

Kier was there in an instant, leaping over the side of the cliff astride Kildare. It was a near-vertical drop. The travelers who witnessed the event were nearly as shocked by Kier's bold actions as they were by the tragic fate of the family whose lives were lost on the mountainside. Fiona joined others who stood at the edge of the trail, watching in awe as Kier chased the mudslide to the bottom of the ravine.

A group of men rappelled down the mountainside to help Kier dig through the debris. They shouted periodically, eager to gauge if any were buried alive. Hearts were heavy when one by one each of the six members of the family was confirmed dead.

As the travelers witnessed this sad drama, Kier and the group of would-be rescuers buried the dead. Brent and Horace led the effort to clear the remnants of the slide and make the trail passable. With pickaxe and shovel, they clawed away rocks and trees. In a daze, the travelers got underway, joining the front of the column that had already stopped for nooning.

The hardships visited on the company cast a somber mood. All were eager to descend from these mountains of gray stone and embrace their first glimpse of California.

After a time, the beauty of the changing scenery had faded to the banal nature of what must have been the ten-thousandth step. Or one hundred-thousandth. Fiona could not decide which. Her feet were tired of walking. Her back hurt. Her legs were sore.

Late in the afternoon, a woman's screams heaped upon sounds of confusion made a hard day worse. Weakened by the heavy rains, a large tree branch crashed onto a wagon a few behind the Lenihans', killing the young couple who drove it. Now orphaned, their young toddler cried pitifully, frightened by the commotion and the absence of a parent to soothe him.

Eight deaths at the hands of nature in the span of one day. Fiona was numb.

Kier ordered the front of the column to continue to the campsite in a high mountain valley, which another two hours of hard slogging uphill. Before the wagons that followed sank even deeper into the mud, Kier instructed their drivers to prop the wheels with sideboards. In some places, the mud was so unforgiving it gobbled up sideboards and wheels alike.

Those whose wagons were behind the crushed wagon went to work gathering branches and twigs—anything that could make a surface strong enough to prevent the wheels from being engulfed by the oozing muck. Everyone was assigned this task, collecting as much as they could carry to prevent the loss of another wagon.

Fiona turned back with worry to see Kier waving at Billy to keep the front of the column moving. There was nothing to be done for the young couple whose lives were lost as quickly as the weather changed, the sun coming out to shine through yet another rain shower.

Nearly three hours after Fiona's cooking fire had brought her soup to a boil, the rear column of wagons pulled into camp. The mood among that group was subdued. Exhausted and covered with mud, the only sound among them was the whimper of the orphaned boy who rode with Kier.

"That poor child," Hope said, coming to Fiona's side. "To lose his parents like that. What will become of him? Surely someone will take him in."

When Fiona saw Kier riding toward her, she realized that someone might be her.

"He must be about Jeremy's age," Hope said quietly. "Does Kier know nothing about children?" she said, her tone changing to one of perturbment. "That boy is likely terrified of that big horse, not to mention that man."

"Will you take him until we can sort this out?" Kier asked Fiona, reining Kildare to a stop and lifting the crying boy from the saddle with his other arm.

In the moment of Fiona's hesitation while the boy dangled in midair, his arms and legs flailing, Hope stepped forward. "I'll take him." Her arms reached hungrily for the boy.

"You are soon to deliver your own child," Fiona said, studying her friend as she embraced the boy.

"He lost his parents and we lost our son," Hope said.

"Hope—?" Silas questioned, arriving to see the boy grow quiet in Hope's arms. She kissed his head as he snuggled against her, burrowing into her comfort.

"God has made this possible," she said, appealing to Silas, Fiona, and Kier in turn. "It's the right thing to do. If he will have us," she finished, pulling away from the boy to regard his face. She cupped his cherub cheek with her hand. "It's Charles, isn't it?" she said gently, smiling at the boy, who nodded, never once taking his eyes from Hope's.

"Why don't you keep him for now," Kier said, considering the matter resolved.

The next day dawned gray and rainy, much like the last. It marked another ten hours of endurance. The travelers were so tired from the rain and mud they did not speak.

A group of men on horseback arrived, seemingly headed the wrong way. Kier greeted some of the men with a handshake and others with a familiar backslap. During nooning, Kier described the men as a U.S. Government-mandated relief team of civilians and soldiers headed east with stock and supplies to aid travelers in reaching California before winter storms set in. After so many emigrants had perished over the years, the government chose to attempt to save as many as it could. He had ridden with these parties in past years.

Similar to the way fortunes had changed for Charles, Hope, and Silas, it was the same for Kier when the crash of a tree branch falling in the forest startled Kildare, who reared up and twisted away from the noise. But the mud held his hind leg fast. The sound of bones breaking was as shattering an event as many of the losses the company had experienced.

Doc and Libby's wagon was just passing Kier's position, with Fiona's wagon following. She heard the snap from more than fifteen feet away and knew at once what it meant. She halted her team and ran forward to help Kier, joined by Doc and Libby. Traveling one ahead of the Pickerings, neither Clare nor Gideon realized anything had happened and continued unaware.

Kier pulled free from his fallen horse and knelt at the great beast's side. Fiona watched Kier lower his head. He said something to Kildare, stroking his face with the tenderness of an old friend. The horse struggled to stand but Kier instructed him to lie down. The horse's eyes were wild. Fiona saw bones protruding from Kildare's hind leg and stopped short, realizing there was nothing she could do to help. She and the Pickerings kept their distance.

Caleb and Maggie caught up to her then. She held them against her as much to keep them from interfering as to comfort them in what she knew came next.

"Why is he doing that?" Maggie asked with alarm when she saw Kier draw his pistol.

"Kildare is badly hurt," Fiona explained, lifting Maggie into her arms and forcing her small face to look away.

The sound of the gunshot echoed for a long time, reverberating off every tree and rock in the forest, its release trapped by the oppressive layer of clouds.

Maggie cried against Fiona's neck, a sadness Fiona shared but felt more deeply when she met Kier's eyes. Tears streamed down Caleb's face. She drew him to her.

"Keep moving," Kier snarled to Fiona in a show of efficiency to distract from his frustration over the loss of Kildare.

Fiona turned back more than once to see Kier remove Kildare's saddle and throw it over his shoulder. Before rounding a bend in the trail, she looked back again to see Billy with Kier, the younger man taking orders from the man who now needed a horse.

That night the rain turned to snow. The children were delighted to play among the flakes, catching them on their tongues and trying to count how many different designs they could hold on their clothing before they melted away.

Their parents were less amused by the dusting of snow. Some of them watched the sky in fear. Others needed reassurance from Kier they were not facing the same fate as the Donner party ten years earlier.

Traversing Donner Pass left a pall over the group. Those who knew what it was were silent at its crossing. Caleb and Maggie noticed the tension and asked Fiona about it. She gave them a sanitized version of the story, which was enough to inflame their imagination.

For the next two hours, they questioned her

nonstop about how the party came to be stranded, how deep the snows were, and how it was they had nothing to eat. Fiona quieted them at last by suggesting they say a prayer for the people who died that terrible winter and for the children who lived to tell of the ordeal.

"If Mr. Moran would have been with them, they would be alive today," Caleb said with certainty, putting it all into perspective for Maggie. And for Fiona too, who caught herself smiling at the thought.

Once west of Donner Pass, many in the company had begun to think they were home free, an easing of vigilance rarely helpful in a wilderness setting.

The snow that day turned to more than a dusting. When a full three inches covered the ground and the snow showed no signs of stopping, tensions returned. The winds kicked up and soon it felt like they were fighting their way through the heart of a blizzard, marching into the wind, regardless of which way they turned.

Kier made the decision to batten down and wait out the storm. Animals were secured on the leeward side of the wagons. Families huddled together among their belongings, wrapped in whatever coverings they could find. It was snowing too hard to make campfires, so people relied on each other for warmth.

"Was Finn MacCool ever in a snowstorm?" Caleb asked as he snuggled beneath the buffalo skin and the tarp, which Fiona pulled over them for extra warmth and protection from melting snow.

"I don't know," Fiona replied, too tired to make up a story. "What do you think?"

"His breath was hot enough to melt the snow, so he was only in rainstorms," Maggie said officiously.

"There's your answer," Fiona said, amused by her daughter's response. With the matter of Finn MacCool settled, Fiona sang an Irish lullaby until they slept.

She awakened with a start to realize the wind was no longer blowing.

The camp was eerily silent. She rose to investigate. Wrapping herself in her winter cloak, which she found at the bottom of her trunk, she opened the flap of their wagon. An insulating layer of snow broke free to reveal a camp swathed in fog. The air was breathless and still.

A half moon lit the snowscape from above. Its theatrical beauty reminded Fiona of Ireland. Warm air had followed the wind, melting the snow until the chill froze it in glass beads on the trees. Watching the night settle, she grew emboldened by a familiar sense of home. The faeries are about, she told herself, stepping into the scene as if stepping into a dream.

Fiona shivered from the thrill of her adventure. She wanted to explore it before day broke and it was gone in a rush of snowmelt.

Seven inches of snow blanketed the earth, blown from patches of bare earth to two-foot drifts. Shafts of moonlight reached into the forest, silhouetting branches against silver beams that reflected over the ground, illuminating the path. Awed by the ethereal quality of the night, Fiona walked among the trees, enchanted by the feel of winter wrapped in summer.

The night deepened. She thought she was alone until she saw another set of footsteps. Following them, she looked up to see Kier ahead of her. Hesitant at first, she pulled up her hood and left the boundaries of camp.

"Kier," she said, calling to him. Her voice was garbled in the fog. The acoustics distorted sounds, making them tinny and muffled. Unnatural. She called to him a second time before he stopped.

"Go back to camp," he said, not turning to face her.

"I like it out here," she said after a pause. "It won't look this way tomorrow, or ever again."

The pair stood together, yet apart. There was a tension filled with sadness and loss. It was a window into what it was to be Kier Moran, a loner, an intentional outsider, at a moment when part of him regretted his nature. Fiona thought to leave, but forced herself to stay, to be there for him if he wished to speak.

"I'm sorry about Kildare," she said.

"He was an animal."

"You don't really believe that, do you?" she said empathetically, her tone soothing.

"You should go back to your wagon. It isn't safe out here. The boughs are heavy with snow," Kier said gruffly.

"You're out here. Seems a tree branch could fall on you as easily as it could fall on me."

Kier did not respond.

Fiona decided she could outwait him.

It was uncomfortable lingering in the prolonged silence. She closed the distance between them.

"I ask myself what I could have done differently," he said, turning to face her.

"Surely you don't blame yourself for the deaths."

"I am responsible for every life on this journey," he said.

"You could no more have stopped the tree branch from breaking or the rocks from sliding than you could have stopped the snow from falling. You can do many things, but I've yet to believe you can control the weather." She allowed her words to wash over him, smiling softly. "I know you're a good man."

"You know nothing," he snapped at her, his words cold.

"I know your heart. It is a good heart," she pleaded.

"You know little of me."

"I know what I see and hear and feel and smell and taste from knowing you."

"Goodnight, Fee," he said at last, turning to walk away from her.

"Don't you find it arrogant when a man takes on a burden only God can shoulder? You are not alone in bearing our sorrows."

He turned suddenly and stormed toward her, eliminating the space between them before she had time to react.

"We could have gone another way. I chose this path, so troubled by storm and tragedy. There are other routes we could have traveled, yet I chose this way because I deemed it the best way, the path least likely to bring us into contact with unfriendly Indians or difficult terrain. All these lives are in my hands. All these people look to me as their leader and protector. Look what I have done to them."

She could not see his face to read its expression. The brim of his hat concealed it in shadow. In silence he lunged toward her. She wasn't sure what he had a mind to do. Her instincts told her he was going to strike her. Her experiences with Simon and her father told her so. She cowered and turned to run but stumbled into the trunk of a broad tree.

"Don't," he said simply, his tone apologetic. "I would never hurt you."

Removing his hat, he stood before her, seeming to tower over her where she half-stood, half-lay against the tree. Their eyes met, two pair shining in the darkness, brimming with uncertain anticipation. He laid his palm on her cheek and slid his hand beyond her face, tangling his fingers in curls that fell free when the hood slipped from her head.

He traced her features, grazing the surface of her skin with his fingertips. She closed her eyes to bask in his tenderness, quietly receiving his affections as he caressed her face and throat, her ears and the nape of her neck. His touch was as delicate as a veil, each point of contact bearing the whisper of a kiss.

She reached for him, yearning to feel the weight of his face, committing it to memory: his cheekbones, eyelids, the bridge of his nose, the cleft in his chin, the space behind his ear, the scars that marred his flesh. It felt good to be near him again.

More erotic than a kiss, it was a symphony of touch. Their lips never met, their hands never traveled below their shoulders. They traded the lead, alternately venerating one another's features with the depth of their emotion. Their exchange became an elaborate overture, a ritualized mating dance.

The moment was perfect. They were alone together, outside the bounds of their pilgrim society where no one dared travel—except Fiona, who had ventured beyond the perimeter of their circled wagons to the borderland where he maintained his existence.

"I don't deserve you," he whispered. "You are fearless, steadfast, and true, and unafraid to pass into the wild unknown."

"Because you've shown me how."

"You give my wrecked soul hope. But other men can give you what you need. I would fail you at every turn."

"You haven't failed me yet," she said, covering his hand with hers.

"You should go, Fee. I have to let you go." His words were heavy with loss.

"I don't want to go."

They stood at an impasse, their emotions constructing a wall between them. He turned his back on her. "Go before I won't let you go."

"No," she said at last, her voice ringing with confidence.

Fiona's instinctive reaction would have been to give in to his rejection of her and sulk quietly away, choking on her tears. But she had changed in the weeks and months since she had come to know Kier. She was stronger. He had made her stronger. She had learned to fight for what she loved. And she loved Kier Moran.

She reached out and placed her hand on his back. The tension in his body felt hard and unfamiliar against her palm. She traced the sharp edges of his muscles and rested her hand at his waist. "There's nowhere else I want to be."

He laced his fingers through hers.

"Can you live with regret?" he whispered.

"Why must there be regret?" she breathed.

"To care for me is to do so without hope, for anything we begin will not be finished to any degree of satisfaction for you. When we reach California, you will stay. I will go. That is how it will be," he explained.

"I will have no regrets," she stated confidently.

Fiona's head began to spin. In a broad sweep, her hand moved to his cheek. As she lifted her other hand to hold his face, he closed his arms around her. She could not discern whether it was he who took her, or she who surrendered to him. All she would remember was that she was firmly in his arms for the duration.

Their kisses deepened as they breathed each other's breath. She opened her lips to him, and he entered her. The force with which he consumed her transcended any of her imaginings. Her voice caught when she gave herself completely to him, reveling in their intimacy. She unbuttoned his shirt to kiss his shoulders and chest.

The sensation of his flesh beneath her hands was exhilarating. Her fingers knew where to travel as if they had caressed him before, perhaps in a dream. Her nightgown slipped off her shoulder when he buried himself in her. She cried out, her voice rising above the canopy of the forest.

Their union was like the terrible beauty of Ireland and the rugged beauty of the West. She knew she would never regret the experience of having him dwelling within her, her body surrounding his, their unacknowledged love surrounding them like a cloak.

Rising above him, she took his face in her hands and ran her fingers back into his hair, losing them in its thick black waves. He shuddered as she moved against him, drawing him more deeply into their experience. She kissed him, wanting to pleasure him, wanting to possess him as he possessed her.

Their bodies trembled with the strain of their passion. She arched back with his release, gazing at the stars above them in their infinity. A canopy of light smiled upon them, a million sparkles that dazzled her

341

mind as he filled her senses. Although she belonged to no one, she was completely his in that moment, making love to him under the night sky.

She looked down into his face. His eyes were on her; she knew they had never left her. With an energy Simon had never possessed, or cared to, Kier continued until she experienced the level of pleasure she had given him.

Her eyes grew wide with the intensity of the experience. A primal yell rose within her, surging through her body until it erupted, echoing in the night. She collapsed over his shoulder, reborn in him. Her curls fell across his back.

"I wish I could offer something better than a bed of snow," he said, easing her to the ground. They sat where they had stood, their limbs as tangled as the roots of the tree that supported them.

"That four-point blanket would be nice to have," Fiona teased as they wrapped her cloak around them.

"Or your buffalo skin."

Once settled, Fiona reached up to brush his lips, wanting to see him before he slept. She took his face in her hands and kissed him. Then he smiled. Her heart surged with joy as dimples creased his face. His eyelids were heavy with happiness. He covered her hand with his before folding himself against her.

Fiona smiled when she heard his breathing change. She wondered if he slept this soundly most nights but supposed he did not. Curled in his lap and nestled against his chest, she listened to the night around them. Its stillness persisted, making her feel as if they were the only two creatures in the world.

He awakened to caress her, running his fingers

over her skin as if painting a set of clothes on her. She relished the feel of his hand as he ran it slowly down her back.

"There is in you something that I cannot—" He took a breath to center himself. She drew away from him to see his face and was mesmerized by the way his eyes probed hers. "You make me—feel."

Her expression bid him continue.

His words came more easily. "You make me feel. I've lived my whole life as a man of whom I have not been proud. You make me want to live anew."

He fell silent, unable to continue. She turned in his arms to kiss him.

She pressed her head against his chest, basking in the comfort of the arms that held her and the warmth of his body against hers. An easy silence covered them, where they found contentment in simply being together.

His hand caressed the sweetness of her thigh and she gave herself to him again, knowing she would never tire of the feeling of her body closing around his, holding him deeply within her.

Kier made love to her with an ardor that invigorated the farthest reaches of her body, his movements confident and certain, his skill delivering them both to a state of prolonged rapture. Their second union did not have the same urgency as their first, but its intensity was something Fiona had never experienced. She would not have believed it possible. But then, since finding Kier on this journey, she had come to believe in the possible.

She knew he was wrong. Clare had said as much. Where there is no love, put love, and there it will grow. It had been growing between them for some time. She felt it. Tonight was but a flowering of all that had been building since their first meeting. It was an experience she didn't want to end.

Suddenly she realized she had no idea how long she had been away from camp. Anyone might be looking for her. She had taken a risk coming to him outside the established boundaries. "I should go," she said, kissing him. "No one knows—"

"I'll take you back," he said, climbing reluctantly to his feet.

He surprised her with an embrace, pulling her to him in another kiss that said what words could not. They separated and held one another's eyes. It was enough to make her realize she did not want to go back to camp.

She reached for him, placing her hands behind his neck and running her fingers through his hair as she kissed him. Kier covered her hands with his and turned his cheek to kiss her palms, first one, then the other. He wrapped his arm around her and walked with her back to camp.

"I should go alone from here."

"There is no need," he said, understanding her wishes but wanting her to know he would stand by her all the same.

He kissed her again before she left him, the kind of kiss that gave insight to his wild nature. Half-beast, she recalled an earlier description of him. He was indeed that, but so much more. Their parting embrace was delivered by the thoughtful man inside of him, its message bidding her sweet dreams.

As she walked, she wound her hair into a knot, wanting to appear intact should she encounter anyone.

Kier was her secret. She could still feel him inside of her. His perspiration covered her skin. His taste was in her mouth. She would sleep well that night, surrounded by his memory.

When she reached the circle of wagons, she turned back, wanting to see him one last time. But he remained concealed by darkness. She knew he was there as surely as she knew that he watched her. The comfort she found in knowing this was beyond words. She kissed her fingertips and extended them toward the woods, blowing him a kiss goodnight. And then she turned, disappearing into civilization.

Kier struck a match, its glow shining for a moment at the edge of the woods. The taste of sweet tobacco filled his lungs.

Chapter 24

The hazy dawn revealed a world iced with frost. Every leaf, every pine needle glistened as sunlight burned through the fading mist, fracturing clouds in pale beams that made her think of heaven reaching out to earth.

Thick with moisture, the heavy air made the cooking fire slow to burn. Fiona fanned it with her skirt and tossed a handful of kindling on its anemic flames. As she watched her handiwork, she pulled her neck to one side and reached back to massage a stiff muscle. His hands took over. His touch made her forget the fire.

"You have the most beautiful hair. Liquid ebony."

He wrapped his arms around her, and she turned to talk to him over her shoulder. "Thank—"

He silenced her with a kiss.

"I'm going to ride ahead with Billy and Tom to scout the route. We'll be back by dark."

"Will I see you then?" she asked hopefully.

"If you can handle a little more regret," he said with a grin that became a kiss reminiscent of their passion beneath the stars.

"Good morning, Mr. Moran," Maggie greeted, climbing from under the Lenihans' wagon.

"Good morning, Maggie," he replied, unable to take his eyes off her mother.

"Will you lift me up, Mr. Moran?" she asked,

planting herself in front of him. Her head tipped nearly all the way back to see his face. "Please?"

Kier obliged until Maggie giggled.

"Coffee?" Fiona asked, producing a cup after Maggie scampered away, spying a chipmunk to chase.

He watched her above the rim as the hot liquid seared his esophagus, warming him all the way to his groin.

"Mom!" Caleb exclaimed, running to where she stood. He was sweaty from a good run. "Mr. Moran showed us a den of foxes! There was a mother fox and five babies."

Fiona looked to Kier for an explanation.

"One way to distract a group of boys from throwing snowballs first thing in the morning."

"You've been up for a while," she teased.

"Maybe I never slept," he said slyly.

****

All day Fiona's face shone with happiness. At nooning she was almost giddy in her mincing of herbs for the soup stock already underway for the evening meal.

That night the camp had a lightness that came from the lifting of collective spirits among a people knowing they were on their descent into California. With the mountain snows and harrowing passes behind them, all that lay ahead were gentle winds and golden light that beckoned from the bountiful land.

Camped on a high plain, the travelers rejoiced with the majesty of the sunset that shone on snowcapped peaks that stood to their east. The alpenglow was a fitting farewell to the rigors of the trail, to the rocks and gorges, rain and fog, and straining beasts. It was a good feeling to have the Sierra Nevada nearly behind them. The travelers reveled in a social evening of music, dancing, conversation, and a shared meal of trout and wild turkey.

Despite Jake's best efforts, Kier had become akin to the beloved head of the clan. He could not walk across camp without being stopped to visit with everyone, old and young. He scanned the crowd for Fiona but did not see her. A second survey located Jake in the midst of a group of women, Caroline among them, who hung on his every word.

"Where's your mother?" Kier asked Maggie, lifting her high above his head before returning her to the ground and crouching before her.

"Do that again!" Maggie exclaimed with a giggle. Kier obliged, his focus on the little girl complete.

"She went to freshen up," Clare offered, nodding toward Fiona's wagon, which was parked in the outer ring. She arched her brow at her son's uncharacteristic cheer. After a scouting day his demeanor was typically standoffish. Tonight, he was downright friendly.

"She promised me her first dance," Caleb said proudly.

"Me, too," Maggie said, not to be outdone.

"I'll remind her," Kier said with a smile, returning Maggie to his mother's care.

It took him a while to make his way clear of the crowd. He did what was necessary in terms of being politic as he moved through the people, stopping to deliver advice, shake a hand, or pat a toddler on the head, but he pressed on, looking for Fiona.

He called her name as he ventured among the parked wagons that encircled the campground. There was no reply.

He stopped short at the entrance to her wagon. The canvas flap was closed, but he could see into the wagon at its imperfect closure. She was centered in the sliver of light, standing with her back to the entrance.

Finding a rare moment of peace, she had taken advantage of the solitude to luxuriate in a sponge bath. Knowing Kier would soon return, she wanted to present herself as well as trail conditions allowed. Stripped to the waist, she washed her dewy skin with lavender water.

Kier was mesmerized by her long, lean back, its creamy flesh illuminated by lantern light that reflected on the fabric walls of the wagon. Black curls were piled loosely atop her head. Stray tendrils spilled onto her shoulders, stuck to her damp flesh like wrought iron volutes.

He watched her as she dipped her cloth into the basin and lifted it to cleanse herself, her arm raised above her head like a flamenco dancer. She turned slightly and Kier saw the curve of her breast. A stray drop of water coursed down her shoulder and onto the breast where it hung, suspended like dew, waiting to fall. Kier watched it breathlessly, his throat thick with desire.

She patted herself dry and pulled a fresh camisole over her head. It had once been crisp and white but was now stained with dirt and blood from those she had nursed.

He cleared his throat to announce his presence. "Fee."

Startled, she peeked at him over her shoulder and pulled a shawl around her in the same instant she opened the flap.

"Kier," she said, greeting him with delight, climbing onto the tailgate and reaching for his hand to help her to the ground. Unable to take her eyes from his, she was transfixed by their blue color. How different they appeared than they had the night before, when they were nothing but a black abyss, a direct window to his troubled soul.

She stepped from the wagon into his arms. He took her face in his hands and ran his fingers across the nape of her neck when their lips met.

"I missed seeing you today," she said between kisses. "Greeting you each morning is one of my favorite parts of the day."

"Why's that?" he asked, taken aback.

"Because I know you're alive," she said with a gleam in her eyes.

"Do I seem on the verge of death?" he asked with a crooked smile.

"You're in a dangerous line of work," she said, covering his mouth with hers.

"Gunfighter, maybe," he said, trying to get at her meaning. "Miner. But wagon master?"

"Snake bites, Indians, falling off horses and over cliffs, disputes between travelers, bears, coyotes, tornadoes," she said, kissing him between each declaration until his laughter made her stop.

"Bears," he said dubiously.

She loved the way he smelled, the feel of his body against hers. Simply inhaling, she drank him in, the comfort of his nearness, the headiness of being with him.

"How was your scouting expedition?" she asked,

as much to hear his news as to distract from her urge to hold him inside her.

"Long. But by tomorrow night people will believe they are in California, even though we have already passed into its territory. What did I miss on the trail today?" he asked with the ease of a husband checking with his wife after a full day apart.

"Maggie has an entirely new bouquet of sunflowers. I've nowhere left to store her artistry. Caleb is looking for signs of Finn MacCool. Your mother collected unusual plants to brew another exceptional pot of tea. The oxen are still walking, and the cow didn't die, so in all I have no complaints."

"If we step into the woods we'll be away from the gossips," he said deviously.

"Why, Mr. Moran," she said with mock indignation. "What sort of lady do you think I am?"

"Your actions, my lady, are all the answer I need." His hand traveled under her skirt.

When her face reddened, he laughed and pulled her to him in an embrace.

"I am to remind you that you promised your first dance to both your children," he said with administrative authority.

"Then why are you tempting me with an interlude in the woods?"

"Pure selfishness," he replied, snaring her lips. "I do have a favor to ask. Now that Jake and Caroline have insisted one of the older boys should drive her wagon so they can travel together, would you consider allowing Caleb to shepherd the livestock with the children?"

"He'll be nine next week," she said hopefully,

trying to keep her voice even as his hand caressed her thigh.

"Making him the youngest. But he is level-headed, and we need him. He'll learn a lot."

"Of course," she replied, resisting the temptation of his mouth only a breath away from hers. Beads of perspiration glistened on her face. "Will you be near him?"

"I'll make a point of it."

"Do you think he can be of help?" Her voice broke as his fingers found what they sought.

"With a little guidance, absolutely. It will be a good experience for him. Show him a thing or two he can use in your new home."

Your new home. The words sounded hollow to Fiona. Devoid of Kier.

"How about those woods?"

Fiona could barely speak. "The dance."

Kier conceded and withdrew his hand, leaving her body contracting in little spasms of pleasure.

"Can I see you later?" Kier asked, pressing his forehead to hers.

"I'd regret it if you didn't," she replied, attempting humor while regaining her composure.

The camp was a whirl of music and laughter, nearly everyone dancing to the fiddle and drum. A smattering of applause further punctuated the sound, the clapping of hands adding percussion. Billy shone in his role as the lead vocalist, charming the crowd with his energizing lyrics.

California! People who had been hesitant to believe in the journey's end had started to accept their near success. There was a far larger crowd on the makeshift dance floor that night than there had been in a long time.

Jake halted the music to announce he and Caroline were to be married when they reached San Francisco. The band insisted on playing a dance just for them. They were twirling around the makeshift dance floor when a dog chased a rabbit through the party. Jake tripped over first the rabbit, then the dog, and crashed to the ground in a cacophony of broken bones and torn fabric.

He howled like a fallen elephant.

Chapter 25

After a long night spent caring for Jake and Caroline, both of whom were hysterical, Fiona struggled to mix cinnamon into cold, lumpy porridge. Putting pestle to mortar, she ground more cinnamon from the small amount that remained in her supply.

Jake had suffered a fracture of his lower leg, breaking both his tibia and fibula. He had thrashed and screeched when Kier had worked with Doc to align the broken bones so they would heal correctly, Kier pulling to lengthen the leg while Doc repositioned the fractures and applied a splint.

While Fiona had seen fellow travelers tolerate far worse injuries, she guessed perhaps this was Jake's way of coping with his misfortune. It took the remainder of Doc's supply of laudanum to relieve Jake's pain.

"We're almost home," Doc had told Fiona. "Hopefully the opportunities for significant injury are behind us."

Jake's immobilization meant not one but two of the older boys were needed to drive his and Caroline's wagons, since she had become his full-time caregiver. Now Caleb had an even greater responsibility driving the cattle that day.

The pestle slipped, and Fiona scraped her hand, immediately wringing it to dull the pain. A dusting of cinnamon stained her yellow blouse and self-made skirt. With a sigh she considered switching to her faded blue dress.

Kier's arms encircled her from behind. She covered his hands with hers and leaned back, allowing herself to dissolve against him. He was a tonic.

"How's Jake this morning?"

"Quiet, at last," Kier replied. "You and Doc reassembled him well."

Fiona smiled at his description.

"I'll find you when we make camp," he whispered in her ear.

With Maggie and an armful of dolls by her side, Fiona put her team in motion. As it had most days, her wagon traveled between the Pickerings' and the Morans'. Kier tipped his hat to her when he rode by, as he always did, and she gave him a private smile.

"Would you look at that," Fiona said, as she and Maggie watched the canyon walls fall away to an open plain. They now traveled through the foothills of the Sierra Nevada. Spectacular peaks of stone had given way to rolling, brush-covered hills. The Central Valley was nearly in sight.

One of Maggie's dolls fell over the side of the wagon. It was all Fiona could do to keep Maggie from following her. The girl responded with a temper tantrum when Fiona scolded her for having too many dolls on the bench with them.

Kier rescued the doll, his attentiveness appreciated by both mother and daughter as the dusty rag doll was once again safe in Maggie's arms.

"How are the cattle drivers?" Fiona asked.

"A little slow," he said with a wry chuckle before urging his horse ahead. "Thankfully we have reached an easier part of the journey."

Kier had sent Billy and another young man out front to scout; their travel goal was sixteen miles that day. The potential for slow-ups lay in the group of children who were driving the cattle. The two teenaged boys who were most experienced with the cattle were driving Jake and Caroline's wagons at the front of the column. Now the task of keeping more than two hundred cattle traveling behind Horace's wagon, the last in the column, depended on a handful of children including an eight-year-old for whom Kier had great affection but little confidence.

Kier trotted past Horace's wagon only to see a beleaguered smattering of animals and children, leaving the observer to wonder who was herding whom. They had not been traveling for long and already fifty paces separated them from the end of the train.

"You all seen a wagon train around here?" he asked, leaning forward in his saddle. His expression was one of amused annoyance.

****

Maggie chattered, alternately talking to her mother and her collection of dolls. They were an odd family, made of rags, carved wood, and prairie grasses. But each was a treasure to Maggie, for Gideon had crafted most of them. Fiona asked her about each one, amused by the vivid stories Maggie could weave, complete with details from their journey west.

"Can we sing a song?" Maggie asked.

"Yes. How about Billy's version of 'Amazing Grace'?"

The dulcet tones of mother and daughter came together on the refrain.

****

Billy staggered, his determination giving him the strength to continue. He fell and stood, fell and stood again. One arrow protruded from his chest; two more were in his shoulder and thigh. His clothing was stained with blood.

The scouting party had been cut down without warning. The Yokuts' attack had been fast and brutal, depriving Billy and his companion of the opportunity to warn the company. He tried to fire his pistol into the sky to alert them to the danger, but his arm was useless. His fingers no longer worked. It was too late.

He fell to his knees, vomiting blood before a well-muscled warrior took his scalp, his death throes negligible, his last breath an apology that went unheard.

****

Travelers in the first wagons did not know what hit them. Suddenly their wagons were aflame. Yokuts on horseback raced past them, creating chaos. Gunshots rang out.

Fiona stopped singing.

Kier stopped talking to his charges.

When shouts and screams followed, Fiona reined her team to a stop. Caleb. Her first thoughts were of her son.

"Horace!" Kier yelled to the rear wagon, ordering him to look after the cattle and their accompanying children. He spun around in his saddle and realized his group had fallen well behind the train. His resources were not promising: a half-dozen children, all under the age of twelve, every one of them but Caleb utterly intimidated by him. More screams followed more gunfire.

It was a diversionary attack, designed to cause maximum fear and confusion while the Yokuts achieved their primary objective: cattle theft.

The men knocked over wagons and set canopies aflame. Jake's wagon caught fire, but he was lying immobilized in Caroline's wagon, which was untouched by arrows. Caroline's second wagon crashed on its side, some of her trunks of clothing spilling open in the dirt.

Fiona screamed when two painted men started to rock her wagon. She grabbed Maggie and leaped to safety.

Kier rode the length of the train, galloping hard to reach Fiona. His mount was far slower than Kildare.

The Lenihan wagon fell over in an awful clatter of possessions, throwing Fiona to the ground before she could jump clear. Her leg was trapped under the sideboards.

"Go to Mr. and Mrs. M," she yelled at Maggie, who stood fearfully, watching the chaos unfold. "Go now!" The Morans' wagon was directly behind theirs.

But Maggie grew disoriented and did not see Clare or Gideon. Instead, she ran toward Silas and Hope, who cradled Charles against her. They were the only familiar faces the little girl could see.

Fiona struggled to free her leg. Her children were in peril and she could help neither of them. At last she wriggled free.

Kier encouraged more speed from his horse. Fiona's wagon was in the middle of the column, beyond where he could see.

"The cattle," Kier hollered at Brent, who had ridden to find him. "They're after the cattle. Horace is alone back there." Tom Thorpe was in earshot and ran to join them.

Brent and Tom nodded and went to aid Horace, while Kier forged on, trying to reach Fiona. He arrived at her overturned wagon to see Maggie running into the heart of madness with Fiona in pursuit. When he saw that Fiona did not see the danger, he yelled to get her attention.

She was so intent on snaring Maggie she did not notice the mounted rider bearing down on her. The Yokuts warrior had his spear drawn, poised to impale Fiona's heart. A second rider materialized from a wall of smoke and swooped down to catch Maggie's wrist. In the same moment he pulled Maggie into his saddle, Fiona heard Kier's warning. She turned in horror, wanting Kier to do something. That's when she saw the spear.

Decorated with feathers and beads, it was a thing of beauty, blessed to be successful in its kill. The arrowhead was fashioned from carved flint with a tip designed to bring down prey. Once thrown, it became an aerodynamic wonder, moving with precision between earth and sky.

Kier had not been close enough to save Fiona, but he could warn her. He arrived too late for Maggie as well. He could only watch from afar as the child fought with her captor, screaming and kicking to break free. He drew his pistol but could not take the shot. From his range, he doubted his accuracy. He might hit Maggie by mistake.

Had Kier not alerted Fiona, the razor-thin tip of the spear would have taken her life. Instead, flint met bone with crushing accuracy, severing tendon and artery, bursting capillaries, and tearing an angry swath from thigh to mid-calf. She fell like a mastodon taking a mortal blow. Despair rang from her mouth as blood splattered around her. She watched helplessly as Maggie disappeared in a veil of dust, her plaintive cries for help fading.

Fueled by rage, Kier killed the Yokuts warrior who had attacked Fiona, bashing his head with a stone axe and cutting his throat with his hunting knife. With his pistol he felled another two marauders before they could inflict additional damage on his people. Yanking his knife from one victim, he hurled it at another, the blade piercing the man's eye before embedding in his brain. Revenge stained Kier's face and hands with angry crimson. He ran to where Fiona had been cut down. She was surrounded by people, all of them overwhelmed. They parted to let Kier kneel at her side.

"Why does this always happen to us?" Caroline wailed from the edge of the crowd of onlookers. "You would think we would be free of these savages by now. Several of my trunks have been smashed on the ground. I need someone to pick them up for me. Well?" she said after a silence. "Isn't someone going to help me?"

Caroline's demands had a grating dissonance. Evangeline led her sister away from the scene.

Fiona lay strangely quiet, staring at the cloud formations above her as she slipped into shock. Despite the tourniquet someone had tied on her thigh, she had already lost a lot of blood. Kier lifted her into his arms but she was barely aware of him. She felt so peaceful, so calm, as the life ebbed from her. She closed her eyes, losing herself in the tranquility.

Kier shook her so hard her nose began to bleed,

and everyone present thought he had caused it until Doc recognized it as a response to shock.

Her eyes opened, glassy and unfocused. "Colm," she whispered, half-smiling at something no mortal could see.

"No!" Kier bellowed, refusing to surrender her to the brother who had come to greet her.

"I will not let you die!" he said, uncharacteristically bordering on frantic. "Fight this, Fee. Don't give in to the peace. Don't drift away. Don't fall asleep." Clare's tears fell at the possibility the woman her son loved could slip away from all of them forever.

Doc worked to cut out the offending object, assessing the damage to Fiona's leg while carefully unthreading the spear from the mess of damaged muscle and cartilage.

"Don't you have any laudanum?" Kier asked, grimacing as Fiona began to react to the pain.

"We used the last of it on Jake," Doc replied quietly.

The Scotch. Kier decided to send someone for his prized bottle of Scotch, which was hidden in the supply wagon. Billy would know where to find it.

Billy. No one had seen Billy in some time. Why had Billy not warned the company of the attack? Was the young man unaware of the misfortunes of the day? Surely, he had seen the Yokuts approaching.

Not finding Billy in the crowd, Kier went in search of the alcohol. He could hear Fiona's screams before making his way through the crowd that had gathered around her.

He met his mother, who was doing her best to bar

Caleb from the awful scene. The boy appeared stricken.

"Find Billy," he snapped at Horace before handing Doc the Scotch and kneeling at Fiona's side.

Kier held Fiona, urging her through the ordeal, and offering his strength. She writhed and cried out, her body buckling with every cut from Doc's knife and every stitch with his needle. When he doused her leg with Scotch, she nearly fainted. What little Scotch Doc did not use he had her drink.

Blood and tissue stained her muslin skirt and the grass around her. Kier offered her the length of the barrel of his revolver.

"That'll break her teeth, son," Doc said quietly.

In an action that left onlookers agog, Kier struck Fiona, knocking her out to spare her pain. Doc reacted with some surprise, then proceeded quickly in the brief time before the pain jolted Fiona to consciousness.

For now, he had done all he could do. He hung his head. Too much of her leg had been opened to the air. Infection would surely set in. The question was whether she could survive it.

Kier gathered Fiona in his arms. She was limp, like one of Maggie's rag dolls. Like the one who now lay trampled in the dirt. He carried her to her wagon, which had just been righted by Horace and Silas. Hope was inside, straightening its contents and making a bed for Fiona.

"Come," Evangeline said, stepping forward to take the hands of Doc and Libby, who knelt on the ground beside where Fiona had lain. A pool of blood stood in a hollow. It had begun to coagulate.

"It's in the Lord's hands now," Evangeline said somberly. "Let us pray for her recovery. And for the lost child."

In silence, Kier and Hope attempted to make Fiona comfortable. Kier tenderly arranged her limbs in the bed while Hope tucked the blankets around her.

"I can stay with her," Hope offered.

"What about Charles?" Kier asked about the orphaned boy.

"Others are watching him. You know Maggie was trying to reach me," Hope said after a heartfelt silence. "She was running toward me. I could not reach her in time."

Kier embraced the young woman, who sobbed bitterly in his arms.

"I was afraid—afraid to leave Charles, afraid to run after Maggie. I could not move, only stand and watch."

"My mother or Libby can sit with her," Kier said when Hope's tears had subsided.

"What of Caleb?" she asked. "He will need someone to comfort him."

Kier nodded.

"I'll look after him. It's what I can do," she said, meeting his eyes before climbing from the wagon, leaving Kier alone to stare at the sleeping Fiona. He took her hand and held it in both of his, fighting emotion.

Libby cleared her throat to alert him to her presence.

Kier kissed Fiona's hand and laid it gently on her chest before nodding his appreciation to Libby. He took a final look at Fiona before climbing from her wagon.

Kier moved the company to a more defensible site ten miles farther along the trail and established a night watch. Horace returned with no news of Billy.

When the Yokuts retreated, they took Maggie with them. The bodies of a half-dozen Yokuts littered the ground, four of them dead by Kier's hand. Maggie appeared to be the company's only casualty. A little over two dozen animals were stolen from the herd. The bodies of Billy and the other scout had yet to be discovered.

"Look at this," Kier said to Brent and Horace. "White men dressed as Yokuts."

"Are the other men Yokuts?" Brent asked.

"Hard to say. I don't know their tribe well. Keep the company quiet. I'll look for Billy and the other scout."

He found them. Billy's head was crusted with blood where his boyish shock of hair had once been. Kier would not bury him this way. He spit on his handkerchief and washed Billy's face. He did the same with the other young man.

Kier was stripped of emotion. He rode back to camp in silence, towing two horses and their lifeless riders. With a heavy heart, he and Horace laid out the bodies for Doc to evaluate and the women to tend.

Kier's next stop was Fiona's wagon. He spelled Libby and sat by Fiona, holding her hand in his. With a flutter of lashes, she opened her eyes, then awakened with a start. Kier stroked her cheek to put her at ease.

Fiona appeared to gaze up at Kier for a long time, trying to read his face to confirm all that had occurred.

"Where's Caleb?" she whispered.

"With Hope."

"Maggie?"

"No."

"Will you find her?" she asked, tears welling in her

eyes.

"I'll go at first light."

"Can you not go today?" she pleaded.

"Too late in the day."

"Do you know the tribe who took her?"

"By reputation," Kier replied, his answers clipped.

"What is it?" she asked after a profound silence, knowing there was more.

"Billy is dead."

Her hold on his hand tightened.

"How?" she cried, tears falling.

"Yokuts, and white men dressed as Yokuts."

"Oh Kier," she said, bringing his hand to her lips. "Did he suffer?"

"Yes."

Fiona held his hand to her cheek, where it was cleansed by her tears.

Kier lowered his head to hers and they lay together, bound by their grief.

****

"How about a cup of tea?" Clare invited Kier. "I could use the company."

They sat in silence on Clare's stoop, watching the campfires grow bright in the lengthening night.

"Does my father drink tea with you?" Kier asked after a long time had passed.

"Coffee, and in the morning only. He says tea keeps him awake. He is up with the sun, you know. Prefers daylight to darkness."

Another long silence settled between them.

"This is my Western Sierra Nevada brew," Clare said with pride. "Has some of those berries in it we saw along the trail. Makes it bitter, don't you think?

Reflects appropriately on this portion of our journey."

"If something happens—."

"She is strong," Clare said, cutting him off. "Has the heart of an ox. She will not leave her children."

"Would you take Caleb?"

"Of course. We have delighted in those children. Does that mean you will be leaving us, then?" she asked.

"Got plans," he mumbled.

"They can't wait?"

"No more than the winter will wait."

"I see," Clare said coolly. "She will heal faster if she knows you are near."

"I don't live where you're going," he explained.

"It's your house," she objected.

"It's yours. I've never lived in it. Its walls will be better with all of you in it."

"I don't think you want to leave her," Clare pressed.

"She knows I am a wanderer."

"A man can change."

"At first light I'm going after Maggie. I don't know the Yokuts, but there's bound to be something I can trade for her. Don't know what they want."

"Do they expect a trade?" Clare asked.

"She has dark hair. Probably a replacement for a lost child."

"They would do that?" Clare said with repugnance. "Steal one of ours to become one of theirs?"

"People salve their grief in many ways. I don't know what they'll take for her. May send the company into the valley while I negotiate with them."

"If they want anything we have, give it to them,"

Clare said, finishing her cup of tea. "There is nothing in our wagon I wouldn't trade for Maggie. Even the whole wagon."

****

Caleb sat with Gideon, feeling grown up but trying not to cry. With his mother gravely ill and his sister gone, and Kier tense and short, Caleb sought the presence of the older man. Gideon rarely said much, so Caleb would not have to put on a happy face while answering some grownup's questions. But just as Kier had a few surprises, Gideon had a few of his own.

"Ever played poker?" Gideon said.

Caleb turned to look at him, unable to hide his astonishment. Caleb shook his head. "You play cards?"

"Usually not when Mrs. Moran is looking," he said with droll humor. "How much do you know about cards?"

"Mother calls them a vice."

"Well, yes," Gideon said dismissively. "Knowing how to play poker is not a bad skill, in my estimation."

"We may need to keep this skill to ourselves," Kier said, joining them.

"How is she?" Gideon asked.

"The same." Kier pursed his lips, a subtlety that was not lost on Caleb.

"How are you doing?" Kier asked the boy.

He merely nodded. He had seen Kier nod in the affirmative and figured it was a response he would understand.

"She's hurt real bad. And I have more bad news. Billy Noble is dead."

Caleb looked at Kier with shock before dissolving into tears. He had been strong for his mother but hearing about one of his idols was too much.

Kier embraced the boy, sharing his grief. He emitted a piteous wail that perfectly captured the company's reaction to the news. It was a terrible day.

"Tomorrow the company is going to rest. After we bury Billy, I'm going to find Maggie and bring her back. Can I count on you to help drive the cattle when we move out the day after tomorrow?"

Again, Caleb nodded. Kier nodded in return.

****

The Reverend and Evangeline Pride led the rite of Christian burial. Billy was well regarded by everyone in the company, and people wanted the chance to pay their respects. Although every funeral had been a tragedy, in a way the loss of the bright young man was among the most difficult for the company to bear.

Billy and the other scout were buried in the foothills of the Sierra Nevada, on a rise with the first view of the Central Valley. They were almost home.

Kier delivered the eulogy. "We are here to mark the passing of an exceptional man whose loss we feel deeply in the absence of his leadership, his enthusiasm, and the silence of his guitar. We are thankful for the time we knew him and blessed that our Maker saw fit to share him with us. Our lives are the richer for knowing him."

There were some raised eyebrows among those gathered. Kier had not struck anyone as a man of faith. That his words came from the heart gave those who heard his eulogy new insight into the man. He continued to surprise those in the company who had misjudged him.

The father of the other young man delivered his

eulogy, and their bodies were covered with California dirt, making them part of the land well before their time.

The next morning Kier visited three Yokuts villages. There was no sign of Maggie, nor had anyone seen her. He visited four more villages that afternoon, with the same results. No one seemed to know the Yokuts who had attacked the wagon train. Some questioned whether the attackers were Yokuts or cattle thieves posing as Yokuts. Whoever they were, there was no sign of them. An expert tracker, Kier was unable to pick up a trail in the heavily used woods. Maggie had vanished. Kier returned to camp at sunset, his body sagging under the weight of failure.

As expected, Fiona had grown febrile. Doc examined her leg but saw no signs of infection. Libby maintained vigil, keeping the wounds clean. When Kier arrived at Fiona's wagon, Libby took the opportunity to stretch her legs.

Fiona was lying on the floor of her wagon. Kier climbed inside, sitting beside her with the flap wide open, in plain view of the company. His smile was tender as he sat at her head and took her hand in both of his.

"Any word?"

"I have been to seven Yokuts villages."

"She must be there," Fiona said. Her voice was strong with belief. "I saw them take her."

"Those men seem unknown to any of the Yokuts I have met."

"Did you watch the villages to see if you saw her after they saw you leave?" she asked hopefully.

"I studied each village before and after entering it.

She wasn't in any of those villages."

"Will you keep looking?"

"Of course, but we must move the company tomorrow," he said, caressing her hand.

"Please find her," she said, her eyes searching his. "I know she's alive. I can feel her."

"She may not be."

"You have to find her. If she's out there alone, wandering—"

"I will go back for her. The company is at risk. I have to think of our safety now."

"Please, Kier," she whispered.

"We need to keep moving. I will look again tomorrow, then make camp with you tomorrow night. I will do all within my power to find her."

He caressed her face and felt the fever.

"Thank you for last night," she said with a wan smile.

"I was glad to have been there to help."

"I mean, for the night before, and the one before that."

He smiled at her, a big smile with his dimples flexing, like he wore when dining with his friends at Fort Kearny. Her message had been welcome. He cupped her face with his hand and brushed a stray curl from where it had fallen across her forehead.

That night Fiona dreamed she was walking along a river's edge. She knelt to draw water. As she submerged her flask in the cool, clear depths, a yellow ribbon floating in the water caught her eye. It looked out of place, streaming out from where it was caught on something under a cluster of willows.

There was a little girl in the water. She had yellow

ribbons in her hair. When Fiona reached forward to pull the child from the river she recoiled in horror, for it was Maggie.

Fiona stumbled back on the bank. She began to shake. Her breath came in jerky gasps as a sob rose in her chest. At last she screamed, a wretch of hysteria and grief.

She awakened bathed in sweat. Her fever had worsened.

Clare patted her face with a damp cloth. "What is it?"

"I dreamed I found Maggie, drowned in a river."

"It was a dream," Clare assured her.

"She had yellow ribbons in her hair," Fiona said, choking on her tears.

"It was a dream."

"She's alive. I can feel her," Fiona said frantically.

"Kier is staying behind to look for her tomorrow. And the day after that. He will find her."

The next day the company reached the Central Valley. For most, the golden hills were an affirmation of all they had risked to come this far. This was California, the land of promise that had inspired them to give up all they knew to go west. They had survived the journey and could now face the more familiar challenges of tilling the soil and building their lives in a land that offered so much opportunity.

As the company rolled past farms and ranches filled with stout animals and healthy crops, Kier went in search of Maggie. Again, he found nothing.

Kier returned to camp to learn Fiona's condition had worsened and that she was counted among the very ill. He found Fiona where she lay among those suffering from injury and the resulting infection, and a second group who had contracted dysentery. He held her hand, not wanting to deliver the bad news, but not wanting to keep the information from her either. He soon realized it didn't matter, for she barely knew him through her delirium.

Doc had enlisted the help of all the boys in camp to harvest maggots from every dead animal, piece of rotting fruit, and other organic matter that was in the process of returning to the earth. He then applied them to people's non-healing wounds, where the creatures debrided the wounds by dissolving the infected tissue.

Where Fiona's presence in the company was missed, Jake's was not. Jake and Caroline complained about the smells emanating from the wagons containing the sick and wanted their wagons reoriented to be upwind of the foul odors. For their trouble, a few of the men rolled both wagons outside the boundaries of camp and left them on their own just inside the perimeter. Jake was not amused.

For the most part, all eyes were fixed on the city that was coming into view before them: Sacramento, the capital of California and the end of their cross-country journey.

Chapter 26

With Jake indisposed and Kier not inclined to speak, he delegated the task of leading the final meeting of the company to the Reverend and Evangeline Pride. It would be an emotional parting for many whose lives had become intertwined. Friendships formed between people who had been complete strangers not four months before were now concluding. Most in the company would never see each other again. The occasion was tailor-made for the eloquence of the Prides.

"From Independence, Missouri, to Sacramento, California, some seventeen hundred miles now lie behind us and are part of our collective history. Today we stand as Californians, and our history has yet to be written. It is a fresh start, with new crops to till, new friendships to form, and new experiences to savor. We will do so with the knowledge we earned these new lives because the Lord saw fit for each of us to stand together on this glorious day where the sun shines down on us in full majesty."

Fiona listened from inside her wagon. Although her fever had subsided, it had not yet broken. She felt too weak to sit in a chair outside her wagon and participate in the ceremony.

"The journey has not been easy," said the Reverend Pride. "Some of us have lost loved ones. Others have lost everything we brought on the journey but our lives."

Fiona rolled on her side, pouring out her grief at the mention of loss. She was unwilling to accept that Maggie was gone forever.

"We have experienced the worst of nature and the worst of man. We have also experienced the best of man with the courage and daring of those in our company. We are stronger for our hardships, for we believe in the power of our resilience. We have faith in the desires of our hearts.

"It has been an honor for Mrs. Pride and me to have had the privilege of knowing you on this journey. You will remain in our prayers wherever life takes you in this great state. Our place is here in Sacramento. Please stop by our church whenever you pass this way, for you are always welcome in our home."

For the last time, the company raised its voices together in song, led by the indefatigable Evangeline. From inside her wagon, Fiona could envision the minister's wife taking the floor. Her fondness for Evangeline made her smile.

"Although we offer our thanks to the Lord for allowing us to see this beautiful day in California, I would like to extend my thanks to the one among us who has lifted us up, helped us keep our footing, and seen us through every challenge with a clear head. That person is Kier Moran, who is truly a gift to us all. On behalf of Mr. Moran and his lovely parents, I offer this song in thanks."

Fiona rolled to her back and listened to the sweet vibrato of Evangeline extol Kier's virtues. She could almost imagine the look on his face.

Evangeline closed the meeting with a final rendition of "Amazing Grace," in honor of Billy Noble. Fiona curled into a ball and covered her ears. Every word cut through her with memories of Billy and of Maggie singing the song. She crossed over to sleep, exhausted by the scope of her losses.

She awakened to the kindly face of Evangeline.

"I could not leave without seeing you," she said, taking Fiona's hand. "Meeting you was one of the finest aspects of our journey. Words cannot express my depth of sorrow at your loss. I will remember her and you in our prayers. After you are settled and well, please come see us here in Sacramento. I would so enjoy hosting you in our home."

"Thank you," Fiona said. "For everything. I shall miss you."

Camp that night had a strange feel. It reminded them most closely of the time they spent in Independence, although without the bustle or sense of urgency. Because the travelers were uncertain in this new dynamic, they kept mostly to themselves. Tom Thorpe and the men who would be leading sixteen wagons north spent a long time with Kier, seeking his advice on how to move the smaller company to the farmlands and forests of northern California.

Kier turned a company of forty wagons south, bound for San Francisco, Los Angeles, and points beyond. Doc and Libby, Hope and Silas, Horace, Brent, and Jake and Caroline traveled among this company. As before, Fiona's wagon was situated between the Morans and the Pickerings. Fiona did not look forward to their arrival in San Francisco because it meant she would need to say farewell to Doc and Libby.

Now that they traveled on established roads, Caleb was able to drive the Lenihans' wagon. The boy was intensely focused on keeping the team moving fast enough to keep pace with the other wagons, but not so fast he could not stop quickly, if needed. The five nights of camp along the main road reminded Fiona of what it was to camp with the Owens company on the road to St. Louis. It felt civilized.

Clare, Libby, and Hope traded off taking their meals with Fiona, trying to get her to eat. Hope was relieved when Fiona smiled and cooed at Charles, who had developed a strong attachment to Hope. Fiona put her hand on Hope's belly and felt her child kick.

"Kier and Silas have been talking business," Hope announced. "Kier said he would help Silas by introducing him to the owner of several lumber mills, hopefully not far from where you will have your farm. It would be nice for Charles and my baby to grow up looking up to Caleb. I want Charles to be like Caleb."

On the second day, Doc applied fresh maggots to Fiona's leg. Although she felt better overall, her leg felt worse. It ached. It was red and swollen. She could see the pockets of infection throughout the wound. Doc lanced them and put the wriggling mass of insects on the oozing mess, covering them with a bandage to keep them in place. Fiona turned away, unable to watch.

Kier spent time with her after supper, sitting by her in full view of everyone, in keeping with the customary interactions of an unmarried man and woman. This kept them chaste, although Fiona did not feel well enough to do much more than visit. She didn't mind the time they had, for in a way it reminded her of their early days on the trail when they talked by firelight.

"You're almost home," he said one night.

"It's because of you that we've made it here," she said graciously.

"I'd like you and Caleb to stay at the house until you're well."

She began to object, so he kept talking.

"A physician friend can look after you, help you get back on your feet."

"Thank you, but I—"

"Don't fight me on this. You're in no condition to set up your farm," Kier said.

"I don't know how I could repay you," she said, swallowing before speaking.

"Stay the wonderful friend to my parents. It means a great deal." A pause. "I'm going to set camp."

He lifted her fingers to his lips and kissed them, one by one. Then he was gone.

In her convalescence, Caleb offered Fiona his journal to read. Although her eyes misted when his entries referred to Maggie, Fiona was impressed by her son's insight. His writing was filled with praise for Kier and Billy, another name that pulled at Fiona's heart. Caleb described Kier and Billy with awe. There were pictures and brief sentences about the weather, Indian sightings, and the mischief Caleb and his pack of friends found.

There were drawings of Balthazar and the other oxen, of Fiona leading the team on foot, and of Fiona doing wash at the river's edge with Clare, Libby, and a very pregnant-looking Hope. There were stories about Kildare, who held nearly as much fascination for Caleb as did Kier.

The tornado, snowstorm, and desert creatures were

the subject of many drawings. Finally, there was a comical portrait of Jake and Caroline holding a parasol.

When they reached the outskirts of San Francisco, Doc climbed into the wagon for the last time to remove the maggots. He carefully unwrapped the bandages and was pleased with the progress they had made with the wound.

"Make sure you see a physician when you get to where you're going," he said kindly. "Kier said you have three more days' travel to Santa Clara. When you can, sit up in a chair. The fresh air ought to do you good. Stand on your leg when you are able. Bodies have a way of forgetting how to work when they are not used."

Fiona nodded. Her eyes filled with tears. "I shall miss you terribly. You were my first friend on this journey." Her voice broke.

"You must come to the opening of the opera. Libby and I would so enjoy introducing you to our children and their families. I would keep you with us to care for you but Kier insists there is ample room at his house. Clare will keep a good eye."

Fiona swallowed, choking on fresh tears.

"You will be happy here," she said, looking at the blue sky outside her wagon. "The air will be good for Libby to breathe. Your children will treasure their time with you."

"We will see each other soon," he said, taking her hands in his before pulling her skirt to cover all but her newly bandaged leg. "Kier said there is a stagecoach we can take in a single day's travel. I anticipate we will make that journey more than once, you and Libby and I. You are a good nurse. A good cook. A good mother. A dear lady."

"Thank you," she said, holding his hand.

"I have something for you," he said, reaching into his medical bag. "It's our last bottle of Château Lafite Rothschild. You weren't feeling up to sharing our third bottle with us, so the last bottle is yours to enjoy in your new home."

"I'll save it for when you visit," she promised.

"It's yours. You'll know when to open it."

Fiona's parting from Libby was no less emotional, for they had shared so much on the trail. They hardly spoke, for words seemed inappropriate to convey their feelings.

"Doc said he invited you to the opening of the opera. I will hold you to it," she said, embracing Fiona. "God be with you and Caleb."

With that the Pickerings were gone, as were Caroline and Jake, whose teamster drove their second wagon behind the Pickerings into the heart of the city. Caroline and Jake did not take the time to say farewell to Fiona.

Ten other wagons parted company, leaving the southbound company under Kier's care.

Fiona slept through the next two days and was only vaguely aware of the progress they made. On the morning of the third day, it was time to say farewell to Hope, Silas, and Charles.

With the departure of the Pickerings and now the Whittakers, and her own tenuous circumstances, Fiona was struck by how she felt life was slipping away from her rather than assuming a fresh start. She loved these people and did not want to lose them. She had expected these to be bittersweet days but was surprised by how empty she felt. It was a new kind of loneliness. With Maggie gone and Kier soon to leave, the world felt as if it was closing in on her rather than expanding with possibility.

"If it's a girl, we're going to name her Fiona," Hope announced, placing Fiona's hand on her belly. "Kier has found us a situation not far from here in a place called Boulder Creek. We are only a half day's journey. Once we're settled, I'll bring the baby to see you. I can hardly wait!" the expectant mother chattered excitedly. "Can you believe we have actually come this far, all the way to California? It's still hard to imagine, even though I know we are here. By nightfall, Silas and Charles and I will be in our new home, sleeping in real beds. I have forgotten the feel of feathers. I'm sure I won't sleep at all, what with those normal things around me. Do you think you will have trouble sleeping tonight, away from all of us?"

Fiona smiled affectionately at the young woman. "Absolutely. I will miss your spirit. It will be strange doing wash without you, for I have fond memories of our time together at the river's edge."

"We'll miss your kindness," Hope said, leaning forward to kiss Fiona's forehead. "But I'm glad to know you are near, so we are assured many chances to share old memories and talk about new ones not yet made."

Fiona reached up to embrace her, and then she was gone.

She heard some discussion about routes and campsites, followed by the sounds of well-wishers and goodbyes.

"How are you, dear?" Clare said, leaning against

Fiona's tailgate. "We are now but four wagons—yours, ours, and Kier's two. Such a strange thing, this parting of ways. Kier said we'll be home by midday. Are you feeling well enough to sit up? You have missed much traveling. It is a beautiful place. It will do your heart good to see it come into view."

Fiona agreed. Soon she was situated behind Caleb, who had become quite the teamster since reaching California. Fiona reckoned he could drive the wagon as well as she.

It was sunny and warm, almost hot—a day so bright Fiona squinted against the glare. The sky was a clear blue with a few white, fluffy clouds.

It was perfect. What's more, it had the feel of something peaceful, entirely devoid of struggle. Gilded hillsides undulated broadly as far as she could see. There were fields and farms, and groves of trees. Orchards. She had never seen a vineyard but guessed at what she was seeing when she recognized clusters of grapes being harvested from groomed vines.

It smelled good, with a hint of salt air. Throughout were the buzzing of bees and the flutter of butterflies. There were wildflowers, too. Maggie would have loved this place.

"Are you excited about school?" she asked Caleb, who looked so grown up driving the team. "I would imagine you could start right away."

"I want to be sure you're okay before I go," he said, his expression grave.

"I'll be fine. Mrs. M will keep watch over me until I am well enough to get around and well enough for us to start our farm. I'm sure there's a school nearby."

Fiona watched him, admiring his focus. She

thought she saw Kier in him and knew Caleb had made a careful study of the wagon master over the past months.

"I'm so proud of you," she said, reaching up to touch him.

"This will be a good place to live," he replied. "The farms are big."

After a few more miles, they stopped. Below them lay the Santa Clara Valley. At its seat was the Mission Santa Clara de Asís, its characteristic architecture visible from the top of the valley. The grandeur of the landscape mesmerized the group that had amassed at the valley's edge: Clare, Gideon, Caleb, and Brent.

Kier lifted Fiona from the wagon to see the view. He carried her to the rim of the valley as a groom carries his bride over the threshold. She was lighter than expected. Fragile. The Irish roses had faded from her cheeks, making her white as death, her black curls appearing even more dramatic against the alabaster of her skin. Her injuries had drained her vitality.

Her eyes were pale and watery, like the sea. She had an unfamiliar dreaminess about her, as if she had become immortal through adversity. Kier was affected by the sight of her, the weight of her in his arms. He stared at her as if seeing her for the first time. Her vulnerability left her unguarded. As he watched her, he saw the subtle yearning.

It was a mutual realization that left them mute. It went beyond lust, beyond affection. They were two people who loved one another. Their unarticulated conversation communicated the depth of their mutual regard.

It was joyous. It was also terribly sad, for they

knew what would happen when they reached his house. She would stay and he would go. He had said so, more than once.

"We have reached the Valley of Heart's Delight," he said.

They were oblivious to the chatter around them until Caleb asked Kier to identify the structures in the valley. Without drawing his eyes from Fiona's, he told him where to find the mission church and the cluster of buildings beyond it. That was their home.

"We're standing on a ridge in the Diablo Mountain Range," he explained while looking at Fiona. "Across the valley you can see the foothills of the Santa Cruz Mountains. The Pacific Ocean is on the other side of those mountains."

"Let's keep moving," Kier said after giving everyone the chance to take it all in. "That way we'll get there for lunch."

He placed her carefully inside the back of her wagon. As he drew away, their hands caught one another. She felt a sense of loss when her fingers slipped through his.

Caleb urged the team forward, following Gideon and Clare. The wagon pulled away, and Kier stood there, watching her as she sat in the back of the wagon, watching him.

****

"We're here!" Caleb announced excitedly.

His voice drew her back from sleep. Drowsily, she sat up to see Kier's house come into view.

What she saw astonished her. At first, she believed it to be a dream. They were driving through a working ranch, with several hundred head of cattle in the distance. Ahead were an old gray barn and a double-sided paddock attached to a large corral that had at least twenty horses in it. A groom was exercising a lone horse in a second corral. A flat wooden structure that resembled a bunkhouse rose above the corral. Beyond it stood a grand stone home, two stories high. It was a house worthy of the Cushings.

It was not at all what she had imagined. As she studied the magnificent stone detail on the house, she felt a new emotion: anger.

The house was an imposing edifice, built to last for generations. Clearly, he did not intend to let the Moran name die with him. It was incongruous that a man who never stayed in one place for long had a home of such permanence.

It didn't fit him. The Kier she knew was a man who lived in flight, moving between destinations, with no place to call home. Yet he had a house that represented order, commitment, and responsibility. The long term. When she saw it, she felt betrayed, as if the man she thought she had come to know she in fact did not know at all.

Anger turned to sadness, all of it filtered by the fact she didn't feel well. She was hot and achy and irritable. She leaned over the side of the wagon, believing she would vomit, but she did not.

She watched him break from their group and gallop down the hill to where his staff gathered excitedly to meet him. An even dozen men and women were clustered around him when he dismounted. Fiona was touched by the affection his ranch staff had for him. Hands were shaken, backs were slapped, and hugs were exchanged. As she watched, she grew increasingly intrigued by this formerly unrevealed side of Kier and wanted to know him as well as she knew the man who had such an effect on her life.

Kier's staff was delighted to meet Clare and Gideon. Once those introductions were complete, he proudly ushered Fiona and her son forward, treating them as equals in importance to his parents. Fiona stood, supported on one side by Caleb and the other by Brent. She would have collapsed without them.

Natch was Kier's foreman. Meredith, his wife, was the housekeeper and cook for the staff of more than a dozen ranch hands. Fiona could see at once the affection Natch and Meredith had for their boss.

Fiona was well received by the staff, to whom she was introduced as a widow from the trail who had been injured during an Indian raid. Other pertinent details about her were left to speculation. When he mentioned Fiona and her son would be staying at the house as his guests, she was immediately given a second inspection by his staff.

Feeling she was being manipulated, Fiona thanked Kier for his generous hospitality but insisted she and Caleb would be continuing to their property, where they would make camp, never mind she had not yet purchased any property.

"I won't hear of it," Meredith said. "When you grow tired of my cooking, you can go. Until then, our hospitality is yours."

"It's settled, then," Kier said, showing a new side. Lighter. Almost fun.

Fiona could not help but stare.

Good-natured bantering followed, a sign of Kier and his staff's mutual affection. Fiona politely declined the invitation again but Kier politely insisted. His parents insisted. His amused housekeeper insisted. Again. His weathered foreman insisted. Caleb insisted. With all eyes on her, she finally agreed.

Kier swept Fiona into his arms and carried her inside the house.

"At last he has found a wife?" Meredith said in confidence to Clare as they followed everyone inside.

"I hope so," Clare agreed.

"I believe so," Meredith nodded sagely. "You can see it in his eyes."

"Yes, but will it be enough?"

"I've seen the way he looks at horses, old men, young women, calves, foals, children," Meredith said. "He ain't never looked at another living creature the way he looks at Fiona."

Kier carried Fiona through the kitchen and dining room, across the drawing room, and up the main staircase, which rose from the front entrance to the house. He carried her to the room at the end of the hall on the second floor. She had no idea he was installing her in the master bedroom.

Fiona took in what she could of the house as they passed through its empty rooms. Not one stick of furniture. It was a shell awaiting an occupant. Kier indeed owned a house, but it was far from being a home.

Curiously, the master bedroom contained a magnificent four-posted bed. Made of hand-tooled mahogany, it was worthy of the house.

"I'm not an invalid," she objected as he set her gently in the middle of the comfortable bed.

"You need your rest," Clare assured her, entering

the room behind them. "You seem warm," she said with concern, feeling Fiona's forehead with the back of her hand. "Are you feeling all right?"

"A bit out of sorts being in this house, I suppose." Although she addressed Clare, her words were meant for Kier, who hovered over his mother's shoulder.

Clare reacted to the strange tension in the room. "I'll leave you two alone. I'll be downstairs if you need me."

Fiona was weak. She felt the fever rage through her when she spoke. "This is—unexpected," she said, taking time to choose the appropriate word. "I don't want your charity."

"This isn't charity."

"Then what is it? A widow of little means sleeping in your bed, relying on your housekeeper to cook and clean for her, and your mother to keep watch over her."

"It's not my bed," he said with a shrug.

"Then whose?" she said with an unmistakable edge to her voice.

"I sleep in the bunkhouse."

An abrupt silence followed.

"Can I get you anything?" he asked, softening.

"No."

"All right, then," he said. He left her alone.

She dozed, giving in to her feelings of malaise. She awakened in the late afternoon, taking in the unfamiliarity of her surroundings. Her eyes blinked once as she studied the draped silk canopy that hung above her. She watched lace curtains dance in a breeze that floated through an open window.

Suddenly she was aware she was not alone. She addressed him as she turned to look toward him. He was a solitary man watching her from the shadows, sitting in a chair at the edge of the room.

"Who are you?" she asked.

"Kier Moran," he replied, his expression puzzled.

"This grand house, a full staff—not the Kier Moran I know from the trail."

"I've been out here a long time, Fee. You know of the lives I've lived."

"I suddenly feel as though I don't know you at all," she said, feeling at a loss for words.

"Then what I've come to tell you may or may not be a surprise. I'm leaving."

It took her a moment to respond. She choked on her emotions, a thousand raging at once, competing for her to act on them. But she refused. Despite his overtures, she knew where she stood with him. "I see," she replied, her sadness crashing down like a Midwestern storm.

He rose and crossed slowly to her, bending to one knee at her side.

"I came to tell you farewell."

"Why did you bring me here?" she whispered, her voice hoarse with tears. She looked up at him, lifting herself to a sitting position, her eyes stormy with fever and heartache.

He was startled by what he saw, by the demon that seemed to have awakened in her.

"To be among good people who will watch over you while you recover."

"Do you ever finish what you start?" she spat at him, regretting it immediately. "I'm sorry," she whispered. "I didn't mean it that way."

"Oh, but you did," he replied, hanging his head.

"I'm ashamed," she said, turning away from him, desperately fighting her feelings. "You've been nothing but kind to us. I have no right to be anything but grateful. You told me it would be this way."

"Fee—"

Her lips quivered. "Thank you for—for so many things. For getting us here safely, for risking your life for us, for inviting us to stay in your home." Her eyes brimmed with tears.

"Consider it a gesture of appreciation for all you do for my parents. You and your children have given them great joy." He took her hand in his.

She noticed no mention of his regard for her. "When will you return?" she asked, still unable to meet his eyes.

"I don't know."

He waited for her response, but none came. Tears had clogged her throat.

"Will you have time to search for Maggie?"

"I will."

He leaned over to kiss her goodbye. Given what had passed between them, it felt perfunctory. But it gave her a final chance to feel his lips against hers. He paused as if to turn and go, then took her in his arms to give her a second, more meaningful kiss, one wrapped in passion and emotion and words unspoken.

"Watch out for that leg. You need to exercise it, or it will go lame. I've told Natch to get you moving tomorrow."

Giving her one last, long look, he rose to leave.

Fiona felt her heart shatter. "Goodbye, Kier Moran," she said quietly when he reached for the doorknob. Tears streamed down her cheeks, but he did not see them.

His shoulders sagged, a gesture of regret. "Goodbye, Fee Lenihan." He hesitated, then walked through the door.

Fiona stepped from the bed, crying out when she put weight on her injured leg. She fought her way to the window and stood with her hands on the glass, watching him ride away.

He turned back and looked to the upstairs window as if expecting to see her there. She lifted her hand in a wave.

He tipped his hat to her and spurred his mount east.

A word about the author...

Bronwyn Long Borne is a nurse by day and writer by night. Her first novels are the self-published Shalemar Trilogy—*Length of Days*, *Poetry of Days*, and the forthcoming *Wonder of Days*—under the pen name Rohret Buchner.

Bronwyn grew up in Wyoming, where you can still see the wheel ruts carved into the land by the thousands of covered wagons headed west. She and her husband live in Denver, Colorado. They share a love of food, wine, the mountains, and the arts.

http://bronwynlong.com

Thank you for purchasing
this publication of The Wild Rose Press, Inc.

For questions or more information
contact us at
info@thewildrosepress.com.

The Wild Rose Press, Inc.
www.thewildrosepress.com

CPSIA information can be obtained
at www.ICGtesting.com
Printed in the USA
FSHW022045030821
83803FS